Champagne Book Group

Presents

The Long Journey Home
Journey Home, Book 1

By

Andrew John Robinson

This is a work of fiction. The characters, incidents and dialogues in this book are of the author's imagination and are not to be construed as real. Any resemblance to actual events or persons, living or dead, is completely coincidental.

No part of this book may be reproduced or transmitted in any form or by any means, electronic or mechanical, including photocopying, recording, or by any information storage and retrieval system, without permission in writing from the publisher.

Champagne Book Group
www.champagnebooks.com
Copyright 2018 by Andrew John Robinson
ISBN 978-1-947128-47-7
August 2018
Cover Art by Fran Armstrong
Produced in the United States of America

Champagne Book Group
2373 NE Evergreen Avenue
Albany OR 97321
USA

Dedication

To Stephen, not just my brother, also my friend and mentor. Without you, this story would not have been possible.

Dear Reader,

Most of the events portrayed in this book actually happened and occurred on Martha's Vineyard, the place of my childhood.

I wrote this book not only to tell a story. I wanted to share my love of this special island and hope that shines through in the pages before you.

One

Arthur held the old quill pen and tried again to get some ink on the well-worn tip. He was still getting used to the ancient instrument and the cool evening breeze of summer that wafted through the window. It made him feel better especially after the day he had. Scratching the pen tip across the parchment before him, he wrote,

> *Hard to believe that I, a man born in the first part of the*
> *Twenty-First Century, seem destined to fight and maybe die*
> *in a terrible battle near the end of the Eighteenth.*

He put the quill aside and picked up the paper. His eyebrows went up as he contemplated where to go next with his tale. Thinking back over their time in this strange *old* world, Arthur couldn't help but recall how they'd come to be here. It had started simply enough in the early part of the summer of 2029 while he'd waited for his girlfriend to come over to the island on the ferry…

Standing on the wharf, he was lightheaded like a kid expecting a visit from Santa Claus. His stomach fluttered. Not a mere butterfly in there. No, it was a seagull or maybe even an albatross. For a moment he wondered why but the answer came to him. Yeah, they'd dated for six months after they met at last year's New Year's Eve party in Boston, but this was different. Hazel was coming to visit him at his home for the *first time*. She was coming to 'The Island', as the natives called it, and he was sweating bullets. Would she love the place as much as he did? Would she want to stay in his house once she saw it? Sure, he'd described it to her, shown her pictures. Heck, he'd given her a virtual tour by hauling his webcam around the place, but none of those things meant squat.

She'd never been there!

What if she hates it? What if she hates the island and my friends, and…well, everything? What if she gets back on the next ferry, and I never see her again?

'There are plenty of fish in the sea, literally and figuratively. Don't stress too much over women', his dad always said.

That'd been easy for him to say. He'd met the love of his life in high school, married right after they graduated college, and been happy for the rest of his life. Arthur had a string of dead end relationships, then Hazel came into his life, and for the first time a soft warm surge bloomed inside him that seemed to signal real love.

The blast of a horn brought him out of his inner turmoil. He spun toward the sea and smiled. The ferry was fast approaching the wharf. Stepping over to the old wrought-iron railing at the edge of the boardwalk he waited for the steamship to dock, and the passengers to disembark. It was so early in the season that there weren't many people onboard, so Hazel was easy to spot. There was also her physical appearance. She tended to stand out from any crowd given her height, her willowy shape, the white blonde hair, and a lean figure that almost screamed athlete. Her clothes were not at all typical for the era and time of year. Her cutoff jeans were super high on her thighs, and her tie-dye T-shirt was better suited to a 1960's protest. He, on the other hand, was the soul of propriety in long pants, a long-sleeved shirt buttoned up to the collar, dress shoes, and socks. Casting his gaze down he saw her running shoes. Yeah, he and she made for quite the pair.

She saw him, smiled, then raced to him. "Arty, dude! Oh, it's so good to see you."

Their arms entwined, and he hoisted her aloft. At six-two and—not to be boastful—pretty damn fit, he could toss her around like a little kid. Their eyes locked, and hers spoke volumes. The world fell away, lost as if enveloped in an early morning fog. Time slowed and seized his mind like when he chewed some saltwater taffy from *Darling's* and his jaw went up and down in slow motion as he ate it. Silence wrapped about them like a quilt on a frigid January night. Her firm yet supple flesh made him feel conflicted as his hands held hers. He wanted to grip harder, to hold her close, and yet her softness commanded his body to gently cradle her. Her warmth trickled down his arms to ensnare his heart and soul. He lowered her until they were face to face, nose to nose, and then their lips touched. Her kiss was like a soft breeze and sweet wine, and he drank in as much as she gave.

Setting her down, he smiled and brushed the hair from her cheek. "I'm glad to see you too. You have no idea how glad!"

"Ah, I think I do. That was a good kiss. It 'said' a lot."

He cocked his head. "Oh really? You can tell so much from a mere kiss? Tell me, what did mine say?"

"Well it was no first kiss, no perfunctory smack on the lips. It was no friendship peck, a light brush to the cheek, but it also wasn't some pushy, manly open-mouthed slobber saying, 'Hey, baby, you wanna do it?' No, it was warm and tender, and just the right duration."

"I had no idea you were an expert," Art said with a chuckle.

"Oh, years of field research," she said and winked. "Now, come on, if we stand around talking about kissing all day, we'll never leave the dock. I'm here to see this island you've talked about. Lead me to it."

"You got any bags?" Art asked.

"Got all I need in here," she replied and turned to show him her backpack.

He smiled, not only at her efficiency, but at the opportunity to see her shapely figure. "The lady travels light. My kind of woman. Come on, my cart is over here," he said, gesturing for her to follow.

She did, falling into pace with him, and Art wondered if the temperature had shot up. She was right there, right next to him, her hand open and available, yet he was unsure about taking it. Now he was truly sweating! If he took it now, he'd get her hand all slimy. What a wonderful start to the weekend that would be. An electrical charge rippled through his body as the air shot from his lungs.

Hazel made the move. She took his hand in hers. "Did you say cart?"

Art's throat cinched down like a halyard pulled tight around a cleat. She was so casual about it all.

"Yeah," he squeaked, cleared his throat, and pointed. "Right there. With a lot of islanders we use electric cars to get around."

"Ah, eco-friendly. Me like."

"Well…ah, yeah," he stammered and added with a whisper, "most of us can't afford a car."

Thankfully, she didn't hear and plopped herself into the passenger seat. He climbed in, and off they went toward town. A more accurate description would be that they entered Oak Bluffs. After all it sat next to the wharf. Hazel spun in her seat to take it all in, which made Art smile. There was something about showing the island to a new visitor that always refreshed his love for and appreciation of the place. Of course, there was the added boost of it being *her*.

"So, that's the Flying Horses on our left," he said as he pointed.

"I remember you talking about that place. Oldest carousel in America, right? Oh, and is that cotton candy I smell?"

"You have a sharp nose."

She shrugged. "Eh, sharper eyes. I spotted the display through the open window. Can't wait to sink my teeth into a batch of that! A chronic sweet tooth is one of my many vices."

"Really, how do you manage to keep so thin?"

"Dieting, Arty. Dieting and exercise. I bike at least a couple miles every day. If I don't do both, I blow up like a balloon. That cotton candy, when I so much as sniff it, I gain five pounds. Hey, what's with the statue?

Was that a weeping angel?"

"Memorial to an old…battle in the Revolutionary War."

"I caught a glimpse of the plaque, but did my sharp eyes deceive me, or was the date the nineteenth of April?"

Art nodded. "Yeah. People talk about the Revolutionary War starting with the shot heard 'round the world, on the nineteenth of April in seventy-five. Well, for us islanders, the nineteenth of April five years later is the day the angels wept. Anyway, come on, you don't want to hear a bunch of gloomy history. Let me show you my world."

"Angels wept, eh? Yeah, does sound gloomy. Hey, what a cute little marina."

She turned to the right as they zipped along the southern edge of the harbor.

"Yeah, not as big or popular as Vineyard Haven, and right now it's empty."

"Slow season?" Hazel said, turning to face him.

"Early in the season. Once the Fourth hits, oh man, this place will be hopping."

"I guess I came at a good time," she said with a smile. "We can have some quiet *alone* time."

She winked. Arthur's chest was crushed in a vise, but he managed to paint on a grin. He became acutely aware of the island's small size. They arrived at Mayhew Manor too soon. Parking next to the towering edifice of wood and stone, a tower atop its main peek, he stood and waited for her. She gazed up at the place, her cute little jaw dropping open. She had such pretty white teeth, and her eyes widened like a camera attempting to encompass a panoramic vista.

"Holy crap, this is where you live? Damn, Art, you been holding out on me? I thought you were a poor college grad like me. I'm going to be paying on my student loans for the rest of my life."

"Calm yourself, my dear, I am no one-percenter. I'll wager my college debt is right up there with yours."

"Then how can you afford this place?"

"It belonged to my parents, and my dad's parents before them. This is the ancestral home of the Mayhew family going back, oh…right around two centuries. William Mayhew built it in the early 1800's."

"Wow, and here I thought my family was a big deal for being in Providence since I was born. You live here all alone?"

"Yeah," he said, his voice cracking. He cleared his throat. "My brother and sisters…died in a boating accident years ago. The waters of the island aren't at all lucky for the Mayhews, but hey, let's not talk about negative stuff. Come on, you can stow your bag, and I'll take you on a tour of the island."

He set off quickly, led her along the serpentine red brick walkway, and blinked fast to staunch the flow of tears. They went up the creaky, bowing steps to the wide, bland porch. He couldn't help but be ashamed of the place. In the years since his siblings passed, this area in particular had suffered the most neglect. It had been one of their favorite play places. The porch was the bridge of their pirate ship, the deck of their hover express, and the command center of their underwater city. Once his siblings were gone, neither Art nor his parents could ever bear to sit on the chairs.

The porch chairs. Oh yeah, they'd lean the rocking chairs over so they lay on their fronts, the tops resting on the railing then stand behind them, and hold onto the rockers. They became the triggers and the chairs their anti-aircraft batteries. It drove their dad crazy, as he always complained about scuffing the paint.

He never complained…*after*.

Now the deck sagged from rot, the chairs sat idle, and the paint peeled from the rough boards. Art brought Hazel inside before she could ask any painful questions. They moved through the snug foyer and entered the sitting room opposite the large parlor. Here was a room Art *had* worked to maintain. It was the main spot he hung out in.

She set her backpack on the low six-sided coffee table and slowly viewed the entire room. "Wow, what beautiful old pieces. Man, I haven't seen a platform rocker outside of a museum."

Art leaned on the high back chair next to the equally high couch and gestured at the chair. "Sit down, try it out."

"Oh, I'd be afraid to. What if I break it?"

"You? Please. You're what, maybe a hundred and ten soaking wet? If it can take my beefy frame, it can take two of you. Why, I bet you won't be able to get it to rock."

She grinned and climbed in. "You're on, my friend. Loser buys lunch."

It took a bit of effort, the springs were strong, but she did manage to rock it, albeit a tad. Art sat on the couch so he was closer, but not crowding her, and stretched out his long legs across the coffee table. He smiled. It brought warmth to his soul to see life in the room once more. Since his parents' passing, this had become his sanctuary, his hideaway from the world. The flat screen TV mounted above the sooty stone fireplace was the true window in the room. The others were kept closed, locked, and the drapes and shades forever drawn. His laptop and Xbox sat on the roll top desk in the corner, and the wrap-around bookshelves, complete with ladder on a track, had enough books to take him on any flight of fancy he might want. What else did he need?

There was one thing, and he hoped with all his heart it sat across from him.

"Art, what's first on the agenda?" she said, still scanning the room.

"Ah, I thought we'd take that tour."

"Sounds like a plan. Let's hit it! Can I leave my things here?"

"Sure. Ah, you don't want to change?"

"What, my clothes? Oh man, you're not going to tell me you're one of those Moral Majority-types, are you? Isn't it a bit late in the relationship to spring that on me?"

"No, not at all. It's just that, while the island is nice and hot during the day, once the sun goes down, it gets pretty chilly around here."

"That's why you want me to change now, before noon?"

He cracked his knuckles, the thing he did whenever he got nervous, and licked his lips. "Well...it's not me, Hazel. Some of our more conservative types might give you some guff."

"And I'll give it right back!"

"Remember, I have to live with these people."

She fell silent, chewing the inside of her lip for a moment. "If anyone says anything, I'm a mainlander who doesn't know any better."

He didn't want to tick off any of his neighbors, but he also valued Hazel's company far more than theirs, so he agreed. They set off, and his heart pounded so hard as to make the blood thunder inside his ears. They hadn't discussed the sleeping arrangements. She had left her pack in the sitting room. He tried to put such concerns out of his mind, and instead focused on the island.

He took her through the sprawling streets of Oak Bluffs, down Main Street in Vineyard Haven, and out North Road toward Chilmark and Gay Head.

"I can't believe it, a town with a main street called that," she said then giggled.

"That's the island for you. Wait until you see the clay cliffs; they are incredible. Back when my dad was a kid, you could climb them."

"We can't now?" she said.

He shook his head. "No, wind and rain have caused a lot of erosion over the years, as have people. A while back climbing was banned to try and slow it."

"Ah, I get it. Sounds like your family and this island are tied together."

"They are. Thomas Mayhew, an ancestor of mine, bought the place back in 1642. His son established a school for the Wampanoag, the natives who lived in this area."

"Whoa, the whole blinking rock, like that guy who bought

Manhattan?"

Art nodded. "Pretty much, yeah. What do you think of the place?"

"It's neat, but isn't it kind of...I don't know...limited?"

"I think of it as a comfort. What, New York more to your liking?"

Hazel shook her head. "Naw, I'm a little tired of the political BS floating around this country. To be honest, I can't stand anymore of 'Sister' Sarah and her ilk. I'll move to Canada or some other place that's more enlightened. Wow, are those the cliffs?"

She leaned forward in her seat and pointed, and Art turned to follow her gaze. Not that he needed to. He could drive this road in a blinding nor'easter. Pulling into a parking space, he climbed out, and doubt crept into his soul. Hazel wasn't in love with the island.

Huh, well, it's early in our first day. Ah, an evening in Oak Bluffs will do the trick. We'll do supper, maybe a movie, and finish off with a few rides on the Flying Horses. Oh, and a big helping of cotton candy.

He smiled as he led her up to the scenic overlook. The cliffs, a colorful mix of red, tan, and white rolled and undulated across the land before them. They stood there, the tall sea grass fluttered in the breeze, and a small pulse of delight rippled through him. Despite the prospect of losing out with Hazel, a pleasant warmth still filled his soul. There was something about the cliffs that always brightened his mood. He could understand why. It embodied so many wonderful elements of his world. There was the countryside, the wide-open vistas of the sea, and the sounds of the gentle waves breaking on the shore. Then there were the aromas of the island: a unique blend of sea salt, honeysuckle and—of all things—a dash of skunk, which he had never found anywhere else.

"Gee, what's that, some sort of museum on wheels?" Hazel asked.

Art shifted his gaze to see what she meant. A pair of horses pulled a carriage along the narrow loop road that ran along the cliffs.

"That is Phillip Davenport and his wife out for their daily ride."

"What, you parade around waxwork figures to remind people of the so-called good old days?"

"Wax? Hazel, that's the real Davenports, as in, in the flesh, alive and kicking."

"You sure? I've seen Greek statues in a museum livelier than those two!"

He chuckled. "Good one, but yes, they are most definitely alive. Trust me, the day one of those two kicks the bucket, the whole island will hear about it. They're the richest family around, and they make sure everyone knows it. They lost a lot during the Depression, but they're one-percenters."

The carriage drew near. He bit his lip as Hazel stood there, hands on her hips, and cast her eyes up at them with a defiant glare. Tiffany Davenport, dry and sour as ever, frowned down at her.

"Clearly a tourist with *no* sense of *decency*," she sneered and sat back as they rode off.

"Huh, seems all that money hasn't bought them a personality, or a sense of humor. They seem like they've been eating lemons all day."

"Okay, enough with the jokes. I get the point. Hey, you want to see something special? There's a beach near here with a place we call the 'Council of Elrond.' Do you know the term?"

"That's from *The Lord of the Rings*, right?"

Art nodded. "Yeah. In our case, it's a cave my friends and I played in when we were kids."

"Awww, a memory of childhood. Yes, I most definitely would like to see it."

A new surge of hope rippled through his chest. He drove her along South Road to that most special of spots. It was remote, almost at the center of South Beach, but it didn't matter, Art could find it at midnight on a moonless night. He grabbed the flashlight from the cabinet under his seat, took her hand, and led her along the old trail he knew so well. They moved down the side of the cliff. The sounds of traffic on the asphalt faded into the distance, and the path grew narrower until it was little more than a thin, bare patch between the tall sea grasses. Once on the beach, Art easily found the cave. For him and his friends it was the best play place in the world. He stepped inside but stopped and turned when he saw her freeze at the opening.

"Um, is it safe? It seems awful dark in there. I don't…do well in the dark."

Smiling, he held up the flashlight. "Got it covered. Come on."

Switching it on, they marched inside. The floor was wide and sandy, the walls and ceiling jagged and rough, and he saw their old 'thrones,' the twisted lumps of stone that had the rough appearance of chairs were where he and his friends used to sit when they called the council to order. He saw the special items, the things that were the whole reason they'd chosen the cave as their headquarters.

"Are those crystals?" she asked.

"Yeah, once you get deep inside, they line the walls and ceiling, and there's one great big one in the floor right here," he said, pointing at the ground before them.

Hazel moved forward to kneel at the spot. Brushing the sand away, she ran her fingers over the large deep blue stone. "Wow, it's awesome. Any idea what kind of crystal it is?"

He shook his head. "No, and believe me, my friends and I tried to find out. We know they're not diamonds or sapphires, or any other precious stone, but when the lights hits them, oh man, are they ever incredible. That's why I wanted us to get here now."

She stood and faced him, her brow wrinkled. "What's so special about now?"

"At high noon on the longest day of the year, a shaft of light comes down through an opening in the roof and illuminates the big crystal. It's said if two people stand before the stone, and if their love is truly pure, a window unto eternity will open."

"Oooo, a test of true love, eh? How many girls have you brought down here for the test?"

He swallowed hard. "Um, well…I've always wanted to do it, but it's never worked."

She blew a raspberry. "Yeah, right, I bet you've said that to all the ladies. Okay, I'll play along. When's the laser light show start?"

"In a moment," he replied, checking his watch. "The light will come down, illuminate the big crystal, and the cave will fill with a soft, blue glow."

A slight glow did in fact appear, slowly filling the cavern. Art and Hazel gazed up at the same moment as the sun reached its zenith. Like a laser, a column of light shot straight down to the crystal, pulsing like a beating heart.

"Wow, what a show." She gasped.

Tendrils of light, like the radiant legs of some giant spider shot from the crystal. Both of them jumped in surprise.

"Holy crap, it *is* a laser show," she squeaked.

"Ah, it's never done this before," Art stammered.

The beams multiplied, as each hit a crystal, it split, and the new ones struck more crystals, and thus they increased exponentially until the entire cave seemed ablaze with dancing rays of pure energy. The center of it all, a spot above them in mid-air swirled like a tornado or whirlpool.

"Arty, please tell me this is your doing. I'm starting to get a bad feeling about this!"

"Sorry, girl, I'm a couple minutes ahead of you on that front."

"What? Why the heck are we standing here like the proverbial deer caught in the headlights? Let's get out of here!"

Clasping hands tight, they bolted for the opening. An explosive roar reverberated behind them, a blast of wind like a nor'easter enveloped them, and it was as if he and Hazel were in the eye of a storm. Total silence, total stillness shrouded them. The ground melted away from their feet and every move was a labor, taking twice as long as it should, as if they'd been dropped in a vat of Jell-O. Art thought they were moving in slow motion like in some lame horror movie. A swirling vortex of white light appeared before them, and they sped up, drawn to it like flotsam to a whirlpool.

Is this it? Are we dying and doing the classic 'go into the light routine'?

He turned to Hazel, held her hand tight, and smiled, hoping to reassure her. Based on her strangely calm expression, it seemed as if she'd accepted their fate. Her grip told another story. She was as scared as he was yet determined to be strong in the face of the unknown. The light grew more intense and blotted out everything. Art was certain of Hazel's presence by the touch of her hand.

Darkness came, oblivion embraced them, and he waited for either harps or pitchforks to appear. Instead, he did a cannonball into deep water. Down, *down* into the blue-green depths of the Atlantic they went. He knew the waters around the island. The sting to his eyes, the icy stabs to his muscles, and the salty taste in his mouth told him where they were.

Opening his eyes, he scanned the area for Hazel. They'd been separated upon splashdown. A long willowy shape kicked by him headed for the surface. He didn't have to be a marine biologist to know it wasn't a dolphin. He smiled, despite their dire circumstances, as he was relieved to see her, and swam after her.

Breaking the surface, he coughed and sputtered for a moment, then sucked in a lungful of refreshing air. "Hazel, you okay?"

"Other than scared enough to almost turn my hair white and chilled to the bone, I'm great. You?" she replied as she headed for shore.

He fell in next to her, swam with ease, and tried to calm down and catch his breath. "I hope I didn't scream like a girl as we were hurtling through the air, but no guarantees."

"Great, we're alive. Frozen stiff, but alive. You want to explain what happened?"

"Me? I'm as baffled as you. Hazel, I swear, the only thing that's ever happened in the cave before was the big crystal lit up."

Reaching the shallow area, she stood and waded ashore, her long thin arms wrapped about her slender frame as she shivered. "Really? Hand to God? You're saying that wasn't your doing?"

"Come on, you think I could arrange something like…that? I wouldn't know where to begin," he replied, stepped out of the water and turned to offer her his hand.

She walked by him, ignored the gesture, and bent to wring out her hair. "Huh, actually, now that I think about it, you must be telling the truth."

"Thank you for believing me. What put the check mark in the win column for me?"

"Well, lasers and wind machines could have started that show, but when we…um, for lack of a better word got *immersed*, we were practically immobilized. As we shot from the cave, my hair didn't budge. You may be some closet geek, who goes to Comic-Con dressed as Wonder Woman for all I know, but there's no way your FX skills are *that* good. Whatever hit us was real. We have to figure out what it was."

He cracked his knuckles. "Ah...thank you for that, I guess. I think somewhere buried in there was a compliment. Anyway, come on, let's get back to my cart, and we'll head home. We both need a change of clothes."

Her teeth chattered. "No argument here, let's go."

They set off, and Art immediately came to a halt. It was so abrupt Hazel ran into him.

"Ooph," she grunted. "Arthur, what's up? Come on, I'm slowly turning blue here."

He turned to face her. "Um...sorry, but we've got a problem. The trail is gone."

"What? That's impos..." She glanced behind him as she bore witness to his truth. Her throat bobbed as she swallowed hard. "Arthur, I am officially scared. Please tell me you know what's going on. This is your island. Did we come ashore somewhere else?"

He shook his head as their eyes met. "Sorry, Hazel, but this *is* the same spot. The cliffs are bigger and further out into the water, but there's no mistaking this stretch of land."

"Then what—? Wait a minute, bigger? Further? So, in a way, you could say the cliffs are...younger?"

The hairs on the back of his neck stood straight up, and he licked his lips. He could see where she was going with this, and he didn't like it. "I wouldn't necessarily put it that way. Oh crap. Hazel, we've got company."

He pointed off down the beach behind her.

She didn't budge, didn't even turn her head slightly. It was clear she was fighting the urge to cast her gaze in that direction. "If I turn around, am I going to see Vikings or some other strange apparition of history?"

"Ah, how do you feel about Colonial America, say...mid eighteenth century?"

She shut her eyes tight and winced in emotional pain. "Oh, this isn't happening, this isn't happening, it's a delusion, a dream, it's all a dream!"

"A shared dream?"

Her eyes popped open. "You had to spoil it for me, didn't you?"

"Sorry, but they're going to be here in about a minute, and we need a plan of attack, so to speak."

"Say little, watch, listen, and figure out what the heck's going on! How are you at improv?"

"Been in a couple plays with the Island Players."

"Good, it'll help. 'Cause either we're caught up in one wild joke, or we've proven Einstein wrong. I don't know which, but we need to figure it out and find a way out of this mess."

Art painted a smile on and waved to the middle-aged couple approaching on horses. Behind them was a gang of half a dozen younger people. They bounced around so much it was hard to get a count of them. Hazel turned to face them; her arm slipped around his waist to cling to him tightly. It made his heart ease off on the cannon volley it was laying down. He took a deep breath as a renewed tingle tore through his body. He hoped it was only a chill as the man and woman stopped their horses, and the man easily dropped to the ground. If they were actors, some sort of re-creationists, they were damn good ones!

"Good day to you, neighbors," the man called out, helping the woman down. "What brings you to our shores?"

Art took them both in. They appeared to be in their fifties. The man was as tall as Art with the same rat's nest of ebony hair and a powerful build. He either worked out daily or was a laborer. The woman was barely five feet, but she was no pixie like Hazel. Not fat, merely curvy, and her long brown hair was neatly tied into a long ponytail.

It was their clothes that truly caught his attention. He hadn't seen outfits like them since his last visit to Sturbridge Village. If these people were fakes, they weren't good, they were incredible. The man wore breeches, what today would be considered knee-highs, although he wasn't wearing white stockings. Maybe it was the heat or being on the beach. Instead he had boots. Then there was his cream-colored shirt, brown vest, and coat—all of them were old and worn. The lady, poor thing, rode sidesaddle in a long green dress with more layers than Art could count. It had to be stifling.

"Ah, we are travelers," Art replied, staying vague.

The man turned and drew closer, and their eyes locked. Instantly, words unspoken passed between them, and they both smiled. Art was worried about their predicament, but he *knew* they were among family.

"Cousin," he and the man said together.

"Arthur, is it truly you? Oh, thanks be to God. We feared the worst when we found the ship's wreckage. Who is this young lad with you?"

"Lad?" Hazel snapped.

The woman gasped and turned to her horse. "Good husband, avert your eyes, and preserve the lady's dignity!"

He did, staring off into the waves as his wife pulled a blanket down and dashed forward to wrap Hazel in it.

"Here, child, cover your nakedness. We will get you home and dressed at once."

"Naked? Oh, ah, yes, a thousand pardons," Hazel stammered.

"Why are you dressed as a common tar?" the woman said.

"Tart?" Hazel said.

"*Tar*, Hazel, she means a sailor," Art explained. "We were asleep when the storm hit. By the time we were awake, the ship was badly listing, and all our clothes tumbled overboard. We put on what was handy and grabbed whatever would float to help us keep from drowning."

"We'll get you decent garments so as to avoid public shame, and feed you," the woman said. "I'll not have my new cousin called a tart by the locals or be sickly due to lack of food. I'm Patience Mayhew, good wife to Joshua, the lumbering clod you see there."

Patience smiled and giggled, and Art could see Hazel grimace. It was clear dental hygiene was a bit primitive in this era.

"I'm Hazel Lo—" she started to say, but Art cut her off.

"This is *Lady* Hazel Puttenham, of the Essex Puttenhams, and my wife."

Joshua turned to face all of them, smiling. "Wife? Why, Arthur, you said nothing of a wife in your letters. You are a sly fox wanting to surprise us and a lady at that."

"Husband, enough mindless prattle. You take the children and ride on ahead. Stoke up a fire, put on some soup and tea, and I'll bring our cousins along presently."

Joshua grinned and bowed to her. "Yes, m'lady. You see, cousin, even here, we still live under tyranny."

He mounted his horse as the others reached them. It was clear these were their children. The 'genetic apples' hadn't fallen far from their 'trees.' Patience shooed them away, and Art almost burst out laughing. There were two boys and four girls, ages ranging from about five to fifteen, and the expressions on the two oldest boys' faces were priceless. Hazel was effectively covered, but her legs were bare from the knees down, and the boys stared at her as if she was a stripper doing her best pole dance. They scampered after Joshua as he rode off.

"Hazel, can you ride?" Patience said.

"Ah, not well, and I'm feeling...weak from our trials and hunger. I'll walk. Could we go inland, and take a road back to town?"

"No, this end of the island belongs mostly to the savages. We cannot be going there. Come, I'll lead you to our home. We have one of the largest farms on the island."

"Ah, is there a problem with the nat...ah, savages? I thought 'Grandfather' Thomas signed a treaty with the Sachems. I also recall that 'Grandfather' Thomas Jr. established a school for them."

Patience nodded as they walked along the sandy shore. "Aye, you know your family history. However, no piece of paper, nor converting to the true faith, can change the truth that they are still savages and must be avoided."

"You have a lot of grandfathers, husband," Hazel said slowly. "And what is a Sachem?"

"The leaders of the Wampanoag are called Sachem," he explained. "As for Thomas and his son, they were great-grandfathers. Actually, there are several greats in there. We find it easier to omit them, eh, cousin?"

Arthur smiled and laughed, trying desperately to lighten the mood. Fortunately, Patience responded in kind, and they continued.

"So true, cousin. Ah, it pleases me greatly that you survived the sinking. I do not know how Joshua would have borne the loss of another family member to the sea."

"Another?" Hazel said.

"You have not told her?"

"I thought it best not to speak of it until we were on dry land again. Hazel, Thomas Jr. drowned in a shipwreck. His dear father never recovered from the loss, and thus our family tends to avoid the sea."

"Hard to do when you live on an island," she replied.

"All the world's continents are mere islands," Art said.

Patience heaved a sigh. Her ample bosom rose under her heavy dress. "Ah, you sound like Joshua, when you say that. You are most certainly a Mayhew."

"I don't understand," Hazel said.

Art gazed up at her and smiled. "Those words, *'All the world's continents are mere islands',* are essentially our family motto."

"I see. Wait, how is it you and Joshua knew you were related? I mean, I see a certain resemblance, but…did you see something else?"

"The eyes," Art and Patience said together.

Their gazes locked for a moment, and they laughed.

"Aye, cousin, there is no denying you are family. I saw it in Joshua's face the moment he beheld you. You share the same hazel eyes. Here is the breach in the trees. Come, our home lies on the outskirts of Edgar Towne."

"Edgar Towne?" Arthur cried, and paused to collect himself. "We've arrived before…? Oh, yes, I remember, they sailed—I mean, *we* sailed from Southampton in the spring of 1779."

"Cousin, are you addled? You seem confused about nothing at all."

"It's the wreck and hunger," Hazel said. "It's affected both of us. Some rest and food will improve our state."

"Yes, most certainly," Patience replied, nodding.

She led them and the horse through a break in some tall oaks trees, and they came out on a narrow tree-lined dirt road. Art sweat bullets and shivered. Fortunately, given the state of their clothes and bodies, no one, not even Hazel, suspected the truth. He tried to put the future out of his mind and focus on the here and now. They needed to eat, get cleaned up then talk about how to handle this brave *old* world they'd been thrust into. His nose crinkled. The stench of raw sewage trickling across the road literally brought tears to his eyes. It was clear Hazel had the same reaction, as she coughed and gagged.

"Cousin, are you ill?" Patience said. "Perhaps you've caught a chill from the vile sea air. Come, we will get you inside. Do you see? It's as I said, one of the largest homes on the island."

Art cast his gaze about the area. The house *was* quite large, a classic New England Colonial home. A low wall made up of simply stacked stones separated the two-story building from the road. The place was different from the paintings and sketches he'd seen in his family archive. It appeared brand new. Stone fireplaces sat at both ends of the house and the back and were in sharp contrast to the white walls, and deep green shutters. A barn, a woodshed, and stables were further back from the road. Fields stretched off across the rolling countryside, and pear and cherry trees dominated the front yard.

There were also a great many people, and all gaped at him and Hazel. Any doubts Art had as to *when* they were evaporated in an instant. Even the folks at Plymouth Plantation weren't this good. It wasn't so much their clothes or physical appearance. It was, of all things, the smells. As rank as the waste flowing around them was, it was also clear these people had no idea what deodorant was, and a good twenty people of all ages crowded around to see them. It quickly became obvious what was the focus of their attention. *Hazel.* At first he thought it was because they hoped to catch a glimpse of her so-called nakedness. Surely the children would have loudly announced that upon their return. However, it wasn't the case. Yes, a number of men cast their gazes down at her legs, but most merely seemed fascinated by *her*. Of the people crowded around them, there were only five women.

Hazel was a rarity.

"Poppa, Poppa, they have arrived," a little ragamuffin in a yellow dress, stained with soot and dirt, shouted.

For one so tiny, she appeared to be no more than five, but she had a big voice. Art grinned. It made sense. In this era, in such a large family, if you wanted to be heard, you had to be loud.

"Charity, calm yourself, child," Patience scolded. "You'll give yourself a case of apoplexy."

Joshua stepped out of the front door and stood upon the large stone threshold. "Come in, cousins, our home is yours," he said, waving his arm to gesture for them to enter.

"Are they the Mayhews from England?" someone said.

"Is that Arthur?" another called out. "What word do you bring us from Parliament?"

Patience hustled them toward the door then turned to the crowd. "Good neighbors, good friends, *please,* our dear cousins have suffered a terrible trauma. Give them time to recover, and we shall present them to you properly tomorrow."

The throng agreed, called out well wishes to the couple and dispersed. They entered the home, and Art's stress levels dropped. Granted, they were no closer to an answer as to what the heck was going on, but they had achieved a measure of safety. As Joshua closed the door Art cast his gaze around. Like the exterior, the interior was classic. They were in a small entryway, what today would be called an atrium. Pegs on their left provided places to hang coats, and a low shelf near the floor held child-sized boots, all of them caked in mud and sand. A narrow spiral staircase led to the second floor.

He didn't need to see more to know the layout of the place. The family records meant he could walk the place with his eyes closed. Two large front rooms sat to the right and left. He could see them through the wide doorways. Each had elaborate panel work on the walls and above the fireplaces. In the back was the large kitchen. From their current vantage point he saw the long table set for a meal. In the large square stone fireplace which had to be at least five or six feet square, a great kettle hung over the roaring fire from a hook, and a teenage girl stirred the contents. To the right and left of the kitchen would be four rooms, which were the children's rooms and storage. Upstairs were two bedrooms and an 'open chamber' for more storage where Patience would do spinning and weaving to make cloth and linen.

The only issue for Art was the heat for it was rather stifling. He tried to ignore it as they were escorted forward. After all, it wasn't like he could ask them to turn down the A/C. Of course, given their wet, cold clothes, the warmth was rather welcome. Here they met Faith, the oldest, who'd been left to watch the baby and tend the household.

"We will prepare the meal," Patience said. "Arthur, take your good woman upstairs to our room. You'll find dry clothes there."

"Of course. Top of the stairs, the back bedroom."

Joshua and Patience glanced at each other than at him.

"Bless me, but so it is," she said. "Husband, your letters home were quite detailed."

"I...um, suppose, but, strike me down, I don't recall being *that* detailed."

"Ack! Do you see why our lands are in such disarray? How can I accomplish anything with an addle-pated husband and disobedient children?" Patience said, wearing a smile. She playfully smacked two of her little ones.

Art smiled and nodded. Hazel did likewise, and he led her by the arm up the spiral staircase. It was beautiful, far better than any old sketch or painting could hope to convey. Wide low steps with a lovely stain, with the thin spindles painted white, supported the deep red railing which was not painted, being mahogany. Some sort of light varnish helped to bring out the deep natural color of the wood. Reaching the top, they moved quickly into the room. Art closed the door and turned the old key in the equally old lock. Although, in studying them, they appeared to be quite new. He turned to her, heaved a sigh of relief, and saw her do the same. In fact, she almost seemed to deflate, as if the stress within her, like a Macy's parade float, was being let out. She tossed aside the blanket then flopped into a chair next to the bed.

"Holy crap, I don't believe this," she said, holding her head in her hands. Taking in a deep breath, she glanced up at him. "Art, I know this may seem like a silly question, but I have to say it out loud once. Have we gone back in time?"

"I know it sounds unbelievable, but I'm hard pressed to come up with another explanation. We're two hundred and fifty years in the past. It's June 1779."

"Amazing. Here I am, graduate of Tufts with a degree in anthropology, dropped into the greatest living lab in history, and all I can think is how to get out of here!"

"Hey, don't be ashamed about feeling that way. I'm right there with you."

"Great. So, how do we do it? This isn't like John Carter on Mars, or Dorothy in Oz, and it sure ain't Narnia. It's the cave, right?"

"Yeah, and that's where we run into a problem," he said.

"Oh, I *so* did not want to hear that." She groaned. "What—? Wait, timing, is that it?"

He nodded. "Yeah, noon on the summer solstice is the only time the light enters the cave."

"Oy! So, we're trapped here for a year? Come on, there's got to be something we can do."

"Right now, what we need to do is get dressed and head back downstairs," he replied, turning for the closet. "If we take too long they'll grow suspicious."

She cocked her head at him and got to her feet. "Of what? As far as they know, we're a married couple, which I assume you said so we *could* be alone."

"Precisely. However, if we're alone too long, they'll think we're...um, engaged in inappropriate activities."

"Inappropriate? Wha—Ah, as we're guests in their home, hanky panky is a big no, no, right?"

"Yeah. Also, it *is* day time."

She rolled her eyes. "Gad, talk about repressed. No wonder most families have a dozen kids."

"As I recall from the family journals, women were in short supply back then—ah, I mean *now*. Between death in childbirth, low immigration, and people left due to the war, young healthy women were virtually unknown here. If you were single, you'd have more suitors than a divorced lottery winner."

"I see. Hey, what was that calling me Lady Something-Ham?"

"Another tidbit I remembered. If they think you're a lady, a member of the nobility, it'll boost your standing in the community. In among my dad's personal papers, I found some genealogy stuff he'd researched on our family back in England. One of our ancestors was related to the Puttenhams, so I figured it was a good ace to pull out and play."

"Ah, I see again. Smart. I recall my classes on Colonial America. Women in this era were not—*are not*—treated well."

"Correct. To say you're a second-class citizen would be a classic understatement," Art said, rifling through the garments. "Here we go."

He handed her quite the plethora of items, both male and female, but mostly female, and she spread them out on the multicolored quilt that covered the large bed. There were underwear, undergarments, a slip, a light green dress with long sleeves, and stockings. The male items were far more modest. He wore underwear, an under shirt, pants, and a shirt.

"Holy cow, do I have to wear *all* that stuff?" she said.

"Hey, be glad we're not in Boston or New York," he replied, moving to the other side of the bed. "Can you imagine the heavy clothes and corset you'd have to wear there? Small communities on the outskirts of civilization tended to be a little less restrictive."

"Good point. How are we going to do this? You okay with turning our backs?"

He cracked his knuckles and nodded. "Sure."

They did so and changed.

"Art, give me the full skinny on what's up with your…relations. I mean, they were expecting you, and you don't have a police callbox, so, what's the deal? Wait, I know, some ancestor of yours was on the ship they said went down."

"You got it. Wait, police…? Ohhh, I get it. Good one."

"Thank you. Just trying to lighten the mood. Your ancestor was also named Arthur?"

"Yeah. See, my full name is Arthur Edward Mayhew IV."

"Wow, which *digit* are we standing in for?"

"Um, Arthur Jr. He was coming to America to…let me think. Ah, he had tried to resolve a dispute the islanders had with the British army.

In…September 1778, General Grey raided the island for sheep, cattle, and other items, promising payment later, but it was never made. The islanders sent an emissary to London, *twice*, to ask for the money, but he was rebuked. Arthur Jr. made an appeal to Parliament and was coming to tell them when his ship went down," he explained, slipping up his trousers. "Huh, linen. Not bad."

"I'm curious, what was the answer?"

He shook his head. "No. As far as the Brits were concerned, the islanders were rebels and unworthy of consideration."

"Wow, that's going to go over like a…what, lead pound note, or shilling? Not to be morbid, but is he dead?"

"Let me put it this way—his body was never found. I think we're safe in assuming he 'sleeps with the fishes'."

"And his wife?"

Art sat on the bed to pull on his stockings. "He wasn't married."

"Whoa! What happens if Joshua writes to the folks back home?"

"Hazel, we're in the middle of a war! According to my family records, there were no direct communications with the family back in England for almost ten years after he died. Let me think…it was…damn, I can't remember exactly, but it wasn't until after the war, word reached England about his death and another son was sent to…um, help with things here."

"I see. So, we're in the clear on that. However, it does bring up another point: the war. How is that going to affect us?"

He swallowed hard. *Oh, I can't bring myself to speak of…it, not now. There's only so much bad news she can take at once.*

Two

Licking his lips, Arthur turned toward Hazel and smiled. As great as she'd been in shorts and a tee, there was something about this old fashion rustic outfit that made her even hotter. The flowing dress, the snug bodice with its intricate needlepoint, and the delicate sleeves all combined to create a vision of true loveliness, despite the outfit hanging from her body. Although, who was he to talk? He had to cinch his belt up to the last notch to keep his pants up. Joshua and Patience were much bulkier than either of them.

Hazel snapped her fingers. "Yo, dude, come back to me."

"What? Oh, sorry, I drifted off there for a moment."

"I noticed," she said with a sigh then grinned. "You were checking me out, weren't you? Even in something this frumpy, I still rock it."

Art chuckled. "That you do, but you might want to watch the modern vernacular. Remember the trouble it caused Marty in *'Back to the Future'*."

"I'll try. Now, about the war. My knowledge of American history is not what it should be, but I guess that's why I have you. This is your…homeland, your area of expertise. What do we face in the coming year?"

"Hazel, we'll talk about it later. Come on, we need to…wait, where are your clothes?"

"I kept them on. One, the antique underwear creeps me out, two, my things are nice and cool, which helps me deal with the heat, and third, I don't want the 'relations' getting their hands on my stuff. You really want them checking out my bra or the things in my fanny pack?"

Art snatched up his wet things from the floor. "Oh man, I didn't think about that. What if they read the tags in my clothes?"

Hazel stepped closer and turned his shirt collar out. "Think they'd even know what Guatemala means?"

"I don't even know if it's a country in this time. Well, come on, let's head back down and eat, and I'll just tuck these off to the side somewhere."

They emerged from the room, headed down the stairs, and a sea of smiling faces greeted them as they entered the kitchen. Their focus was

Hazel, and thus Art was able to set his things by the fire to dry. He softly announced that, but no one heard, not with Hazel taking center stage, so to speak. Joshua stepped forward to bow, take her hand, and kiss the back of it.

"Dear lady, you are a *true* vision, more radiant than Venus emerging from the surf, and we Mayhews are *not* fond of the water. For you, even I would brave the trials of Odysseus if it meant you were my Penelope."

Hazel smiled and gazed at Patience. "My dear, I can see how it was that such a clod was able to win a prize as great as you. He has the tongue of a poet."

The children giggled and moved closer to take turns hugging her. Art slipped in among them, and they expressed their affection for him as well.

"Ah, now you are presentable," Patience said, the joy clear in her voice as her bosom heaved again. "Come, sit by me. Arthur, you take the seat of honor, the second head. Joshua, will you slice the bread?"

He nodded as he sat at the main head of the table, which was to be expected, as he was head of the household. "Aye, dear one. Faith, serve the soup. Everyone, sit, and you shall be on your best behavior, little ones, we have guests."

"Yes, Father," all the children said.

They took their seats, which consisted of only five chairs. Most of the children sat on long benches. Patience was on Arthur's right, Hazel next to her, and Charity sat on his left. She gazed up at him with eyes as blue-green as the Vineyard Sound, a dusty small face, and long flowing auburn hair. Introductions followed as Faith served the soup, but Art had no hope of remembering all of the names. Perhaps he'd do better in time. Faith was quite the adorable girl, a grownup version of Charity. She appeared to be about sixteen and did her best to be neat and clean. Joshua sliced up a large loaf of fresh bread, the children passed the chunks around the table, and he reached for his spoon.

Patience frowned. "Ah-hem!"

Joshua sighed and lowered his head a bit. "We give thanks," he said quickly and snatched up the utensil then started eating before she could voice another complaint.

Art's eyebrows shot up, and he cast his gaze at Hazel. She appeared equally stunned, but it was clear she wasn't going to say anything. He gave her a tiny nod and slapped some butter on his bread. One bite, and he almost moaned in delight. Never in his life had he tasted anything so delicious. He quickly chewed and swallowed.

"My compliments, cousin. It's clear someone around here knows how to bake."

Patience's face took on a slight, reddish hue. "You'll turn my head. It is nothing, merely our fine island grain and water, and a good dose of family love."

"Well, I guess the island water is particularly pure," Art said with a grin.

Joshua laughed a hearty Santa Claus-type laugh. "Ah, you are a witty one. You'll fit in nicely here."

"How are things here?" Art said. "I don't recall what you wrote in your letters about the…rebellion, but I would imagine things have changed. Will Hazel and I be able to find some land here?"

"The rebels continue to make mischief, nothing more," Joshua grumbled.

"Now, husband, be honest. Arthur and Hazel need to know the truth of what they face in the coming months. The colonials have managed to be victorious several times, but they are on the mainland. We remain safe and well here, other than the sorry episode regarding our stock."

"They have been lucky, nothing more," Joshua snapped. "In fact, I would say it has not been a case of Washington and the other rebels being good leaders, it's that the British commanders have been overconfident, or incompetent!"

"Enough," Patience said, frowning. "Let us not scare the children. I asked for honesty, not anger. Now, all the island is waiting to hear your news. So, tell us, what has Parliament decided in the matter of our petition for payment?"

"No, Arthur, speak not of that here," Joshua ordered. "As it concerns the entire island, it should be told to all of them. I'll not have you or the children sneaking off to tell others and get tongues a-wagging on the matter."

"Husband, you dare accuse me of being a gossip?" she snapped.

"I thought it more a statement than an accusation," he replied simply.

The children giggled, but instantly fell silent at their mother's scowl.

"Fine, we shall speak no more of it. Our cousins deserve a chance at a new life. Let us leave the dust of the past at the door and speak to them of the future."

Joshua grumbled under his breath something about there not being much future, but seemed to force a smile on his face as he moved his gaze from Arthur to Hazel. "We've set aside a small farm for you to start with. It's only a hundred acres, and it has a fine cottage for you to live in. I don't suppose it's up to *your* standards, m'lady, but it's the best available. By the contract with your father, you may work it for the next seven years and keep half of all profits."

Art tilted his toward Hazel and found her eyeing him. No words were needed; her expression spoke of concern and uncertainty. He knew she thought the same thing—she was wondering about those seven years.

What in the world are we going to do? What about the payment for the stock? Should I tell them no money is coming? In the original time stream, they don't find out for years. Will that knowledge change history? Oh, what have we gotten ourselves into? "Most fair and equitable, Joshua. On behalf of my wife and I, we thank you."

"I'm sure it will be a fine, fine home," Hazel added, trying to sound upbeat. "…and I'm sure we can…furnish it…somehow."

"No worries there," Patience replied. "I've set aside a few things we no longer need, and the children have been working on gifts. We have chairs, a table, and a good sturdy trunk for your clo—oh, apologies, where is my memory? We'll make you some new clothes and ones that fit better than our old garments."

"Did your father speak of the money I owe him?" Joshua said.

Art cracked his knuckles. "Ah, no, I don't recall him mentioning the details of it."

Joshua rolled his eyes. "Aye, he is a forgetful one. If his head were not attached to his shoulders, I think he would leave the house without it."

The children giggled. Patience silenced them with a single scowl. Even Hazel sat up straight at her glare. It was clear she was not a woman to trifle with.

"Husband," she said slowly and with a firm tone.

He nodded. "Yes, I know. Put simply, I stand in his debt for the sum of a hundred pounds, and he sent instructions I was to turn it over to you. However, what with the rebellion, times are hard. All of our sheep were taken, and we await payment. I cannot come up with such an amount all at once."

"Not that we do not have it, you understand?" Patience said, the words rolling from her mouth. "We merely do not have it in *cash*. We have goods aplenty and can easily give it to you in those. The Mayhews are not paupers!"

Art raised a hand to cut them off. "Cousins, speak no more of it. Whatever you can provide will be sufficient."

"Thank you, Arthur," he replied with a smile.

The oldest boy, Art had to think for a moment then recalled that his name was Jacob, fifteen, and quite the mini-me to his dad, poured the tea. Art instinctively reached for the cream and sugar but saw none.

"Cousin, is something amiss?" Patience said.

"Oh, I…ah, I'm used to milk and sugar."

Patience threw a sly look toward Hazel. "Well, well, it seems the lady is intent on turning you into a gentleman. Faith, fetch the honey."

The children giggled and were once more silenced by a glare from their mother.

"Oh, don't trouble yourself, child," Art called out.

"It's no trouble," Patience replied. "We are only too happy to share our *bounty* with family. I trust when you write your father, you will speak of that, and how *well* we are doing."

Art felt a tiny tug to his sleeve. Moving his eyes downward, he found Charity watching him.

"We have biggest house in town," she parroted.

"One of the biggest," Patience said with a forced laugh. "*One of,* children, where do they learn such things?"

Art patted Charity's small hand smiled at her and glanced at Hazel. She had a smirk on her face that said it all. It was clear she knew what sort of woman Patience was. Faith returned from the store room and set a small clay pot before Arthur.

"Thank you, child," he said, lifting the tiny lid.

She nodded and resumed her seat next to the baby, asleep in a bassinet, and Art had a brief struggle opening the jar. The rim, encrusted with honey, was sticky, but he managed and dropped a small dollop in his cup. Hazel did the same and both took a sip. The expression on her face told him she also thought it excellent. Never in his life had he tasted anything so wonderful. Not sickly sweet like those artificial sweeteners back home, merely…natural. Yes, that was the right word.

The same was true for the soup. It was rich and creamy, yet not overly filling and bloated. The carrots and potatoes crunched, the greens and peas snapped, and the meat was tender and tasty. Art's only complaint was that it was a bit salty, but that was to be expected. These people had no refrigeration. Salting was one of the few means of preserving meats they had.

As they ate, Hazel engaged the other couple in conversation, clearly intent on learning as much about them and this world as possible. As she was a true stranger, she could play dumb and ask all manner of questions. It worked to perfection. Inside of five minutes Patience was off like the Energizer Bunny. They learned a great deal. There were about fifteen-hundred people on the island. Most of the able-bodied men had left to join the fight, some with Washington, and a few as loyalists. It was clear the fight for independence was a source of considerable friction within the community.

Oh, if the conservatives back in our time could only hear this! Although, how will the islanders react when I tell them about their sheep and cattle?

The savages, as Patience repeatedly called them, lived primarily in 'their area,' as she referred to the village of Aquinnah. Christians, yet they preserved many of their traditions. Most people called them pagans and heathens. She made it clear their children were forbidden from interacting with 'those red people.' There were also the towns, Tisbury, Chilmark, and

Edgar Towne, which had originally been Great Harbor. It sat on the shores of the eastern harbor of the island, across from Chappaquiddick Island, and included Cottage City, present day Oak Bluffs. Tisbury, known as Vineyard Haven in the present, wrapped about the other harbor, Holmes Hole, and then stretched out to West Tisbury. The tiny hamlet of Chilmark was next to it. In between were fields and wild open countryside. This made Art smile. It was perfect with plenty of untamed vegetation and unexplored land for them to make use of. If they were truly going to be stuck here for a year, they'd need a base of operations, a place where they could sit and plan.

There's also the matter of finding a safe place to hide next April when the troops come, but we've got time for that. I wonder if the old abandoned sand pit is—what am I thinking? Old? If it is there, it's new, and Oak Bluffs isn't there, nor even Sunset Lake. Man, finding our way around here may be harder than I thought. They sure as heck don't have GPS.

"Cousin, what's wrong? Am I prattling on too much?"

Art snapped back to reality. "Oh, ah, no. Why do you ask?"

"You had a dark expression about your brow. I feared I spoke too long."

"No, not at all. Your voice is like…a nightingale's song."

Joshua grinned and gazed at Hazel. "Ah, with such flattery, it's easy to see how Arthur ensnared such a prize as you."

"True, it certainly wasn't his *looks*," she replied with a smirk.

Everyone giggled over that one.

"Come, come, enough of my mindless chatter," Patience said. "Let us hear from you. Tell us of your wedding. Was it truly opulent?"

Art swallowed hard. He was out of his element. Plan a wedding! He'd never even attended one.

"Oh, it was a modest affair, only two hundred of our closest friends and family," Hazel said with a casual tone. "As I'm not the oldest of the girls, and not Daddy's favorite, that would be my baby sister, Constance, I didn't get a big fancy wedding. Oh, to see how she wraps him around her little finger, it just… just—Forgive me, I don't want to say something I'll regret."

"We understand," Patience said and nodded her head toward Charity. "We are *quite* familiar with that situation."

A low giggle rippled around the table, and Jacob, who sat next to the girl, playfully jabbed her in the ribs. She batted him away, stuck out her tongue at him, then turned to Hazel.

"Did the king come?" she said.

"No, child, but the Prince of Wales did send a gift, which now rests on the bottom of the Atlantic." Hazel heaved a sad sigh and brushed a false tear from her cheek. "Oh, forgive me for becoming so emotional."

Patience turned to comfort her. "Not at all, it was entirely my fault for calling up such a painful memory."

"No, how could you have known? After all, a lady's wedding is supposed to be joyous."

"We will speak no more of it. As I said before, leave the past at the door and move on."

Art grinned, fighting hard not to smile from ear to ear. Hazel was a genius. In one fell swoop she'd not only cemented her standing with the family and, in time, the town, but she'd given them a reason not to pester her with details on her life. The meal continued, Patience using the time to quiz the children on their schooling. They were asked to do arithmetic, quote the Bible and other works, recite poems and lines from Shakespeare, and know history and the classics. Art was impressed with their knowledge and abilities. Without Google and a calculator, he wouldn't be able to answer half of the questions.

Once the meal was over, Faith led the children in cleaning up. All but Jacob helped. He stood with his head down before his father, who didn't appear pleased. The boy had *not* done well in the little lesson review.

"Son, you will oblige me by going to your room," he said, his tone firm.

"Yes, Father."

He departed, and Patience led Art and Hazel back to the entryway and through a large open doorway into the sitting room.

"Ah, I'm so glad he went easy on the lad and didn't take him to the woodshed," she said, keeping her voice low. "I know he is the eldest boy, but sometimes I think Joshua expects too much of him."

Hazel positively shuddered. It was clear she was upset and trying to control herself. Art could understand. After all, in their time the mere *idea* of corporal punishment had disappeared from many places. Here it was sure to be a daily occurrence.

"I'm certain the boy will do fine," he said, trying to distract Patience.

"Hazel, are you all right?" Joshua said as he entered the room.

"Just… a mild chill," she replied, practically glaring at him.

Art let out a small low whistle. *Wow, if her eyes could speak, she'd have ripped him a new one.*

"Well, it's no wonder," Patience said. "Look at you, so thin. No worries, we'll get you healthy in no time. Please, sit. Shall we play a game?"

"Dominos sounds nice," Hazel said.

They all took seats in the lovely wooden chairs around a strangely familiar table. Art's eyes grew large. It was the six-sided table from his parlor. He knew it was a family heirloom, but he had no idea how far back it went. A memory remnant now awoke within his head. He remembered

Grandpa Steve telling him that *his* grandpa had found the table in the ruins of the old house, cleaned it up, sanded away the scorch marks, and given it a new coat of varnish. It appeared quite nice now.

Patience pulled out a small wicker basket with cards, dominos, and other items in it from under the table, while Joshua stuffed a pipe with tobacco. Art scanned the room. As with the house in general, the old sketches and oil paintings didn't do it justice. There were lovely needlepoint works framed on the walls depicting the countryside or famous quotes. A sideboard had silver candlesticks and a decanter and glasses on it; they were seated in the centers of delicate white lace circles. The sideboard itself was beautifully carved and painted. The wall opposite the large doorway had a fireplace with small windows on either side of it. The late afternoon sun filtered through the cream-colored curtains.

Stretching his neck, he turned in his chair a bit to gaze behind him. He smiled. It had the appearance of his sitting room back home. A lovely floor to ceiling bookcase was full of leather-bound books. Reading was clearly encouraged here. He remembered. The islanders considered education vital to the community. In the early 1700's a law was passed that any town with fifty families had to have a school.

"Arthur, feel free to use one of my pipes," Joshua offered, striking a match under the edge of the table.

Art almost laughed out loud. Now he knew why the table had so many scratches there. He checked behind Joshua. On the opposite side of the doorway from the sideboard was a small round marble-top table, and a fine little pipe stand where a tobacco tin sat upon it.

"I don't smoke. I mean, I don't want to smoke now," he said quickly and patted his chest. "All that seawater has clogged my innards."

"We understand," Patience replied, helping Hazel to mix the dominos. "A good night's rest and you'll feel much better. Oh, and you'll take our bed. No, no, no arguments. It is the least we can do to help you in your new life here in the colonies."

"Aye, that new home of yours has plenty of bedrooms," Joshua said with a wink. "You best get to filling them right quick."

Hazel almost sent some of the dominos flying into the fireplace, but she managed to control herself. "Oh, sorry, just…little anxious about…the future."

Patience glared at Joshua. "How can you speak of such a thing? Look at this poor creature. Thin, sickly, we must fatten her up before any thought of children can be entertained."

"What? Fatten?" Hazel said. "Oh, yes, of course. Yes, I was always a delicate child, afflicted with all manner of maladies. I think that's another reason my father was so keen to marry me off to this great oaf."

They all chuckled and froze as a pounding came to the front door.

"Ack, I do not need the gift of second-sight to know who that is," Patience grumbled. "Faith, you will tell the gentleman we are *not* receiving company today."

"Yes, mother," the girl called out, making for the door.

Art cracked his knuckles. *Damn, who could this be?*

"Bah, the 'squeeze crab' rears his ugly gob," Joshua mumbled.

Breathing through his nose, Art tried to act as if he wasn't paying attention to what was going on at the front door, wasn't straining to hear every sound, every word, every nuance that might be conveyed by the creak of a floorboard or the rattle of the door. He heard it open, a man instantly spoke, made it clear he demanded to see Joshua, and didn't wait for Faith's reply. Heavy footsteps moved quickly through the entryway. Art was surprised by Joshua's reaction. He sat and puffed on his pipe, his back to the doorway. Hazel bit her lip, and Patience seemed on the verge of losing hers. A man entered, and Art almost choked on his own spit.

It was Mr. Davenport. Of that there was *no* doubt, as he was the spitting image of his descendant, and Art grunted to keep from laughing. Joshua was right to use the term 'squeeze crab', as it fit this man, he was sour-looking and shriveled. Behind him came a young man, maybe mid-thirties, who was probably his son. Again, familial features made that fairly certain. Art crinkled his nose. The young fellow needed a bath, and he had his right pinky buried deep in his ear. Faith dashed in behind them.

"Mother, Father, forgive me, they—"

Joshua raised a hand, and she fell silent. "It's all right, child. Go, tend to your chores. Isaac, to what do we owe the…pleasure of your company?"

"Mayhew, you know full well the laws of the island," he snapped. "New arrivals are to present themselves to the governor before sunset of their first day here. Take a look out those windows. The sun nears the horizon, and who are these people?"

"This is my cousin Arthur and his dear wife Hazel," he replied, his voice calm and quiet.

"The *Lady* Hazel Puttenham, of the Essex Puttenhams," Patience added. "They are the only survivors of the *Cricket*. Come now, Isaac, you cannot expect them to follow some silly law after so severe a trauma."

"Arthur survived? Wife?" Isaac grumbled and locked his eyes on Arthur. "You, Mayhew, speak. What of the money we are owed?"

"No, not a word," Joshua snapped. "You are governor, Isaac, not king here! The full council shall hear the news tomorrow. Also, if your presence here is merely to belabor a point of law, why is Obadiah with you?"

Art did a double take. *How in the world did he know Isaac's son was with…? Ohhh, I would guess his…aroma is quite distinct.*

Isaac stepped up to the table, right next to Joshua, yet didn't meet his gaze. "Yes, you're quite correct. I have another agenda to fulfill this day. There is the matter of Obadiah's request for Faith's hand in marriage. Joshua, I'm a reasonable man, but even my patience has its limits. Your answer?"

"Will be forthcoming in all due time," Joshua replied. His tone was soft and slow, yet conveyed rock-hard resolve. "How can I be expected to give proper consideration to so weighty a matter now? My dear cousins have just endured a terrible ordeal."

Hazel put the back of her hand against her forehead. "Oh, my heart, such palpitations, all this tribulation and stress is making me weak. Arthur, dear husband, the room is spinning."

Art raced around the table to kneel before her, playing the dutiful and concerned husband to the hilt. He almost smiled. Hazel was making use of her acting skills, he well remembered her at the last Comic-Con doing her own *Supergirl* routine. She was good.

"I'm here, my beloved! Governor Davenport, with all due respect, can you not grant us time to recover? My poor wife is a weak, sickly woman unaccustomed to strife."

Patience moved to the sideboard, poured a glass of wine or whatever was in the decanter, and handed it to Hazel. "Here, child, drink this. Isaac, enough, leave our home! We will bring them to the council chamber tomorrow."

He grumbled something about, "This isn't over," but complied. He marched out, pushing his son before him, who had a bad limp, and a moment later the door slammed.

Hazel drank the entire glass. "Thank you. My, my, such delightful wine. Is it local?"

Joshua nodded. "The island is well-named, although not all the grapes are fit for wine. We have labored to improve them over the years, and now our vineyard produces a fine 'fruit of the vine.' Cousin, another matter I wish to discuss with you is to obtain a letter of introduction to Lord Puttenham. If he would help us to import our wine to England, it would be a profitable enterprise, one I would gladly make you a full partner in."

Art's throat tightened. It would appear he'd made a mistake in linking Hazel to a known individual. He had to think, to come up with an excuse.

"I fear my father would not be amiable to such an endeavor. He took the pledge some years ago. However, I'm sure I can think of someone, who can help us. Give me some time to consider it."

"The… pledge?" Joshua queried.

Art bit his lip. *Uh-oh. Ah… when did the temperance movement start? Gee, I don't know!*

"Um, it's something new in England," Hazel said quickly. "People abstain from strong drink, and they call it that as they pledge not to drink."

Art couldn't help himself, he smiled ear to ear. Hazel to the rescue! They resumed their seats and started playing, and the evening passed in peace, for which Art was incredibly grateful. As the sun set, the room cooled, and the chill of evening crept through the thin walls. Joshua summoned Faith and Thaddeus, the second son, to stoke up a fire. Art watched in amazement as Thaddeus crawled into the fireplace to arrange the kindling. It was quite spacious. Like the kitchen fireplace, it was easily six feet square at the base, and made of crude bricks. He remembered his dad telling him the mortar was made by burning oyster, clam, and other shells. It was quite excellent and hard as rock. Once a roaring fire was lit the children retired to see to the young ones.

Patience was silent for a long time, casting her tiles down as the game continued, but finally lifted her gaze to fix upon Joshua. "Husband, we must discuss the marriage."

"Now? In front of our guests?"

"All the more fitting. Hazel, you understand the need for making a good match," she said, gazing at her.

"Um, of course, but love is vital as well. How does Faith feel about the lad? He *is* much older than her. Also, he has a limp. Is he in poor health?"

Joshua grumbled. "Fie, I don't recall him being lame before hostilities broke out."

"Huh, a politician's son avoiding military service," Art said under his breath. "Guess things never change."

"Her feelings are of no importance," Patience snapped.

"*My* feelings toward Davenport are simple," Joshua said. "He is a Capulet to my Montague."

"Which is precisely *why* we need this union," Patience said with passion. "It will seal the breach and bring peace to the island. Husband, look at the strife and conflict being waged across the colonies. Let us set a good example."

Joshua sighed and hung his head, bathed in the soft flicker of the flames. "So be it. Come the morrow, when we present Arthur and his good woman to the council, I will give my bond to Isaac, but *not* my hand!"

Patience clapped in glee. "Wonderful," she squealed and cast her eyes from Art to Hazel. "Tomorrow we will have your initial presentation to the community. Husband, we should make plans for a good and proper welcome."

"Is that wise? After all, what with the rebellion still going on."

"Nonsense, a proper and *sizable* party will not only demonstrate the

Mayhews are no pikers but show that stability reigns. It will be a calming effect on the citizens."

Another sigh of resignation escaped his lips. "Again, so be it. Now, the hour grows late. Come, we should retire."

Art turned to check out the mantelpiece, where a small steeple clock sat, and saw the time. It was close to nine, which wasn't late, at least by their point of view. Of course, he also knew they'd be up before sunrise, so an early bedtime was definitely called for. He got to his feet.

"I agree. It has been a most trying time for poor Hazel and myself."

While the ladies put the game away, Joshua doused the fire and checked the barometer hanging next to the fireplace.

"Glass is rising, and there was a red sky tonight. Good weather tomorrow for the hunt."

"The glass is what?" Hazel asked.

"That's a barometer," Art explained. "When the air pressure rises, it causes the water to rise inside the tube."

She nodded. "Ah, I understand, and high pressure is a sign of good weather, correct?"

Joshua chuckled. "Cousin, you appear afflicted with a curious wife. God help you!"

"Eh, I prefer to think of her as a challenge worth overcoming."

They all chuckled at that, although Art could tell Hazel's laugh was rather forced. He then slipped away to the kitchen to fetch his clothes, yet wondered what sort of hunt Joshua talked about. He decided not to ask then gasped when he saw that his things were gone. His chest tightened, and he tore about, being as quiet as possible, desperately searching for the garments.

Joshua asked, standing behind him. "Cousin, what troubles you?"

He spun to face him. "Oh, ah…I…my…clothes, I left them by the fire to dry and now…I seem to have misplaced them."

Joshua frowned. "The children! Faith, come here this instant," he bellowed.

A thump, a bump, and the door facing Art opened. Faith, in her nightclothes and hastily throwing on a robe, emerged as Patience and Hazel entered from the front.

"Y-y-yes, Father," she squeaked.

"What have you done with Arthur's garments?"

The poor girl trembled. "I-I know nothing of his clothes, Father, upon my honor."

Joshua turned to face her. Art didn't have to see his face to know he was fuming. "As eldest, it is your responsibility to see that our guests are properly cared for. Fetch the strap."

Faith trembled and seemed to shrink in size, her eyes filled with tears in clear anticipation of what was to come. Yet, she said not a word, just nodded and turned to go. Art saw the expression on Hazel's face. It was a blend of terror, rage, and concern. He knew she was about to say something, and so he acted.

"Wait, they are merely waterlogged clothes that were not even mine. If you recall, I said we threw on what was handy as the ship foundered. They are a mere trifling, unimportant. I want them back so as to cut them up for rags to help clean our new home."

Everyone froze. All eyes were on Joshua as he considered his words.

"Very well, we'll let the matter be. However, young lady, you replace those items with some decent clothes for your dear cousin, and thank him for saving your hide."

Faith nodded again and again. "Yes, sir, yes, Father, I'll make him a fine outfit, and I thank you with all my heart, Cousin, my thanks forever."

"It is nothing, child," Art replied with a smile.

She zipped back to bed, Hazel heaved a sigh of relief, and they climbed the stairs to their room, a small whale oil lamp in his hand. Only when the door was closed and locked did they relax and sit on the bed to talk in low whispers.

"Wow, have we dropped into a colonial Game of Thrones, or what?" Art said.

Hazel giggled. "Definitely. Did you see Faith's reaction to Isaac's son?"

He shook his head. "No, I was blocked by Joshua."

"Oh, she does *not* like him. I can't believe her mother is pushing the marriage."

"Hazel, face it, it's the norm in this era. He's the only son of the governor, which means power and social standing in the community. Add the Mayhew wealth and lands, mix in the wealth of the Davenports, and I'm surprised they've waited so long."

"Arthur, the girl's what, sixteen?" Hazel squeaked in protest. "I mean, I know…youthful marriage is accepted here, but…damn. Reading about it is one thing, to see it live in front of you is quite another. Huh, Faith and Charity, what about Hope?"

"Doesn't sound like there's any for these girls," he said, cracking his knuckles. "Although, maybe we can do something to help."

Her brow wrinkled. "*Do* something? Ah, should we?"

Art did a double take. "What happened to your rightful outrage at the situation?"

"Well…there's the one little issue of time travel. This place is an anthropologist's dream, social dynamics, jockeying for position and dominance, and family structures that haven't been seen in living memory, but if we do something, as much as I'd like to—heck, *love* to—won't that change history? What will the consequences be to *our* world?"

"I agree, but our presence has already changed the time stream. Tomorrow, they're going to ask me about their appeal for payment on the sheep and cattle and other goods taken by the army. No matter what I say, it's going to contradict history, and presto, we've changed things."

"What are you saying, in for a penny, in for a pound, as the old saying goes?"

He shrugged. "Yeah, I guess I am. So, why not help the poor girl?"

Scratching the back of her neck, she slowly nodded. "Okay, I'm in. What do we do?"

"Um, I don't know. Let's sleep on it and see if we can come up with something."

She smiled and kissed the end of his nose. "Okay. Oh, I hope we come up with something good. That Davenport guy creeps me out, and his son is a troll! Did you see the glare he shot you when he found out who you were?"

"Yeah, but that's to be expected. According to the island records, he wanted the land set aside for Arthur Jr. In the original time stream, he bought it once Arthur was declared dead."

"Ah, I see. Huh, you know, given that you invited me to stay with you for this trip, I had decided to take our relationship to the next level."

She giggled. He laughed and brushed her cheek with the back of his fingers.

"I'm so glad you say that, Hazel, I hoped we would too. I understand if you feel this is most definitely *not* the time to do it."

Taking his hand in hers, she kissed it, and smiled at him. "To be honest, I'm torn. On the one hand, this would be the most awesome first time for any modern couple. I mean, come on, think about it, making love in the past! I once made out with a guy in an elevator riding from the lobby to the top of Freedom Tower. That doesn't even come close to this."

"I'll grant you that. What's the 'other hand' you've yet to mention?"

"I'm afraid of...pregnancy. If we're going to be here a year and I get pregnant now that means going through childbirth without the benefit of modern medicine. I'm sorry, but no amount of love can overcome *that*."

Art clamped his hand over his mouth and snorted so hard his ears popped. He was desperate to not laugh too loud. What would Joshua and Patience think of that? It took a minute for him to control himself.

"Hazel that is the best excuse for refusing sex I've ever heard. Come on, how about we get into the nightclothes they've left us, and we'll cuddle. Bet you never expected to hear a man say that, huh?"

It was Hazel's turn to control her laughter as she nodded and rose to her feet. Given that she had her old clothes on underneath, and that she had trouble with some of her new things, Art helped her get undressed down to her garments. He then turned his back, she did likewise, and they changed into the pajamas one of the children left out.

"This flannel straightjacket isn't what I had in mind for tonight. I brought my fanciest nightie, it really is awesome, but…it's in my bag back in your place. I guess I should say back in our time."

"Well, it'll be something for us to look forward to when we get home. Hey, I was wondering, how'd you know to use the phrase about 'taking the pledge' to mean your 'father' didn't drink?"

She grinned. "I'd like to say it was my studies of societal norms, but nothing so intellectual. I heard the term used on an episode of 'Doctor Who'."

Art chuckled. "Oh, Hazel, you are one in a million."

She agreed, carefully bundled her clothes up tight and hid them under the bed with her fanny pack, and they climbed in bed and spooned. Art heaved a sigh of delight and relief. She was so warm next to him and fit perfectly against his large frame. His arms wrapped about her and she rested her small hand on his forearm. Her hair was soft and smelled of salt water, but he didn't mind, and it tickled him as she turned her head to gaze back at him.

"Arthur, no matter what happens to us in this…weird world we've been thrust into, I'm glad we're together."

"Me too. I wish I had some profound words of comfort and encouragement about the future to say right now, but I'm no fancy talker."

"I think you do just fine."

Three

The first rays of the day filtered through the delicate curtains and fell on Hazel's face. Her cheek was warm. Opening her eyes, she managed a small smile. Despite knowing everything that had happened to them yesterday was not a dream, she still had a warm good feeling about her. Arthur was wrapped around her, albeit snoring in her ear, but she didn't mind. When she was a kid, her dad was King of the Snorers. The way her mom had put it, he could rattle the windows, peel the wallpaper, and be heard in every room of the house.

Disentangling herself from his beefy arms and legs, she sat on the edge of the large comfy bed and yawned and stretched. The mattress was incredible, plush and firm, yet giving to her form, and she'd had the best sleep in her life. No blare of traffic from the street, no pounding on the walls or arguments from the neighbors, and most definitely, no roar of jets from Logan Airport. She flexed her muscles, stood and did her morning routine, a little warm up to get the blood flowing and ease the ache of her bones. Today, she was particularly sore. A foul tar-like taste also assailed her. When she smacked her lips, her mouth tasted like the bottom of a birdcage. She wanted mouthwash or a toothbrush.

Unfortunately, she knew neither was available. *Huh, we're going to need to work on that. Damn, there's something else I need to take care of, and it can't wait.*

She had a full bladder. Hazel was no history major, but she didn't need to know the Wikipedia entry concerning bathrooms to know flush toilets weren't around. Last night, while playing dominos, Patience said the privy was out next to the stables. Hazel had smiled and nodded, unsure what she'd meant, but now it was obviously some sort of outhouse. She cringed but resigned herself to using it. Slipping off the bed, she headed for the door, but froze. She wasn't an expert on this era, but she knew she couldn't skip on out to the 'facilities', despite her nightclothes being more cumbersome than the dress she wore to her prom. It would be indecent. She put her own clothes on, slipped on a new dress without all the petticoats, then tiptoed down the stairs.

"Good morning, Cousin," Faith chirped.

Hazel jumped and spun toward the kitchen. "Oh! Sorry, you gave me a fright. I wasn't expecting to see anyone up—ah, awake."

"Mother and Father will be awake presently, and they expect breakfast ready so we can get to work."

She gazed behind Faith, who stood by the table set for a meal, and saw a large griddle hanging from the hook over the fire. Hazel's nose and ears told her eggs and bacon were cooking, and tea brewed on the table. A typical morning meal for her was coffee and toast, maybe a bagel, but she knew that wasn't possible. She did not relish the idea of trying to stomach a huge meal.

I know these people mean well, and in this era a hefty woman is equated with health and wealth, but I'll be dipped in who-ha before I eat as much as they do. "I can see you're doing a fine job. I just need to go…out, and I'll be right back to help."

"Oh, didn't Mother show you the chamber pot under the bed?"

Hazel's eyebrows shot up, and she suppressed a squeak. "Chamber…pot? Ah, no. It's fine, I'll just…and be…back."

She hustled out the front door before Faith could say anything more, like offer to let Hazel use her pot. The cool crisp morning air enveloped her. She shivered and tingled, stifled an inhale, and slowly drew in a long deep breath. The air was clear and fresh, and *so* invigorating. Never in her life had she, for lack of a better word, *tasted* air so clean. That was what came of breathing pre-Industrial Revolution air. Walking along the large stone steps that led to the front gate, she veered off to her left toward the outhouse, and was a little taken aback by the presence of several people at the stone wall. Correction, several *men*. They stood there, all smiles, leaning on the wall, and gave her a collective bow of their heads.

"Good morning, Lady Puttenham," an old white-haired one said, offering a toothless smile.

"Peace and blessings to you, Lady Hazel," a strapping young man with broad shoulders and rippling chest called out.

"My-my, she has a fine 'apple dumpling shop', hasn't she?" someone snickered.

Chortles rippled through the crowd, and the other four gave similar greetings. She tried to be polite and respond in kind, but she had to be brief. Zipping over to the small shed-like building, she opened the door, and her eyes began to water. The smell was *quite* powerful. She coughed, stepped inside, and slid the wooden latch into place. Given the dimensions of the place, and her unfamiliarity in handling her stupid gown, she pulled the whole thing off. Dealing with her shorts was much easier, and she did *not* cast her gaze down the hole. If its appearance was only *half* as bad as if smelled, one glance would make her puke.

Once she was done and dressed, she peeked out the small crest-shaped opening before leaving. The men had left, which was a relief. The idea of guys hanging around was bad enough, but them seeing her go to and from the toilet doubled her embarrassment quotient. As she emerged, she caught sight of the clothes' line and smiled. Arthur's clothes were flapping in the gentle breeze in among the family's things. She snagged them and headed inside as he came down the stairs, and once more she envied him his wardrobe.

He smiled. "Hey, you found my clothes. Where were they?"

"Out on the clothes' line. Do you understand the phrase 'apple dumpling shop'? One of the men outside said I had a good one."

He blushed. "Ah, well…it's slang for your…breasts."

She rolled her eyes, and while he needed to go to the bathroom, he first dashed back upstairs to hide his clothes. She went to the kitchen to help Faith and the younger children finish preparing breakfast, despite their protests.

"No, no, it's quite all right, I insist on helping. It's the least I can do to thank you for all you've done for us."

Faith blushed, Charity beamed with joy, and Mary and Amity, who were ten and twelve, respectively, finished setting the table and poured the tea. Hazel learned a little tidbit of information. Thaddeus was the one who'd taken Arthur's clothes. He'd hung them on the line to dry and gone to bed without telling anyone.

A moment later, Patience and Joshua joined them, and Arthur dashed in. They sat down to eat, after another brief blessing, and made plans. Hazel could not believe the mountain of food set before her. There were eggs, giant slabs of bacon, ham, bread, and fruit. She didn't know where to begin and was amazed to see the other adults chow down with relish, even Arthur, albeit with a little less gusto. Taking a sip of tea, she was disappointed. This was the one time she craved coffee, and tea didn't cut it. A slight smirk cut across her face. She thought of her old boyfriend Reggie. He had jokingly said she loved coffee more than sex. When it came to first thing in the morning, he wasn't far off.

"Hazel, what ails you?" Patience said. "You're not eating. Is something amiss?"

For once, Hazel didn't have to come up with something in the spur of the moment. She'd planned for it. Patting her stomach, she grimaced. "It's nothing. All the salt water I drank yesterday upset my stomach. I'm sure I'll be fine, but I shall eat light this morning."

"Quite understandable," Joshua said. "Eat as much as you wish then give the rest to the girls."

Faith and the others perked up at those words. Casting her gaze about the table, Hazel realized the young ones had some sort of porridge. She almost laughed out loud.

Sheesh, this is practically a page out of a Dickens' book. I wonder if they're allowed to ask for more.

Yet, Hazel was wise enough to hold her tongue. She ate some eggs and bread with butter, it was heavenly, drank more tea, and passed her plate to the girls. They were almost drooling, but Faith kept them civil. She divided the portions among them, taking the smallest for herself, and they ate.

"We will need to go at once to the council, Arthur," Joshua said. "After that, we can show you your home, and discuss the planting of the fall crop."

"I understand. Ah, where are the boys?"

"Already at work," Joshua replied. "The summer harvest is close at hand, and I want to insure the corn crop is a good one."

Hazel bit so hard on the inside of her lip, she almost drew blood. It's what she did when she walked through Boston Common alone at night or she got an overdraft notice from the bank. Her thoughts were of poor Faith. The expression of dread on her face told Hazel so much, as she knew what awaited the girl after the meeting today. Hazel wanted to scream, to shout, to beat some sense into these mindless clods, but she knew she couldn't, which only served to make the blood explode in her ears more. Yet, she had one consolation—she always did best under pressure. Sitting there, watching the girl shuffle about the room with her head down and a black cloud hovering over her was as if lightning shot from that cloud to Hazel's brain.

She smiled. "Joshua, a word, if you please, before we depart."

"Certainly, m'lady. What is it you wish to discuss?"

"Arthur and I talked last night. Oh, and by the way, the bed was most comfortable. We have a proposition to set before you."

She almost laughed. The expression on Arthur's face was priceless. He had no clue where she was going with this, but he quickly painted a knowing expression on and slowly nodded.

Joshua turned to him. "Oh, and what might that be?"

Arthur sort of snorted, as he was helpless to response.

Hazel ground her teeth. *Damn, I forgot, it's a male dominated society.*

"Ah. Why not let Hazel tell you?" Arthur stammered. "It is her idea."

"Thank you, dear husband," she said, not giving Joshua a chance to disagree. "Given my poor health and lack of knowledge of some household tasks, due to my *privileged* upbringing, we desperately need help around the house. Faith is clearly a capable girl, and there is the matter of the hundred pounds."

Patience's chest heaved as she took a deep breath. "Was not that resolved last night? Arthur, you said—"

He raised a hand to cut her off. "Ah-ah, wait a moment, let my beloved finish her proposal."

Hazel smiled and nodded at him. "Thank you, dearest. We are willing to forgive twenty-five pounds of the debt in exchange for her as a maid."

Hazel pressed her lips together to keep from smiling ear to ear. Arthur lit up like a neon sign. He got what she was doing. Patience sat up straight, her face a mass of contradictions. It was clear she was conflicted. The reduction of debt was a godsend, but she was keen on the marriage. Joshua slowly nodded and grinned.

"That is most generous," he said to Arthur. "I would have given her services to you for ten. Done and done again."

Hazel smiled and held out her hand to shake his, but he ignored her, and instead shook Arthur's. She seethed. Her jaw clenched so hard her teeth throbbed. The only thing that got her to relax was the prospect of colonial dental service. Taking a deep breath through her nose, she slowly counted to ten inside her head.

It's working, it's working. Let it go that he slighted you, let it gooooo...

"Ah, husband, are you sure about this?" Patience said, sort of choking on the words.

"Patience, our cousins are in need, and they are being helpful to us. How can we refuse such an offer? Yes, Isaac will be upset. He will have to understand family comes first. Faith, come here," he called out.

The girl, who had hovered in the background since hearing her name, stepped up to the edge of the table. Now Hazel's heart truly soared. Faith was happy, of that there was no question. She stood tall, head up, and smiled broadly.

"Yes, Father," she said with a bright chipper tone.

"I would imagine you heard the discussion. As of today, you will move into their home and serve them, and I best not hear a word of complaint from them!"

"Y-yes, Father, thank you, sir, I will work hard and bring honor to the family," she said quickly.

Hazel looked her in the eye. "I'm sure you will, child."

Arthur gave the girl a stern glare. "And, Faith, I want you to remember what a delicate creature Lady Hazel is and how unaccustomed she is to heavy labor. So, if she asks you what seems to you a silly question about...candle-making or cooking, you will not be surprised. You will answer her, is that clear? Otherwise, you will answer to me."

"Y-yes, Cousin Arthur, I will help her as best I know how," she squeaked.

Now it was Hazel's turn to be conflicted. While she hated Arthur scaring the girl, she understood why he did it. Not only was it expected, but it also gave Hazel an excuse for asking Faith to help her with things she should know and not arouse suspicion from her or anyone else. Arthur was proving to be a pretty sharp cookie, despite being a man. After that, they finished eating, and Faith was sent to pack her things.

It was time to go before the council. Hazel knew a good deal about social interaction, which might be a help to Arthur, but this was a place he needed to take the lead. They went upstairs, using the excuse one of her slips was falling, and he needed to get some notes he'd written. He helped her get her dress and petticoats off, and she put his clothes on over hers.

"You going to be okay like this?" he said.

She nodded, getting dressed in her appropriate outfit. "I'll be fine. Once we get to our new house, I'll strip."

He smiled and hugged her. "This is such a great idea. I have to say, Hazel, you are a genius, first Faith, now my clothes."

"Eh, I try. Now, come on, let's go…get presented."

They headed downstairs and out the front door. Joshua was getting the horse and carriage ready, Patience sat up front, and Faith stowed her bundle in the back. She climbed atop it and hung on. Hazel eyed the girl and chewed on her thumb nail.

"Will she be safe back there? Perhaps she should wait here, and we can come back for her."

Joshua adjusted the bridle. "It is nothing. She will be fine. We cannot ride to the council chamber, come back, then go to your farm. It's in Cottage City. The trip would waste the day."

Hazel had to think about his words for a minute. Arthur stepped close and whispered a quick outline of the geography of the area. The Mayhew house was sort of southwest of Edgar Towne, where City Hall was located, and Cottage City was northwest of town beyond the area that would become State Beach. She understood. She didn't like it, as she thought Faith was being made unduly uncomfortable, but she remained silent. They climbed into the simple carriage in the back, its seats had rather thin cushions, and Joshua sat up front and grabbed the reins.

"Giddy-up," he cried.

The horse took off. The carriage lurched forward, and Hazel let out a squeak. *Yeah, extremely thin cushions and bumpy roads. Sheesh, I will never complain about potholes in the roads again. This place is more holes than road.*

She gazed over her shoulder at the small deck out back. Two trunks sat there. They probably had the clothes and household items intended for them, and Faith sat between them on a sack, which must have her things. Hazel couldn't help but be amazed at how little the girl had. Yet, it was the custom, and the Mayhews were a family of means. Hazel could only imagine what life was like for the poor. Patience acted blissfully unaware of the girl's plight at staying put. She yammered on.

"You see there, that's our main crop of corn," she said, pointing to the right. "Looks fine, eh? Wait until you taste it. Nothing is sweeter than summer corn. Oh, and see there, the main well for this area. My father dug that well and set the stones in place. Have you ever seen such workmanship?"

"Patience, remember the dangers of pride."

Arthur nodded. "Yes, what's the saying? Ah, pride goes before destruction."

"Destruction?" Hazel said. "I thought it was fall?"

"I can never recall," Patience said, her nose in the air.

"Ah, Joshua, do you remember it?" Hazel said.

"No," he mumbled. "I…oh, it seems others are headed for town. No doubt to see your appearance before the council."

Hazel leaned out the side a bit to look around Patience and saw carriages and wagons come onto the road from little side paths from homes. Most were simple, little more than open wagons with people sitting on sacks or kneeling on the bare floor, but a few were fancier than theirs. Then she saw a truly ornate one, and her jaw dropped. It was the Davenport carriage, and it was the same one from the present!

Sheesh, I know these New Englanders love to hold on to old things, but…damn.

"Would you look at their yard? All of her linen clothes on the line to dry. All their garments cannot be dirty at the same time. Bathsheba is being boastful. She wants everyone to how rich they are." Patience spun around in her seat to face the rear, her face sour. "Do you see her in their carriage? She's wearing her finest silks, *silks*, to a council meeting."

Hazel now knew the name of the governor's wife. *Man, I always thought my name was a bit old and outdated, but… damn, Bathsheba?*

"Maybe she does it to…honor Hazel and I," Arthur suggested.

Patience grumbled and hung her head, and Joshua turned to him. He grinned and winked. It seemed Arthur had hit her with something she couldn't rebuke. Hazel sat back and scanned the area as they rode on. The air was so fresh, so clear, the sky bluer than she'd ever seen, and a gentle breeze wrapped about them. Her nose crinkled at a light stench of sewage in the area. Maybe she was getting used to it. The rustle of the trees that lined the narrow road was soft and mild, and she saw more pear and cherry trees. They were quite common.

She rubbed her chin as a memory came to her. When Arthur took her around the island, he hadn't brought her to Edgar Towne. She wondered why and made a mental note to ask him. As they neared the center of town, the buildings became more frequent and larger and more ornate. The City Hall was easy to spot. The large red brick building had classic columns along a narrow front porch. It was also the only place with a well-maintained front lawn.

Joshua pulled up right smack in the middle of the front of the building, and silence descended across the area as all eyes turned toward them. At that moment, Hazel wished with all her heart for some antiperspirant. She was sweating like a turkey the day before Thanksgiving. Joshua climbed down and helped Patience. Hazel's heart pounded so hard she truly thought it would shake the front of her stifling dress. She took in a deep breath and pressed the tip of her tongue against her teeth. It was time for her to use her education. Her knowledge of colonial America was limited to classes in high school, but anthropology was her thing, and thus she understood the patriarchal society. She didn't bound from the carriage and introduce herself to the first person she met. She sat and waited and tried to be patient as Arthur got out and offered her his hand. Her eyes almost rolled, but she caught them at the last moment, and forced a smile on her face.

It actually hurt.

"Come, my dear," he said, trying to sound serious.

His expression told her he was as conflicted as she was. He wanted to laugh, but she saw the fear and concern in his eyes. He was clearly worried about facing the governor, the council, and essentially the entire town. Offering her his arm, she took it, and tried to appear prim and proper as they walked up the wide stone walkway. It was made easier by the fact she was in her sneakers. Arthur had objected, voiced concerns about anyone seeing them. She countered that, given her long dress and multiple layers of clothes, there was little chance of that. Besides, she'd never worn heels in her life. If she tried now, she'd probably fall flat on her face, and how would that seem? The stroll into the building was slow due to Patience. She hung on Joshua's arm and turned to face from side to side, happily chatting away.

"These are our cousins newly arrived from England. She's Lady Puttenham, *favorite* daughter of Lord Puttenham."

Now Hazel couldn't help herself and rolled her eyes. *Damn, woman, what's your family crest, a strutting peacock?*

Slowly the throng made their way inside to a large meeting room. It appeared like a sort of courtroom, a long low table on a slightly raised platform faced the front door. Benches and chairs ringed the other three sides. A small open area separated the seats from the table, and Governor Davenport was seated 'center stage' with half a dozen other men. People milled about, and Joshua ushered Arthur and the ladies to seats right down front.

Looking around, Hazel was impressed with the room. The people had made an effort to dress the place up. Four huge brass chandeliers hung from the ceiling, and they had oil lamps not candles. She knew that meant they were a gesture, a symbol of the wealth and standing of the community. Actually, as she thought about it, the townsfolk could be poor as church mice, as the old saying said, but they might be trying to impress the other towns.

Her eyebrows shot up. *The other towns, I hadn't thought of those places. Oh, I hope we can visit them. I'd love a chance to study their people. Although...damn, getting around by horse and buggy ain't going to be like Arthur's electric cart.*

She put such thoughts out of her mind for now and focused on the things around her. The walls, beautifully finished paneling, had fine oil paintings hanging depicting island life, farming, fishing, whaling, and church services. She noticed the natives were conspicuously absent from everything, and the largest paintings of all were portraits hanging behind the council. Right at the exact center was the biggest and fanciest of the lot, Isaac's, and it was almost laughable. The real man was old, slightly bent at the back, his face lined. Like so many high society men of the era, he wore a towering wig of fancy brown curls. The painting showed him strong, robust, and with a mane of thick black hair. At first she thought it was an old picture, but she scanned the other portraits. Each showed a past governor. Joshua's was quite nice, but they all showed the men as they were then, not in their youth. Although, in Isaac's case, Hazel had a feeling it was his wished-for youth.

Sheesh, what an ego.

She also studied the people, and a pang thrust into her heart. There were women, girls, old men, and boys, but few young men and even fewer young women. Jacob and Thaddeus were two of the oldest boys she'd seen. Would they be called on to fight soon, and if so, on which side?

Patience grunted next to her. "Would you look at Isaac? Have you ever seen such an owl in an ivy bush?"

"Um, apologies, Cousin, I'm not familiar with—"

"Of course, what was I thinking? You know nothing of our slang. It refers to a person with a large frizzled wig, which is what he always wears when he wants to put on airs."

Isaac banged a gavel. "Good people, please be seated, there are important matters to discuss."

"What news do you bring from England?" someone called out.

Isaac struck the gavel harder. "Order! This is not Haymarket Square in Boston. We will conduct these proceedings in a proper manner. All of you be seated. Neighbor Mayhew, step forward."

Hazel almost laughed. Arthur was halfway to sitting when Isaac called on him, and he did the classic 'reverse engines' sort of move and practically jumped to his feet.

"Ah, yes, yes, Neigh—Governor, I'm… ready."

Hazel saw him crack his knuckles behind his back. Arthur was nervous, and with good cause. While an expert on this era and particular place, no amount of book knowledge could prepare him for this. Would he know enough to answer their questions? Would he say the right things in the correct manner? America, the colonies were at war, and loyalties were divided. What if they thought he, and by association she, were on the opposite side? Hazel practically chowed down on the inside of her cheek. She was powerless to help, didn't even know what she could do to help, and had to trust someone else to take the lead.

It started simple enough. Isaac asked a bunch of boring routine questions like his full name, age, birthplace, and profession. The only one that surprised her was when he gave her age as being twenty.

Why'd he knock five years off? Oh, wait, it was the custom for women to marry young. He didn't want people thinking I was an old maid.

Isaac droned on. In Hazel's opinion, he asked nonsense things such as who were Arthur's siblings, friends, and business associates. Casting her gaze about the room, she saw two expressions: frustration and boredom. The people wanted to move on. Even some of the councilmen seemed angry, one on the verge of falling asleep.

Is he trying to trip Arthur up, catch him in a lie? Maybe I should faint. I scream, fall to the floor and this whole thing ends. Yeah, perfect plan.

Shifting in her seat, so as to make a dramatic fall that would avoid the chairs in front of her, Hazel froze as the answer came to her. It was so simple she scolded herself for not seeing it sooner. She'd given Isaac too much credit. He was a little fish in a little pond, and he wanted to make himself feel important. By drawing this out, by making everyone wait on him, he asserted his dominance.

Huh, well okay then. I understand Mr. D a bit better.

"Thank you, Neighbor Mayhew, for being so forthcoming. I know this has been a bit tedious, but it was necessary."

A snort sounded behind Hazel. She suppressed one of her own.

"I am happy to answer any questions I can," Arthur replied, his voice a bit weak.

"Good, because now we come to the most important one, the one I'm sure our citizens came to hear. What news do you bring from Mother

England? When will payment for our livestock and other goods be made?"

There was an instant change to the demeanor of the room. Hazel could sense the energy level rising, and everyone was focused and alert.

Arthur cracked his knuckles. "With regrets, I am the bearer of bad news. Parliament has rejected your petition. No payment is coming."

"What?" Isaac bellowed. "Why?"

"Ah, they consider you…rebels," he stammered.

Pandemonium reined for the next few minutes. Hazel was terrified, excited, and fascinated. She was seeing history play out in front of her like no play or musical could ever present.

Damn, and to think I waited five years to see 'Hamilton'. These people are out for blood!

Isaac beat the table hard with his gavel, to no avail. He threw it aside and pointed at Arthur. "You, Mayhew, this is your doing! Ruin, you've ruined me."

"Me?" Arthur squeaked. "I'm the messenger, nothing more."

Hazel rose and tried to move forward. If he was about to be arrested, or worse, lynched, she was going to fight at his side, and damn any social conventions about women being dainty.

"Isaac, curb that vile tongue of yours before it says something you will regret," Joshua said. "You know full well we were warned in March of seventy-seven to move our sheep and cattle to the mainland for safekeeping. You chose to ignore that. The fault is in you."

"No, this is your doing. You wrote to parliament, didn't you? Told them we were disloyal. Well, so be it."

A modicum of order was restored as everyone watched Isaac, with his son's help, climb up on the table. The effort was not without a mishap as his wig tumbled off, exposing his thin almost pure white hair. To see him stand there in front of his imaginary self was almost comical.

"Citizens, I call the question," he shouted. "Those against England, cry aye."

"Aye," the room said as one.

"Motion carries," he replied.

Out of the corner of her eye, Hazel saw that Joshua hadn't spoken. *Is he not in favor of independence? Damn, seems we've been thrust into a history mystery.*

Joshua grabbed Patience by the hand and took Hazel's elbow as he called out to Arthur. "Cousin, we are leaving!"

He didn't have to say it twice. Arthur almost beat them to the doors. Despite being extra wide double doors and both open, the surging throng made exiting difficult. All the while, Isaac could be heard shouting after them. Once in the carriage, Joshua took off and urged the horse into a full gallop as they headed west along some back road. As if their speed wasn't enough to jostle their hair about, once they were out along Sengekontacket Pond, the strong onshore wind from what would become State Beach struck them.

"Husband, slow down before we all catch our death from this frightful sea air," Patience called out.

He did so then turned with a grin. "Well, I don't suppose Isaac will be disappointed at the marriage being called off."

At his words, Hazel thought of Faith and gazed back to check on her. It was amazing. The girl was curled up on her bag and fast asleep.

Damn, girl, you are something.

Sitting straight, she cast her gaze out over the pond and beach. It was a wild and untamed area. She'd never been there. She figured Arthur wasn't a big fan of swimming, so she turned to Joshua and Patience.

"Cousins, the shore off in the distance is sandy and open and the waves gentle. Do you ever come here to play or…swim?"

They turned to gaze at her, confusion positively burst from their expressions. "S…win?" they said together.

"The word has no meaning to us," Patience said. "Is this something new?"

"Yes," Hazel said. "It's all the rage in Err—ah, on the Continent. People go in the water for recreation and exercise."

"I've never heard such nonsense," Joshua snapped. "Wander around the shore, out where bandits and pirates can see you, not to mention the vile creatures of the deep that could attack you. Why, just last week another gang of Picaroons raided the salt works on East Chop."

"Pick-a-what?" Hazel said.

"They're Tories, ah, loyalists from the mainland," Art said without thinking.

Joshua strained to turn around in his seat, amazement written across his face. "Why, so they are. Cousin, has word of such things reached England? I never would have thought our little troubles would warrant the interest."

"I…ah," he choked out.

"It was the crew of our ship," Hazel said quickly. "They spoke of bandits and pirates and told the ladies on board all manner of scary tales. I thought it was all bluster to try and impress us with their bravery."

Joshua snickered and turned back to face forward. "Ah yes, sailors do like to woo the ladies, yet another reason not to wander the shores. Those 'hungry' sailors would love to snatch up a pretty girl. I take it this swim activity is something the *nobility* partake of?"

"Now, husband, judge not," Patience said, touching his arm.

"However, dear, he is right, it sounds quite dangerous and uncomfortable. I've been caught outside in numerous downpours. Running around in wet clothes is not pleasant."

"Well, people wear special clothes to swim. They aren't heavy, but I suppose it'll be a while before it becomes popular here."

"Most definitely," Joshua said his voice firm with resolution. "People parading about in light garments? Why, who knows where that might lead?"

Hazel and Arthur exchanged knowing expressions, and both fought hard not to laugh. The carriage made a turn to the right, which, if Hazel remembered correctly, put them on what would one day be County Road, and into the outskirts of Cottage City. It looked nothing like its future counterpart. Not one building was familiar, only a few dirt roads were in roughly the same locations as some present day streets.

"Are these Picaroons dangerous?" Hazel said. "I notice how few homes there are here, and it makes me wonder if they see Oak—ah Cottage City as easy pickings for their raids."

"They can be," Joshua replied. "However, they tend to be small in number, and we have watch towers around the shore to warn us of their approach."

"Aye, but I would put no stock in Huzzleton's Head," Patience said. "That is the tower in Holmes Hole and is owned by Master Daggett, a known Tory."

"Patience, he is merely…diplomatic," Joshua said.

"Bah, what nonsense! A few months back the British kidnapped a pilot from Falmouth to lead them through the Nantucket Shoals," she said, turning to Arthur and Hazel. "Before departing, who do you think they called on to dine with?"

"Daggett?" Arthur said.

She nodded. "Aye, and while they ate, the pilot's friends sneaked over, kidnapped two of the officers, and forced the British to exchange them for their friend."

"Yes, which caused us still more trouble," Joshua snapped.

"Which means my words at the meeting have caused you even more," Arthur said. "I'm sorry, Joshua. The governor seemed quite angry with you."

"Fie, it is of no concern, and has nothing to do with you. Isaac has been consumed with bile since the *Unicorn* incident."

"The *Unicorn*? The Liberty Pole? Ah, I thought that an apocrypha."

Patience gasped. "They know of the incident in England?"

"Only vague stories, and none that agree with each other."

"I know nothing of it," Hazel said. "What is the *Unicorn*? I assume you are *not* referring to the mythical animal."

"It was nothing," Joshua said. "A minor fracas turned into a rabble-rousing tale. The *HMS Unicorn* stopped in Holmes Hole for supplies. They were stored near a warehouse and one night three little girls were playing there. They accidentally set fire to some kindling, and the whole place was consumed."

Patience gave a harrumph. "My great clod of a husband likes to tell the story that way because he, nor any *man*, can conceive of the notion that *mere girls* had the courage and marrow to do what no one else would, and that's to deny the English anymore of our goods! They sneaked passed the sentries and set fire to the supplies, among them our Liberty Pole, which the sailors had cut down. Some say it was to use as a spar on the ship, but that is utter nonsense. It was ill-suited to such a purpose."

"Then why did they cut it down?" Hazel said.

"Pure spite! They sought to cut down our spirit by cutting down the symbol of our liberty, but that was where they made their critical mistake."

"How so?" Hazel said.

Patience turned to her, a sly grin on her face. "Because a symbol is merely a symbol, the spirit is within us, and how can they cut that away?"

Hazel smiled back, pure energy and delight rippling through her. At that moment, she wished she had her phone. She would have taped that speech and put it up on *YouTube*, and Patience would have been elected governor.

Damn, woman, you are the Spirit of America!

"Patience, calm yourself. It was one act by three girls, hardly the actions of soldiers on the field of battle."

"Oh so? What of the widow Luce?"

Joshua groaned. "Oh, not that tale again."

"What, what?" Hazel said. "Another story of brave island ladies? Patience, I simply must hear it!"

Patience needed no more encouragement, she was off.

"It was back during the raid. Out near Lambert's Cove, a squad came upon the home of the elderly widow Mrs. Luce and her grandson Joseph, he being twelve at the time. Despite her prayers and pleas, they took her sheep, pigs, and cows. They were about to leave when the sergeant spied a pig hiding under her petticoats as she sat by the fire. 'Well, boys,' he said, 'you have left the fattest of the litter behind.' The men approached her, and in an instant her prayerful tone changed to one of rebellious defiance. She grabbed a broomstick and brandished it in their faces in, as has been told to me, a manner terrible to behold. 'Away with ye, cursed seed of the oppressor, the despoilers of the widows and the fatherless! Take what you have of mine and be gone, but this is Joie's pig, and not a hair of him shall ye touch.'"

"Whoa, talk about one brave old lady," Hazel said with a grin. "What happened next?"

"The Red Coats, impervious to fear and pity, advanced on the prize, her broomstick rattling among their bayonets so fast they had to call a halt to their advance."

Hazel laughed. "Oh, I can picture it in my mind. What a sight that must have been. I'm sorry, please go on."

"No apology needed. The tale does quicken the heart, eh? The sergeant handed his musket to a comrade and rushed her, intent on grabbing her about the waist and wrestling her to the ground. However, it was a rash assault. He got such a terrible whack to the head he must have thought he saw a signal flare from the fleet as he at once retreated to his men. The widow then seized her coal scuttle and let loose a volley of red-hot coals from the fireplace, thus the men elected to withdraw."

"Yeah! Way to go, granny," Hazel said, shooting her fist in the air. She realized she was acting in an inappropriate manner for the time and meekly lowered her arm. "I mean, she sounds quite the brave and noble lady." *A perfect running mate for Patience.*

"She's another troublemaker," Joshua grumbled. "Enough of these fanciful tales."

"Yes, husband," Patience replied.

Hazel took a deep breath and pressed her lips together. As much as she wanted to tell him off, she knew it would lead to trouble, and so she contented herself with relishing the mental movie playing out in her head as they moved through the sparse town. Reaching the harbor, they couldn't go up New York Avenue to East Chop. It wasn't there, and the harbor was much bigger and encompassed Sunset Lake. Joshua rode them up the gentle slope next to it. If Hazel's memory was accurate, he was taking them along what would be School Street. A single farm sat about halfway up the hill, and that was where they stopped.

"You will find the island soil good for farming and grazing," he said, reining the horse. "Our climate is mild, and we have plenty of oak and pine."

"We own the biggest sawmill," Patience added, climbing down from the carriage.

Joshua clapped his hands. "Faith! Wake up, girl, time to work!"

Hazel jumped higher than Faith did. She saw her head bop up from her little bench in the back. As Arthur and Hazel climbed out, she didn't wait for his hand this time. Faith grabbed her bundle and raced for the front door.

"Yes, Father," she called out over her shoulder.

Hazel stood before the building and took it all in for a moment. The place appeared to be roughly the same as Joshua and Patience's place, albeit smaller and not maintained as well. The lawn was overgrown, the pear tree needed trimming, and the green shutters had faded from too much sun. A small barn sat off to the right and behind the house with a small spring further up the hill next to it. The field was on the left stretching down the hill and was wild and overgrown, it obviously hadn't been tended in a long time. Hazel was no farmer, but even she could tell that much.

"Have no worries about the field," Joshua said. "I have made arrangements to clear it. Cousin, would you help me with the trunk?"

Arthur darted over and grabbed a handle. "Of course."

They hoisted it up and headed through the dew-covered grass toward the open door.

"Your nearest neighbor is Edward Norton and his family."

"Edward Norton? *Ed Norton* is our neighbor?" Arthur said with a smile.

Joshua's brow wrinkled. "Aye, that he is. Do you know him?"

"No, no, the name is merely familiar to me."

Hazel rubbed her chin. *What's Arthur going on about? What's so special about that name? Sheesh, don't tell me it's a friend who went back in time before us.*

"Ah. Well, he's a fine man, his wife's a good woman, and they have many strong children. I've made arrangements for him to drive his cattle over here sometime next week. They'll make quick work of these pesky plants and lay down a good layer of fertilizer."

"Fertilizer?" Hazel said. "How can cows do that?"

Everyone, even Faith, chuckled as the men carried the trunk inside. Patience and Hazel followed them to the kitchen, and she was struck by how similar the layouts of the houses were.

Huh, guess it's a popular model, or maybe just the standard.

"Oh, Cousin," Joshua said as they set the trunk on the dusty table, "she has a lot to learn, ay?"

He nodded. "Yes, but that's why we have Faith. I'm sure she'll be a big help."

The girl beamed and opened the trunk. Inside were all manner of kitchen supplies.

"She will, or she'll answer to me, and you. Aye, that strikes a chord in my mind. Faith, which room are your things in?"

"The one closest to the kitchen, Father, so I can easily tend to the cooking."

"Good girl. While Arthur and I bring in the other trunk, go get *them*."

The girl cringed and swallowed hard, but nodded. "Yes, Father," she squeaked.

Faith slipped away, the men headed back outside, and Patience unpacked the trunk and put the things away. It was how casual she was that caused a knot in Hazel's stomach. What could fill Faith with fear, yet leave her mother acting so nonchalant? Hazel tried not to think about it and instead helped put the plates and other items in the cabinets that ringed the room. The heavy clomp of feet on the bare wooden floors—the place had no rugs like back in the other Mayhew home—told them the men were returning. As they set the other trunk down, Faith stepped out of the shadows and handed Joshua a stick and something else then he turned to Arthur and Hazel.

Here it comes, the 'big reveal'. Okay, Joshua, lay it on us.

Four

"Here is Faith's strap," Joshua said, handing Arthur the item. "Should she be disobedient or displease you, a taste of this will set her right."

Arthur's eyes grew wide as he took it, clearly at a loss for words. He gazed at it and then Hazel as if to say, 'Help!'

Joshua turned to Hazel. "And this is her cane. If Arthur is away, and you feel you cannot wait, a dozen or two strokes of it will suffice."

Hazel stood there, her arms bolted to her sides. *Is this man suggesting I beat his child with that thing?* "Her...cane? You want me to...use that?"

He offered a warm and friendly smile, full of compassion and understanding. "Of course, a mere woman, particularly a lady as dainty as you, cannot be expected to wield a large strap. If you have any troubles, ask Faith. Honesty is one of her chief virtues. She will instruct you on how to punish her."

Hazel's head spun. She reached up to stroke her neck to appear thoughtful. Actually, she checked to make sure it wasn't puffed out like a bullfrog as her body felt as if it had indeed inflated with rage. She winced in pain from the clamor in her ears. There was no point clamping her hands over them. The pounding wasn't church bells—it was her blood exploding through her arteries.

Must control rage. Different time, different culture. Don't say it. Don't tell him what you think of him. Let it go, just let it goooo...!

Patience grabbed a chair and pushed it behind Hazel. "Cousin, sit, you are having a fit of apoplexy. Faith, fetch water from the well!"

"Aye, Mother," she cried, and dashed out.

Joshua chuckled and turned to Arthur. "I had no idea how weak and womanly your wife was. The mere talk of simple discipline, and she is overcome. It's clear you will have to take Faith in hand."

"Weak? Womanly?" Hazel choked out, almost spitting the words.

Arthur took the cane and dashed to her side, putting his hand on her shoulder. He squeezed *quite* hard.

"Oh. I'm sure once she's fully recovered from our journey and trials, she will rule this house with an iron hand. Hazel has an inner strength that even surprises me at times."

All her rage, all her anger dispersed like water shooting out a geyser from the top of her head. Hazel deflated. Arthur had done the right thing at the right moment. The dig at her shoulder had been a not so subtle signal to wait, and he'd given the perfect reply. She was learning to trust the big goof.

"Well said," Patience replied. "Some rest and decent food to fatten her up, and she'll be a lioness. Eh, Cousin?"

"Most certainly," Arthur said with a smile. "Ah, here's Faith."

The girl entered, out of breath, ceramics pitcher in hand and poured Hazel a glass of cold refreshing water.

"Ah, never have I tasted better," she said. It cooled her tongue both literally and figuratively. Now she could face Joshua, and she rose to stand before him. "Do not worry, Cousin, Faith will return to you a better woman than you can ever imagine."

He smiled and nodded, blissfully unaware of her true meaning. "I leave her in your capable hands. Faith, come, say your goodbyes."

She did, embracing her mother long and hard, and gave her father a curt bow. Hazel sighed and started to shake her head in disgust but smirked as the late morning light caught the glint of a tear on his cheek.

Why, the big old softy. He may act like a grizzly, but he's a teddy bear.

They departed quickly, Joshua not saying a word. He seemed cold and aloof, but Hazel knew the truth. He couldn't open his mouth without sobbing, and she intended to tell Faith as soon as possible. Another thought came to her as they stood on the wide porch and waved as her parents drove off. She turned to face the girl.

"All right, young lady, let's establish something right off the bat," she said, trying to sound firm.

"Bat? Did you see a bat in the house?" she squeaked, gazing about.

Hazel winced and chided herself. *Damn, forgot, modern idiom.* "No, sweetie, I…misspoke. What I meant is I want to establish something right now. You are not to set foot in our room, ever. Do that and I'll cane…no, I'll send you back to your parents."

Her words had the desired effect on Faith. She almost literally became white as a sheet, and her chin trembled.

"Oh no, Cousin, mistress, not that, I beg you! I swear, I give my pledge to God, never will I set foot in there, not if I was offered all the riches of Midas."

"Fine, we will speak no more of it," Hazel said, putting the back of her hand against her forehead. "Now, I feel myself growing fatigued. Husband, help me to lie down."

Arthur took her other hand and slipped his arm about her waist. "Yes, dearest. Faith, finish putting everything away then fill the cistern as best you can then we'll sit down and review the household chores."

"Yes, sir," she said.

He and Hazel climbed the stairs, and Faith headed for the kitchen. Part way up, Hazel stopped and called out to her.

"Faith, I want you to know, your father loves you very much. He may not show it, but I saw it in his eyes as they left."

She smiled up at Hazel. "Oh, I know."

"You do?" Hazel replied, taken aback by the girl's casual demeanor.

"Yes, but social constraints make it impossible for him to show it. I feel so sorry for Daddy."

"Ah…all right then." *Damn, I underestimated this girl. She's not only sharp, she's a regular genius.*

Once in the room, a musty dusty place, Arthur grabbed a chair, and Hazel used her petticoat to clear the dust from the mattress to sit.

"Okay, what was all that business about our room?" he said. "I think you scared her out of five year's growth."

Hazel cringed. "Yes, I know, and I feel terrible about it, but I had to do it. Arthur, if we're going to get through this year we're going to need to plan and prepare, and we're going to have to be able to talk."

"Ah, the clouds part, and I see the light. By making this room forbidden territory to our own little '*Olivia* Twist,' you insure we get privacy."

"You got it."

"Thank you, but what I don't 'got' is why being sent home is such a terrible thing. How'd you know that would work best?"

"It's part of the social dynamics of this kind of society. If we reject Faith, it won't just reflect badly on her. Her parents will be publicly humiliated and lose face. About the only thing worse would be an out of wedlock birth."

"Wow," Arthur said slowly. "Yeah, I can see where that would be a real kick in the teeth. I mean, what, as recently as the 1970's that was still something that would get a girl kicked out of her home."

Hazel nodded and stood. "Yeah. So, now that we've scared the poor child, we'll start building her up. Here, would you help me get these clothes off? I'd like to take your things off, and we can stow them in the bureau."

"You got it," he said and started in on the buttons down the back of her dress. "What's your plan for Faith?"

"At this point, I don't know, other than giving her lots of positive reinforcement and *never* using that…*thing* on her! Ahhh…that feels better," she sighed, slipping out of the gown.

Arthur put the dress aside and helped her with the petticoats. "No arguments there. I mean, use a strap on her, really? No way. Can you believe they've actually done that to her, and the other children?"

"Arthur, it's the custom now," she said, heaving another sigh and finally got down to his clothes. "As for the whole 'Rubenesque Figure' being the height of attractiveness, did you hear Patience? Sheesh, she sounded like a Jewish mother with her talk of me needing to eat."

He laughed as she handed him his shirt and pants. "I got news for you, my girl, a whole lot of ethnic groups have maternal figures who advocate food as a curative for everything. I had an Italian mother, and all she ever said was, 'You're so thin. Eat.' I could be going out with friends to supper and she'd want me to eat before I left."

Hazel, down to her own T-shirt and shorts, wriggled and shook in delight at her physical freedom then giggled. "She wanted you to have food before going out to have food? Okay, you win the mommy competition. Now to business. We need to plan out our year. To get home we have to be in that cave on the next solstice. Everything we do from now on has to be with that goal in mind. So, how we going to do that?"

He paced the room. "Well, if we just work this farm, produce enough food to get through the winter, we should be fine. We're lucky in that we don't have to worry about producing enough to sell to make money. As long as we and Faith can eat, we're good. Plus, we also have the money Joshua owes us. With even a few pounds we can buy anything we need to survive."

"Okay. Ah, do you know anything about farming?"

"Well…I grew some beans and exposed half to rock music and half to classical as part of a grade school science project."

"Oy!" She groaned. "That still puts you ahead of me."

"What about running a household? You know anything there?"

She blew a raspberry. "Run a house? I can't balance my checking account or pay my credit cards on time. My cable and electric have been turned off for lack of payment more times than I can remember."

"You've been that short on money?"

"No, I just forgot to pay the damn bills!"

He slapped his forehead. "Ohhh brother, we're in good shape."

"Now, now, don't throw in the towel yet. We've got Faith, literally. The girl can at least keep us alive. I mean, provided there isn't some major disaster headed our way. You're the expert on island history. What's coming up in the next year?"

"In the next several months?" he squeaked and cleared his throat. "Ah, well…"

A bead of sweat trickled down the side of his head, and his jaw muscles twitched. That knot returned to her gut. She had a bad feeling about his sudden silence.

"Arthur, talk to me. Is something...wrong?"

He licked his lips. "No, sorry, lost in thought for a moment, and it's so hot in here. I need to open some windows. Huh, no screens. Wonder if I can use my degree in mechanical engineering to invent something to help us in that department. Think I'll go down and talk to Faith, outline her chores, and check out the farm. If we're going to be stuck here a year, we might as well be as comfortable as possible."

He moved to the door quickly. As Hazel's dad, who was ex-army would say, he 'moved with a purpose,' and that bad feeling inside her did not diminish. She sat on the bed, her gaze playing about the room as she contemplated *things*. A dreadful sensation cut through her like an icy wind off a frozen lake. Another saying of her father's came to mind, 'Someone just walked across my grave.'

Arthur seemed to be hiding something, but she couldn't understand why he would do that. If there was a storm or battle, or some sort of attack coming, why not tell her? After all, they could easily plan for it. For now, she decided to put such worries aside and also keep her eyes and ears open. If need be, she'd confront him, but for now, she thought 'playing nice' was best. Why get all up in his face over nothing and poison their relationship when they had so much to get through, and they had to depend on each other? No, she was not going to damage the trust between them over a mere gut feeling.

Getting to her feet, she scanned the room that would be their home for the coming year. It was a quaint little place, much like the bedroom of Joshua and Patience, albeit dustier and dirtier. It was clear no one had lived here for at least several months. The spool bed, nice and large and firm, sat against the north wall of the house and had a beautifully varnished headboard and footboard. Tall narrow windows were on either side, and cute little tables sat under each window. A large and beautiful quilt covered the bed. She patted the mattress. The detail and workmanship of the quilt was incredible. A large map of the island dominated the center of the quilt. Each town was shown along with symbols representing their produce, for lack of a better word. Edgar Towne had barrels and bottles, Cottage City fish, Tisbury fish and cattle, and Chilmark general farm products and lots of barrels. A grapevine pattern encircled the whole image.

Hazel sighed and slowly shook her head as she realized Gay Head was not even shown. That end of the island was multicolored, probably to symbolize the cliffs. She tucked her fanny pack in the bottom drawer of a bedside table, opened the windows on either side of the bed, then moved to the west wall to open the window above the long low bureau. She ran her fingers over the bureau and smiled. The hardwood was smooth, well polished, and painted to resemble a vineyard. The drawer handles were carved with a grape pattern, and she was amazed at the smooth movement of each drawer. She sighed and rolled her eyes at the large number of petticoats neatly folded in them.

No, there is no way I'm wearing all of those all of the time.

A matching bureau sat under a matching window in the opposite wall and she opened that window so as to create a nice cross breeze. After that, she thought it best to go downstairs and help. She'd seen Arthur head for the barn and wanted to check on him and Faith. She sighed again. Leaving the room meant dressing. With the windows open and her in *her* clothes, she was quite comfy, but they had work to do. Slipping on *one* layer of undergarments, she pulled on her dress, then headed downstairs. She could not believe how busy Faith was and how much she had already gotten done.

The pots and pans were put away, the tables and counters wiped down, a small fire crackled, and a wash tub sat on the main dining table. Faith was heating water to wash the dishes she had piled in the tub, and she was kneading a pile of dough, clearly with the intent of baking bread. Hazel smiled as she stepped into the room. Faith had also gathered some wild flowers and set them in the middle of the table in a tall ceramic vase. The floor creaked. She spun toward the doorway.

"Cousin, ma'am, is everything all right? I was cleaning up and cooking."

Hazel nodded. "You're doing an excellent job, Faith. Oh, and drop— I mean, there's no need to be so formal. We're family. So, you can call us… 'Auntie' and 'Uncle.' I'm going outside to help Arthur then we can prepare lunch."

Hazel moved through the room on the left, which was used for storage. There were shelves with blankets, cooking supplies, sacks of sugar, flour, and other staples. The next room was farm equipment such as shovels, hoes, an auger, bags of seeds, and a bunch of things she didn't recognize. She sure hoped Arthur at least had a clue as to how to use all these things. Stepping out the wide back door onto the narrow porch, she scanned the area. The spring was at the top of the nearby hill, which meant that's where they'd have to go for water.

"Arthur, a word," she called out to him, standing near the barn.

He turned to her. "What's up? Actually, we need to watch the modern lingo. It'll confuse people."

Coming down the simple wooden steps, she moved close to him. "You're right. I'll work on that. I know these may sound like silly problems, but I'm wondering how we bathe and brush our teeth? Or…ah, do we at all? I hate the idea of getting a cavity while we're here."

"Huh, to be honest, I don't know what sort of teeth cleaners are available in this era, but I might be able to mix us up something, and I can cobble together brushes. As for bathing, I don't know if tubs exist now, and I'm sure showers don't. If I remember correctly, those people who chose to bathe usually stood in a small basin and poured water over themselves."

She grimaced. "Sounds cold and...minimal. They also don't have deodorant, do they?"

He shook his head. "Nope. Those who can afford it buy perfume, yet, you know what? I think I might be able to work something out for us."

"What kind of something?" she replied, totally confused.

"I've checked the lay of the land, literally," he said and pointed at the spring. "Look at where the water is relative to the house. It comes out of the hillside at roughly the same elevation as our second floor, and that is something I can work with."

"In what way can you 'work' with it?"

"Even a simple gravity fed pipe system will have a decent head to it."

"Pipe? Head? Arthur, you're not making any sense. You sound like you're talking about a glass of beer."

He chuckled. "I guess I am. Sorry about the technical term. In this case, head refers to the amount of pressure in the lines."

"There you go again, lines. What sort of lines do they have in this era?"

"Technically, they don't, but I can cast pipes out of clay."

"Pipes out of clay?" she squealed, her jaw dropping. "Are you crazy?"

He shrugged. "What's so crazy about that? It's not like we have a shortage of the material around here, wouldn't you say?"

"No, quite true. We've got cliffs literally made of clay, so I'm sure you can find the material. That's not the issue. My concern is you building a pipe system—period. What are the people going to think about that? Aren't you concerned about changing the future?"

"Oh, come on, a few pipes won't amount to a hill of beans."

Hazel rubbed her chin. "Well...are you saying you could make some sort of bath tub?"

"Yeah. Now, it'll have to be down cellar, but I can do it."

"In the cellar, why?"

"In a word, weight," Arthur said. "Not yours, my sweet, but the water and tub. Together, they'll amount to quite a bit, and I doubt these old wooden floors could support it."

She slowly nodded. "Ah, I see. Yeah, I don't relish plunging through the house in my birthday suit and ending up with broken bones, at the least. Given the state of medical science, I'd never survive."

"And 'Death by Bathing' would not be a fitting epitaph for you," he replied with a grin.

She giggled. It warmed her soul to joke with Arthur. Considering the difficulties they faced in the coming months, they were going to need each other to get through it, and a positive mental state was critical.

"So, how do we begin?"

He cracked his knuckles. "Well… I guess we can start today, right after lunch. I'll begin with the molds to cast the pipes and sketch out the design. Oh, pen and paper, that's what I'll need. You and Faith could even help with the other components. Hey, now that I think of it, I might be able to work this out so it helps in other aspects of the household."

Her brow wrinkled. "Oh, how?"

He grinned. "You'll see, my sweet, you'll see. I'm saving it as a surprise."

"Arthur, you're not going to build some huge waterworks system to supply the whole bloody town, are you?"

He laughed. "No, nothing so grandiose, merely something to make us more comfortable."

Hazel had to admit she was torn regarding his proposal. While it sounded interesting and definitely something to make their lives easier, and a totally awesome project to help pass the time, there was that whole time paradox thing. What was he truly planning, and what affect might news of his design have on the locals?

He seemed so confident everything was going to be fine, and she wanted so much to trust him, but doubt nagged at the back of her mind. There it was again, the desire to trust him, which was something she'd never known with any other man. She had to wonder: was it their odd circumstances that influenced her, or was it something else? Hazel had never before used the 'L word' in any relationship, other than Jimmy Vickers back in kindergarten, and that was only because he gave her his chocolate milk, so she was hesitant to trot it out now. She'd heard how extreme emotional trauma could cause people to form emotional attachments too quickly and that they never lasted, but she had a feeling that wasn't the case with Arthur. She wasn't sure, she only had a feeling, and so she was willing to give him the benefit of the doubt.

For now.

Going inside, Hazel set to work helping Faith make lunch, and Arthur went upstairs to the front bedroom. Faith told him an old desk was in there, and writing equipment was stored inside it. Hazel so wanted to go with him and watch him sketch out his ideas, but she decided to help Faith. Not only did she not want the poor girl doing everything, she figured it would help if she started learning some of these things. It almost made her roll her eyes, the thought of standing in the kitchen to stir the pot of soup.

Talk about being a stereotype!

When everything was ready, she cupped her hands to her mouth, and called out, "Come and get it, or I'll throw it away!"

Faith shuddered. "Auntie, you mustn't cry out so! Speaking in such a loud voice is not ladylike. What would your father say? There's also the matter of threatening to waste good food. Most inappropriate."

"Oh, it's all right, I was only kidding. It's a little joke Arthur and I have."

Actually, they didn't, but she wasn't going to tell Faith that. It'd upset her. It *was* her little joke, something she always said, which was why she'd said it without thinking, and she hoped he'd get it. The heavy clomp of his footsteps told them he was on the move then came the creak to the stairs, and a moment later he appeared.

"I guess I need to get down here," he said with a smile and sniffed. "Ah, smells delicious. Ladies, sit, and we'll eat and talk."

"Talk, Uncle?"

"Your uncle is a bit of an…inventor, and he's come up with…well, let him tell you."

Arthur set out the pages he'd brought down with him on the table and outlined his idea for a water system for the house. Hazel was amazed. He'd worked out a way for the water to simply flow into several chambers that would provide them with water for the kitchen, hot water, well, *heated* water, and a sort of cooler in the basement for food storage. She could see the awe in Faith's expression. She sat there, jaw hanging open, eyes growing wider with each passing minute, as her gaze moved across the papers to take it all in.

"Uncle, I don't mean to speak…ill of your idea, but how will a little pipe like my father's fill a cistern?"

Hazel and Arthur stared at each other. She was impressed. The girl was trying to understand, but she clearly misunderstood the concept of a water pipe. All she knew was the pipes her father used for smoking.

Arthur smiled at her. "Faith, when you see what we're planning, you'll understand. The pipes we're going to make are *much* bigger. After we eat, we'll get started."

After cleaning up from the meal—something Arthur helped them with, which got the most incredulous expression from Faith—they set to work. From the back storeroom they found a pickaxe and shovels, a large washtub, some rags, a bunch of short wooden dowels, and a small low table. From its aroma and knife marks in the top, it had been used to gut fish.

Once outside, Arthur got them organized. They set the table in the shade of a nice pear tree, put the tub next to it, and filled it with water from the spring. While Hazel and Faith did that, he poked around with the pickaxe until he found a good outcropping of clay, and they used the shovels to pile up a nice mountain of it next to the table.

He cracked his knuckles as he scanned the other items, now spread across the table. "Hmmm, we need a lubricant. Faith, is there any grease or oil, or maybe lard or something like that in the house?"

"Yes, Uncle. Mother gave me a tub of her finest chicken fat."

"Perfect, go get it."

The girl once more appeared confused but obeyed without question. Meanwhile, Arthur got things organized. They put some clay in the water to soften it, while Arthur set out their tasks. Hazel and Faith would take the clay in small clumps, smooth it, roll it, and create two large, for lack of a better word, pour spouts. Meanwhile, he took the dowels, spread some fat on them, and covered them in clay. By the time he had all of them covered, the first one was firm enough to slide the dowel out from inside the pipe.

Faith was totally fascinated. "Uncle, those are such large pipes."

He smiled. "Correct. Now do you understand how they will carry water?"

She nodded. "Yes, but… each piece is only about four feet long. How will they… unite?"

"That will come later, when we're ready to put the pipes in position. We'll wrap them in more clay to connect them."

"And these spouts we're making, how do they figure in your plan?" Hazel asked.

"At the beginning and the end. Once everything is in place, we'll direct the spring into the first one, and the water will flow through the pipes. The second one will flow into the cellar at the end of the hot trough, and we'll also have the cistern in the cellar. That way, when you need water for cooking or cleaning, Faith, all you'll have to do is go down there with a bucket or pitcher."

Her eyebrows shot up. "You mean, no more hiking up to the spring?"

Hazel smiled. "That's exactly what he means. So, Arthur, what next?"

"Well, the spouts look fine, so we'll leave them to dry, and make several more lengths of pipe. I'm not sure how much we'll need, and better to have too much than too little."

Faith picked up one of the dowels. "You… you mean *I* can make one?"

"You go right ahead," he said, smiling and nodding.

It was as if he'd given her the right to vote. Faith positively glowed with delight and set to work. Granted, it took her twice as long as Arthur or

Hazel to form a single pipe, and she'd almost completely covered the front of her dress with clay, but she did it. Arthur worked on several Y-shaped pipes to allow for multiple flows.

Finally, hours later, the three of them red from the clay, hot and sweaty as well, sat back and gazed over their efforts. Two spouts, three dozen lengths of pipe, and several Y-joints sat in the grass to dry. Arthur poured each of them a large cup of water, and they sucked them down in no time. Never had Hazel tasted such cold refreshing water. No chemicals, no water treatment plant, no nothing. Just water. It was very, *very* good. Getting to his feet, he stepped close to the back wall of the kitchen. The house was essentially U-shaped in the back. The kitchen was at the center, and there were two rooms on each side. They formed the sides of the U. He kicked at the dirt and studied the ground then moved to the left of the fireplace, which sat at the center of the back wall.

"I'm thinking this is where we'll build the troughs. So, we'll need some stones and mortar."

Smiling, Faith rose to face him. "Stones are no problem, Uncle. Look about you. There are plenty to be had. As for mortar, I don't know how to make that, but Mr. Norton is coming tomorrow with his cattle. We can ask him."

"Splendid, Faith, thank you for the suggestions. All right, I'll gather some stones and stack them here to use when we're ready," he said and gazed off to the horizon. "It's getting late. Why don't you ladies go in and start supper?"

She nodded and darted off. Hazel stayed rooted to her spot for a moment. She couldn't believe what she'd heard. Arthur expected her to play 'Little Suzy Homemaker.' Then she achieved clarity. Of course he said that. He had to. It was expected.

She gave him an exaggerated curtsy and squeaked, "Yes, dear."

He snorted. His belly actually twitched for a moment as though he fought the desire to burst out laughing. "Thank you for understanding," he whispered.

"I'm trying. You going to be okay, or do you need some help?"

"I'll be fine. I'll be careful not to overdo it."

Hazel headed inside and found Faith already changed and cooking a supper of chicken, potatoes, and mixed vegetables. The girl was nothing if not fast and efficient.

She turned to face Hazel as she entered. "Auntie, if you'll give me your dress, I'll put it to soak with mine."

"Fine, I'll go upstairs and change and bring it to you."

Climbing the stairs, she reached back to work the buttons. She was getting better at that and was able to get undressed without help. It was calming and comfy to be in her own clothes, if only for a few minutes, and she realized she was going to have to wash them sometime soon. That was a task she needed Faith to teach her, among other things.

Hazel was beginning to figure out the whole 'household chores' routine, and they were considerable. She now understood why it was that people used to talk about 'wash day' and 'ironing day.' Those tasks used to take an entire day. There was cooking, bringing in wood for heating, filling lamps for lighting, basic housework, emptying—yuck—chamber pots, making clothes, doing the laundry, tending the sick, childcare, and taking care of livestock. It was a relief to Hazel that there were only the three of them to take care of and that Faith was there to help her.

Man, if we ever get home, I will never complain about having to go to the laundromat every week to wash my things.

In the bureau was one of Patience's older dresses. Hazel could tell that by the patches on the elbows and the smaller size, and so it fit better. Once she handed the dirty one over to Faith, she zipped off to add it to the laundry tub, and Hazel set the table. She could hear Arthur outside stacking the stones. Everyone couple minutes, there was a thump and the bang of stone hitting stone. She sniffed and smiled. Faith was nothing if not a good cook. The chicken, browning in the fire, made Hazel's mouth water.

She chuckled to herself. *Patience complained about me being too thin. Well, a couple months of classic meat and potatoes and I'm going to blow up like a balloon. Although, considering how active we are, maybe I can stay trim.*

Arthur joined them briefly. He also changed and handed over his soiled things to Faith, and they sat down to supper. He made a point of saying a nice blessing and mentioned what a good job Faith had done and what a big help she'd been.

She smiled. "Thank you, Uncle Arthur! Will you test me on my lessons?"

"Oh. Ah, I would, but I don't know where you are in your studies."

"Faith, that brings up an interesting question. Do you go to school?"

She shook her head. "Oh no, only the boys attend classes. Father can't afford to pay for the rest of us to go."

A surge of fire coursed through Hazel's stomach and throat. She and Arthur locked eyes, and by the expression on his face, he understood her mental communication.

"Well, we will see about you going to school," he said.

"Me? Oh, no, I can't do that," she squeaked. "Uncle, Auntie, I could never repay the debt."

"Now, now, don't you worry about that," he replied. "We will bear the cost, and there will be no talk of repayment."

"It is our pleasure to help you in your education."

"I…yes, Uncle Arthur, thank you, Aunt Hazel," she choked out. It was clear the girl didn't know what to think or say and was quite overcome with emotion, but she managed to hold it in and not burst into tears.

He cracked a single knuckle. "Besides, how much can it be? If I remember correctly, from your father's letters, there is no tuition to attend school. Isn't that correct?"

She nodded. "Oh, yes, but there are the books and supplies."

Hazel sighed and grinned ever so modestly. *Huh, in more than two centuries, education in America doesn't change.* "We will take care of them. I must say, I'm impressed that school is free. Your island is most progressive, Faith."

The girl smiled. "Thank you, Auntie. Not only does each town have a school, but in 1748 we established a 'moving school.' It stays in Holmes Hole for two months in the fall, Chilmark for three, Kiphigan, which is between here and Edgar Towne, for two months then the schoolhouse near the meeting hall in Tisbury for the next five. Any child can go to any of them."

"A moving school," Hazel said slowly. "I've never heard of such a thing, but now I'm doubly impressed."

After supper, Arthur further amazed Faith by helping to clean up.

"Now, how about a game of cards?" Hazel suggested.

"A…game?" Faith said. "Oh, no, Mother wants me to work on your new clothes."

Hazel opened her mouth to tell Faith what she thought of her mother but checked herself. No, she didn't want to go there. Better to let things go, for now, and work on getting Faith to lighten up in the coming weeks. What was Hazel thinking, weeks? They were going to be there months! Oh, she hoped life in this era would be easier than in theirs.

"Well, how about I help with the clothes, and at the same time I'll…um, ah, tell you a story?"

The girl smiled. "A story? I'd like that."

Hazel smiled back. "Good, and while I tell it, you can show me how you sew. I've had a few lessons, but it's been a while, and I'll need to know how so as to be a good wife to Arthur."

She almost choked saying the words, but managed to hold the smile without, she hoped, it appearing too fake. Just *thinking* the words was repulsive. Yet, she knew learning to sew would be helpful for them, and it would make Faith feel good to teach her. So, they went upstairs to the large center room where the spinning wheel and other equipment were set up. Lighting two oil lamps, they took seats in a rocking chair for Hazel and a small simple chair for Faith. Arthur joined them briefly so Faith could measure him, then he held the notepad while she measured Hazel. After that, he sat and read a book while they worked.

Hazel sat and rocked and thought a moment. *Huh, I've got to use a story that's appropriate for this era and this...audience. Now, let me see.* "Ah, I have a tale. Once, long ago, there lived a giant who had a big house and a big garden full of lovely trees and flowers. However, the giant was selfish. He didn't like the children of the town playing in his garden. So, he built a tall wall around his garden to keep them out."

"That wasn't quite nice of him," Faith said.

"Well, he *was* selfish," Hazel replied. "Winter came, and spring followed, but not in the giant's garden. The Spirit of Spring passed the giant by as she didn't like him being selfish, as did Summer. Now, Lady Snow and Mr. Sleet, and Ian Icicle were delighted, as they had a place to spend the hot summer, but the giant was confused. 'Why is winter staying so long?' he wondered. Fall gave way to winter again, and the next spring something different happened. One morning, the giant glanced out his window and saw the children playing again in his garden. The flowers were blooming, and the trees had leaves."

"How did they get into the garden?" Faith asked.

"That's what the giant wanted to know. He saw that a hole had opened in the wall, and thus the children could climb through. He also saw one tree was still bare. A little boy stood before it, but he couldn't reach to climb it. The giant sighed. 'Oh, I have been such a fool,' he scolded himself. 'No wonder spring has passed me by.' With that, he went outside. The children, quite naturally, ran in fear. All but the little boy, as he was crying so hard he couldn't see the giant coming up behind him. Gently, he hoisted the boy into the tree. The child smiled and reached out to embrace the giant, as least as much of him as he could reach. The giant smiled back and blushed as the boy kissed him. Then the children knew it was safe to come into the garden. That day, the giant knocked down the wall and sat and played with the children as they enjoyed the garden. 'You must come again tomorrow,' he told them, as they prepared to leave. 'And bring the little one with you. Who is he?' The children explained that they didn't know him or where he lived but would try to find him. Well, they never did. The years rolled along. The giant was a good friend and good neighbor to the people and always let the children play in his garden. As he grew old and infirm, he could no longer play with them, but he would sit in his huge rocking chair and enjoy watching them play."

"Did he never see the boy again?" Faith said.

Hazel playfully wagged her finger at her. "Ah, ah, I'm coming to that. One day he looked out his window and saw the boy again and raced out happily to see him."

"He was still a little boy?" Faith said.

"Wait and listen, and all will become clear. The giant dropped to his knees and smiled to see his small friend, but then frowned. On his hands were nail marks, and he had similar marks on his feet. 'Someone has hurt you,' the giant boomed. 'Tell me who that I may thrash them!' The boy smiled and shook his head. 'No, it's all right. These marks mean nothing. Once, long ago, you let me play in your garden. Now come, come and live in my garden and know eternal peace.' The giant's weak bones grew strong, his muscles firm, and he was able to toss aside his cane. Following the boy, he departed this world for paradise."

Faith smiled and sighed. "Ohhh, Auntie, what a sweet story! Is it from the Bible? I don't recognize it."

"Ah, no, I heard it in England from a friend. Oscar is his name."

"Well, if you're ever able to write to him, you must tell him what a wonderful story it is, and that he should publish it. Thank you for telling it to me."

Hazel smiled back. "And thank you for the sewing lesson. It's been so long since I did it that you've helped me a great deal in remembering. Now, I think the hour grows late, and we should all retire."

Once more, Faith was fast and efficient. She had the place cleaned up and the sewing things stowed away in no time. Their new things were ready for them to wear the next day. A quick curtsy, a wish for pleasant dreams, and off Faith went. Hazel and Arthur could finally relax. They got into their nightclothes, climbed into bed, and cuddled up close. The night air gave them goosebumps, and they both groaned about their sore muscles.

"Man, and here I thought I was in shape," Hazel said. "You think Patience is this active every day?"

"I doubt she works with clay much, but work hard? Yeah, I'm sure of it."

"Damn, I will never say the folks in colonial times had it easy not having to deal with the stresses of modern life. I will definitely never call these the 'Good Old Days' again. They had it rough!"

"That they did. Hey, where did you hear that story? It was a nice one."

"I read it as a kid. It was in a collection of stories by Oscar Wilde."

"Oscar Wi—? Ohhh, hey, isn't that tampering with history?"

Hazel shrugged and smiled at Arthur, wrapped in her arms as much as she was in his. "Who knows? Maybe he hears the story from someone visiting from America. At any rate, I don't think we're in danger of copyright infringement."

He chuckled and squeezed her tighter. She loved the feel of his large hands, despite the calluses, against her back. His long arms gave her warmth and comfort. Despite everything, it was as if she was curled up safely with a friendly bear in its cave, and that meant she could sleep.

"I'm glad we got through another day," he said, kissing her cheek. "I worry about tomorrow and the day after that, and…well, you get the picture."

She gave him the warmest smile she could, rubbed his back, and kissed him full on the lips. "No matter what happens, we'll face it together."

She was scared silly but bound and determined not to show it. So much about the future was uncertain, but she thought if they worked together, they could overcome any obstacle.

Five

Art winced as he stretched in bed. His back and arms throbbed. It was clear he wasn't in as good a shape as he thought. Still there was a nice compensation—he awoke spooned up next to Hazel's warm and supple body. He'd have kissed the back of her neck, but as he ran his tongue around his mouth, he got a bad taste rippling across his taste buds.

Okay, today, somehow, I come up with mouthwash or toothpaste, 'cause I'm not going a year without both. Man, my breath could knock over a tree!

Unwrapping himself from Hazel, he rolled away. She opened her eyes and smiled.

"Where you going, my man?"

He covered his mouth. "I'm trying to lose this morning breath."

"Right there with you, dude. Any thoughts?"

Swinging his legs around to sit on the edge of the bed, he sat and scanned the room. "For now, I guess good old fashion water, but I remember some things I read once. I'll see about getting to town today and buy the ingredients to whip us up something."

On the bureau on his side of the room was a pitcher and bowl. He smiled at the sight of it. He hadn't seen one since going to a museum in Boston last year. He'd filled it with water last night, while the ladies sewed, and Hazel told her story. While there was no glass, with a bit of skillful manipulation, he poured some in his mouth, and rinsed.

"I must say, Arthur, waking up with the same man two days in a row, and not 'doing it' is a first for me. I'm becoming quite the virtuous woman."

He almost choked on the water, but managed to spit it out the window rather than bother with the bowl and have to clean it.

"Hazel, you have quite the sharp wit."

She bowed her head. "Thank you, my man, I try."

"Be careful," he replied as she got out of bed. "A witty woman in this era is a dangerous thing. Can get you into trouble."

She smiled, opening a window. "Bring it!"

Art sighed and shook his head sure his grin went ear to ear as she leaned out the window. What a figure she had, even covered by a nightgown. He was careful to move his gaze away before she turned around, and he got dressed as she also rinsed her mouth. Here again he caught himself staring. Even swishing water in her mouth, her cheeks puffed out like a chipmunk, she was still hot. He was comfortable with her as he stripped down to his briefs without hesitation. She followed his example and spit out the window. Somehow she managed to make it sound sexy then she turned to him.

"Not the best cleanse I've ever had, but at least it's something. I checked out your little Erector Set Rube Goldberg creation. Any chance of including indoor plumbing with the deal? I don't relish the hike out to the outhouse when winter comes."

"Oh, I don't see it as poss... hmmm, wait a minute," he said slowly, tapping his upper lip. "I remember a show I saw on one of those history channels. It talked about the Roman forts along Hadrian's Wall and how they used flowing water to create toilets. Maybe I can do the same."

"Who's Adrian?"

"No, no, *Hadrian*, Roman emperor, built a wall across northern England to keep out the tribes to the north in Scotland."

"Wow, sort of like the Chinese, right?"

"Along the same lines, but not so long. Now, I'm off to avail myself of the facilities, limited as they are, and I'll see you at breakfast."

"Good, at least the seat won't be cold," she said with a smile.

With one swoop of her arms, she hoisted her nightgown up and over her head and stood before him in her underwear. It seemed she was comfortable around him too. Art tried not to stare as she washed her face and got dressed. He headed for the door, but it wasn't easy. A figure as good as hers, encased delicately in matching red lace bra and panties was a true vision of beauty. He was glad to step out the back door into the bracing morning. It cooled him in more ways than one. By the time he emerged from the outhouse and walked back through the dew-laden grass, Hazel exited. They later sat down to another wonderful breakfast of Faith's.

"Ah, Uncle, will we make more of your pipes today?"

"I think we have enough for what we need, but it wouldn't hurt to make extra."

"Oh, it will not hurt me at all, I'm strong," she replied, grinning.

Art was confused for a moment then he realized he'd fallen back into modern idiom. "Yes, so you can make some more, and Hazel and I will prepare the troughs. Oh, but, Faith, don't tell anyone about our pipe system yet. It's my invention, and I don't want people to know about it until it's ready."

"Yes, sir, I will not say a word," she said.

Several loud moos bellowed outside, and he and Hazel both jumped in their seats.

Faith casually turned to stare out the window in the store room. "Mr. Norton is here to clear the fields."

Art chuckled and helped to get the dishes off the table. "Ed Norton, I love it," he said in a soft voice.

"Faith, why don't you go and welcome him?" Hazel said. "We'll join you presently."

She curtsied. "Yes, Auntie."

Once she was out the back door, Hazel turned to him. "All right, out with it, what's so funny? Tell me now before you do or say something to upset him."

"You don't know? Geez, didn't you ever watch classic TV? Ed Norton was the neighbor and friend of Ralph Kramden in *The Honeymooners* show."

"I have no idea what you're talking about; the only Ed Norton I know is the actor. Sorry, Arthur, I never cared for old things," she said, then scanned the room. "…although, I am learning the importance of knowing the past."

"Maybe some night I'll do story time and tell you about it."

She laughed. "Hey, that's a good idea. Translate a modern story into something for this era. Right now, I would imagine there's a social protocol we should follow regarding neighbors coming to help us."

Art gazed around and nodded. "Yes, and it appears Faith is way ahead of us. She's made extra bread and put on water for tea."

"What would we do without her?"

"Starve," he said, chuckling as he offered her his arm. "Shall we go make nice with the neighbors?"

Out the front door they headed, and before them were arrayed quite the variety of people, yet clearly a family. The man, obviously Mr. Norton, limped up to them on a stout walking stick.

"Good morning to you, Neighbor Mayhew," Edward called out to him.

Art stepped forward, responded in kind, and introductions followed, not that he had a chance of remembering all the names. Edward had brought the entire brood, and he and his wife Mary were nothing if not prolific. The two oldest boys, Phineas and Solomon, stayed at his side, while the younger six rug-rats dashed about and sounded more like a chorus of feral cats than children. However, Art wasn't about to say anything on the issue. Edward resembled his future TV namesake in height and build, but that build rippled with powerful muscles. There was no doubt he worked a farm and worked hard all day. Mary and Tabitha—their oldest daughter, a cute little strawberry-blonde cherub of twelve—stepped forward with two baskets of goodies.

"A few things to help you find comfort on our island," Mary said.

Art smiled. "Oh, neighbors, such generosity. I have no words to express my gratitude."

The baskets were large and overflowed with household items of pie pans, pots, spoons and ladles, a jug of something, a jar of honey, and an old fashion toaster. He almost laughed at the sight of it. Appeared to be just like the one his grandfather had, only newer. Although, come to think of it, it probably *was* the same one! It was so simple, but he remembered using it once when he was a kid. The metal cage held one or two slices of bread in it and went on the end of a long pole so one could hold it over the fire or hot coals. The trick was keeping an eye on the bread so it didn't burn.

Art also remembered asking Grandpa Steve why people used it. Wasn't it easier to stick the bread on a fireplace fork? He'd explained that having one of those gizmos was like so much in life, a status symbol. Art understood the meaning of it as a gift. The Nortons were making it clear how well they were doing.

"Tabitha, help your mother take these things inside," Edward said.

"Yes, sir," she said.

Hazel moved forward, arms spread wide. "Here, let me help."

"No, ma'am," the girl squeaked. "I am strong, it is my duty."

She hustled inside. Hazel gasped for a moment then visibly calmed down. A knife thrust stabbed Art's stomach. He so wished he could do something to help her cope with this patriarchal society.

"Such a thoughtful and obedient child," Hazel choked out through a forced smile.

Edward smiled at Art. "She is, but she can be a bit trying. Boys, get these other supplies inside and stowed, and then tend the cows. One of them wanders off, and it'll be your hides that pay for it."

"Yes, Father," they said together.

They grabbed several small sacks sitting on the ground behind them. Art realized they were flour, salt, and other staples. He was impressed. The boys, maybe fifteen and sixteen and skinny as rails, easily hoisted them over their shoulders and marched into the house.

Mary fell in behind them. "No worries, Husband, I'll see to it they don't waste time."

"*Tempus fugit*, eh?" Hazel said.

"Don't you worry about your fields, neighbor," Edward said, still fixed on Art. "My cows will clear them by nightfall."

"And fertilize them too," she said, her volume going noticeably up.

Art cracked his knuckles. *Oh boy, got to do something here before this escalates into all out war, but what?* "You must excuse my wife. She is accustomed to speaking her mind. Her full *title* is *Lady* Hazel Puttenham."

It was all Art could do to not explode in a fit of laughter. His words had the desired effect. It was as if Edward had been struck by lightning. He practically snapped to attention and snatched off his hat.

"*Your Ladyship*, a thousand pardons. Joshua said nothing of your position. I had no idea a Mayhew had married up."

A positively demonic grin crept across her face as she lifted her nose ever so slightly in the air. "We will say nothing more of this *insult* to my honor. In future, I hope you will remember your *place*."

"Certainly, ma'am, certainly. Is there anything else me and mine can do to help you and your good husband?"

Art saw Hazel's throat rise and fall as she swallowed, and silence followed.

"Actually, there *is* something, good neighbor," Art jumped in with. "I want to build some water troughs, and I need mortar. Would you have any to spare?"

"Say no more. I shall return home this instant and bring all I have."

"Oh, no," Art said. "We don't—."

Edward raised a hand to cut him off. "No arguments, good fellow, it is the least I can do. If you need help with the work or with the farm, my boys are available. Ah, at a reasonable rate of pay."

"Of course, we would not expect less." *How are we going to handle that little matter? I wonder if Joshua can spare some money.*

Edward departed, giving Hazel a quick bow as Mary and the boys emerged from the house. The latter raced off to watch the cows, but Phineas, the oldest, seemed as if he'd forgotten something. He kept gazing back at the house.

"Such fine strapping lads," Hazel said, her gaze trying to keep pace with the others. "As for the young ones, so…energetic."

That's putting it mildly. Where's a bottle of Ritalin when you need it?

"We must be going now," Mary said. "The children must get to school."

"Oh, what a pity," Art said, trying to sound sincere. "I hoped we could all sit down to lunch together."

"You're welcome to return," Hazel said.

"With regrets, I must decline. I help at the school and am thus needed there."

"Really?" Hazel replied. "Perhaps when I bring Faith, I can help too."

"Faith? Is she not too old? I heard talk of a fine match with the Davenport boy."

"A mere rumor," Hazel said. "She is bound to us now, and I shall see her educated."

"My wife is a firm believer in education. As for Obadiah, that was mere gossip, and I'm sure a woman as fine and upstanding as you wouldn't engage in such a thing."

Art smirked as her back stiffened, and her face took on a slightly reddish hue.

"Certainly not," she squeaked. "Tabitha, children, come along, school."

They hustled off. Tabitha dashed out to join them, and Mary had to smack the occasional head or bottom, whichever one she could reach, to herd her little miscreants in the right direction.

"Sheesh, you sure winged her with that one," Hazel said. "What got her panties in a bunch?"

"The mention of gossip. Not only is it considered quite unladylike, it can be a punishable offense in some areas."

"You're kidding." She gasped.

He shook his head. "No, I'm serious, or maybe I should say, I'm in earnest. In some areas, a woman convicted of being a gossip could get the dunking stool, be put in the stocks, have to wear a large 'G' on her clothes, or be subject to other forms of public shaming. One of the worst was being forced to wear the Scold's Bride."

"Huh, sounds innocent enough, but so does the iron maiden. I may not know much history, but I do remember that one. If memory serves, it was a big metal cabinet shaped like a woman, hence the maiden name, and full of spikes inside pointing at the poor person locked in there. I'm guessing the Bride thing is the same?"

"You're not far off. It's a device that locks around the head and has spikes positioned to make speaking painful."

Hazel's eyebrows shot up. "Spikes? Painful? Damn, remind me to never gossip. Hey, the letter 'G' thing, is it that *Scarlet Letter* story I heard about?"

"Close. That was about a woman who had a child out of wedlock and was considered an adulterer. She wore an 'A' on her clothes."

"Huh, figures, men always want to see a woman's 'A'. Oh, and I bet the *man* who knocked her up didn't have to do that, did he?"

He shook his head. "Nope."

She heaved a sigh of frustration and threw up her arms. "Of course. Arthur, I have to say, I don't know if I can last a year in this…testosterone nightmare. Isn't there a way to trigger the portal sooner?"

"Not that I know of. The light only comes through on noon on the summer solstice."

"Well, what about…I don't know, use a mirror?"

Art rubbed his chin. "Not a bad idea. Although, who's going to hold it? You and I have to be in the cave."

"Faith?"

"That could work. Oh, wait a minute, one big problem, we don't know where the opening is. My friends and I spent a good portion of our childhoods searching and never found it."

"How hard can it be? It has to be directly overhead."

"Does it? Think about it, the cave is full of crystals that reflect light. Who's to say there isn't a long, convoluted passage leading to the surface?"

She wore a sour expression, as if she'd eaten a bad batch of clams. "Why'd you have to be so damn smart?"

He shrugged. "Just lucky I guess. Oh, paint a smile on, dearie, we've got company a-coming."

Hazel turned to check where he was pointing and was able to see the wagon approaching. It was the 'in-laws.'

"Huh! Are they coming to see us or Faith? Think they miss her?"

"Maybe. Let's play it all smiles and happy to see them, okay?"

She smiled so big Art thought prolonged exposure would give him a cavity.

"How's this?" she chirped.

"Like you should be in a Disney movie. Please, take it down a notch and play nice."

"Hey, as long as they bow and curtsy properly, I'm good."

He sighed and rolled his eyes. "'Angels and ministers of faith, defend us.'"

"Hamlet," she said with a sly grin.

"What the…?" He literally did a double take.

"You're surprised? Hey, I do know some of the classics."

"Ahoy, cousins," Patience called out, waving to them. "We come bearing gifts aplenty!"

Joshua reined the horses and hopped down from the old style wagon. It was quite different from the carriage of yesterday, a plain means of transport. Joshua helped Patience down and moved to the back to lower the tailgate.

"Come, Arthur, lend a hand," he said.

"My husband is all business." Patience sighed, throwing open her arms. "First, come, give me your love, both of you."

Art hugged her then helped Joshua with the crates as the ladies embraced.

Are they moving in?

Joshua handed him a box of clothes. "Now, these are *gifts*, we wish to make that clear. Some of our old clothes that should fit better, pears, cherries, flour, and other goods, oh, and some fine plantings from our herb garden."

Patience smiled and nodded. "Yes, and you be sure to tell your father when you write to him. You tell him the Mayhews of Martha's Vineyard know how to treat their relations."

"I most certainly will," he replied, heading for the door.

"Mother, Mother, Father," Faith cried, rushing out to greet them.

She and Patience hugged each other tight, and then she came to the back of the wagon. Her father handed her several bolts of fabric.

"It's good to see you, Faith," he said. "Are you tending to your chores and serving your cousins properly?"

"Yes, Father," she squeaked, her tone soft and full of fear.

"You do honor to the family. Take those inside."

Hazel waved to her, gesturing for her to follow. "This way, Faith, I'll help you to put that away."

Art led the way inside. He and Faith took their supplies up to the center room and set them down. He told her they could put everything away later. By the time they came down the stairs, Joshua and the ladies came in with more boxes.

"Faith, get the chickens and rooster into the barn and penned," he ordered.

"Chickens?" Hazel said. "Ah, *live* chickens?"

Patience nodded. "Of course, you'll need fresh eggs, and we've given you a dozen of our finest fowl. Faith will help you build a coop, and we've brought you plenty of flour, salt, honey, butter, eggs, and my best vegetable oil. Joshua, come, we'll need your long monkey arms to reach the high shelves."

"Yes, m'lady, I shall be with you presently. I need a word with Arthur, upstairs, in private."

Art looked at Hazel, who returned his gaze, and her expression spoke confusion and concern. He smiled at her, trying to seem confident. Based on her reaction, he had *not* pulled it off. Joshua headed up the stairs and Art followed and wondered about the small item he was carrying. It was heavy yet wrapped in a light linen cloth. Joshua headed into the front bedroom.

"Oh, Cousin, we use the back bedroom," Art said.

He turned to face him. "Aye, I can tell, this room is still dusty, but what I have needs privacy."

Art was intrigued and accompanied him, and, with a heavy thump, Joshua set a small box on the long low table next to the desk. When he'd first used the room to sketch his plans, Art figured it was set up as a sort of office, guest room and nursery combo. There was a twin bed, cradle, a sort of changing table, a tall storage cabinet, which resembled a free-standing closet, and two bureaus. Joshua pulled the cloth away to reveal a strongbox. It appeared to be quite solid, the hardwood and metal straps forming a crisscross pattern over it.

"My old box," he said, holding out the key to Art. "It's solid, and the lock is smooth, but not what it appears. You see the keyhole here? It's a fake, put there to confound thieves. The real one is here."

He took the key and watched as Joshua pointed first at the apparent keyhole in the front, and then slid a piece of metal on the top aside to reveal another one.

"Ah, good. Thank you, Cousin, this is something we need."

"There is another gift inside, ten pounds, and it's good money too. It is the first payment in my debt of ninety pounds."

"That is *very* good. Wait, ninety? I think you're confused, the debt is seventy-five."

He shook his head. "No, I'll not take twenty-five for Faith, a mere girl. Joshua Mayhew honors his debts. Ten is fair payment for her services."

"Ah...all right. The money will come in handy, all of ours was lost in the sinking, and I will need it to hire the Norton boys to help around the farm. Wait, *good* money?"

Joshua nodded. "Silver and gold, no worthless colonial money. So, already hiring laborers, eh? That is wise, as I and the boys cannot help you."

"Oh, your sons are not available?"

He sighed and shook his head. "With regrets, Cousin, they are not. My bones grow weak. I cannot work the farm or go on the hunt any longer, and the boys are needed to tend our crops. They can help a day or two a week, but no more."

"No apology needed, Joshua, I understand. What is this hunt you mentioned?"

"It is a matter we need to discuss, but not now. If I delay in helping Patience, she will lose *her* patience, and I will lose sleep for the next fortnight listening to her complain."

He chuckled, and Art laughed, heading downstairs to help put things away. Edward arrived with the mortar and put it in the barn. They invited him to stay, but he had his farm to attend to. He and the boys rounded up the cows and headed home. The fields were cleared and *quite* fertile. Later, sitting down to a nice lunch Patience launched into a report on all the latest doings in Edgar Towne. For that matter, she knew the goings-on everywhere on the island except Aquinnah.

Geez, the woman has a better network of spies than General Washington ever did.

"Now, on to more important things than Bathsheba and her linens," she said. "I have arranged for a hall in Tisbury on the twenty-ninth for the party, all the *proper* people will be there. Hazel, you will need a gown. I apologize for the short schedule. A week is not enough time to make a decent dress, but I'm sure the shops here in Cottage City have a nice selection. Perhaps Faith can help you to personalize one, give it some flare."

"We'll come up with something," Hazel said, offering a smile.

Art could see the pain in her face. The idea of wearing some stifling dress was repugnant to her. Joshua tapped his cup on the table and cleared his throat as he stood up to address the room.

"Arthur, it is time for me to speak of an important matter—the hunt. You may think of the gifts we've brought as the 'molasses.' Now I must feed you the 'sulfur.' Whaling brings in a good income for the island, but I can no longer go on the hunt, and, as I told you, the boys are needed on the farm. I need you to go in my stead."

"Go on a...*whale* hunt?" he said, his voice rising an octave.

"You...*kill* whales?" Hazel snapped. "How can you do that?"

The expression on Joshua's face spoke volumes. He was shocked at her words. "Hazel, they are a vital natural resource. Where do you think the oil for our lamps comes from? There was a time when the occasional dead whale washed ashore and was enough to give us a fine income, but those days ended years ago. Now we must hunt."

"Joshua, while I would gladly help you in any way I can, I don't know anything about whaling."

"Arthur, there is little to know, and the crew will instruct you, but you *must* do this," he insisted. "If a Mayhew doesn't go on the hunt, we'll lose our share of the profits from it, and that will devastate the entire family."

"Husband?" Patience squeaked.

He sighed and hung his head as he resumed his seat. "Patience, with regret, it is the truth. The rebellion has made working the farm difficult. The harvests have been lean, and prices are down. I missed the last hunt. If a Mayhew does not go on this one, we will be cut from the crew list."

Arthur *truly* cracked his knuckles. He did it so hard they ached. He was torn. As much as he wanted to help, the mere thought of killing a whale made the bile burn his throat. What was he to do? If he refused, what would Joshua and Patience say? What would they do, both to survive and to him? He didn't think Joshua would become violent, but it would end their relationship and have a ripple effect on his and Hazel's relationships with the Nortons and...well, everyone. They could end up social pariahs, outcasts. How would they survive the year?

Maybe if I go on the hunt and...sort of...help out, but not do anything cruel, maybe that'll work. "Cousin, yes, I will do it," he said as he slumped his shoulders in defeat.

Joshua and Patience beamed with delight. Hazel gasped.

"Arthur, you can't be serious?" she snapped.

"Hazel, I *have* to do this," he told her, hanging his head.

"Cousin, you have no idea what a help this will be to us," Joshua said. "Not merely the money, which we shall split evenly, but it will preserve our standing in the community. Isaac has grown more belligerent."

"In one day?" Art said.

He nodded. "He has become like Cato the Elder. Last night, he ended every speech at the town meeting with a reaffirmation of the island's devotion to the cause of liberty and breaking from Mother England."

"He hurls the most venomous insults at Joshua," Patience snapped. "And Bathsheba has taken to flying a rebel flag from their home. How she managed to get it sewn in one day, I will never know, but I heard she paid a seamstress *double* rate to get it done. Can you believe such wasteful extravagance?"

Art heaved a sigh. Their presence was most definitely changing history, the island was becoming as politically polarized as the present. From his knowledge of island history, he knew that the Davenports had always been quite reserved, and now the governor had become a hot-headed rebel. He wondered what such passion would lead to, and what a character from the old *Green Hornet* TV show had to do with anything. He mentally slapped himself in the head.

Wait, I know what he's referring to. In Ancient Rome, Cato the Elder was a senator, and he used to call for the destruction of Carthage, Rome's chief rival, every time he spoke in the Forum. God, how could I be so dumb?

He put such thoughts out of his head and focused on the present. Once he agreed to help, they finished lunch and prepared to depart.

"Be at the dock at dawn in three days' time, that is when the next hunt takes place," Joshua said. "The ship is the *Silvana*. Report to the mate, Mr. Bacon, and tell him you have come in my stead."

"I'll be there. Again, thank you for everything."

They left, and Art led Hazel and Faith out to the backyard. They set to work on the new plumbing system. Faith mixed the mortar while he and Hazel dug a trench from the spring down to the area where the troughs would sit. First though, he dug a little diversion swale for the water to go into. That way it didn't flow into where they were digging. For the next few hours, they worked in silence. Faith was quite the good worker. She was able to start the troughs, building them side by side so they shared a wall. That wall she built halfway up, per Art's instructions, the three sides of the hot one she finished, and one side of the cold one, the long side.

Pausing for a break, Art wiped the sweat from his brow, and took a cold drink of water. No cup was needed. He stuck his whole face into the stream, let it wash over him, and drank until he thought he would burst.

"Ohhh, that's good."

"What's *not* good is what you're doing," Hazel grumbled.

"What are you talking about? We're only building—."

"You know what I mean!" she snapped. "Whaling, *killing* a whale. Arthur, how can you?"

"Hazel, talk to me. What would you have me do?"

He explained his reasons. She listened in stoned silence. Her jaw clenched and twitched at every word and spat out her acceptance of the inevitable.

"I hate that you're right. You know that, don't you?"

"I do. Let me be honest with you, I hate it too. Maybe we can take some solace in the fact the whale will die—*did* die—with or without me there."

"It's not much, but it's…something. Let's move on to happier thoughts. Tell me about these pipes."

"We put the spout at the top and lay sections of pipe in the trench. Faith, go get some rags from the kitchen, please," he called out. "We wrap the ends in a piece of cloth and cover them with clay. Once it hardens, it'll be an adequate seal."

"And the troughs, how do they work?"

"Ah, now that's where my engineering expertise comes into play. The water will flow into the first trough. Once it reaches the level of the pipes we'll put in the shared wall, it flows into the other trough and fills it. Now, note the pipe at the far end of the first trough. Its rim is higher than the others, but lower than the top of the troughs."

"I get it. The water fills the troughs until it gets to that pipe, and then it flows…um, where?"

Art moved to the area between the troughs and the house and gestured at the ground. "That's why we now need a ditch here. The pipe will run into the cellar, that's where it'll feed a cooling trough to sort of refrigerate food, turn a water wheel, and go to our new toilet."

Hazel's jaw dropped. "Holy cow, Arthur, how many things are we building? Wait, a water *wheel*? What does that do?"

"Nothing, yet, but I figure it's better to have it set up ahead of time. It's a power source, and you can never have too many of those around, especially in this era."

"After that where does it go?"

"I've thought of that too. A pipe will take it down to the pond next to the fields, which is the natural course of the spring. From there it pops off to Sunset Lake. Well, to where the lake *will* be. For now, we'll allow it to flow on, but we can block and divert it to the fields when it's needed."

"Wow, this is something, my man. I can't wait to see it all put together."

Art was happy to see Hazel excited about something, not focused on the negative aspects of their existence. They continued working. He did the pipes in the troughs, Faith the sides and other pipes, and Hazel dug. When she grew especially hot, she went inside and took off all but one layer of clothing Faith was shocked but said nothing. Art couldn't help but smirk, but he also kept silence. He installed the pipes in the troughs. The one at the end stood straight up and almost went to the top to hold the water in, and then it came out the end of the first trough and headed for the house.

They got a lot accomplished, but not finished, and all went to bed aching and sore. They were also so dirty they had to bathe, even minimally. Faith used a large kettle to heat some water, and each took their turn standing in a wooden tub in the kitchen to clean up as best they could.

Later, crawling into bed, he groaned. "Wow, talk about achy muscles."

"A couple weeks of this, and you'll be super buffed," Hazel said, brushing the damp hair from his forehead. "Arthur, I'm…I'm sorry about the whaling…thing. You're right, we have to fit in here. It just…oh, it rubs me the wrong way."

"I understand. It does me too, and I'll do all I can to avoid it in future. Hey, I wonder something. Why is our party in Tisbury? We're here, and they're in Edgar Towne. Why not in one of those places? You're the anthropologist, what's your professional assessment?"

She smiled. "It's in a faraway place, which means it's more expensive. It's symbolic of the family's social reach and the expense shows their wealth."

"Ah, I get it. Everything is status and position for these people, isn't it?"

"Do things ever change? Now, come on, sleep."

He agreed, and sleep came easily.

~ * ~

The next day, they worked more on the waterworks. They ran the pipe into the cellar, and there split it in two. One went into a wide trough. As Art explained to the other, the cellar was already cool, but the open expanse of cold water would keep it even colder, which would help keep eggs, butter, milk, and other produce fresher longer. They built a waterwheel that was turned by the flow of the water. For now, it did nothing, but he had some ideas about what to do with it in the future. Then there was the second pipe. It ran under their new toilet seat. When someone needed to go, they could now come down to the cellar, sit and use the facilities, and everything was flushed away with the water as it flowed out the other side. From there, the two pipes came together, went out the front of the house, and down the hill to the small pond. Faith was amazed.

"Uncle, this is…I have no words!"

"That's best, my girl. Remember, I said tell no one, and I meant it. This is based on an old Roman design, and until I'm sure it works, no one is to know, understood?"

"Yes, sir," she said with a nod, moving to check out the toilet. "Oh, I understand how it works. It's like how Hercules cleaned the Augean Stables in a single day."

"He cleaned the what?" Hazel said.

"Auntie, do you not know the labors of Hercules? The stables were labor number five."

"Well, I saw the movie—ah, a…*moving* play about him, but it only told one story."

"Oh, Auntie, you don't know what you've missed," Faith said with a smile.

She smiled back. "It sounds as if it's one of your favorites. Hey, how about you tell a story tonight? You can tell me all about his labors."

Now Faith truly glowed with delight. "Oh, yes!"

"Just think, Faith," Art said, "from now on, when you need water for cooking, no more hike up the hill. You can come down here and fill your pitcher from the trough."

"Yes, it's wonderful. Ah, Uncle, what of the metal you had me cover with pitch?"

"Those are for the second trough outside. Come, it's time we try it."

They hiked outside and placed the U-shaped metal pieces in the water. Hazel slowly nodded. It was clear she understood.

"So, the metal is painted black and heated by the sun, and in turn heats the water," she said. "Brilliant! But how do we get it in the house?"

Picking up the second clay spout, he moved to the side of the house, and set it in place. "Well, that's where things get a little…primitive. I couldn't figure out how to make a valve system. So, when we want hot water, we have to scoop it out of the trough, pour it in here, and it'll flow into the tub in the cellar."

"What tub?" Hazel and Faith said together.

He rubbed the back of his neck and grimaced. "Ah, the one we have to build."

Hazel groaned. "What, more work?"

"Oh, but, Auntie, consider that we have done so much already, and Uncle has made such wondrous things, a little more effort is not so much trouble."

Hazel chuckled. "I can see you're a 'glass half full' sort of person."

"Half…full? Sorry, Auntie, I do not understand."

"Sorry, modern phrase I learned in England. It means you're an optimist. You're right. All right, let's get to work."

It took the better part of the next day, but they finished the tub and filled the shelves in the cellar with their produce. Standing there, hot and sweaty, covered in dust and dirt, they all smiled.

"Hazel, would you like to baptize our little creation?"

"Arthur, it's your invention. The honor belongs to you."

He playfully wagged a finger at her. "Ah-ah, ladies first. Besides, when I come back from the hunt tomorrow, I think I'm going to need a long hot soak."

She smiled and agreed, and they set to trying it. First, Art stuck a large wooden plug in the drain pipe of the tub. It wasn't a tight seal, but it was good enough. Then, using buckets, they got some cold water from the cellar trough and filled the tub about half full. After that, Art and Faith went out to pour a couple buckets of hot water into the tub via the spout. Hazel stuck her hand in the water to test it, asked for a little more, and declared the temperature comfy. Art and Faith made a point of staying away so as to give her privacy. He turned to continue work on the chicken coop when he saw Faith standing next to the trough watching the hot one slowly re-fill.

"Uncle, it's working! I…ah, could I…?" she stammered.

He grinned. "Would you like to try it next?"

"Y-yes please," she said uncertainly.

"You go right ahead and do so."

The girl practically exploded with glee yet managed to not scream too loudly. She and Art worked on the coop until Hazel was done bathing. She went upstairs to dress then Faith and Art went down cellar to re-fill the tub. Art put the plug back in the bottom and they poured more water into it.

Faith stood by the tub and checked it out. "Ah, the plug is like the Beetle Bung stoppers we put in our barrels and kegs. Is that it, Uncle?"

He nodded. "Exactly. Although, because it's a clay pipe and a wooden plug, the seal isn't tight. It leaks, and so the water will eventually seep out of the tub. I'll go outside and pour some hot water down the spout. You let me know when the tub feels right for you."

"Yes, Uncle."

After he did so, she took a quick bath, giggling and squealing the whole time. Hazel came out to help him finish with the coop. They shooed the chickens in there and stood off to the side to take in all they'd accomplished.

"I have to say, my man, I know a bath isn't much, but…damn, it sure *feels* like a lot. It sounds like Faith is enjoying hers. Did she have enough hot water?"

"Oh yeah, the trough had plenty. I look forward to trying it next."

He did so, while the ladies fixed supper, and they relaxed for the evening playing cards and telling stories. They taught Faith Liverpool Rummy, which she thought meant the game came from there. They saw no reason to correct her. While they played, Faith told Hazel about Hercules, and the smile on her face as she became animated at the tale spoke volumes. The girl truly enjoyed herself.

As they prepared for bed, Art had another idea. He went down to the kitchen for some apple vinegar, it was in a jug the Nortons had given them, and brought it up to their room. Mixing about two tablespoons of it with some water in a jar, he set it next to the pitcher and bowl.

"What you got there, Mr. Mechanic?" Hazel said.

"I remembered something my dad taught me, a homemade mouthwash, a little apple vinegar in water, and you give it a shake before using. It's not much, but it's better than nothing."

"Hey, at this point, I'll try anything."

She did so, and so did he. While nothing like one of the store brands, it wasn't bad. It was surprising how a simple creature comfort made their lives so much easier. Yet, stretching out in the bed, he thought about tomorrow and the hunt and wondered.

The closest thing I've ever done to hunting is build my own lobster trap. What's it going to be like on a whaling ship?

That thought and others tormented his mind as he drifted off to sleep.

Six

Next morning, Faith made Arthur an especially big breakfast of eggs and ham, several large slabs of bread and butter, and plenty of hot tea. She said it would keep his belly warm out on the open water. It was something Joshua always told her before going on a hunt. After that, he and the ladies made their way down to the harbor. He to find the *Silvana*, and they to shop. He gave Hazel some money and the key to the strongbox.

"Try to stay on a budget, dear," he said with a wink. "Remember, we're in the colonies now, prices are different from what we're used to."

"I'll try," she said, winking back. "I'm sure Faith will be a help."

A final kiss and a hug, which made Faith and the men working the dock gasp, and she and Hazel walked away. He realized what the issue was with everyone, their PDA. For people, even a married couple to kiss in public was, in some communities, unheard of and even illegal. He hoped it didn't come back to bite them in the ass, so to speak.

He watched the ladies stroll off toward the center of town. He couldn't help himself. Even in all those layers of clothes, Hazel was totally hot. He turned his attention to the matter at hand, the whaling ship. Actually, calling it that was too much of a compliment. It was little more than an oversized boat. Art was confused. Every book he'd read, and movie and TV show always showed whaling done in large ships. This was only a three-masted schooner.

The answer came to him. *Of course, they don't need a big ship around here because they drag the whale back to shore to carry out the process of getting the oil out of the blubber.*

He moved to the end of the gangplank and studied the craft. It was old, the deck and masts were cracked and well-weathered, and the hull, while solid, showed its age. Its black coat of paint was faded, and the occasional board was warped and split. He could see the name arcing across the stern in brass letters—all were dented. A man stood at the top of the plank, and he was a human version of the old boat. A face deeply lined by years of experience and exposure to wind and sea. Clothes faded and hanging on his bony frame, yet lovingly maintained. Every hole was patched, each tear mended by someone who knew what they were doing.

"Mr. Bacon?" Art called out.

"Call me Israel, and you are?"

"Arthur Mayhew. I've come to take Joshua's place on the hunt today."

"Ah, well, come aboard, lad, and lend a hand," he said with a smile and a wave of his beanpole arm.

Trotting up the plank, Art shook the man's hand and winced. Israel was lean, but he made up for it in pure muscle. He also had quite the strong aroma. Art's eyes watered as the man reeked of dead fish. It was as if he bathed in them, which probably wasn't far from the truth. Art was grateful to be put to work untying the boat from the dock then helping raise the sails. It got them away from land and the stiff offshore breeze helped clear the air. Art quickly realized the whole boat stank, and for good reason. It must have been used as a fishing boat all of its life. The blood and guts of countless fish and whales had infiltrated every fiber of the vessel. Art was a good sailor, zipping around the island in a little sunfish was a favorite pastime of his, but he had trouble keeping his footing on the slick deck.

A snap of rope, the flutter of canvas, and the groan of old timbers told him the sails had caught the wind. He gazed up and the breeze wrapped about him, pushing his hair into his eyes. The sails were like Israel's clothes, old and worn, yet patched and cared for. The vessel eased its way out of the harbor, sliced through the blue-green waters of the Vineyard Sound, and headed east toward the open waters of the Atlantic.

Art stood off to the side, trying to stay out of the way of the crew, all of whom knew what they were doing. They zipped about smartly, pulled ropes, unfurled sails, and sharpened the various harpoons for the hunt. He had mixed feelings about everything. As a Mayhew, the sea was not his friend, yet, holding onto the rigging, gazing off to where sea and sky became one, ripples of delight coursed through his body as the ship slid through the churning waters of the sound. There was simply something about the open waters of the island that breathed new life into him. Perhaps that was why, at an early age, he'd overcome his fear of water to become an excellent swimmer and learned to sail. His parents had hated every minute of it. At all swim meets they stood, not sat, and watched him like proverbial hawks, ready to raise the alarm at the first sign of trouble. He used to chide them.

"Mom, Dad, it's an indoor pool. Would you chill and enjoy it?"

They never did.

When it came to sailing, they were ten times worse. He had to sail only in the sound, stay within sight of land, keep his life vest on, and never be without his GPS. Now, standing on the massive deck of the whaler, he thought of how tiny his boat was in comparison. This ship was almost as big as the *Shenandoah*, so there was little chance he could help sail her. It made him wonder how much of a sailor he could be. The clang of metal against metal made him jump. The crew finished with the harpoons and the sight of them made him sick to his stomach. He knew the invention of the Toggle Iron, the harpoon with a head that twisted once in the whale's blubber so as to hold on better, was decades away, and so these whalers used harpoons with broad pointy heads. They were disgusting. Then there were the lances, long and sharp, and with an oval-shaped flat point. They were used to make the final kill. Once the whale grew tired, the mate would thrust it into the whale's lungs over and over until it drowned. Art couldn't imagine ever doing that to such a magnificent creature.

He tried to put those thoughts out of his head and focus on the scene around him. It was a beautiful morning, clear blue sky, crisp salty air, and the sea open and clean. No oil slicks, no massive clumps of floating trash and plastic. He smiled. This was the sea as it was supposed to be, full of life, and brimming with potential. Thoughts of what was to come, not merely today, but in the years leading up to his era were enough to break his heart. If there was one good thing to come out of this odd journey of theirs, it would be to instill a love and appreciation of nature in these people. Yet, what chance did he have of doing that? Besides, come April, all of this would be gone. So, what was the point?

"Avast there, friend, you're a stranger to my ship," a gruff voice said.

Art turned and knew he was face to face with the captain. The man had the appearance and bearing of someone used to giving orders and being obeyed. The white of his hair was in contrast to the deep ebony of his eyes. The crow's feet told Art the man had spent many years squinting at the sun-sparkled sea, and his wrinkles spoke of how long he'd trod the earth. He was easily in his late fifties, maybe older. As Art's Grandpa Steve would say, the man had been 'Ridden hard and put away wet.'

"Greetings, Captain," Art said.

Israel, at the wheel, explained who he was.

"A Mayhew who has his sea legs, eh? You're off to a good start, my boy," he said, offering Art his grizzled hand. "Jonas Ahab, master of the good ship *Silvana*. Welcome aboard. I hope you bring us luck."

"I hope so t—ah, Ahab? Your name is Ahab?"

"If my parents are to be believed. What ails you, lad? I've seen canvas darker than you. If you're about to lose your breakfast, go down wind of us, and aim overboard. We scrubbed the decks yesterday."

"No, I'm fine, I just...ah, the name sounded...familiar." *If this old tub is this rank after it's been cleaned, I don't want to be around it when it's filthy. A whaling captain named Ahab. What is this, some sort of cosmic joke?*

"Thar she blows," someone in the crow's nest cried.

"What did I say about luck? It seems we have some today. Lend a hand, and we'll clear away the boats."

"Yes, s—I mean, aye-aye, sir!"

Jonas smiled. "Ah, a man who shows respect to his captain. You'll do well here."

He directed Art to the starboard boat, and he and a tall lanky young man lifted it from its cradle. Art was amazed the two of them were able to do that, but he remembered what he'd learned about whaling. The small boats used to hunt whales were sleek and light, tightly built and powerful, and able to stand up to the punishment the activity could dish out. Slipping the boat over the side, Abe, the young fellow, held onto one end of a lanyard, and the crew lined up to climb aboard.

"Can you row?" Jonas said.

"Ah…I was on the school sculling team," Art said without thinking.

He waved toward the boat. "Then climb aboard, lad. Timothy, you're in command. Israel, same bet as last time?"

Art turned his head as he got into the boat. Israel was on the port side getting into the other small boat.

"Aye, Jonas," he called back.

Climbing into their respective boats, the men pushed off with their oars. Art gazed around. He was in the middle row of three pairs of men. Abe was at the bow, Jonas at the stern, his hand on the tiller, and the men starting rowing. Art had always thought of himself as strong, but he was hard pressed to keep up with the others. The boat rolled and pitched up and down the waves as Jonas scanned the seas. Art's muscles strained, practically every one of them clenched and released as he bent forward, swung the oar back, and heaved with all his might to thrust it through the water. The boat shot forward, moved away from the ship, and the other boat came into view. Harder and harder they pulled on the oars, Art's lungs burned, his bones ached, yet they had only just begun.

I think I'm going to have a heart attack! How do these guys do this on a regular basis?

"Thar she blows," Abe shouted.

"Pull, lads, pull," Jonas cried. "A pot of gold is escaping. You want to eat tonight?"

"Aye," the others called back.

"Then pull with all you've got. Pull 'til your hearts burst from your chests like shot from a gun!"

The men responded by stepping up the pace. Art couldn't believe it. How these men had such strength and endurance, he would never understand.

He tried to keep up. His muscles strained as if they would tear free from his bones. The boat practically took flight. It seemed to skim across the sea and knife through the waves.

Jonas sang out, "A Yan-kee ship comes down the ri-ver. Blow, boys, blow! A Yan-kee ship with a Yan-kee skip-per, blow, my bul-ly boys, blow!"

The men sang back. "Who'd you think is the captain of her? Blow, boys, blow! Why, Jonas Ahab, and there is no other, blow my bul-ly boys, blow!"

It was long about then that Art got the point of the song—it gave the men the proper rhythm to pull their oars in sync. A roar filled the air. A mist settled across Art's neck and head. He squirmed and tingled at its coolness and cast his gaze around. The whale was alongside them and shot spray from its blowhole. Out of the corner of his eye, he saw movement at the bow. He turned in time to see Abe pick up a harpoon. Swinging back his arm, he threw. The harpoon arched through the air, a stout rope trailed behind it, and with a mighty *thunk* it imbedded itself in the creature's thick hide.

"A hit," Abe shouted.

"Ship oars and secure the line," Jonas replied.

The men slid the oars into their slots, turned toward the bow, and grabbed the rope. Abe looped it around a small post in front of him as the whale took off. The boat shot forward. Abe staggered back but managed to stay on his feet. Art wasn't so lucky, ending up with his head in the lap of the man behind him.

"Wet the line," Jonas shouted.

"Eyes front, son," the old salt looming over Art said with a grin. "I ain't about to carry you on this sleigh ride."

With the heave of one hand, the man got Art back up. He sniffed and saw smoke. The rope spun around the post so fast it was about to set it on fire. He grabbed the small bucket at his feet, dunked it overboard, and hurled it at the post. It hissed and cooled the smoke subsiding. The men held the line, played it out a little at a time, and they were off on what he knew was called a 'Nantucket Sleigh Ride.' The whale strained and heaved, raced through the surf, up one wave and down the other. Spray washed over the boat, drenching them. He blinked, the salt stinging his eyes. He licked his lips and lent a hand at holding the rope as the wind slapped him in the face. Abe weaved his way through the men to take the tiller as Jonas moved to the bow. Art ground his teeth until his jaw ached. His arms strained as if they would to tear from his body any moment, and he heaved and pulled together with the others as they slowly drew closer to the great beast.

He was amazed. How Jonas and Abe could stay on their feet as the boat rocked beneath them was incredible. Talk about having good sea legs. The whale rose next to them. Art gasped. Never in his life had he been so close to such a huge creature. Jonas struck. The long lance in his hands plunged into the whale's hide up to its hilt. He pulled back and struck again. The beast shuddered and groaned and rolled away from the boat. The rope snapped taut, pulling the bow and causing the boat to spin to the left. Jonas plunged overboard. Art and the men tumbled into each other and spun around as they searched for him.

"There, there, do you see him?" Abe said, pointing toward the whale. "It's Ahab, and he beckons for us to come to him."

Art turned. Jonas was atop the whale, his lance buried deep in its side, and he waved to the crew to come help him. Art jumped without a moment's thought. The beast was like a super thick mattress. It heaved and rolled under him and trembled. He fell to his knees. He could feel the creature struggle for breath. Clawing at its flesh, he tried to stand, his body alive with adrenaline. The whale shuddered and a geyser of red erupted from its blowhole. Art and the others were drenched in the hot fluid. He sucked in a lungful of air and gazed down at himself.

It was blood.

The crew cheered. The whale settled in the water and became still. Its life force dimmed. Art dropped to his knees on the poor animal. As it died, as its energy dissipated, he experienced the same agony. His heart slowed, he gulped air, and red tears trickled down his face. He couldn't believe what had happened. He'd helped kill a noble creature of the sea, and it tore a hole straight through him. He ran his hands over his chest.

Funny, I could have sworn a harpoon struck me as well.

"Lad, on your feet," Jonas called. "Come on, we've a whale to haul back to shore. You did fine today. I'll be pleased to have you on my ship anytime you want."

"I…ah, yes," Art choked out.

By the time all of them were back in the boat, the ship arrived, along with the other boat, and they worked together to lash the whale to the side of the ship. After that, they made for shore, Edgar Towne where the facility to reduce the whale to oil was located. A flock of seagulls trailed them the whole way there and more flew above the broad and heavily stained building. They marked the site like vultures hovering over a place of death, which was quite accurate. The stains on the walls and deck were blood. Art grimaced as they pulled into the dock. Whale bones were strewn across the shoreline and black smoke rose from the massive cauldrons on the dock area. The stench was positively toxic.

The ship docked, the crew disembarked, and celebrated their good luck and good fortune. Art had nothing left inside of him. He was numb as he shuffled along, while the shore crew moved in to slice up the whale's carcass. He couldn't bear to watch so he hiked away from the factory. He wasn't a block away when Joshua rode up in his wagon. Smiling down at Art, he hopped from the seat.

"Arthur, I saw the smoke and came at once. What part did you play in the hunt?"

"What...part? Ah, I...rowed in one of the boats."

"You didn't get left on the ship? Aye, this is fine. Did your boat make the kill?"

"The...kill? Yes, yes we did," he said, his voice cracking in sadness.

"The lad did fine, Joshua," Jonas said, his voice coming from behind him.

Art turned. He and Israel walked toward them.

"Arthur, this is excellent news," Joshua said, his smile going ear to ear. "It means a higher share of the profits."

"And here's a little extra," Jonas said, holding out his hand to him.

Art took a coin from him and checked it over. It was silver, a Pine Tree Shilling, which he recognized as a typical Colonial coin of the time.

"What's this for?"

"We won the bet I had with Israel here. We made the kill, so he owed me ten shillings. I always make a point of sharing my bounty with my boat crew."

"Oh, ah...thank you, Captain," he replied, pocketing the money. "I...I suppose I should go home and get cleaned up."

"What ails you, lad?" Jonas said. "You did fine for your first time."

"I was troubled by...killing."

"Arthur, have you never hunted anything?" Joshua said. "These whales are God's bounty, put here for us to enjoy. Why should we not reap what He has sown?"

He cracked his knuckles. *What can I say that they could ever understand? Ah, maybe this'll work.* "True, but remember He entrusted us with the world. It would be an affront to Him and His benevolence if we were not good stewards of nature. Look at the mistake of the Native—ah, the savages in clearing all the trees from the western shores. What, are we no better than them?"

A cone of silence descended around them. Art gazed from one to the other of the men and smiled. They all seemed to be considering his words.

Jonas slowly nodded. "Aye, lad, I understand your concern. Joshua, you remember the days when we had no need to hunt the great beasts?"

"I do. The occasional dead one would wash ashore, and the oil it provided was more than enough to meet our needs."

"And then the hunts started," Jonas said. "Now we find it harder and harder to land a decent whale. Perhaps, once the rebellion is over, we should discuss with the other captains some measures to ensure the whales don't die out."

Art smiled, and an ounce of redemption swelled within him. It wasn't much, but maybe, just maybe, he'd planted a seed of conservation in the hearts and minds of the whalers. The big question? Would they remember it in the coming years? Would any of them survive the massacre? He tried to put such concerns aside as the captain insisted on taking Art to a pub.

"It's your first hunt and your first kill, lad. Such events in a young man's life must be celebrated. Come, we'll get you some ale as strong as your stench!"

The men laughed and marched off to St. Elmo's Fire, a nearby public house, a place of strong drink, strong men, and loose women. Art almost laughed at the concept of such ladies on the island. Given the small population, it was kind of like the old joke about a city being so small, the town hooker was a virgin. The four of them sat at the creaky and leaky old wooden bar on high stools, all of which were in desperate need of new upholstery, and Jonas bought them a round of ale. The old pewter tankards were beaten and dented, and Art had serious doubts as to their cleanliness. However, he wasn't going to insult his host by not drinking.

Oh well, maybe the alcohol will kill any germs.

"That's it, lad, sluice your gob," Jonas said, hoisting his drink aloft.

Art had to think about his words for a moment, as he wasn't familiar with the slang, but he was pretty sure Jonas was telling him to take a hearty drink. They all did so, and Art was hard pressed not to gag. His favorite beer was Guinness, which was strong, but it had nothing on this stuff. It was also clear the others were used to the vile concoction. They emptied their cups in no time, and Joshua ordered a second round. At the rate they were going, Art would be falling down drunk in no time. He wanted to beg off but didn't know what to do. He took another sip. A little excess dribbled down his chin and onto his chest, and he patted his shirt.

"Oh, I am a mess. Joshua, could I go by your home and change?"

"No need, lad," Jonas said. "This is a whalers' pub, which means they know how to take care of us."

He was confused. He had no idea what that meant, but he learned. There was a changing room in the back with full bathing facilities. Well, *contemporary* bathing facilities: a tub to stand in and a bucket to dump over his head. It was cold, but at least it was cleansing, and they even gave him fresh clothes. Although, 'gave' was a relative term. Sold would be a better word, but they only cost five shillings, which he had to spare. The garments were also not new, but it made sense that they would have the cast off clothes of numerous seamen. He returned to the others in time to hear them discuss money.

"Joshua, rest assured, the oil will be capped and sold within the week," Jonas said.

He nodded. "Very well. Arthur, if you are agreeable, Jonas will pay me our share, and I will give you your portion."

"That's fine, Joshua, I have no objections. There's no rush about the money. Now, if you will all excuse me? A day on the high seas and hard work has left me famished. I would like to get home and eat."

"No troubles there, lad," Jonas said. "Barkeep, fetch food, you've some hungry seamen here! Oh, and some Adam's Ale for the lad. I think he's getting a bit unsteady from that last round."

In no time they had more food than Art thought he could ever choke down and a pitcher of water, the Adam's Ale. There was a thick stew, bread, potatoes, and a couple dishes he didn't recognize. An hour and four tankards of ale later, since the men couldn't stand drinking much water, he had barely made a dent in his platter. How these men could inhale theirs and not blow up like balloons, he didn't know. Finally, he figured out how to slip away.

"Gentlemen, I must be going. I have a young wife at home, and she requires my…attentions."

The men chuckled.

"Lucky man," Jonas said, gazing about the pub. "An old dog such as myself must make do with any harbor he can drop his anchor in. The waters here are…mostly barnacles and reefs, not safe for the likes of me."

Israel chuckled. "Captain, how many whales have you brought in? How many gales have you faced and even chased the likes of St. Elmo's Fire off our decks? Are you saying you can't also tame a mere woman?"

"My mate," Jonas said, patting his shoulder, "one day you will learn there is no creature of the Seven Seas, not the kraken, selkie or siren, or even a force of nature to equal the dangers of the fair sex."

They all laughed at that, then Joshua and Art departed.

"Joshua, are you all right to drive? Perhaps you need some Adam's Ale."

Joshua's brow wrinkled. "Nonsense, why wouldn't I be?"

"Well, it's just that you had quite a few pints in there and—oh, what am I thinking, it's only a wagon."

"Cousin, sometimes you do and say the strangest of things. Come along, and we'll get you home."

They headed back to Cottage City. Art did the neighborly thing and invited Joshua to stay for supper, but he declined. As he told Art, if he wasn't there to corral the children, Patience would make his life miserable for at least a week. So, he took off for home, and Art went inside. Faith was busy in the kitchen, and Hazel was working in the cellar. He went down to see her.

She cast her eyes up and down his body and said, "What's wrong?"

"What makes you say that?"

"*Is* something wrong?"

"Well…yes, but that's not the point. How did you know?"

She smiled. "Arthur, you're one of those people who wears his feelings like a new suit. What is it?"

"The hunt, I…I went on it."

"Yeah, okay, I knew that. What about it? Oh, did you see them kill a whale?"

"Ah, not…exactly, I…I helped, and I…enjoyed it, for a moment, for one brief moment. Now I…I don't know how to feel about it. I mean, not the killing, I feel terrible about that."

"Oh, how to feel concerning the moment," she said, slowly nodding. Strolling around the pantry area, she turned to him. "Well, from a…clinical standpoint, it's understandable. You got caught up in the mob mentality. It's how riots and lynchings take place. There's more to it as well. The hunt, the act of…of killing appeals to a basal instinct within all men."

"What, you mean the old hunter-gatherer of the Neanderthal?" he said. "I'm surprised, Hazel, with you being so understanding, given how opposed you were to me merely *going* on the hunt."

She lowered her gaze to the floor for a moment. "Arthur, I know you had no choice, and I know you couldn't resist your feelings. What's important to me is you realize it and feel remorse."

"I do, and I even tried to change attitudes. In a way, I may have planted the seed of conservation among the whalers."

"Oh really? Do tell," she replied.

Art related the events of the day. Hazel sat in rapt attention and was clearly caught up in the excitement of the hunt, even with the knowledge it ended in the death of a whale, as she was literally on the edge of her seat.

"Wow, Arthur, I have to say, I can understand your feelings, and I think I'm starting to understand the attitudes of the whalers. I didn't think that was possible, but I do see things from their point of view. Although, truth be told, I sure hope you don't have to go out on another hunt."

He nodded. "So do I, but…well, let's not dwell on the future. Tell me, how was your day?"

"Oh, now that is quite a tale. Come on, let's go upstairs and sit in proper chairs, and I'll tell you my adventure."

Seven

As the *Silvana* pulled away from the dock, Hazel's thoughts turned to her shopping needs, a stupid gown for the party, some household supplies and food, and some sort of substitute for deodorant. Granted, the latter was a silly concern, but like the bath and toilet, it would make their lives here a bit easier. So, they set off for the center of Cottage City and the shops located there.

She stopped short as she heard a bell ring. "What is that?"

"The school bell," Faith explained.

"School? Huh, we should go check that out. After all, we want you to get a good education."

"What about shopping?"

Hazel waved her off. "That can wait. I want to know what's available for your schooling. Do you know where the school is?"

She shook her head. "No, Auntie, I went to school in Edgar Towne, but if we follow the sound, and the trail of children, we'll find it."

She smiled, took Faith's hand, and off they went. The air positively crackled it was so sharp and clear. Yes, puffs of smoke rose from various buildings, but they were nothing compared to the pollution spewed by all manner of factories and vehicles back in the present. At every inhale, Hazel was invigorated and alive, and it gave speed to her steps.

The bell stopped after a couple minutes, but children strolled, while some dashed along, the wide dirt roads leading away from the harbor giving a clear sign as to which direction was the right one. A mild breeze shook the branches above them. Hazel's hair wafted about, and soon she saw the school.

It was *not* the classic little red schoolhouse. No, it was a fine-looking building, one-story, nearly-new shingles on the roof and sides, a narrow porch with a narrow roof, and two wide stone steps that led into it. The children streamed in while the teacher, yet another non-stereotype, stood next to the door and welcomed each of them with a smile and the occasional pat to the head. She was tall, solidly built, and it was clear she could handle any fuss or trouble any five or even ten children could cause. Her long walnut-shaded hair wasn't in the classic schoolmarm tight bun but flowed across her broad shoulders. She eyed Hazel up and down as they approached but gave only a glance at Faith. Hazel decided to play nice.

"Good morning, ma'am, I am *Lady* Hazel Puttenham Mayhew. How do you do?" she said, trying to make herself sound important.

She thought that might help, yet, checking out the teacher's face, it didn't seem to have impressed her.

"Hurry along, children," she said, then nodded at Hazel. "Good morning. Miss Rebecca McCarthy. To what do I owe the pleasure of your company this day?"

She gestured at Faith. "This is my niece. My husband and I would like her to attend your school."

Her gaze narrowed as she studied the girl. "How old are you, child?"

"Sixteen," she squeaked.

"Is she not too old? She might become too educated to get a husband."

Hazel's back stiffened to the point she thought it might break. *Must not kill, do not react, do not tell this woman what I think of her. Calm, remain calm, remember the era you're living in.* "It isn't something we're worried about. A truly strong and worthy man will not be intimidated by an intelligent woman. Now, can she attend?"

Rebecca's nostrils flared, and she gestured for them to enter. "Come in, and we'll see what can be done for the child."

They did, and Hazel smiled. The place reminded her of the library she visited as a little girl when she stayed with her grandparents. The way she put it, the place smelled like knowledge. It was only years later she learned that had been the smell of moldy books. Here at last was a stereotype. The rows of desks faced a large blackboard, bookcases full of books and supplies on either side of the room, and even a dunce cap and stool in the corner, right below a rack of canes. The children took their seats, younger ones up front, older ones to the back, and they got out what could only be called their school supplies. Granted, they were nothing like Hazel had used or ever seen, but she figured they were what were appropriate for this time: small individual blackboard slates, various books, paper, and quill pens. There were inkpots on the tables before them.

"Children, begin your arithmetic lesson. Solve the problems on the board. Mrs. Mayhew, Faith, come this way."

She led them into a snug office where her desk and chair and another child-sized chair sat. Rebecca took her seat and gestured at the smaller one. Hazel gawked at it, unsure if she could balance atop so tiny a thing. Granted, she was proud of her firm butt, but even its petite size had to give way to the laws of physics. Still, she wasn't about to let Miss McCarthy intimidate her.

She sat and saw pictures on the walls around them, all strong women of the past: Joan of Arc, the Virgin Mary, Queen Elizabeth, and someone who appeared to be an ancient Egyptian.

"Comfortable little place you have here," Hazel said. "I'm curious, who is that?"

Rebecca's gaze followed her to the third picture. She smiled and nodded. "Ah, I would not expect you to know that lady, she *is* rather obscure. That is Hypatia, author, scientist, and one of the last librarians of the Great Library of Alexandria."

"Alexandria, that's in Egypt, isn't it? Wait, I remember learning about that. It was the greatest library of antiquity, correct?"

"Quite true, you know your history. The foremost repository of knowledge of the ancient world, but it was destroyed by the folly of war and violence. Let that be a lesson to you, Faith, violence is never the answer."

The girl nodded. "Yes, ma'am."

Hazel was unsure what to make of Rebecca. She respected knowledge and learning and admired strong women, yet she resisted educating Faith. There was also her latest comment. Did it mean she was against the revolution? Hazel decided not to press the issue and instead focused on what was important, and that was Faith.

"So, is that an indication you will accept her as a student?" Hazel said.

Rebecca bit the nail of her little finger, chewing on it. "Mrs. Mayhew, it's not that I don't want to teach her, it's merely I'm unsure there's anything I *can* teach her. At her age, she has probably learned all the island schools have to teach. If it weren't for this silly rebellion, you could send her to the mainland."

"I see. Well, I would appreciate you evaluating her and seeing if there's anything she can learn. I could help. Back home, I always made a point of assisting in the community in any way possible."

Rebecca perked up at those words.

Huh, I guess there's nothing like the PTA now, so a parent volunteer is probably unheard of. Hazel cast her gaze toward the children and squirmed in her seat. *Damn, a room full of children. What am I getting myself in for?*

"Help is always appreciated," Rebecca said, offering a smile. "Very well. Faith, I will give you the same oral exam I was given upon graduation. Mrs. Mayhew, if you would help the children with their arithmetic and do their geometry lesson, I would be much obliged to you."

"Geometry?" Hazel said, her eyebrows shooting up, as did the pitch of her voice. "What sort of lesson do you want me to give them? I don't know what level they're at."

"The outline is on my desk before the blackboard. You have merely to follow it."

She got to her feet. "Ah, I see. I'll do my best."

"I would expect nothing less. Faith, be seated," she replied, gesturing at the now-vacant seat.

Appearing to be a bit worried, she did.

Hazel stepped to the doorway and paused. "Oh, and please, call me Hazel. Um, I left all the... ah, formalities of my title when I left England."

"Thank you. Hazel is so much nicer, and you must call me Rebecca."

She nodded and left the room. As she moved to the teacher's desk in the classroom, she was struck by how well-behaved the children had been while the teacher was away. Granted, she'd only been in her office, but it was impressive. Of course, there was the matter of discipline. Hazel didn't know much about Colonial schooling, but she'd seen several movie versions of *Tom Sawyer*. She knew teachers back in the old days were allowed to be quite strict. Forget a spanking or the paddle, they could cane the children for even minor offenses. She introduced herself to the children.

They responded with a collective, "Good morning, Mrs. Mayhew."

She practically jumped in surprise. The arithmetic was easy, although she was impressed with the sums the children were able to handle without a calculator. The geometry was another matter. She hadn't done that stuff since high school, and she barely remembered any of it. Having the lesson plan was her salvation, and it became clear why it was taught. Most of the kids would be farmers, so figuring out acres of land, bushels of crops, gallons of water, and so on were important to them. Still, she was glad when the lessons ended. Having all those little eyes on her was a bit unnerving. She was like a gazelle surrounded by a pride of lions. Her first instinct was to run, but she remembered why she was there. It was to get Faith educated. No matter what, Hazel was going to help her. By then, Faith and Rebecca were back, and it was break time.

Faith smiled as she drew up next to her. "It went quite well, and Miss McCarthy said she can teach me all she knows, world history, art, French and Latin, and many other subjects."

Hazel heaved a happy sigh. She loved seeing the twinkle in Faith's eyes. She was excited about learning, and that right there was enough for Hazel. It made the whole crazy journey of theirs worthwhile.

"That's wonderful. I hope you do well. Rebecca, is there anything I can do for the children during their break?"

"Well, I normally tell them a story. Would you like to do that?"

Faith let out a little squeak of glee and quickly recovered her modesty. "Auntie, why don't you tell them the story of the selfish giant?"

"Oh, but you've already heard that one."

"I don't mind. Please," she begged.

Hazel chuckled and nodded. "All right."

She did. The children sat in rapt attention. It was so popular they asked for another.

"Another?" Hazel said, casting her gaze over at Rebecca. "Ah, I don't know if we have time."

"It's quite all right. When a story can teach a life lesson, it is more than a mere story. Please, Hazel, tell them another."

"All right, let me think."

Hazel wasn't sure what to do. She was no storyteller, and she didn't know many fairy tales, even the standards like *Hansel and Gretel*. All she remembered of that one was the latest movie version, and it wasn't appropriate for children so young. She leaned against one of the benches and thought a bit and got desperate. Casting her gaze again about the room, she saw all the little faces fixed on her, and they leaned in as they waited for her to start.

Come on, girl, think of something. The 'natives' are getting restless here. Ah, wait, I've got it! "I know, I can tell you the story of Lysistrata. It's a tale from the ancient Greeks. I saw the play back in college."

"Oh, is it like Hercules?" a boy said.

"It most definitely is not," Rebecca snapped. "I'm sorry, Hazel, but I forbid you telling the children that story. It is…inappropriate."

"I see. I have another, a tale of knights and ladies fair. Well, one fair lady. This is a story of a knight who lost his way, Sir Rick, and how the Lady Ilsa helped him see the error of his ways."

She launched into the tale, the children enthralled by all of it. Hazel couldn't help smiling. If her film buff friends could see her now, they would bust a gut laughing. The one odd thing was the sensation that she was being watched. Now, of course she was being watched, the children were all focused on her, but that wasn't the sensation she had. It was as if two eyes were lasers burning holes through her. As she drew near the end of the story, Ilsa and King Victor flying off on a dragon, she became animated in her gestures and movements as an excuse to spin around, and thus she got to scan the room. She wasn't sure, but she thought she caught a glimpse of a little face at the window next to the blackboard. That didn't make sense. If it was a child, why wasn't he or she in school? She almost mentioned it to Rebecca, but she realized it was best she didn't. Unlike Arthur, she didn't know much about this society. Who knew why a child might not be in school yet spying on it? More importantly, if she said anything, what might happen to that child and/or their parents? Better to let it go. After all, she wasn't sure of anything.

After the break, Rebecca did lessons in public speaking, as a nod to Hazel, then grammar, logic, music, and finished with astronomy. She gave Faith books to read and some lessons to work on, and the children were dismissed. Filing out of the building, they paused to thank Hazel for her stories, and she and Faith headed for the center of town, such as it was. Strolling along a dirt road that wound its way through the small homes that dotted the area, Hazel found a strange feeling course through her. She was happy! Considering their situation, considering her discomfort at being around children, such a feeling wasn't unusual; it was downright amazing.

Damn, why am I feeling so good? I've never in my life been around so many tiny humans, never wanted to be around them, and now I'm a...what, female Pied Piper? I don't know. I think all this fresh air and clean living has pickled my brain. Ah, here we go, the town and its shops. This'll get my mind off those rugrats.

They'd reached the business area, a collection of modest shops. Here they found more people, horses, carriages, wagons, and the hubbub of activity. People passed each other along the dusty trail, Hazel coughed as the dust irritated her throat, and the stench of manure assailed her nose and choked her lungs.

Wow, and to think I used to complain about the smell of diesel in the city. How do these people stand it?

"Auntie, here is a dress shop," Faith said.

She turned to check where Faith was pointing. It was a cute place, white with yellow trim, and lots of fancy clothes on their version of mannequins. Hazel's heart sank to her ankles. Fancy was an inadequate word to describe these gowns. No, these were museum-worthy pieces. They were large billowy dresses with more layers than she could count and cinched down little waistlines that didn't seem big enough for her to get a leg through.

"Um, is this the only shop in town?"

Faith nodded. "The only one in Cottage City that sells such garments. Edgar Towne has two, but I don't know about Tisbury."

"I guess we'll have to try this place. Come on, let's go in."

They entered and met the shop owner, Mr. Daniel Archer, a man so flaming, Hazel was amazed even Faith couldn't tell he was gay. However, considering how closeted people had to be back in the present, this era was probably ten times worse. He showed her several gowns, all of which she hated, but knew she had to pick one. She did like one thing, the smell of his shop. It reminded her of her grandmother's sewing room with the aromas of different fabrics and threads. She'd never thought about threads having a smell, but they did, and they summoned up many pleasant memories of her childhood.

Her big problem was that trying a dress on was more complicated than an upgrade to her computer. It wasn't only a matter of lacing up the back, there were the layers of undergarments, buttons and lace everywhere, and the rigid lining. She could understand why a woman would have a maid or at least a couple daughters around. Putting on something like this was for sure a group effort.

Damn, now I know how it was for those knights of old in their suits of armor. Sheesh, I think this stuff could stop a bullet. What is it, Colonial Kevlar?

Mr. Archer gasped when she asked about a long red gown that appeared as if it would be a lot more comfortable.

"Madam, *red* at a coming out gala? Some things simply are not done!"

Faith softly cleared her throat. "Um, Auntie, he's right. That color is…inappropriate. Let's find something else."

Hazel chewed her lip for a moment. *Huh, what's so bad about red? Wait, red is the color of passion. That's it. Damn, could these people be anymore sexually repressed?* "Ah, that's fine. What else do you have?"

He showed her, all the while chatting happily away. Hazel moved behind a changing screen to try on a long flowing green dress. Faith helped her, of course.

Daniel moved close, all smiles. "So, you are newly arrived from England, eh? That explains your accent. Come, come, you simply must give me some gossip. What is happening in court? What are the latest fashions? Ah, I know, it's something French this season, isn't it? The 'frogs' always dominate the world of high fashion, don't they?"

Hazel wished Arthur was there. With his knowledge of history, he might be able to bluff his way through a discussion of the goings-on at court and what people were wearing. She had no idea.

"Yes, yes they do. I'm afraid I can't tell you much. My…parents kept me at home mostly, I never got into…um, London to attend court."

"Ah, such a pity," he said, heaving a sad sigh. "This war is terrible for a man's social life. Now come, let me see you in tha—oh! No, no, no, my dear, this will not do."

Hazel had stepped out from behind the screen. Daniel took one look at her and reacted as if she'd handed him a dead fish.

She gazed down at herself. "What's wrong with it?"

"Oh, my dear, everything," he said, practically gagging. "It is *so* unflattering to your figure, the color doesn't go with your lovely eyes, and the bodice…well, it's revealing, but *not* in a complimentary fashion."

She grinned. "The apple dumpling shop is not…open for business properly?"

He chuckled. "Aptly, if crudely put, my dear. Yes, the bosom must be *presented*, but not exposed. Displayed, but tastefully, so as to entice the men to approach you without being so overly exhibited as to be an insult to common decency. You do that, and the men will take you for a common tart and run from you, at least in public."

"Ah, well, but I *am* married. It's not like I'm out to get a man," she pointed out.

He cast his eyes around the room. "Oh, tut-tut, a true lady knows the value of teasing the men folk. Ah, there we are, blue is more your color."

He brought the dress he'd pointed at over to her. It turned out the fanciest gowns were lined with some sort of whale bones or material. She wasn't sure, she didn't get a clear answer, and she didn't want to ask too many questions that would give away the fact she didn't know what in the world she was talking about. She settled on the nice blue one he recommended. Daniel took some measurements and promised to have it ready in time for the party. After that, they made a few stops for groceries and, most importantly, bottles of perfume. Hazel had never been one to bother with that sickly sweet smelly stuff, but when that was all there was to deal with body odor, she'd use it.

Coming out of the emporium, Faith appeared a bit troubled, or at the very least confused.

"Sweetie, is something on your mind?"

She squirmed and stared at the ground for a moment before lifting her gaze to meet Hazel's. "I... Auntie, I'm confused about Mr. Archer. I've heard father and his friends speak of some men being 'backgammon players', and Mr. Archer seemed to be one of them. Does he seem a bit odd to you?"

Hazel smiled and chuckled. "Yes, yes he did, quite odd, but remember, odd is not necessarily bad. Odd usually means different, and different is good. Rebecca is going to teach you about many things, many peoples and lands, and they're not going to be the same. The important point for you is that word, *people*, they're all people. Respect them, respect their beliefs and cultures, and ask the same of them. If you can learn that, you can be a friend to anyone."

"Yes, Auntie, I'll try," she said, the smile returned to her face.

They headed home to eat, and Hazel got an idea. They went down cellar and hung the curtains Patience gave them to create enclosures around the pantry, toilet, and bathtub. Faith was confused about the curtains around the pantry.

"They'll help to keep in the cool air," Hazel explained.

She slowly nodded. "I understand, it'll keep the food fresher longer."

"Exactly. Now, why don't you get to your chores? I'm going to try my hand at baking bread."

"It would be easier and faster if you used both hands."

Hazel's brow wrinkled. "What? Oh, yes, I'll use both. That was merely a saying."

Faith headed outside to feed the chickens and tend their vegetable and herb gardens, while Hazel tried hard to make bread. It didn't go as she'd hoped, which mystified her. It wasn't as if the recipe was the secret formula to Coke. She ended up with yards and yards of goo up to her elbows. Heaving a sigh of frustration, she moved to the window to get a breath of fresh air and saw Phineas and Solomon work the fields. She smiled. It was good to have the Norton boys around to help them. She frowned.

Phineas was drawing quite close to Faith. Back in her time, she knew what that typically meant, but she wasn't sure about now. Rather than rush out and cause a scene, she stood at the window and watched. The two stood together talking in low voices. Faith looked around once in a while, and Phineas moved ever closer.

"Come in the barn with me," he said, raising his voice.

Faith gasped. "Aunt Hazel will be upset if I ignore my chores."

She angled toward the house, moving closer with every step, and he stayed right with her. Hazel's frown grew deeper, and she practically growled.

"We've heard about her. A pale sickly thing," he sneered. "She'll be no bother. Now, I'm ordering you to come with me."

The air shot from Hazel's nose so hard and so fast it hurt. *No bother! No bother, eh? I'll show him!*

Wiping the dough from her hands, she marched out the back door, threw it open so hard she heard it crack as it slammed against the wall. All three of the young people jumped in surprise, but it was Faith who seemed terrified. Solomon sort of shrank away, but Phineas stood his ground and tried to appear the picture of innocence.

"So, Faith, *boys*, how are we getting along?" she asked.

Faith trembled. "Ah…"

"We're fine, Mrs. Mayhew," Phineas said with a smile. "You can go back inside."

"Oh, I can, can I? Well, *you* can go back to work in the fields. That is what we pay you for, isn't it?"

He stood up straight and took a step toward her. "Your *husband* pays us, ma'am, and we will do the work we're paid to do. Right now, it is the hottest part of the day, and we are pacing ourselves so as to not become too fatigued. If you worked as hard as we do, you'd understand that."

"Work hard?" she snapped. "Young ma…*little boy*, if you understood all that women do, all the things your dear *mother* does every day, you'd know what real work is."

"Pshaw, go back to your baking. I'm a man, I take no orders from a mere woman."

"Oh, I see, you give orders, is that it? Like ordering Faith about, eh?"

He swallowed hard and lost a bit of his confidence at that remark. "What of it? She's a fair-looking girl. I merely want to educate her in the ways of the world."

The vein in Hazel's temple pulsated and almost exploded with a pounding as her blood pressure soared into the stratosphere. "Is that what men tell girls in this era, I mean, this part of the colonies? I don't think so. Phineas, you will leave my property at once!"

He stood his ground and met her gaze with one equally strong. "Or what?"

Hazel lost it. That was the proverbial straw that broke her back. In a flash, she seized Phineas by the ear and dragged him toward the barn.

"You want to go to the barn? Fine, you and I shall go there, little boy, and I'll show you what I have in mind for you," she snapped.

"Ow," he squealed, his hands flew to hers. "Let go of me! What do you think you're doing?"

Stumbling through the doors, she plopped down on a small barrel sitting right inside and pulled him across her lap. "I'm going to introduce you to an ancient form of discipline you clearly have not gotten enough of in the past."

Hazel's blood and anger were up, and she wasn't thinking clearly. However, she was not about to let some snot-nosed boy push her or Faith around. Internally, she chided herself for what she was doing. Her whole adult life, she'd been opposed to corporal punishment; she thought it demeaned children. Yet, she now saw its value in certain circumstances, and this was most definitely one of them.

She held the boy tight across her lap, raised her hand high, and closed her eyes as she brought her hand down. Yeah, she might see it was appropriate here and now, but that didn't mean she liked it. She smacked him hard and fast, hoping he'd apologize quickly and she could end this sad sorry episode. However, it was clear he was as lean and muscular as she was. Spanking him literally made her hand hurt.

Damn, what's this kid got a cast-iron butt? Is this what's meant by that old saying of this hurting me as much as it does you?

Phineas yelped and complained, but didn't yield, and so she kept at it.

"You can't do this to me. You're not my mother," he screeched.

"No, I'm not, but I can stand in for her. Now, you going to behave, apologize, and be a good and proper gentleman around Faith?"

He growled and spit but remained silent. A small squeak of a gasp caught Hazel's attention and she turned toward the door. Solomon and Faith were outside and sort of sneaking a peek in the door. They both appeared shocked. Faith stood there, her jaw hung open, and her eyes seemed to get bigger and bigger with each moment. It took the better part of five minutes, but Phineas changed his tune.

"All right, all right, I'm sorry, ma'am, I'm sorry," he whined.

Hazel stopped, lifted him to his feet, and stood. She needed to assume a more dominant posture in order to make her point. From what she remembered about social structure, she had to be seen as the alpha of the group, and that required a degree of physical superiority.

"Good, that's what I wanted to hear," she said in a firm tone and pointed out the door. "Now, you march yourself outside, apologize to Faith, and take your brother home. I will discuss your deplorable behavior with my husband, and he'll decide if he wants to employ you further."

Those final words made her stomach turn. She sounded so house-wife-y and submissive to Arthur, and that burned her bacon, yet, she knew such things were the norm now. Phineas winced and rubbed the dusty seat of his trousers. He meekly nodded and hastily darted out the door. Hazel hurried to catch up with him. She wanted to see the apology.

"Faith, I'm sorry for how I acted toward you," he said quickly. "It'll never happen again."

He zipped away, got as far from Hazel as he could, and glared at her.

Faith painted a weak smile on. "It's all right, Phineas, I forgive you."

"Yes, but my father will not forgive you," he snapped at Hazel. "I'm going to tell him what you did."

She snorted. "Really? Fine, bring it."

"Bring what?" he replied, confused.

"I mean…bring him, ah, bring him here, and I'll face him gladly."

"You will not be speaking so once he's done with you," Phineas said with a smirk. "Solomon, come on, we're going home."

They took off. Hazel turned to Faith. The expression on her face spoke volumes. She seemed beyond terrified. The girl stood and shook from head to toe.

"Faith, calm down, child. What, do you think you're next? I'm not at all angry with you."

"Y-y-you're not? Why? Did I not cause all this trouble by defying him?"

Damn, I've got to do something to build this girl up, give her a backbone so she'll stand up for herself when I'm not around, but what? I'd love to tell her about Susan B. Anthony, Harriet Tubman, and all the other 'sisters' in history she should be proud of and want to emulate, but none of them exist yet. Huh, what would be an age appropriate and era appropriate story? Ah, got it. "Faith, being obedient to your father and Arthur, and other…men is one thing, but never forget how strong women are."

"We are?" she squeaked in surprise.

Hazel nodded. "Of course. When they took Jesus down off the cross, who was there for Him?"

"Ah, His mother."

"Correct. Where were the disciples?"

"They…ran off."

"Correct again. In fact, what did Peter do?"

"He…he denied our savior," Faith said, her voice gaining in confidence.

"Yes, he did, and not once, correct?"

"Aye, before the cock crowed twice, he denied Him thrice."

Hazel nodded. "You remember that the next time a boy tries to…force his attentions on you."

She beamed with pure delight. "Yes, ma'am!"

Great, I may have kicked off the women's movement a little early. Climb down off your soapbox, girl, rein it in. "All right, today's…lesson in religion is over. Let's get back to work."

Faith went off to feed the chickens. Hazel headed for the house, and she froze as she reached the back door. She had that feeling again, eyes were on her. Spinning around, she scanned the area. There didn't seem to be anyone there. She half expected Phineas to try to sneak up on her, but he wasn't there. No one was, but she sure had the sensation, as if someone was hidden nearby. She tried to ignore the feeling and instead focused on the bread. For some reason, this had become quite the *thing* for her. It was a challenge she was determined to master.

Sometime later, she wasn't sure how long it had been, she slid a decent-looking loaf into the oven. Sitting back, she smiled and wiped the blend of flour and batter from her face and heard Faith sort of squeak outside. Hazel moved to the window to see what troubled her and let out a squeak of her own.

Holy crap, here comes Ed Norton and the boys, and he's got a strap. Huh, what are the rules regarding hitting a woman in this era? Well, seems like I'm going to find out. Hazel breathed in through her nose, a deep cleansing breath, and blew out her mouth. Cracking her knuckles, she flexed her fists. *Might as well get out there and get it over with, but if he thinks I'm going to meekly accept whatever he dishes out, he's got another 'think' coming. If I'm going down, I'm going down swinging. This is where 21st century woman meets 18th century man!*

Eight

Hazel made up her mind she wouldn't go out the back door. No, this was her house, she was the lady of the house, and so she would march out the front to face Edward. Tossing aside her apron, so as to not appear too submissive, she pushed back her hair, stood up straight, and headed for the door. Her heavy footsteps echoed against the hardwood floor, as she threw open the front door and took up a proud stance on the porch. Out of the corner of her eye, she saw Faith hiding at the corner of the house. It was clear she was unsure what was about to happen.

Hazel chewed her lip. Actually, maybe Faith knew what was going on. Given the societal norms of the era, it was possible a grown woman getting beaten was not that unusual an event. Well, Faith was about to see something completely different.

Hazel gazed down at Edward as he reached the bottom of the steps, leaned on his cane and brandished his belt with his free hand. "Good afternoon, Mr. Norton, what brings you to my home today?"

"Hazel, I would have words with you," he snapped.

She ground her teeth. He used her first name deliberately. Taking a deep breath, she forced herself to put it aside. "Certainly, Edward, what would you like to talk about?"

"My son and your actions toward him. Is it true you beat him?"

"No, it is not. I disciplined him for his *disrespectful* actions toward Faith and me."

Edward calmed a bit at her words. He lowered his arm carrying the strap, and his muscles relaxed. "Tell me what he did," he said simply.

She did, giving details on his words to Faith and to her, and what she did to him. Edward stood there, stone-faced, and never said a word throughout the whole story. Only when she was done did he signal to the boys to draw near.

"Phineas, what do you have to say about this?"

"It's a lie, father, a foul, foul lie!"

"I see. Solomon, come here," Edward said, turning to the boy.

"Yes, father," he squeaked.

"What do you say?"

"Phineas is right. She's a mean lady, who beat him for no reason."

Silence followed as his gaze went from one boy to the other. Hazel played with her hair, twirled it about her index finger as she tried to get a feel for what he was thinking. She wondered if she should tell Faith to give her side of the story.

"Phineas, Solomon, you will oblige me by returning home and waiting for me in the woodshed."

The boys practically snapped to attention and both let out squawks of surprise and fear.

"Why, father?" Phineas protested. "We denied it."

Edward nodded. "Yes, you did. I heard what your voices said, and I *saw* what your eyes told me. Which do you think I believe?"

The boys hung their heads. Hazel grinned. They had no answer to their father's question, and so they both turned and plodded toward home.

He turned to Hazel. "I apologize for anything inappropriate my boys did to you and Faith. They will work an extra week for you for free, and I give you permission to discipline both of them as you see fit. I shall inform them of that once I'm done with them."

"Thank you. Oh, but, Edward, don't be too harsh with Phineas," she asked. "After all, he's already been punished once today."

He snorted. "Fie, a mere spanking? The lad has tasted the strap three times in a single day and still had the gumption to get into more mischief. Have no worries, I shall be firm, but fair. Good day to you both."

Turning, he marched off, leaning on that old cane of his, and it was as if Hazel's body was deflating. All the stress and tension she'd held in since she saw him approach the house melted away, and she believed she might fall asleep on the spot.

Faith sprinted to the bottom of the steps. "Auntie, never in my life have I seen anything like that."

She grinned at the girl. "Well, when the truth is on your side, being brave is easier."

"You're the most courageous woman I've ever met. You have the spirit of Joan of Arc in you! Do you not feel fear at all?"

"Ah, now there's a difference, my girl. Bravery and fear are not mutually exclusive. You can be terrified and still be brave."

"You…you mean you were afraid facing Mr. Norton? You didn't appear to be."

"That's where the courage comes into play," Hazel said with a nod. "Bravery is going into a fight knowing you'll probably lose but going because it's the right thing to do. Now, how about we get back to work, and put this sorry episode behind us?"

"Yes, ma'am," she said, her voice rising with glee.

Faith raced off to tend to her chores, while Hazel watched as she slowly turned to go inside. Reaching for the front door, she got a prickly feeling to her skin as the hairs on the back of her neck stood straight up. There it was again that sensation that she was being watched. She turned and scanned the area. Was it one of the Norton boys? No, that didn't make sense. They'd never dare defy their father and stay near the farm. Her back stiffened as she saw a filthy little head bob above a berry bush at the edge of the field. Clenching her muscles, she made like she was going to race after the intruder but managed to stay put.

No, if I do that, I'll spook him or her. I've got to exercise finesse here. Let's see, what can I do? Ah, I know. That's a current bush, and the berries are good for us. I'll grab a basket and make like I'm going to pick some.

She did, walking casually, and she made a point of *not* looking at the bush or even in that general direction. Whistling a tune, a song no one from this era would know, as it was *California Girls*, she strolled across the front of the barn as if she was heading for the fields. She even made a point of angling away from the bushes on the far side of the barn, and she stopped and sort of gazed at the marsh and harbor off in the distance.

A twig softly snapped behind her.

Her toes curled inside her sneakers. If it weren't for the damn big, billowy skirt she wore, she could easily run down whoever was there.

Okay, I've had enough of this nonsense. I'm going for it.

Dropping the basket, she bent, hiked up her skirt and layers of silly whatever then turned and ran. The bushes shook in a line starting with the one closest to her and going away from her fast. Yeah, someone tiny was zipping away. She tried to speed up, but when she reached the bushes, her clothes slowed her down. A slap-slap of flesh against wood sounded. The runner was between the row of bushes closest to the barn and the barn itself and hitting it somehow.

"Come back here, you ruffian," she called out. "I won't hurt you! I only want to know who you are."

Her pace slowed more, her skirt tangled in the shrubbery. A small head, its blond hair practically black with filth popped up and down as the boy ran like a gazelle and emerged from behind the barn. He sprinted toward a line of trees off to the left. Hazel struggled and pushed her way through the bushes, but it was pointless. There was no way she could catch up with the little guy. Heaving a sigh, she stopped her efforts, turned, and walked back to the front of the barn.

Faith moved to meet her. "Auntie, what's wrong? I heard you calling. Was someone there?"

She nodded. "Yes, a boy, but I couldn't catch him. I don't suppose you know who he might be or where he comes from?"

"Well…it might be the Silent One," Faith said.

Hazel's brow wrinkled. "Wait, you *do* know? Silent? So, he's a mute?"

"I don't know much, only what I heard my mother and some of the other ladies in Edgar Towne say last winter. They met with women from Tisbury, Cottage City, and the rest of the island, and made plans to give food and clothes to the needy."

"Ah, and the Silent One is probably quite needy."

"Um, they weren't sure. All they knew about him was that he was a boy who lived out among the tombs of the cemetery."

"Cemetery?" Hazel said, gazing off at the trees. "Is that what's out there?"

Faith nodded. "Yes, Auntie, and one of the ladies said she found his…nest."

"Well, why hasn't anyone tried to catch him or at least talk to him? He needs help."

"The ladies talked about it, but…" She cast her eyes down to the ground.

Hazel frowned and ground her teeth. "But what? Faith, you tell me what's going on right now or I'll…um, cane you!"

Faith just about shot into the air, snapped to attention, and trembled before her. An ache, as if she'd been slapped in the belly, tore through Hazel. She didn't like saying such a thing, as she'd never do it, but she also knew it would prove effective, and she was tired of all this verbal dancing.

"Bathsheba pointed out we shouldn't interfere with God's will," Faith blurted out. "If the boy had been rendered mute, it must be for a good reason. Maybe his parents committed some terrible sin, and he was punished for it."

Hazel heaved a sad sigh and hung her head. *God, give me the strength not to tell this girl what I think of her mother and those other…women.* "Faith, do you know anything else about him?"

"No, once they decided to leave him be, the matter was dropped. I did hear it said some of the women here in Cottage City make a point of leaving baskets of food for him out by the tombs, but that's only a rumor."

"I see. All right, thank you for telling me what you know. Go back to your chores."

The girl did, and Hazel moved off then strolled among the bushes and trees as she tried to cool down and think. She really couldn't blame the women for thinking the way they did and doing what they did. In fact, if it was true about the food, and she was pretty sure it was, that was downright decent of them. After all, some of them could argue fending for himself was also God's will. From an anthropologic point of view, everything they did made perfect sense. Of course, that didn't mean she liked it or thought it was the right thing to do.

She stood there, the afternoon breeze rustling the leaves above her, and saw the occasional small footprint in the soft earth. It seemed the Silent One had been moving around here for some time. Hazel wondered how far it was to the cemetery, and if she had time to search for the little guy. She checked the sky. The sun hung close to the western horizon. It was getting late, which meant Arthur would be home soon. She decided a search for the boy could wait. So, she went down cellar to get some things for supper, and that was when Arthur returned home.

"Wow, you had quite the day," he said, leaning back in his chair as they sat in their bedroom. "So, let's see, a tough school teacher, a gay dressmaker, a near beating from our neighbor, and a feral child. Did I miss anything?"

"Well, I wouldn't call Rebecca tough. She's just...feisty and determined to teach the kids as best she can. Um, but I wondered something that maybe you can tell me. If Ed had...tried...something, what could he have done?"

Arthur rubbed his chin. "Let me think. If I remember correctly, I think the 'Rule of Thumb' was in effect in this era, but it might have applied to a husband."

"What's that mean?"

"A man could discipline his wife with a rod or cane no bigger around than his thumb."

Her eyebrows shot up as she felt her eyes grow huge. "Discipline? Thumb? Damn, this world is wacko! Wait a minute. So, was he bluffing?"

"Afraid not. You did...um, strike a member of his family, which was not only assault, but an affront to his honor."

"Ahhh, the old saving face and defending his honor routine," she said, slowly nodding. "I'll try and watch it from now on, but I can't promise anything."

Arthur laughed. "Oh, I can tell we're in for an interesting year. How many days until the next summer solstice?"

"Um, actually, I don't know, and it seems to me it's something we should keep track of."

"Good idea. I'll make a point of finding out."

"I bet I can find out before you do," Hazel replied with a sly grin. "Rebecca gave the children an astronomy lesson today. I wonder if Faith knows."

He snapped his fingers. "Hey, good idea. Why don't you make it part of her quiz for tonight?"

She agreed, and as they sat down to eat, she started in on the questions. Arthur was fascinated by the subjects Rebecca had assigned Faith, and Hazel was amazed at how much the girl had already learned. It was clear she had an excellent mind, and she was able to tell them Tuesday June twentieth was the next summer solstice. Supper passed pleasantly. They cleaned up afterward, played cards, and Faith asked for a story.

"Another story, eh?" Hazel said with a smile. "You're getting spoiled, young lady. Stories at school and stories at home. All right, let me think. Ah, I have one. Once upon a time, there was a little girl who lived on a farm with her aunt and uncle. One day, her dog Rex bit the mean old neighbor lady, um...Mrs. Palin and Dor—I mean, Faith, the little girl, got in trouble."

~ * ~

Over the next several days, their lives fell into something of a routine. They worked the farm, Faith went to school, and Hazel helped out. She told *a lot* of stories, and she and Arthur got to know each other better. She found she really liked the big lug, even if he lacked confidence, and she had the feeling he was keeping something from her. They went for several long walks in the woods to search for the silent boy. The cemetery was on the top of the hill, and while they found his nest, they never caught sight of him.

Hazel made a point of leaving food in his little hovel every time they went there. Arthur also went into town to buy a pair of horses and a nice carriage. If they were going to get around on their own, they'd need transportation. It was a beautiful carriage with two broad and firm benches nicely stuffed and black leather upholstery. Considering the fact the carriage didn't have shock absorbers, well-padded seats were important. The backseat meant Faith would not have to hang onto the rear when they went for a ride. It also had a pretty green canopy with trim to keep the sun off them. When he rode up in it, Hazel was all smiles, but Faith seemed worried.

"Um, Uncle, I don't mean to question your judgment, but..."

"What is it?" he said, climbing down. "Go on, speak your mind. I won't be angry with you."

Her brow wrinkled. "You...wo...n...t?"

He gasped. "Oh, ah, sorry, new word people use in England. I meant to say I will not be angry."

"Ohhh," she said slowly and nodded. "I was merely concerned about your money. Is this carriage expensive?"

"It's good of you to think of such things, but don't worry, we're fine. Now, let's get the horses in the barn and cared for. Hazel, why don't you help me? Faith, get supper started."

The ladies agreed, and Hazel helped to get the horses out of their harnesses, rubbed down, and given food and water.

"Arthur, what's the issue with your word usage? She didn't know the word 'won't'?"

He nodded and patted Polaris, the larger of the two horses. The other was Orion. "That contraction is a fairly modern creation. I can't say I know when it came into popular use, but I think it was in the latter part of the 1800's. Oh, and the term 'okay.' I think that's at least fifty years away."

She sighed and rolled her eyes. "Damn, now we have to watch what we say when it comes to *simple* words? This world gets tougher to deal with daily, huh?"

He shrugged. "Well, maybe we can watch out for each other. Come on, let's eat, and relax for the evening. You can tell Faith another story."

That got Hazel smiling, and the night passed pleasantly. Then came the afternoon of the twenty-eighth, and Arthur brought two small glass vials to the table. Faith groaned and stared at her plate. Hazel was confused, but also had a sense of foreboding.

"Arthur dear, what are those?" she said, trying not to sound afraid.

He licked his lips and cracked his knuckles. "Um, these are something I picked up when I was in town getting your gown this morning. They're...laxatives for you to take today."

"Lax...? Who...why would I take that?" she stammered in surprise.

Faith cocked her head at Hazel. "Auntie, have you never attended a large festival before? A lady always takes those before a party."

"I...um, only had my...coming out party, and that was several years ago. I've forgotten many of the details. I mean, I've forgotten the *preparation* details. Of course I remember the actual party, it was a lavish affair. So, why do I take this?"

"Because of your gown, my sweet," Arthur replied. "While we're at the party, going to the bathroom will be a...logistical nightmare. So, you pretty much can't."

"Ah, now I understand—I mean, *remember*. Putting on that gown is like suiting up for battle in chainmail armor."

He nodded. "Exactly. So, you need to...kind of...take care of *it* today. Now, Faith, I got a second bottle in case you wanted to come with us. It's your choice."

The girl's face lit up like a lantern. "I-I can attend? Oh, Uncle, Auntie, thank you so much. I have never gone to any sort of gala!"

Hazel sat back and slowly and minimally shook her head in amazement. The girl was facing the prospect of gastrointestinal distress, and she wasn't the least bit phased by it. In fact, she looked forward to it as she saw it a means to an end—attending the party. Yeah, Faith was a glass half full type. So, the two of them took the medicine after supper. The stuff tasted like some sort of witch's brew containing eye of newt and leg of toad. However, it was effective. As Arthur said, the ladies were clean as a whistle by nightfall.

Come the morning, both ate light, some bread and broth, and then it was time to prepare which was quite the process. First came the linen underwear, then Hazel allowed Arthur in the bedroom to help with the layers of undergarments. She would have preferred to skip some of them, but she realized that wasn't possible. This was a lavish affair, possibly the biggest party the island had seen, and would see, all year.

She had to dress in her best and follow the standards of the day.

Then came the actual gown. She got down on her knees, Arthur climbed up on the bed, and she just about literally clawed her way inside the leviathan. It was like burrowing into a satin and silk tunnel, and she almost thought she needed to hold her breath. The long sleeves were soft against her arms yet confining and extended all the way to her wrists. Given the layers of undergarments, she couldn't feel the rest of the gown anywhere else on her body. An odd sensation. Popping her head out of the top, she stood, and Arthur got off the bed.

"This is where the straightjacket aspect comes in, right?" he said.

"Aptly put," she replied, turning her back to him. "Although, I'm not as obsessed with my figure as these island ladies are, Arthur. You don't have to cinch me down to nothingness."

"Got it. So, you're saying leave you with the ability to breathe," he said with a chuckle.

He did. The gown got laced up tight, but not so it was horribly uncomfortable. It was only slightly uncomfortable. She ran her hands across her stomach and out around her sides. Making a fist, she tapped it.

"Man, I bet this stuff could stop a bullet, or at least musket ball," she said.

"You're not far off. Dress gowns of this era had whale bones sewn into them to give them their shape."

She turned to face him. "Don't remind me. Whale bone, I've got...*dead* stuff in my clothes. Ewww!"

He chuckled. "Relax, my sweet, they clean it up, boil it, and polish it. Be glad you're not laced into one of the corsets they have around these days. Those puppies are practically like an iron maiden."

She grimaced. "Double ewww. Well, come on, let's collect the girl and get going."

They headed out, Hazel taking the stairs one step at a time, as she couldn't see her feet. She was glad to be in her sneakers, the one element of her outfit she refused to give over to the requirements of the era. Reaching the ground floor, she made her way to the kitchen and discovered yet another aspect of the dress—it was nearly impossible to bend over or twist. If she wanted to turn, she pretty much had to do it with her whole body.

"Faith, are you ready to go?" she called out.

"Almost, Auntie," she replied from her room. "I'm having trouble lacing up the dress."

Arthur headed for the door. "I'll help her."

"Arthur, no!" Hazel snapped, grabbing his arm. "That would be inappropriate. I'll go."

"It would?" he said, appearing confused. "Oh, I get it. Even though I'm a relative, I'm a man, and she's unmarried, right?"

She nodded. "Exactly. You get the carriage; I'll help her."

He departed. She rapped on the door and was admitted then helped Faith finish getting ready. Her dress was merely a regular one, nothing fancy. As Hazel would have said back home, 'it was off the rack.' So, a few buttons and lacing, and she was ready to go. Faith glowed with childish delight.

Hazel chuckled to herself as they made their way out the front door. She walked slowly and stiffly, every movement a labor, and Faith bounced like a child going to Disney World. Arthur stood next to the carriage. Hazel was confused as to why he'd gotten out, but she figured it out. It took the efforts of all three of them to get her in the carriage! Finally plopped into the front seat, she caught her breath and waited while he helped Faith climb into the back. He joined them, and they were off.

Sitting next to him, she was downright amazed at what it was like to be encased in her heavy clothes. She literally couldn't feel the seat under her. It was as if she sat on a massive pillow of linen. As the carriage bounced along the dirt road, she found that quite advantageous. She was tossed about so hard she almost fell out of her seat. Gazing over her shoulder, she was surprised to see Faith sit calmly and take in the scenery.

Damn, what's the girl got on the seat of her dress, glue? Well, she's used to hanging onto the back of a wagon. So, this must be a cakewalk for her. Wow, what a view.

Hazel turned to look across the countryside. They moved through East Chop, but it didn't have the appearance of what she remembered from Arthur showing her around when she'd arrived. Thick with trees and bushes, a few simple homes dotted the area, and the open waters of the Vineyard Sound were off in the distance. Eventually she saw more water in front of them and knew it was Vineyard Haven Harbor, but it was called Holmes Hole now.

Arthur reined the horses to the left, and they journeyed along the east shore of the harbor. She released a happy sigh and inhaled slowly and deeply. The air was soft and gentle in her lungs, the sun warm without being hot, and the waves beat gently against the nearby shore. Each splash, splash of a wave break was like the beating of her heart, and it was quite soothing. The salt air tickled her nose and further invigorated her mind and soul.

Wow, now I know why people live near the ocean. There's something about it that infuses a person with new life.

Nearing the harbor, quite the bustling center of commerce and nautical activity, she saw warehouses, docks, shipyards, and hotels. It seemed this was a major business area. Men bustled about, saws ripped, hammers pounded, and the occasional dog barked. The latter was confusing until she realized they were watchdogs, which made sense. After all, the businesses didn't have security systems. She took note of several large black dogs run around. They appeared to be Labradors, but she wasn't sure. The breed seemed popular.

The smell of sawdust, the rattle of chains, the squeak of ropes, and the shouts of the workers surrounded them. A few minutes later they reached the fancier part of Holmes Hole, the place with restaurants and inns and an elegant hotel. It was only three-stories, but it was the tallest building in town. White with yellow trim, it had a wide covered porch with lots of white wicker furniture. A string of brightly colored small triangular-shaped flags hung from the eaves, which Hazel figured were the eighteenth century equivalent of balloons and a sign saying, 'This is where the party is.' The line of horses, carriages, and wagons were also a dead giveaway. Arthur pulled into the queue to wait their turn.

"Gee, seems we're late for our own party," he said.

"Oh, that's all right," she said, catching herself. "After all, we're the guests of honor. Social etiquette dictates we should be fashionably late."

"Wow, Auntie, you know all kinds of things," Faith said from behind them.

Hazel turned as much as she could and smiled at the girl. "Well, I know some things, your uncle knows other things, and together we make a good team. Ah, here we go, it's our turn."

Faith bolted from the back. "Wait, let me help you!"

She positioned herself to sort of catch Hazel as she climbed down, and a valet moved to help. Hazel heaved and shifted her entire body to swing out of the carriage but paused and glanced over her shoulder at Arthur. "Can you give me a push? I don't think I can do this on my own."

His hands came to rest on her back and his mouth drew close to her ear. "Right here to assist you, dear. On three."

They whispered the count together. He pushed, while she pulled and heaved forward then she landed like a gymnast doing a dismount from the balance beam. The valet caught her left arm, Faith her right, and thus Hazel didn't do a face plant right there at the foot of the steps. By the time she was steady, Arthur dismounted and joined them, and the valet got into the carriage. They headed across the stone steps, up the wide wooden stairs to the broad double doors then entered the atrium.

The place was a virtual palace.

Standing there, despite her sneakers, she could feel the thick carpet under her feet. She could see the oil lamps mounted on the walls, the sheer number hinting at the expense of the place. The freshly cut flowers blended with the various foods. All around them were fancy furniture and well-dressed people. Some were staff and the others were the crème de la crème of the social elite of the island. Hazel was in awe at some of the outfits the people wore: long fancy gowns of silk and lace, wigs that made them appear to be drag queens, and elaborate whale bone jewelry that indicated their standing in society.

As she now understood how important whaling was to the local economy, it was clear the more whale-style items you had, the richer you were. Bathsheba Davenport had a multilayered necklace with many large decorative tiles. It took a moment, but Hazel realized they were teeth with some sort of patterns etched into them and painted. She recognized the work as scrimshaw and knew it was quite valuable.

Lots of introductions followed, more than she could hope to remember, and Patience swooped down to latch onto her arm. Around the main room they went, the place ringed with tables and chairs, and everywhere was food and more food. Despite being a little hungry, Hazel made a point of nibbling. This was another social convention she'd learned about. A proper lady didn't eat a lot at such a gathering. Although, truth be told, she knew that one before ever taking any of her anthropology or sociology classes. She learned it from watching *Gone with the Wind*. Patience wore the single most incredible gown Hazel had ever seen. Bright purple, which she knew was the color of royalty and expensive, was long and flowing, cinched super tight at her waist, and had big puffy sleeves that made it impossible for her to bring her arms close to her sides.

"Do you see, my dear cousin?" Patience said, gesturing about the room. "It's as I said. Only the best of island society here. This is the Great House, the oldest inn in Tisbury. You'll find this of great interest, dearie. One of its owners was a woman. Jane Cathcart, widow of Thomas, maintained it until she passed in 1750. There are rumors she and her servant Ishmael engaged in an illicit affair after Thomas passed."

"Why would it be considered illicit?"

"He was a mulatto, and some things simply aren't done!"

"I...um, I see," Hazel stammered. "Patience, not everyone feels that way."

"We'll speak no more of it," she replied, waving her off. "I'll have you know we've even had some uninvited visitors try to slip in, but I made sure the staff knew who was allowed."

Hazel looked around, literally having to turn her entire body at times to take in the room. "Really, there were people who wanted to sneak into our party? Are we that important?"

Patience smiled from ear to ear. "Oh, Cousin, you have no idea. It's not merely that you're a lady or you're both newly arrived from England. You are Mayhews, which means our family grows stronger and more powerful. Is it any wonder the other families now come, hats in hands, asking Joshua for a favor or a business deal?"

"Ah, I see. Well...that's...good. I'm happy to hear the family is doing well."

"Oh, do not worry. We will make sure Arthur shares in our good fortune, especially once you produce an heir."

Hazel swallowed hard and let out a squeak. *Damn, I should have seen that coming. In this era, a married woman's chief function was as a baby factory.* "Um, yeah, we both look forward to that too."

"Yes, but not until we get you healthy. You're still far too thin. Isn't Faith feeding you properly? Do I need to speak to that girl?"

"No, no, I'm fine. I'm just...um, not used to the local food yet. Give me time, and I'll settle in. Oh, do I see someone sneaking in a window over there?" she said, pointing across the room.

Patience spun to check where Hazel indicated. "What? Where? Where is Elijah? He's the owner, it's his responsibility. Never mind, I'll fix them!"

She took off, which Hazel found amazing. How the woman could practically sprint across the room in her long flowing dress was nothing short of amazing. Hazel was now able to get a moment's respite. All this fancy social interaction was downright exhausting. The floor creaked behind her. She rotated her entire body and found Joshua coming up behind her. He seemed quite dapper in his fancy suit with bright white leggings and jacket with brass buttons, but he was way underdressed compared to her and his wife.

He smiled and eyed her up and down. "So, my dear cousin, you look quite nice. Your gown is rather...modest. Did Arthur not allow you to purchase a proper dress?"

"Not at all, I picked it out myself. Have you seen Arthur, or is he hiding in some dark corner?" she said, wearing a grin.

"I left him regaling Isaac and some of the older men with his tale of the hunt. It seems every time he tells it, the whale grows larger."

She giggled. "Ah, men and their heroic tales, they do seem to inflate over time. I imagine St. George started out fighting a bear or lion."

Joshua laughed and patted her on the shoulder. "Hazel, you are a delight, and so very...different from the ladies I know. I see you brought Faith to the party. Not many women would do that. They would want the focus to be on them not their unmarried younger niece."

"Well, as you say, I'm different."

"Yes, you certainly are. Faith said you've enrolled her in school that you want her to get more of an education. Very different. I understand some of the Puttenhams helped to settle New *York*. Once the rebellion is over, will you journey to visit them?"

"Um, possibly. We will have to see if we can afford such a trip. Perhaps I'll write to them. Will you excuse me? My throat is dry. I need a drink."

"Of course, *Cousin*," he replied.

Hazel moved before he spoke but paused at his final word. There was something about the way he said 'cousin' that sounded off. She tried to put it out of her mind and moved to the punch bowl. It was like everything else in the room, huge and fancy. The massive glass bowl sat in the center of a long table adorned with a crisp, white tablecloth and row upon row of mugs. Using the ladle, she filled one with some of the pink concoction and took a small sip. Given her layers of garments, the last thing she wanted was to have to use the bathroom. The drink was sweet, but didn't seem to contain alcohol, which suited her fine. She'd been to far too many parties where heavy drinking led to trouble, even fights.

She froze and nearly dropped her cup. She couldn't believe what she saw across the room. Taking another sip, so as to keep up appearances, she knew all eyes were on her and if she didn't appear to like the punch, it would be an insult to the host and hotel. She put her cup at the end with the other discarded ones, and slowly moved off to the side. It was important to have an unobstructed view of the people she was curious about. Standing there, trying to focus on the three of them as people milled about, her jaw fell open as Patience stepped up to the group and joined in the 'conversation.' Now Hazel was amazed beyond belief.

Patience knew some form of sign language!

"Hazel, are you having a good time?" Arthur said.

She jumped. Somehow he'd materialized right next to her. "Oh! Sorry, you startled me. I didn't hear you coming."

"Is something wrong, Auntie? You seem troubled."

Making a slow turn so she could face both of them, she smiled at Faith. "No, I'm fine, I'm surprised to see people using sign language. Is that common here?"

"Do deaf people not use it in England?" Faith replied, clearly confused.

Hazel cast her gaze at Arthur, hoping he would chime in with an answer. He said 'No idea' with his expression, and so she drew a blank.

"I've never met any such people," she said. "However, I've heard of people using…signals to talk. Are there many deaf people here?"

"Yes," Arthur and Faith said together.

Faith turned to him. "Uncle, you know of our deaf ones?"

"Um, yes, I think your father or someone mentioned it in a letter. Tell your aunt about them."

She nodded and turned back to Hazel. "It started about a century ago. Jonathan Lambert was born deaf, and several of his children were the same way. Now many families, the Hammetts, Tiltons, and even the Mayhews have deaf members. They mostly live in Chilmark, and some people wondered for a while if it was a disease anyone could catch, but now we know better."

"What about the Silent One in Cottage City?" Hazel said. "Maybe he's deaf too."

"Oh no, he can hear. Several of the ladies in town have called out to him, and he reacted. That's how they know he's different."

Hazel chewed her lip. "Ah-huh and why they say he's…cursed," she said softly. "Thank you for telling me about your deaf citizens. Perhaps I can meet them and learn their language. What about you, Faith, do you know it?"

She shook her head. "No, Auntie, but I would like to learn."

"Maybe Miss McCarthy knows it. I'll ask her the next time we're in class and see if we all can learn it. For now, could we meet them?"

Faith smiled and took her hand. "Of course. Come, I'll have mother introduce you."

A true surge of delight tickled Hazel's skin, rippling along her spine. Here at last was something she could enjoy about this world, the opportunity to meet some unique people no one else had ever contacted, deaf people speaking what was essentially an unknown language. She knew ASL a little, and while a few gestures were similar to those she remembered, most were a total mystery. Like finding Lost Atlantis or Brigadoon or being the first person to translate the Rosetta Stone. Gave her such a rush, she trembled as they neared the group.

Faith spoke to her mother, and Patience made the formal introductions. The first was Theodosia Mayhew, a cousin, a mighty oak of a woman who sort of resembled Joshua, the poor thing. Then Hazel met the three people with her, none of whom were related. No, the only common thread was their affliction, as she heard someone say under their breath as they walked by. She ignored it and focused on the group, picking up a few of their gestures. Actually, she did quite well. By the time they trotted out to their carriage to head home, she was able to 'speak' in a few basic sentences.

"Auntie, you're amazing," Faith said as they rode along. "You learned their language as if born to it."

"Well, it's something I want to learn, something I'm passionate about. Here's a little lesson for you, when you love a subject you learn it quickly. Sweetie, would you loosen my ties please?"

Faith gasped. "Auntie! Undo your gown? In public?" she squeaked.

"Just loosen it a bit. It's lovely, but it's so blessed tight it's hard for me to breathe."

"Um, ah, very well."

Small hands played across her back, the straps relaxed a bit, and she took in the first deep breath of the evening.

"Ohhh, thank you, you're a lifesaver," she said with a happy sigh. "Huh, now I know why women are considered the weaker sex. Who can be strong when you're short on breath?"

Arthur chuckled. "I think that might be why women are known to swoon. Anyway, look on the bright side, my sweet, it's over, and with any luck you wo—ah, will not have to wear such a gown again for a long time. So, relax, breathe deep, and enjoy the ride home."

She nodded and smiled, stretching out as much as she could on the narrow bench. The cool night air wrapped about her like a gentle blanket. After all, given her massive layers of clothing, it was as if she was wearing a winter parka. The trees rustled. The sea appeared black, but the waves crashed upon the shore, and the stars blazed across the black sky. She thought back to her home in Boston and how dim the stars always were there, but that was to be expected. It was a big bright city, and now they were in a quiet and dim community, and thus the island lights were minimal. Even the moon wasn't dazzling. It was waning, and so they rode in near total darkness all the way home.

Hazel yawned, her eyes heavy as if weights were tugging them down. Between the gentleness of the ride, the soft air swirling about her, and the stress of the party being relieved, she became calm and relaxed. She blinked and sat up as much as she could. They were home.

"Did I nod off?" she said.

He shrugged. "Eh, not for long, and don't worry, your snoring wasn't too loud."

"Oh, don't believe him for a moment, Auntie, you didn't snore one bit!"

Hazel giggled and sat up. "I never do. Now, how about you help me down, and we'll get changed into more comfortable clothes."

With Faith's help, she got out of the carriage, and the two of them headed inside while Arthur took care of the horses. By the time he came in, she had managed to get free of her colossus and was *only* in her underwear.

She flopped onto the bed and poured herself a glass of water.

"I feel completely drained," she groaned.

He chuckled. "Bet you lost five pounds in sweat alone, huh? You feel up to a meal?"

"Oh yeah," she said with conviction. Pausing, she sniffed. "Wait, do I smell something cooking?"

"That's Faith for you. Seems her mom told her she needed to work harder at cooking for you. So, she got changed and already has supper in the oven, so to speak."

Hazel sighed and shook her head. "Oh, that woman. She's going to be gray before her time and make me *and* Faith gray as well. Oka—I mean, all right. Let me finish changing, and I'll go help the poor girl."

"I'll leave you then," he replied and grabbed the gown. "As for this… I'll find someplace to store it."

Gathering the massive mass of satin, silk, and other 'ingredients' up in his arms, he left, and she slipped into something comfy. She had to laugh as she finished. Back when they arrived, she found these clothes downright confining. Now, they were what her body took comfort in.

Who'd a thought such a thing was possible?

Nine

Hazel's dress took up an entire trunk in the front bedroom, but as they weren't using the room, it wasn't like it would be in the way. He also put the money Joshua had given him, his share of the whale hunt, in the strongbox. By the time he got downstairs, Hazel was there helping Faith, and they soon sat down to supper.

"That's not one of our chickens, is it?" Hazel said, eying the bird Art was carving.

Faith shook her head. "No, Auntie. Mother gave me some heath hens that were all cleaned and dressed for the party but weren't used."

"Heath hens?" Art snapped.

Both ladies jumped in their seats at his outburst.

He cleared his throat and calmed down. "I mean, I didn't know there were any of those left. I thought I read in a letter the British took most of them."

"Oh, no, that was the cattle," Faith explained. "Heath hens run wild all over the island, and they're good eating."

"That's good, but, like the whales, they must be protected so they're always here. Add that to the lessons you learn at school, Faith. The bounty of Nature will only remain if you take good care of it."

"Yes, sir," she said with a nod.

They enjoyed a pleasant meal, a quiet evening, and retired early. Curling up together in bed, Hazel heaved a contented sigh.

"I'm glad that's over with," she said. "I hope that's the last time we're the center of attention around here."

"Me too. With any luck we can lay low and try to get through the coming months."

"Well, we're coming up on July, and I know the fourth is not a holiday, so what are the issues we have to face next?"

He swallowed hard. "Um, just plan for the year. We've planted and are tending the crops. We'll need to prepare for the fall harvest, maybe get some fish and other staples then salt the fish and preserve things for winter."

"Sounds complicated. Makes me glad we have Faith with us. Arthur,

I have to say, the things that girl knows are amazing. For that matter, the kids at school are amazing. Their knowledge and ability to remember details is phenomenal! My dad used to make fun of his dad for only having an eighth grade education. Let me tell you, there's nothing 'only' about it. How in the world do they remember all these things?"

"There are all kinds of memory tools for that, some have been around for centuries. I still remember the rhyme my dad taught me about the weather: 'Red sky in the morning, sailor takes warning.' It may not be accurate, but it's close."

"Oh, I get it, neat. However, I don't see where that'd work for all of their studies."

"What, is Rebecca giving them a classic education?"

"What's that mean?" Hazel said.

"Back…oh, I don't know how many centuries it was, the classic curriculum was established. Let me see if I can remember the subjects. Um, astronomy, arithmetic, logic, public speaking, grammar, music, and geometry. I would imagine she's teaching them that. People developed what was known as a 'memory house' to help them remember things."

She squirmed around to face him, curiosity written across her face. "Okay, I am officially intrigued. I don't care how tired I am, I've got to know what that is."

Art chuckled and smiled, brushing the hair from her cheek. "It's a powerful device to help you remember things. I'll give you an example. Picture in your mind a house. You walk in the front door and find a knight, like out of King Arthur's court, and he's sitting on the couch in his armor reading a book. So, a knight studying…night study…?"

She chewed her lip. "Ah, astronomy! Hey, not bad. So, the kids fill up their 'houses' with mental images that remind them of what they're trying to remember. Arthur, it's like I've said before, I'm glad we're going through this together, and…and I hope at some point we can truly be…together."

He cupped her small chin in his hand. "So do I, but I understand your need to wait until you feel the time is right. I will never press the issue. The final decision is yours. Good night."

They shared a sweet kiss then settled down to sleep in each other's arms.

~ * ~

In the morning, after breakfast, they set about their usual tasks. Art went out to tend the crops with the help of Phineas and Solomon, who were extremely respectful, and the ladies puttered around the house doing laundry and other household chores. Art remembered how his grandmother had talked about wash day and ironing day, mystified by the use of the word 'day.' Now he understood. There was a time when it took all day to do a task.

Pausing in his efforts to eradicate the weeds, he stood up straight and chewed on the inside of his cheek.

Hmmm, I've got an idea rattling 'round inside my head. Actually, a couple of them, and I'm going to try them out.

Once they were done in the field, they all sat down to lunch, and the boys headed home. Art made his way into the barn and set to work. He enjoyed himself as the minutes seemed to melt into hours in the blink of an eye. The next thing he knew, Hazel was rapping on the door.

"Arthur, you've been in here for hours. What's with the tools and stuff? Are you inventing something else?"

He turned and nodded. "You got it. Come on, help me carry this stuff down to the cellar, and I'll show you what I've made."

She was mystified and grabbed the bits and pieces without another word and dashed after him. Once there, he got to work assembling his three little gizmos. Hazel stood off to the side, out of the way, and watched in growing awe. As the first item, a water-powered butter churn took shape, he asked her to help by handing him parts and holding the tools.

"Wait a minute, I know what this is," she said. "I saw one in a museum. That's one of those things to make butter."

"You got it. I got to thinking, churning butter takes a long time, so, why not use our little water wheel to help out."

"Nice," she replied with a smile and cast her gaze about the other items. "And these?"

"A gristmill," he said, pointing at the first. "We can use it to grind wheat into flour and corn into cornmeal. The other is a washing machine to do our laundry in. Granted, it's far from high-tech, but at least it'll speed things up a little, maybe turn wash day into wash half a day. Come on, let's get them put together."

It took the better part of two hours, but eventually three new household appliances were lined up next to the bath tub. As they had plenty of butter and flour, they didn't need to try those two, but they did have several dirty items left over from the day's efforts. He stuffed the plug in the tub. It was the bottom of a barrel he'd sawn in half. They dumped the clothes in, added water and soap, and turned it on. The crank spun, the plunger-like shaft went up and down, and the clothes got agitated.

Faith stood next to it. Her mouth hung open for a moment. "Uncle, this is the most wondrous device I have ever seen. What do the others do? Wait, I know, a butter churn and gristmill. Uncle, there are no words to describe this. You are a genius as great as Archimedes."

"Well, I wouldn't go quite that far, but I appreciate your praise. Now, can you handle the wash alone?"

She nodded. "Yes, sir."

"Good. If you'll excuse us, I have something to discuss with your aunt. Hazel, if you would please?" he said, gesturing at the stairs.

The ladies exchanged confused expressions. Hazel started up the stairs, and Art followed. She waited until they were in their room before speaking.

"Arthur, why all the cloak and dagger? What's up?"

"Oh, it's nothing, honey," he said with a chuckle. "I wanted to show you my other invention, a little concoction I've whipped up to make our lives a bit more comfortable. I figured saying I needed to talk to you was good cover in front of Faith. Here, let me show you what I've got."

She watched as he pulled out a clay jar and removed the top.

"What in the world is that?" she said. "It looks like…chocolate and strawberry pudding."

He smirked. "Yeah, I guess it's less than entirely appealing. This is an eighteenth century version of toothpaste."

"Toothpaste? What kind of… stuff is in it?"

"Clay, some sugar and baking soda, a little vegetable oil, and a couple cacao nibs."

"Huh? Cacao, what's that?"

"Essentially chocolate. I got some from the candy store when I picked up your gown the other day."

"Chocolate, in toothpaste? Wait, did you say clay too?"

Art nodded. "They work together to form a mild abrasive that'll scrub the teeth without damaging the enamel. I remembered the stuff my grandfather used to mix up to brush his teeth."

"He made his own toothpaste?"

"He made his own *everything*. The man was so frugal he made Scrooge McDuck seem as generous as Santa Claus."

"Scrooge, isn't he a Disney character, Donald's uncle?"

"Yeah, I always thought he was kind of cool, a very colorful character."

"Based on Ebenezer Scrooge, right?"

"Right you are. Anyway, if we put some of this stuff on the brushes I made, we can brush our teeth."

He held up one to her and took the other for himself.

She checked it out; turned it over in her hands. "Well, not something approved by the American Dental Association, but a nice effort. What's next, floss?"

Art chuckled. "No, I'm good, but I'm not that good. Shall we try it?"

Hazel nodded. They smeared some of the paste on their brushes and scrubbed. Art slowly nodded as he worked the tough bristles in and around his mouth. The paste didn't taste too bad. They scrubbed their teeth, rinsed their mouths, and cleaned their brand new brushes and put them aside.

She smiled and smacked her lips. "It's not much, but having clean teeth feels pretty damn good! Now, Arty, there's something I wanted to ask you about. How about we take a trip to Chilmark and maybe even Gay Head? I would love the chance to spend time with the deaf people and the natives."

"I don't see why not. Mind you, it's going to be a bit of a trip. This won—ah, will not be something we do in a day."

"Oh, it's really so far?"

He shrugged. "Far? Eh, that's a relative term. It's more the terrain and our mode of transport. Using our carriage will mean not traveling at the sort of speeds we're used to. Well, hey, we're here, why not? The opportunity to see the history of my island first hand is one I simply can't pass up. Let's see, it's Friday, it'll take a couple days to prep, and we can't do it on Sunday. So, how about Monday?"

She smiled. "Works for me."

They spent the next three days getting ready for the trip and settled into the routine of working the farm. Faith squealed with childlike glee every time she used one of their new appliances. She and Hazel did complain about one thing, and that was theft. They noticed eggs went missing from the coop, some clothes got snatched from the clothes' line, and an old worn blanket vanished from the barn. Hazel was sure it was the silent boy, but they never caught sight of him. He was like a ghost—not that they said that in front of Faith. The poor girl was so nervous about the little guy already, that Hazel didn't want to do anything to make her more afraid of him.

Come Monday morning, right after breakfast, they loaded up the carriage and prepared to set off. Hazel insisted Faith come along, despite all her protests.

"Auntie, the house, the chores, my schooling," she whined.

"The Nortons will watch the house, and Rebecca told me you're doing well on your studies. In addition, she said learning island history and culture, especially the quiet ones, as she put it and the natives will be good for you. Now, no more arguing or I shall have to…punish you."

She squirmed and sat back in her seat. "Yes, ma'am."

Art smiled and snapped the reins. "Giddy-up! Here we go, ladies. Next stop Holmes Hole."

Riding along, it was like he was a prim and proper gentleman of the turn of the century. Granted, he seemed more like someone out of the late 1800's because of movies he'd seen like *Life with Father*, but the concept was close. It was warm and refreshing to bounce along the uneven road, the clip-clop of the horses marking the time. He glanced over his shoulder. Faith was engrossed in a book, and his eyebrows went up when he caught sight of the subject. While he couldn't read upside down, it was clear the book was in

Latin.

Yeah, that girl is going to get one fine education. I only hope we're able to give her the chance to make use of it.

As they'd made the journey before, he settled back in his seat, and let the horses set their own pace. Cottage City and Holmes Hole were less than three miles apart, and thus they arrived there in under an hour. Passing through the center of the harbor district, Art let his gaze wander around the area to take it all in and was amazed. The basic pattern of the roads was unchanged, but not one building was the same. He didn't mind. This was his island, his home. All he had to do was close his eyes and let the myriad sensations of the place wash over him, and he was home. Well, minus the horse manure.

The waves broke upon the shore, the trees rustled in the light breeze, and the shouts of people going about their day filled the air. Art almost laughed out loud. The people didn't sound much different from his era. There were workers building ships, mothers calling to children, the squeal of more children at play, and the chatter of sailors and businessmen. Dogs barked, the horses got a little spooked, and Art had to concentrate on controlling them as they made their way out of town and headed toward Tisbury.

"Auntie, Uncle, that's what we need, a dog! That'll keep the Silent One away from the chickens and our clothes."

"A dog?" Hazel said. "Say, that's not a bad idea, but I wouldn't want ours to bite the poor boy. Arthur, what do you think? After all, there are plenty of them around. I think I've seen at least half a dozen black dogs alone. Is there some reason they're so common here?"

He shrugged. "I don't know, but I do know Vineyard Ha—I mean, Tisbury is known for its black dogs. We'll see about getting one, once we get home. Now, we've close to ten miles to Chilmark, so we'll stop there for lunch. Ladies, settle back, relax, and enjoy the ride."

Faith did, putting her book aside, and gazing around with stars in her eyes. He was momentarily confused. After all, it was just the ordinary countryside of the island. Why the big excitement? It came to him. Despite living her whole life on the island, she'd probably never gotten this far up island, as it was called, and thus this was quite the adventure for her. A warm surge coursed through his chest. Considering the horrors of war being waged on the mainland, and what was to come here next year, it made him feel good to be able to give Faith a few simple pleasures in life.

"By the way, my ladies, if you need a rest or to use the…facilities, speak now."

"Facilities, Uncle? Oh, I understand," Faith said with a giggle. "No, I'm fine."

"Several hours?" Hazel said, her voice going up. "Really, it's that far?"

"Not so much far as roundabout. There's no direct road connecting the two towns. We have to go south to the main road, west until we see the Chilmark meeting house, and then turn north onto the road into town."

"Wow that is convoluted. So, North Road doesn't exis…I mean, they haven't built any other roads yet. Well, it's a good thing Faith and I have our books."

"Actually, if I get bored, I could read something too," Art observed.

Her brow wrinkled. "You could? Ah, of course, what was I thinking? It's not like in our time—territory! The horses will follow the road."

"Uncle, would you like one of my books? Or, I could read aloud from one. Right now I'm studying *Caesar's Commentaries on the Gallic Wars*."

"Thank you, sweetie, but maybe later. Right now, I want to take in the beauty all around me, the beauty of my isl…*our* island."

Faith went on studying the countryside. Hazel patted Art's hand and smiled at him. He smiled back. The joy on her face, the twinkle in her eyes told him she was coming to understand what the island meant to him. As far as he was concerned, no matter what dangers and violence the future held, all of it was worth it to see that glow of love grow within her. He suppressed a laugh. Here he was, sitting next to the girl of his dreams, and he wasn't concerned with whether or not she loved *him*. No, it was her feelings toward the place he called home, even if it was more than two centuries out of date.

Sitting back, he lightly held the reins and took it in. Around them were all the glories of nature and all Art wanted to do was absorb it, let it soak into every fiber of his being, and be one with it. This was the island as he always imagined it could be, peaceful and quiet, and populated by happy and friendly folk. No stench of gas and oil assailed his nose. Trees, tall and strong, stretched as far as he could see, and there was no roar of chainsaws signaling their untimely demise. He desperately wanted to throw his arms out as if it might help him embrace the powers swirling around him. Instead, he closed his eyes, inhaled the clear air as deeply as he could, and let the stresses of life drain from his body. They were replaced by, for lack of a better term, the bio-energies that ebbed and flowed around the carriage.

Despite his eyes being closed, it almost seemed as if he could see, and yet his vantage point wasn't himself. In a real sense, he had an out of body experience. His legs extended down into the soft moist soil like roots. His arms and fingers stretched into the clear blue sky as if transformed into branches and leaves, and his heart and lungs seemed to cease functioning. He didn't feel dead. No, far from it, his body was in tune with the rhythms of nature, breathing in and breathing out, and merged with the life around him.

"Arthur, is that the meeting house?" Hazel said.

He sat bolt upright. His eyes snapped open, and a great sense of loss thrust into him. He'd been rudely shoved back into his body, the connection severed, and he was like a freshman at a senior mixer, surrounded by people, yet alone. He well remembered going through that at college. Scanning the area, he saw a modest building by the side of the road. Clearly not a home, it had an official air about it, but smaller than the hall in Edgar Towne, so it was probably the meeting hall. Besides, it was the only building around.

"That's it," he said, signaling the horses to turn. "Goodness, the journey seemed so brief."

Hazel shrugged. "Well, time flies when you're having fun."

"Oh, that's good, Auntie. Did you come up with that saying?"

"What?" she replied, turning slightly in her seat toward the girl. "Um, no, I-I heard it somewhere."

They made the turn, and Art slowed the horses as they passed the low stone wall that separated the building from the road. Two little boys tossed a ball back and forth, and he wanted to be careful around them, especially as one had his back to the road.

"Boys, can you tell us how far it is to town?" he called out.

The one facing them gazed blankly, and the other didn't turn around.

"Boys, come on, speak up," Art added, raising his voice. "What's the matter, you dea—? Oh!"

"Yes, they probably are," Hazel said.

The second boy turned to them as she launched into her signing. They smiled and gestured back.

"Less than a mile down the road," she said.

Art waved and smiled at the boys and urged the horses on. "You picked up their language so quickly. Amazing."

"Not really," she replied with a slight shake of her head. "Some of the signs are the same as ASL—I mean, I recall seeing some similar gestures from some deaf people from...um, Asia."

"Auntie, you met some yellow people from the Far East? What were they like?"

Hazel's jaw muscles clenched for a moment, and she took a deep cleansing breath. "Well, to begin with, they were *not* yellow. They were people, young lady, no different than you are from me, except for their features, their language, and how they chose to live their lives."

"Y-yes, Auntie," the girl squeaked.

Art cast his gaze sideway in time to see Hazel, who worked her way around in her seat to glare at Faith, ease off, and soften her expression. She realized she'd scared the poor thing.

"I mean...I...I'm sorry, dearie. I didn't mean to scare you. I...I'm just passionate about people tolerating others. Your...characterization of

Asians as yellow is offensive to them, but there's no way you could have known that."

"No, it's all right, Auntie, I spoke without thinking. In his commentaries, Caesar berates the Gauls by calling them barbarians, but it seems he and Vercingetorix were cut from the same cloth."

"Who?" Hazel replied.

"The leader of the Gallic tribes. Auntie, didn't you study Ancient Rome in school?"

"Um, yes, but history was never my best subject. Please, go on."

"Well, it seems to me that had circumstances been different, they could have been friends."

Hazel and Art locked eyes for a moment and both grinned. He knew from one of their dates in Boston, when they attended a sci-fi convention, that she was as big a Star Trek fan as he was. So, he knew the same scene was flashing through her head.

"You're right, sweetie," she said. "In a different sort of reality, they could have been friends."

Art wanted to high-five her. *Yeah, she nailed it. Beat me by one second.*

"I've also learned something else," Faith said. "History is written by the winners. Had Caesar lost, would *he* be called the barbarian?"

"Faith, I'm most impressed," Art replied. "You are wise for one so young."

He gazed back at her in time to see her blush.

She gasped. "Uncle, be careful! Remember, many in Chilmark cannot hear the carriage approach."

"The girl's right. Eyes front, mister."

"Oh, aye-aye, m'lady," he said with a grin.

A moment later, they reached the town, and Art smiled bigger. It was a quaint peaceful little spot, and the people didn't seem in a hurry about anything, yet, it was clearly a center of commerce. There was a blacksmith shop, inns and stores, and a carpenter's shop where tools and a great many barrels sat on display. For a moment, he was confused by them, but then remembered what Chilmark was famous for: the Beetle Bung Trees. Their wood was used to make plugs for kegs. The road widened out, the trees parted, and sunshine washed over them.

"Wow, I never thought I'd be glad for the warmth of the sun," Hazel said.

He nodded. "Yeah, it's a nice change from the blistering heat we're used to."

"Is England quite hot?" Faith said. "Mother always says it's a cold, dreary place."

"There are places in the big cities that get stifling in the summer," Hazel replied.

"Isn't it so nice and quiet here?" Art added quickly, trying to change the subject. "We need to let the horses rest," he added, pulling over to the side of the road.

"Let's have lunch," Hazel suggested. "Faith, get the basket. I'll grab the blanket, and we can sit in the park over there."

He checked out where she was pointing. If his memory served, the area was known as the commons, and she was right, it was a public park. Most communities had one. The one in Boston was still maintained in their time. He remembered going there as a kid with his family at Christmas time to see the decorations and sing carols. The big difference was that in this era it was not unusual to see sheep, cattle, or other farm animals grazing there.

Oh well, so long as we watch out for cow pies, we should be okay.

While the ladies set up the meal, Art led the horses over to a long low water trough and let them drink. Turning, he smiled at the tableau before him. It was almost straight out of a Norman Rockwell picture, except the time period was at least a century too soon. That didn't matter. Here he was, standing by two fine animals, and a vision of loveliness washed over him. The grass of the commons was thick and lush, no doubt due to the 'fertilizer' it got regularly. The sky was crystal clear blue with a few wispy white clouds, and he could see the two prettiest girls he'd ever known sitting before him on a beautiful patchwork quilt. That they also had food was icing on the cake.

"Uncle, are you dazed from the journey? You have the same faraway gaze as my father after a trip to the public house."

"I'm just happy," he said, joining them. "It's a lovely day, this is a delightful place, and I'm here with two beautiful young ladies. What more could any man ask for?"

They both blushed.

"Unclllle! You'll turn my head with such talk. A proper lady must be modest."

"Modest, but not rigid or cold," Hazel said, wearing a grin and winked at Faith. "Pay him no mind. I think the lack of food has addled his brain. Give him something to eat before he says another silly statement."

The girl giggled and pulled a sandwich from the basket. Hazel had wrapped each in small cloth, as foil, paper, and plastic were unavailable. He took it and started eating, while Faith filled their ceramic cups with water from the pump.

Thank God she didn't go to the trough.

Returning with their drinks, she got something to eat, but didn't take a bite. The quizzical expression on her face was comical.

"Uncle, what did you say this was called again?"

"A sandwich," he replied simply. "They're all the rage in England now. Invented by the Earl of Sandwich as a means of eating a meal with one hand without getting his fingers dirty."

"How did he come up with such a thing?"

"The Earl is fond of games and hates to stop playing, even to eat," he explained.

The girl's eyebrows went up. "My goodness, he must love his games like Auntie loves telling stories to the children!"

Hazel smiled and tousled Faith's hair. "Now who's trying to turn *my* head? You certainly are your uncle's niece."

Art snorted as he swallowed a laugh. Given their points of origin in the time stream, it was more accurate to say he was her nephew. That fact echoed and resounded within his mind. Here was an ancestor of his, a member of his family, and he was instantly reminded of every regret, every missed opportunity to tell his grandparents, his parents, and most especially his siblings what they meant to him. He recalled one of those advice books he'd read in some bookstore, a collection of quotes, and one hit home for him. It spoke of spending time with those you loved while you had the chance as there would come a day when you were left with two things to remember them by, memories of what was and regrets at what might have been. It suggested always striving for more memories and less regrets.

Hazel touched his arm. "Arthur, are you all right?"

"What?" he said, snapping out of his bleak thoughts. "Yes, fine, why do you ask?"

"Something *is* troubling you," she replied. "You went from happy to sad faster than…um…a bolt of lightning."

He managed a small smile. Clearly she'd been stuck with thinking of an era appropriate phrase. "I'm all right. I was just…lost in a memory, thinking of the family gone to me. Ah, I mean, separated from us because they're back in England."

She blinked, her eyes growing watery. "You have me now."

"And me," Faith piped in with. "And mother and father, and the whole family. We will always be with you."

"Thank you, both of you, and you will have my love, always. Faith, I want you to know, I love you like my own. I have no wish to replace your father in your heart, but you may think of me as a second father and ask anything of me you would from him."

Now both ladies fought back the tears. Faith reached out to take his large hand in her small one.

"Oh, Uncle, thank you, I will always try to be worthy of your devotion."

After that, they settled down to eat and tried to avoid anything that might get the tears flowing. Sitting there, happily eating, he wondered about the future, the distant future. What about his family? Could he tell them all he wished to? Could he warn his siblings and save their lives? Maybe that was the *real* reason for this journey. Maybe he was being given a second chance. If he wrote them letters and entrusted them to Faith, could he somehow arrange things so they were delivered to his family?

The thing is, I can't send them a telegram like in Back to the Future *or give letters to my grandson like in* Doctor Who. *I can trust Faith, but what about the person she gives them to? I'm going to have to give this some serious thought.*

He tried to put the future aside and focus on the now and sat back to enjoy the meal. It was the best picnic he'd ever had.

"This sandwich meal is quite nice," Faith said, finishing hers. "I must tell Mother about them. Oh, and Miss McCarthy. If the children brought these to school, lunchtime would be far less messy."

Hazel nodded. "A good idea. Arthur, it would seem this sandwich thing is going to catch on."

They exchanged grins and winks. Once they were done, it was time to see the village. Art almost had the sensation of walking on a cloud. It wasn't merely the chance to see a part of the island's history come to life. It was Hazel's expression as they strolled around the snug little shops and along the wide paths. She was like a child on Christmas morning. The minutes blurred together as the sun descended across the sky and long before they were ready to move on she was a virtual master of Martha's Vineyard Sign Language. It got to the point where she did it automatically when she spoke. Faith picked up on it and even Art managed to learn a bit.

"Arthur, this is the most incredible place I've ever been!" Hazel said. "To see deaf people being so… so… ingrained into society is something I never thought I'd live to see."

"Are there many deaf in England, Auntie?"

"Not that I've met, but I know people with disabilities struggle in their daily lives and to be accepted. Here, all I see is acceptance. Remember this always, Faith, and be proud of your island for being so… progressive."

The girl beamed brighter than the glow of the setting sun behind her. "I will, but remember, pride goes before destruction. You taught me that, Uncle. Maybe I shouldn't be too proud."

"Once again you show wisdom beyond your years," Hazel said. "Moderation is best, in all things."

"I'm one lucky man to have two such wise and knowledgeable ladies in my life. Now, given the lateness of the hour, I think we'll have to stay here for the night."

"Shall we seek out Cousin Theodosia's house?"

Hazel chewed her lip. "Oh, um, isn't it too late to call on her? I mean, we didn't call—ah, let her know we were coming to town. Isn't it an imposition to show up at her door?"

"Auntie, nonsense, it will be a great insult if we leave town without visiting her."

"I think Faith is right, dear. Remember, the rules of etiquette here are different from what you were raised with," Art said, trying to sound convincing.

He knew his statement was risky, but relatively safe. It was highly unlikely the girl knew much about the social graces of English nobility. The nod of recognition Hazel gave him was reassuring. It was clear she got the message and was playing along.

"Oh, yes, what was I thinking?" she said with a haughty wave of her hand. "Your island is so quaint and free of our rigid social manners."

Thus it was decided. They returned to the carriage and set out for the house. Getting directions to the Mayhew home was easy. While Chilmark was quite the large community by island standards, it was only a few hundred people. Everyone knew everyone, and they most especially knew Theodosia. Hers was a modest home, not at all like Joshua's, sitting atop Abel's Hill, which gave it a 'delightful' view of the town's cemetery. Art almost made a joke about it being a great place to set up a haunted house for Halloween, but he realized the holiday didn't exist yet.

Two of her seven children spotted them as they rode up and notified the other five, who were tending chores in the side yard. It was quite the contrast to what Art remembered as they'd approached Joshua's house and little Charity announced their arrival with a shout. Here, the boy raced in the front door as the girl signaled to the others and turned to wave at the carriage. They stood ready to help with the horses. Art was careful to rein them in well before they got too close to her. The poor thing was a waif and couldn't be more than ten, yet, she took hold of the bridle and secured them like a pro.

"Good day to you, neighbors," she said. "What brings you to our door this evening?"

"Good day to you, little one," Art replied, trying to sound the strong determined man. "I am Arthur Mayhew, my wife Hazel, and this is Faith, daughter of Joshua and Patience."

He never got to say more. The girl squealed in delight and bounced up and down at the prospect of meeting relatives. By then her five siblings joined her, and she informed them as to the identities of their visitors. As Faith and Hazel got down, they were surrounded by bouncing brown and black-haired heads. When it became clear the two ladies knew signing, the hand gestures flew faster than a baseball manager signaling to runners on base. All Art managed to get out of all of it was their names, of which he remembered only Hannah, the hearing member of the group. By then, Theodosia and Reason, her oldest boy, at age fifteen, and the other hearing member of the family, joined them. Theodosia was almost as gleeful as the children and instantly insisted they stay for supper and the night. While Reason tended the horses, the three of them were practically dragged inside the snug home.

Art stood in the center of the small parlor and slowly turned a full three-sixty. This was no large home like what Joshua and Patience had, yet it had a warmth and softness to it that told him it was a place of love. All around were touches that spoke to him. Theodosia's knitting lay spread across her rocking chair. She was mending a boy's shirt and a girl's skirt. Dolls sat at a tiny table clearly in the middle of a tea party, several sketches in progress were on the floor, and on the wall were nine lovely silhouettes representing the whole family. Art understood, these were the eighteenth century version of family portraits. It was clear they were well-tended. The simple wicker furniture was a bit beaten and battered. With seven kids, was there any wonder? It was sort of stitched together with whatever was handy. They were also rather dusty and a bit stained. The portraits, on the other hand, were dust-free, clean, and protected from direct sunlight.

Yeah, well taken care of.

"Um, Hannah, is your father not at home?" Art said.

The girl got kind of a sour expression about her, at least that's how it appeared to him. He wasn't good at reading her.

"Father left last year to fight in the militia," she said, her voice cracking with sadness. "We've not heard from him since."

"I see," he said slowly. "Well, I'm sure…I mean, I hope he'll come home safe and sound someday."

He corrected himself as he didn't want to sound too optimistic to the girl. Given the uncertainty of their lives, he knew it was best to be cautious in his words. Hazel chatted with Theodosia and the children, and they all marched into the kitchen to get ready to eat. Given the size of the family, a sizeable meal was already in the works, and thus three more didn't matter. Art tried to help, but he was pretty inept when it came to figuring out some things, and in addition Theo, as she told him to call her, told the children to take care of the guests. He and Hazel exchanged smirks at Faith's reaction to being waited on. The girl glowed as if she'd gotten a private performance by whatever boy band was popular with the girls back home. Art had also never seen a meal prepared and served in silence. It was like some sort of ballet. The children moved about the room and put plates and silverware on the table. They served food and poured tea, all without a word. They seemed to know each other's moves so perfectly they knew where to step, how to move, and when to shift so as to never bump into each other.

Once everyone was seated and the main course, a brace of roasted heath hens, was on the table, Theo gestured to Art to say grace. He was a bit surprised, as most of the family wouldn't hear it, but he realized she was honoring him as both a guest and the temporary head of the house. So, he did, and the one difference being he noticed no one bowed their heads.

"For everything on this table, and everyone gathered around this table, we give thanks."

Hannah and Reason signed his words to everyone else, and they started eating. The meal was fascinating. Watching people eat and carry on conversations, while they chewed was something Art had never seen before. As the meal continued, he picked up the gestures, and by the time the children went off to bed, he was pretty good at it. He and Theo teamed up to play bridge with Hazel and Faith, and they spoke in virtual silence.

"How is the farm, Theo?" Hazel said.

"It goes…well," she replied, her hands moving slowly.

"Theo, there is no need to be brave or reluctant to speak freely," Hazel said. "We all know the war has led to difficulties, and you are working the farm alone. Now, are you and the children all right? Do you need anything?"

"You are quite perceptive, cousin, but it is nothing. I need only gird my loins and work harder, and all will be well. The corn crop should be fine this year."

"I heard my father complaining to his friends it wasn't the size of the harvest that worried him, it was that the rebellion would keep it from getting to market. Surely you have the same problem, Cousin."

Theo fell silent, *truly* silent, her eyes downcast and misty.

Art reached across the table to tap her arm to get her attention. "Cousin, if you are in need, say so, and we will help you. We have money and could gi—ah, wait, I know, we will buy your entire crop and put it together with our own, and sell it or use it for our own needs."

Theo positively shuddered so hard she almost shook herself out of her chair. The tears trickled down her cheeks and she spoke so fast Art barely caught any of it, but Hazel filled in the blanks.

"She's overjoyed, but she can't accept."

"What? Why not?" he snapped.

Of course, as that was spoken, she didn't hear his harsh words, but she did reply.

"Arthur, I have fifty acres of corn."

"Oh my," Faith squeaked.

Art turned to her. "What's wrong?"

"Uncle, our yield is typically one hundred and sixty bushels of corn per acre. Fifty acres will produce eight hundred bushels, and those will sell for about five shillings a bushel."

He did the math. At twenty shillings per pound that was two hundred pounds!

"Oh, I see what you mean, that's more money than we have. Then let us lend you a few pounds to help you."

"No, Arthur, that is unnecessary. We have all we need to survive the winter, but..." She paused, her hands dropping to her side for a moment. "What we chiefly need is help around the farm. I've been working with Mr. Tilton and Mr. Skiffe, our closest neighbors, and we've helped each other, but it's not enough."

Art cast his eyes at Hazel, who nodded, and he turned back to Theo. "While it is a bit of a trip, we will do all we can. Perhaps we can manage a day or two a week."

Theo let out a series of squeaks and blinked fast. "Arthur, Hazel, you have no idea what this will mean to us, and we will repay you in kind. Patience told us how Joshua will not allow Jacob and Thaddeus to help you. I and the children know the value of family, and we know devotion to family. From this day forward, we will come and work your farm one day a week."

Arthur tried to refuse, but Theo would hear nothing of it, so he let it go. Frankly, he was a little surprised at himself. He'd allowed himself to get caught up in the moment and spoken without thinking. Yet, he could understand why. Theo and the children were so nice, the house a true home, and he found himself wanting to help them with all his heart. He thought about the future, the massacre to come, and wondered if there was some way he could help them. It was something for him to work on. Later, settling down to sleep in the main bedroom, also at her insistence, he and Hazel discussed this new wrinkle to their lives.

"Seems we're getting a whole collection of farmhands," she said with a grin. "I look forward to coming out here as often as we can. I love immersing myself in this wonderful subculture."

He smiled and hugged her. "I thought you'd see that as a bonus to the bargain. Honestly, I figured some money would do the trick. I had no idea we'd get caught up in a quid pro quo arrangement. However, you don't object to making the trip?"

"Not a bit," she replied, and kissed him on the end of the nose. "Good night, man of mine. This has been a great day in this weird world of ours."

He chuckled, kissed her back, and they settled down to sleep.

Ten

Come the morning, they were up with the dawn, which they were now used to. Truth be told, Hazel did better at it than him. She was a morning person, up with the sun and ready to hit the ground running. Art, he was the polar opposite. Back in the real world, midnight was when he was just getting started. The irony of that was never lost on him. Here he was, mister night owl, and he lived on an island where they essentially rolled up the sidewalks at sunset.

Standing next to the bed in her shorts and T-shirts, she did her yoga stretches. The woman could contort herself into the proverbial human pretzel. He hoisted himself up off his back and sort of leaned forward, supported by his elbows, and smiled. Her taught and trim body looked *quite* good. Keeping her legs straight, she bent over so far it almost appeared her head would touch the floor. Instead, it emerged between her ankles and frowned at him. At least that's how it seemed, what with her face being upside down. He squirmed. Her shorts rode *way* up and were quite cheeky.

He liked it.

"Good morning, sleepyhead," she said in a bright and happy tone. "Nice to have you back among the living."

Straightening up, she spun to face him and grabbed his hand.

"No, five more minutes," he whined.

"Lazy man of mine, there's no sleeping in around here. Come on, up and at 'em, rise and shine, and all the other standard clichés."

He groaned but climbed out of bed. "Yes, m'lady."

Like her, he was in his regular clothes, which he'd modified to be more comfortable and serve as night wear. He'd snipped his shirt into a tank top and his trousers into shorts. Once they were both properly dressed, they headed down the narrow and winding back staircase and came out in the kitchen, which was a hotbed of activity. They were the last to rise. While they weren't able to help with the meal or clean up afterward, both of them made it clear they'd help with chores before setting off, no matter how much Theo refused. It was rather comical.

He stood by the back door, arms crossed, and eyes closed. "I'm not listening, Theo. We're helping with at least something and that's final."

"Mother says, 'All right', Uncle," Hannah said.

He opened his eyes to find a somewhat grumpy lady before him, but the slight smile told him she wasn't truly upset. Everyone headed outside. Theo and the children set to work. It was clear they had a routine established. Hazel and Faith helped pull weeds, while Art went with Reason to fill the cistern. Art was impressed. The boy was thin and wiry, but no weakling. As they carried the buckets from the stream to the house, he saw some of the children talking among themselves. They were watching Hazel work and were amazed one so scrawny could be so strong. She bent over, heaved at a stubborn root, and managed to tear it free by herself. He laughed thinking about this era's concept of what was a healthy woman.

Theo was most insistent they not do too much. Art figured she was worried Hazel would injure herself, and so they departed by mid-morning. She also forced wine, fresh greens, and half a dozen heath hens on them, still alive, but caged. He didn't need a lecture from Hazel to know social etiquette required them to graciously accept. After that, they set off for Aquinnah, which confused Art. He couldn't wrap his head around that name. To him, it was and always would be Gay Head.

The trip was brief, by the standards of the day. The road curved below where Menemsha would one day be and went up and down the hills of Up Island, which was what gave it the name. It was a wild untamed area, the road so narrow the spinning wheels trimmed the occasional grape vine with their spokes. There were no signs of homes or buildings until they emerged from the dense vegetation to reach the actual village.

"Wow, it's like we're out in the plains of the west or something," Hazel said.

"The west what, Auntie?"

"Um, western England," she replied, turning to face Faith. "Child, are you cold? I've never seen you shiver so."

"No, I'm fine. It's merely…um, the…savages. Are you sure we'll be safe? Obadiah told me they *eat* white people and sometimes take young girls as…concubines."

Hazel's jaw twitched. "Oh, did he now? Faith, you have nothing to fear. The natives are friendly, peaceful, and live in harmony with nature. Although… I must say, I'm a little surprised to see no trees around here. What would my professor back home say?"

"Perhaps it's a lesson about not making hasty generalizations about people," Art suggested.

"I guess so. It's a bit like Easter Island. My tutor did say the culture there collapsed due to overpopulation and deforestation. It seems human nature sometimes wins out over how we'd like things to turn out."

"Easter Island?" Faith said. "Where's that?"

Hazel's face went blank, and she turned to face Art. She cringed, and it was obvious she didn't know what to say. Art's mind raced as he tried to think, to remember what year the island was discovered. Other than the day, which was kind of a given, the first Europeans landed on it on Easter Sunday, he wasn't sure.

It was either the early seventeen hundreds or early eighteen. Oh well, let's hope Faith doesn't make an issue of it. "Um, it's a small island in the South Pacific. I attended a lecture at the…Royal Academy and learned of it. I told Hazel about it."

"And then I asked my tutor about it. Enough prattling about far off places," Hazel said. "Let us learn about this wondrous community."

She practically jumped from the seat, and he piled out after her. Turning, he saw Faith sort of cower in the backseat. She was clearly unsure what to do. While the carriage offered a degree of safety, staying there alone didn't inspire confidence, and so she joined them. He found it difficult not to burst out laughing. Faith sandwiched herself between the two of them. Her iron grip on his right arm and Hazel's left meant neither of them could anywhere. Her heart pounded against his arm.

"Faith, calm yourself," he said. "There's nothing to fear."

"Y-y-yes, Uncle," she gasped out on a breath.

Her hold on them didn't diminish as they strolled about. The place and people were not the stereotype natives and their village. It was a small community, a few simple buildings clustered around a well, and snug little cottages dotted the landscape. One virtue of a treeless terrain was the ability to see for miles in all directions.

He searched his memory. If he recalled correctly, there weren't many Wampanoag on the island at this time, less than two hundred. Casting his gaze around, he could believe it, there was little activity in the area. What people they saw were dressed in the manner of the day and smiled as they went about their lives. A carpenter worked on furniture in the large open doorway of his shop, a blacksmith pounded hot metal on an anvil, the stench of burning wood and hot metal made their eyes water, and several potters spun clay on wheels. Next to them was a kiln, a fire smoldering under it, and Art's skin grew hot as they walked by it. He smiled to see artisans use what he in his time called 'Indian Paint Pots' to hold the pigments they used to decorate the clay. The memory of playing on the stony beach below the cliffs with his siblings and finding the occasional pot burned bright in his mind and warmed his soul.

None of these normal activities did anything to ease Faith's terror.

A man stood tall and regal, his salt and pepper hair cascading down his shoulders. He dressed better than Art had ever seen Joshua or Isaac. He crossed the small open space toward them. It was clear he was a native. His features, the hues to his skin, which was deeply lined, spoke to an American heritage without the influences of Europe. Faith almost turned into a block of ice as she dug her nails into their arms. Art winced.

"Good day to you, neighbors," the man said. "I am Ebenezer Smith, Sachem to the Wampanoag of Noepe. Peace to you, and welcome to our village."

"Thank you, neighbor," Art replied.

Introductions followed, and Faith calmed down a bit.

"Ebenezer Smith?" she managed to say.

He nodded. "Yes, little lady. I took that name at my baptism. Most people call me 'Ebbie'. Your name is quite lovely. A lovely name to go with a lovely young woman."

"I-I..." Faith stammered, turning bright red.

Hazel smirked and turned to him. "Why, sir, you are clearly a great leader, as you know the way to win people over."

He bowed to her. "I do my best, good lady. Are you new to Noepe? I thought I knew all the Mayhews here. Oh, forgive me, Martha's Vineyard. I do tend to slip back into our old ways."

"No apologies needed, fine sir," Hazel replied. "I am curious about your culture, history, and ways. Noepe, does it mean anything special in your language?"

"Yes, the 'land amid the streams', which seems quite appropriate," he said.

She nodded and explained about them being new to the island. Art was surprised. Ebbie stood there, took it all in, nodded where appropriate, and continued to engage her directly in conversation. Hazel ate it up. After being slighted by so many people due to the social structure of the era, it was refreshing to be treated as an equal. As they talked, they strolled about the village, met some other members of the tribe, and made their way to an open promontory that overlooked the cliffs. Art found it all fascinating. Never in his life had he seen them so large and sprawling, and so far out into the water. Here at last was something to distract Faith. She loosened her grip and stepped forward, her eyes growing wide in wonder.

"The cliffs, they're...they're made of clay," she said softly and turned to Ebbie. "How is this possible? And the colors, so many different colors, how?"

He chuckled. "Well, little lady, among the tribe is a legend that speaks of one of our gods and explains the cliffs."

"God-*sss*? Gods plural? You believe in multiple gods like the ancient pagans of Greece and Rome?"

"We did, child, before we found the true faith."

"Can you tell us the story?" Hazel said.

She was as curious and excited as a child going to visit Santa.

"Of course. Long ago Moshup was a giant and our protector. He sought to maintain balance to the world, and so he married Granny Squannit, leader of the magical little people. They lived in a den at the base of the cliffs. When he grew hungry, he waded offshore and scooped up a whale in his bare hands."

"A whale?" Faith squeaked. "He must have been a big giant."

"Quite large, child. He would bring it ashore, carve it up, and pull up some trees by their roots so granny could cook it for them. He'd then toss the blubber and bones and ashes on the cliffs."

Hazel slowly nodded. "Ahhh, and that's how they got their colors."

"Yes and why there are no trees here. I remember as a child asking my grandfather about that. After all, if Moshup wanted to maintain balance in the world, he didn't do a good job of it. Grandfather never did have an answer for that."

Art shrugged. "Eh, to err is human, to forgive divine."

"Alexander Pope," Faith and Ebbie said together.

She positively shuddered, the expression of total shock on her face was priceless.

"I…you…how?" she choked out.

"I am quite well-read, young lady," he said his voice steady and even, a broad grin on his face. "As it happens, I have a copy of his *An Essay on Criticism* in my library at home."

"*Library*, you have a…library in your…home?" Faith replied.

"Yes. According to Cicero, if you have a library and a garden, you have all you need."

"You…know about Cicero too?" Her eyes widened.

The two of them fell into talking about literature, poetry, and the history of his people. The grin on Hazel's face was so huge Art thought it might split her face in two. He and she sort of stepped back and walked on, hand in hand, and watched as Faith's horizons truly broadened. The girl's entire demeanor changed. She stood tall, met Ebbie's gaze, and spoke to him as an equal. Strolling around the open square, they met with other members of the tribe, sat outside a small inn to share a meal of cornbread and fish, and talked more.

"I see two more islands nearby," Hazel said. "Can you tell us anything about them?"

"Of course," Ebbie replied with a smile. "To the northwest is Cuttyhunk, to the south is No Man's Land, and both feature quite prominently in other tales of Moshup."

"Oh?" Faith said, sitting up particularly straight in her chair. "Tell us, please!"

"It will be my pleasure. Moshup was a kindly old fellow and a hard worker. Yet, in this legend he was outwitted and his work brought to naught by a crafty old woman."

Hazel grinned. "Oh, I like it already."

Ebbie chuckled. "Then I'm certain you will love the ending. Those on the Vineyard wanted easy access to Cuttyhunk and asked Moshup to build a bridge. Now, the Cuttyhunkers had no desire for such an intrusion and begged him not to. His friends prevailed, but he stipulated he would begin at sunset and stop at the crowing of the cock, whether the bridge was finished or not."

"Ah, a time limit," Hazel said. "I smell the beginnings of a plan. Please continue."

"You are quite correct. The Cuttyhunkers were alarmed and unable to devise any means to stay his hand, but an old woman came forward and said if a watch was kept and she was informed when he drew near, she would stop him. The people thought her crazy. How could a poor, weak woman stop a giant when all the men of Cuttyhunk could not? She persisted, and they agreed. A sharp watch was kept as the sun took its evening dip in the western waters. Soon came rocks in a shower, some as large as their biggest wigwams, and the bridge rapidly grew. Only when it became too dark to see did they remember the woman and ran to her. Going to her coop, she waved a bright light before her cock, causing him to wake with the thought of dawn, and he crowed. Moshup, by the bargain he had made, was compelled to stop his work. Yet, the rocks remained and fell into the waters, and many a good ship has gone to pieces on the Devil's Bridge."

"Devil's?" Faith said. "Should it not be called Moshup's Bridge?"

Ebbie nodded. "Aye, fair lady, but not all of your people are as kindly disposed toward our beliefs as you fine folk. Some consider our ancient gods of sea and land to be demons, and thus they sought to stain their memories by invoking the Devil's name. They did the same with the tale concerning Nantucket."

"Oh, Moshup is connected with that island?" Art said. "I had no idea. Can we hear that one next?"

"Certainly. Moshup was kind-hearted and wise, and those in trouble came to him for advice. A maiden, whose poverty prevented her marriage to her true love, begged his help. The fathers of the two were chiefs of equal rank, but the wealthy father would not permit his son to take a poor girl to wife. Moshup promised to help and commanded the lovers meet him on Sampson's Hill in one week."

"Way out on Chappaquiddick?" Art said. "That was quite the journey, for those days."

"Uncle, you know this Sampson's Hill?" Faith said. "I have never heard of it."

He swallowed hard. "I...ah, I think I saw it on a map of the island the captain of our ship had. Hush now, and let's listen."

"You are quite correct, it was a long trip," Ebbie said. "They all met on the hill, and while discussing the matter, Moshup took out his pipe and smoked. Now you must know the pipe was in proportion to his size, and thus it took many bales of tobacco to fill it, so when he was through and knocked the ashes out into the sea, there rose a tremendous hiss and great clouds of smoke and vapor filled the area with a dense fog."

"Was the couple scared?" Faith said.

"No, but they did not appreciate it, thinking he was a poky old giant and slow to suggest a remedy for their woes. However, there was method in all this on the part of Moshup. They were astonished when, as the fog lifted, they beheld a beautiful island gilded by the rising sun. Nantucket was born to meet the needs of two Vineyard lovers. The cold-hearted parent relented, and the ceremony was performed that very day by Moshup. After celebrating the nuptials in a fitting manner, he sent the pair off to their new home with his blessing, and ever since, Nantucket has been called 'The Devil's Ash Heap'."

"Such a pity to again insult your heritage," Hazel said with a sigh. "So, what of No Man's Land? Is it a convent?"

"Con...vent?" Ebbie said, his large brow wrinkling.

"A dwelling place exclusively for women," Art explained.

Ebbie smiled. "Ah, your fine wife makes a jest, most amusing. There was a time when it was part of the island, but Moshup changed it. The day came when he thought his time as part of the tribe was over. The spirits of sea and land grew dim, crowded out by the one God. Moshup decided to remove his gigantic tribe from the earth. First, he sent his sons and daughters to play on the beach that joined No Man's Land to the island. He then gouged out the sand at each end with his big toe, so deep the sea flowed in and rapidly cut away the sands. Moshup called out to his children and told them to act as though they were going to kill whales, and he used his magic to turn them into killers."

"Killers?" Hazel cried, her eyebrows shooting up.

"It's all right, Auntie, a killer is a type of fish that swims in our waters."

She nodded. "Ah, I see."

Ebbie smiled at Faith. "You are quite right, child. He and Granny Squannit took the trail along the beach toward the rising sun. They passed Molitiah's Ledge, Peaked Rocks, and Black Rock then finally came to Zach's Cliffs, and here they found repose in a beach hummock."

"Did you say hammock?" Hazel said.

"No, hummock, it means a small hill," he replied.

"I see," she said. "Please continue."

"It's there the story ends. They've never been seen since. Although, it is said the smoke of their campfire is sometimes seen by those gifted with great vision, and every now and then Granny appears to certain merry ladies and gentlemen returning late at night from a visit to a sick friend or some other place."

Faith giggled. "Aye, I once heard my brothers say Isaac and Obadiah saw her when coming home from the Public House."

Art rose to his feet. "Thank you, fine sir, for your hospitality and stories, but I see the sun starting its descent toward the horizon, and we have a long journey ahead of us. Hazel, Faith, we should be on our way."

Sadly, they all agreed, and said their goodbyes. As they rode out of town, Faith slid from one side of the backseat to the other, waved to the people, and called out to them. Art chuckled softly at Hazel's expression. He knew what she was thinking. Here was a wisp of a girl who used to shudder at the prospect of raising her voice or meeting a 'savage', and now she was coming into her own. She was becoming a strong and confident woman.

"Auntie, Uncle, did you know the original name for Chilmark was Nashowakemmuck and Holmes Hole was Nobnocket? I had no idea the natives used to live there. Can we go back and visit Ebbie again sometime?"

Art turned to Hazel, the grin on her face was as big as his, and then shifted to face Faith. "I'm sure we can arrange that. Perhaps the next time we come to help Theo with the farm."

The squeal that emanated from Faith's lungs was almost high enough to shatter glass, if there'd been any around. She sat back, smiled, and sighed, a truly contented sigh. He and Hazel fell into casually chatting about the village, the cliffs, and how nice a day it was. Trying to engage Faith in the conversation proved difficult, she was off in her own little world. They made their way along the main road and eventually came to the fork in the road to head to Tisbury.

"Arthur, what are you doing?" Hazel snapped as he made the turn.

He jumped in his seat and reined in the horses. "What, what? This is the road to home. What's wrong?"

She leaned in to whisper. "Arthur, we can't go home without stopping in Edgar Towne to visit the family."

"Really? Even though it's out of our way?" he whispered back.

Hazel turned her head toward Faith slightly, and Art did likewise. The girl was engrossed in a book and not paying attention.

"Of course, it's the social convention of the era. Here we are, going to visit family in Chilmark and even the 'savages' in Gay—ah, Aquinnah, and we don't...ah, what's the term? Oh, break our journey with our closest relatives? When they learn of it, and they will, it'll be seen as a great insult."

"Ohhh," he said slowly, nodding. "Well, in that case, here we go."

He got the horses to change direction, they settled into their seats, and took in the view. Here was another area of the island they hadn't seen, and Art drank it all in. They passed the largest farms and fields. Everywhere he looked golden grains wafted in the corn crops, simple farmhouses stood, and finally, as they entered Edgar Towne proper, the true mansions of the island could be seen. It was a long trip and was late in the afternoon when they arrived. As they entered the center of town and reached the City Hall, Art leaned forward. There was a large crowd gathered there and some activity was taking place at the center, and he got a bad feeling about what he was seeing.

It appeared to be a lynch mob.

Stopping not too close, so as to not scare the people closest to them, he turned to Hazel to ask for her interpretation of the event, but never got the chance. Faith leaned forward, her head popped between them, and she groaned.

"Oh, someone is in trouble," she said, practically recoiling and drawing back. "The council is meting out justice. I wonder what crime has been committed."

"Um, why don't you go find your parents?" he suggested. "We'll secure the horses and wait here for you."

She agreed and bounded from the carriage.

"Hazel, what do you think is up?" he said.

"Well, if it's like she said, someone in town may have been caught breaking the law, which in this era can cover a lot. Any idea what are common crimes now?"

"Let's see…it could be something as simple as swearing, not attending church, a PDA, inappropriate behavior on the Sabbath, and even plain old theft."

"What will they do to the criminal? Do they even have a jail?"

He shook his head. "No, in this era, justice was swift, and punishment was the order of the day, at least for some crimes. For others, it'd be a fine. So, it could be the dunking stool, the whipping post, stocks, and even the pillory. The criminal's social status will also be a factor, and their gender."

She snorted. "Let me guess, men get off easier than women, and the rich get a pass on most things, am I right?"

"Well…yeah."

That was all she needed to hear. She shot from the carriage and weaved her way through the crowd to see what was up. He took flight after her, and both of them tried to learn who had done what. All he heard were things like, "No-good thief," and, "She's like her father." Finally, reaching the center, he stepped up next to Hazel, who was positively shaking. At first he thought maybe she was tired and breathing hard.

She wasn't.

Before them were several people, Isaac Davenport, his wife Bathsheba, their son Obadiah, and a terrified little girl who appeared to be about five or six, wearing a filthy dress. That Obadiah held a small whip, while another man dragged the girl toward a post, giving a strong indication as to what was playing out here. Art checked out Hazel. Her face was red with pure rage, and her eyes spit fire.

"What's going on?" she bellowed.

He cringed. The entire area fell silent. He stole glances around them. Yeah, everyone was shocked a lady should dare raise her voice. He quickly stepped forward.

"What my dear wife meant to ask was, what crime has the little one committed that she should be punished in this manner? She is curious as she's never seen such a thing before."

Isaac snorted. "Oh, has 'm'lady' led a quiet and sheltered life? Has she never suffered loss due to theft?"

"Theft?" Hazel said, stepping out from behind Art. "What, this girl stole something?"

Bathsheba nodded and shook a small dress before her. "Here! This, a new dress for our daughter. Cost me three shillings to have it made in time for her birthday, and now it's ruined!"

"Ruined?" Art said. "It seems fine to me."

She hurled it to the ground. "Fie, this…this…urchin has soiled it. I'll not have my child dishonored by wearing such a thing, and so she must pay. Obadiah, do your duty. Three dozen lashes, one dozen for each shilling. Mr. Melville, secure her, and let this be a lesson to every child of the town."

The young man—Art recognized him as Abe from the whale hunt—hauled the squealing and sobbing girl toward a tall pole. Art's blood practically boiled inside his veins. They were going to lash the poor thing over a dress, and not a nice one at that.

"No, no, I didn't do it, I didn't do it," screeched the girl.

"Stop," growled Hazel. "What is the evidence against her?"

"Evidence?" Isaac replied. "She was found in possession of the dress."

"That doesn't prove she's the one who took it," she snapped.

A general chortle of disbelief rippled through the crowd, and Isaac and Bathsheba laughed.

"Someone stole my precious daughter's lovely new dress merely to gift it to a worthless waif?" she sneered.

Art's eyebrows shot up, and he practically had to catch his jaw to keep it from hitting the ground. Never had he seen Hazel so angry. Actually, never had he seen *anyone* so angry. About the closest he could think of, was Bruce Banner right before he changed into the Hulk.

He angled closer and seized her by the wrist. "Be careful what you say," he whispered. "One wrong word and you'll be in the stocks or pillory, or worse."

"Arthur, some days you win, some you lose. What's important is being able to face yourself in the mirror at the end of the day."

"No, what's important is that girl. Now, going to bed with a clear conscience is fine for you, but will it ease the sting in her back?"

Hazel's jaw muscles clenched. "I hate it when you're right. So, what's your idea?"

"I don't know. I only know we have to do something to let the Davenports save face."

Her gaze darted back and forth, and she smiled. "Got it. Follow my lead," she whispered and spoke up. "Good people, neighbors, friends and relations, lend me your ears. I do not argue for a pardon for this criminal, nor even leniency, merely a just and proper punishment. Let the punishment fit the crime."

He gazed around as a general murmur of approval echoed about him.

"Oh, that's good," someone said. "I'm going to write that one down."

"Fie, what nonsense." Isaac sneered. "Everyone knows it is spare the rod, spoil the child, and this one is most certainly spoiled. This is her third crime in a week. The strap and the rod failed to correct her, so now she shall taste the whip."

Art was momentarily startled. *Geez, what is this kid, a one girl crime wave? Well, wait a minute, what these people consider a serious crime could be quite mild.*

He remembered that in this society an orphan was pretty much on their own. Unless they had a relative willing to take them in, they had to fend for themselves. So, the girl could have done something as simple as steal bread. He suddenly understood where Victor Hugo got his ideas for *Les Miserable.*

"Good governor," Hazel said, sounding sickly sweet. "Just and merciful *Christian* man that you are, it's not your methods I argue with, it's the proportions. Three dozen over a dress? If you punish severely for a small crime, how will you hand out justice for something major? Why, you'll have to hang the chi—criminal."

"Small crime?" Bathsheba screamed, snatching up the dress to shake at Hazel. "You call the ruination of my daughter's new gown small? How dare you insult our honor?"

Hazel took a step back, and Art's body went on high alert. Things seemed to be turning against her. Was he going to have to leap into the fray like Robin Hood saving Maid Marian? He gasped as she plucked the dress from Bathsheba and held it up.

"Clearly I misspoke, 'tis a fine, fine dress. Three shillings you say? Why, I'd pay *five* for it. Let us reason together to resolve this matter. Bathsheba, grand dame of Edgar Towne, I will give five for the garment. Will that not settle the matter?"

Art chewed his lip. Bathsheba seemed pleased, but Isaac and most of the people were silent. An idea came to him, and he stepped up next to Hazel.

"Governor Davenport, this undisciplined urchin disturbs the public peace—give her over to us. Not only will we take her away from these fine and noble people, but she shall feel our *daily* brand of discipline. What could be more just than that?"

Another murmur of approval came from the crowd, yet Isaac still scowled, and Hazel's jaw dropped as her eyes grew large. She stepped as close to him as her dress allowed.

"Arthur, are you out of your mind?" she whispered. "Since when did we become foster parents to some kid?"

"Hazel, she's all alone in the world," he whispered back. "You want to leave her in this town where clearly she has no friends and no one who will defend or help her?"

"How can we be sure the miscreant will get what she deserves?" Isaac snapped. "Arthur, are you up to the task? Lady Hazel, you not only left your *title* in England, but your reputation. Can you control this wayward misfit?"

Art chewed his lip as he saw Hazel bite her nails. It was clear she was unsure how to respond. She also seemed troubled, her expression a mix of pain and deep introspection. He slowly nodded, and fiery pain swelled in his stomach. It had to be his words about taking the girl in. Was she feeling guilty or angry about the idea? Movement on his right caught his eye, and he turned. Faith arrived with her family.

Art grinned and stepped forward. "Here, here is proof of my wife's resolve at ruling her household. Faith, tell them of her strictness."

The girl squirmed at being thrust into the spotlight, but recent events had imbued her with a new strength. She stepped between the two of them, turned, and faced the crowd.

"Aye, aunt—ah Lady Hazel has set before me the more stringent of rules."

"Faith, what have you done?" Joshua snapped.

"Nothing, Father, upon my honor, but she has commanded I never set foot in their bedroom. Should I do so they will…they will…send me home!"

The collective gasp that reverberated around them was so strong the sound waves almost tickled Art's skin, and the silence that followed practically hurt his ears. It seemed the point had been made. Abe released the child, and she raced to throw her arms around as much of Hazel as she could reach.

She pried the imp's arms from her and held her out toward Faith. "Take charge of the child," she said.

A small smile crossed Art's face. Hazel was *trying* to speak with contempt and aloofness, but he could see softness in her face. Faith took hold of the girl's hand and led her away. Art gave Bathsheba the money, and the crowd dispersed. A quick contract was drawn up. Little Abigail was indentured to Arthur for the next seven years. Once signed and witnessed, Isaac took it to record at City Hall.

Art slowly shook his head as Joshua, and the family walked with them back to the carriage. *A simple contract, and he charges me three shillings for it, the colossal…jerk! I bet Isaac still has the first pound he ever earned. No wonder his family is so rich in the present.*

He tried to put his anger aside and focus on being with the family. Joshua had the single biggest grin Art had ever seen, and he kept winking at him.

"Why, Arthur, you great horny toad, you," he smirked quietly.

"Excuse me?"

"Oh, come, come, there's no need to dissemble, we're both men of the world, and you newly-wed. Ah, it must be delightful to prance through Cupid's Grove on a daily basis, and Hazel has such fine firm love pillows. I understand the need to keep Faith a goodly distance from your wedded bliss. You can always send her to market should you want to get especially frisky."

I…um…well."

He elbowed Art in the ribs. "In fact, that's how we *got* Faith. Patience had *no* patience that day!"

They reached the carriage, and Faith got her and Abigail in the back. Art was still trying to process the mental movie playing inside his brain and desperately searching for the delete button to his memory. Who knew colonial sex-capades could be so embarrassing?

Oh well, could have been worse. At least he didn't say they played schoolmarm and the naughty student. I think I would have passed out at that.

He helped Hazel in and followed then turned to the family. "Well, not the sort of visit we had planned, but I'm happy things turned out all right. We must be going now."

"Nonsense," Joshua replied in a happy booming voice. "Come all this way merely to leave? You will stay for supper, and the night."

"No, husband," Patience grumbled.

All eyes turned to her.

"Patience, what are you saying?" he said, his glee deflating from his body. "Our cousins, Faith, our…position. We cannot—."

"We cannot accommodate them this night," she snapped. "There is not enough food in the house, the linens hang on the line, and I must review the children's lessons. With apologies, cousins, it simply cannot be."

Art stole a sideways glance at Hazel, hoping she had some idea what was going in. It seemed quite the breach of protocol, but he wasn't about to say anything. She seemed as bewildered as the confusion swirling inside him, but quickly painted a smile on and turned to the family.

"We understand completely. What woman wants company seeing her home any less than perfect? We have just come from Chilmark where we broke our journey with Theo, and we must hasten home. The Nortons have been tending the place while we were away, and heaven help us for what those boys may have done to it."

The children all giggled.

Joshua nodded. "Aye, they're as troublesome as this one you've acquired. That being the case, perhaps it is best you depart. Good luck to you both, you're going to need it. Faith, you help them tame this wild one."

"Aye, Father, I shall do my best," she called out.

Waves and well wishes followed, and they started for home. It soon became apparent Abigail had not bathed in an over extended period. Never was Art happier to get out to the stretch of road along Sengekontacket Pond as that day. The breeze and open air did wonders for the air quality.

"Please, please don't beat me badly," Abigail begged. "I swear before God I did not steal the dress. The girl gave it to me, said she hated it, and for me to take it and go."

"Did you tell them that?" Hazel said.

"Yes, mistress, but they said it was a lie, and the girl denied it."

"Ohhh, that Mercy Davenport," Faith grumbled. "She's a weasel, she is. Face of an angel, but heart of a demon. How one can be so artful and sly after only eight years upon this earth, I shall never know."

"Artful?" Hazel said.

"The word has a different meaning now—I mean *here*," Art explained.

She nodded. "I see. Huh, so, it seems things never change. The wealthy are seen as good and virtuous, while the poor are bad and deceitful."

"What will become of me? What are you going to do to me?"

Art sniffed. "I think a bath is the first item on the agenda."

"Agreed," Hazel and Faith replied.

"After that," Hazel added, "clothes and a hot meal, and then…let's see. I think perhaps Rebecca will get a new student."

As they rode on, Hazel questioned the poor thing to learn more about her. She didn't even know her own last name! Her mother died birthing her, and her father left to fight in the war, entrusting her and the farm to neighbors. When word came he perished at the Battle of Newtown, their farm was seized for taxes and bought by the Davenports, and she was turned out.

"And you were left with a queer bung?" Faith said.

"Yes, ma'am, they said it all went to the taxes."

"A what?" Hazel said, turning as best she could to face them.

"Oh, apologies, Auntie, it means an empty purse."

Hazel gave a loud harrumph. "Nothing left for her, eh? Faith, you take note of this and learn from it. When those in power abuse that power, the weak and innocent pay the price, unless the people come to their defense."

"What people?"

"All of the people. They are the same all over and are also the true source of power in any community, town, state, and nation. When united, there is nothing they cannot accomplish. See what Washington and his forces are doing in the fight for liberty?"

By the time they arrived home, they'd managed to convince Abigail to call them uncle, auntie and cousin, and she was Abby. While the ladies took her and their things inside, he got a report from the Norton boys on what went while they were away, and they helped with the horses. Phineas and Solomon asked a host of questions about Abigail, and Art told them.

"A little girl like that is a criminal?" Solomon said in surprise.

"Well, she does come from Edgar Towne," Phineas sneered. "You remember what Pa said about that town. The people are all dandy prats and squeeze crabs."

"Phineas, shut your bone box," Solomon snapped. "Mrs. Mayhew's relations live there. Think what she'll *do* to you if she hears you speak so."

They and Art jumped as a scream unlike any he'd ever heard resounded around them. He truly thought someone was skinning a cat alive. Focusing on the noise, he concentrated, and realized it was the wail of a little girl, which meant it was Abby.

"Good Lord, what's going on in the house?" he wondered. "You'd think Hazel was caning her."

"Caning!" Phineas squeaked.

He and Solomon shrank away from the house, pure fear written across their faces as their hands slid back in the classic protective stance.

"Um, will you be needing us further, sir?" Solomon said, trembling.

Art's brow wrinkled. *What in the world has gotten into these two? Geez, you'd have thought they'd have seen a ghost, for real. Ohhh, wait. I get it.* He grinned. They thought Hazel *was* caning the girl. He knew that wasn't the case; Hazel would never do such a thing.

However, he decided to encourage it as it would boost her standing in the community. "No, you best run along. If my wife is at all displeased with how you've tended to the farm, well…who knows what she'll do now that her blood is up."

The boys let out squawks. Their eyebrows shot up into their messy hair, and they turned and ran full tilt away from the farm. Not once did they cast their eyes back. Art couldn't help it. He burst out laughing and went inside to see what all the fuss was about. Following the chorus of wails and howls, he made his way down to the cellar and found Hazel struggling with Abby.

"Goodness, Hazel, to use the vernacular of the era, what ails the child?"

Still wrestling, she shook her head. "I don't know. She saw the tub, and the yelling started. Abby, calm down!"

"No, no, I'll be good, I'll be good," she screeched.

"Auntie, it's the tub," Faith said from behind Art.

He turned and saw her coming down the stairs. "What about it?"

"She…she thinks you're going to drown her. Auntie, on a farm, it's quite common to drown a sickly newborn piglet or weak whelp of a bitch in a horse trough. Abby, that's where we wash ourselves."

"Whelp of a *what?*" Hazel snapped but paused and slowly nodded. "Oh, wait, right, female dog. Abigail *Mayhew*, you will get a bath in that tub. Now, you settle down this instant or I'll…cane you!"

Those words, plus Faith's explanation did the trick. Abby became quite the contrite and docile little girl. Art grinned and stepped back against the wall to let Faith come down and help Hazel.

"Well, I'm sure the child would feel more comfortable with me not around," he said. "I'll go outside and pour some hot water in."

"*Hot* water?" Abby said.

Faith smiled and nodded. "Yes, Uncle Arthur is quite the inventor. He's built us a way to get hot water without building a fire."

"What's…in-vendor? Sounds all hubble-bubble to me."

The ladies giggled. Art sighed and rolled his eyes then made his way outside. Yeah, to her, he probably did sound like a man of confused ideas, if he remembered the meaning of her expression correctly.

Pouring a couple buckets of hot water down the spout, he soon heard laughter and splashing, and knew it was time for him to busy himself with something else for a while.

He decided to get as far from them as possible, so as to not chance embarrassing the poor girl. There was task he'd been thinking about for a while, and he thought now was the time to do it. Climbing the stairs, he went to the front room, got one of the quill pens, and wrote.

Hard to believe I, a man born in the first part of the Twenty-First Century seems destined to fight and maybe die in a terrible battle near the end of the Eighteenth. He put the quill aside and picked up the paper.

Maybe I'm being too morbid and pessimistic. Granted, I don't know all the details of the massacre, but we've got a good chance at surviving.

Crumpling up the paper, he stuck it in the flame of the oil lamp and let it burn. He was careful to stomp out the ashes. Instead, he wrote some notes on the events of their lives, and eventually got the shout from Hazel to come down for supper.

Coming into the kitchen, he found three smiling ladies, and the littlest was freshly washed and in her new dress.

"Well, well, doesn't someone look nice now?" he said with a smile.

Faith turned from the pot she was stirring over the fire to tickle Abby. "Yes, and do you see, Uncle? Now that she's all clean, we can see she's carroty-pated."

He chuckled as she ran her fingers through Abby's straight red hair. She also had milky-white skin and a splash of freckles. While she had no idea as to her last name, it was clear she was probably of Irish extraction.

"That she is," he said, taking a seat across from her.

"And bran-faced," Faith added, playfully tapping at some of her freckles.

Abby giggled and blushed.

Hazel turned to face them. "Is that more Colonial slang?"

Faith nodded. "Aye, Auntie, it means she was christened by a baker. She carries the bran in her face."

They sat down to a pleasant meal. Abby was positively ravenous, and Art wondered when she'd last had a decent meal. Given how pencil-thin her arms and legs were, it had to have been a while.

Huh, so much for the Christian charity of Edgar Towne.

After supper, Abby was like a human Dynamo. She was bound and determined to prove herself a good member of the family. The kitchen was neat and clean in record time, and then everyone went upstairs for games, lessons, and story time. It was clear Abby hadn't received *any* formal schooling, so she would start tomorrow.

"So, Auntie, Uncle that means I will not be going any longer?" Faith said, slumping her shoulders.

"Of course you will," Hazel said. "Why would you stop?"

"Well, two in school, neither your blood offspring, and both girls? What will people say?"

Hazel sat back in her rocking chair. "Perhaps they will say we value education. Now, we will speak no more of this, or you shall earn my wrath."

Abby trembled and meekly nodded. Faith nodded, but Art detected a lack of fear on her part. He grinned. It seemed Faith was learning Hazel was more bark than bite. While it made him happy the girl didn't fear her, he did wonder if it might lead to trouble. After all, it was important she remain obedient.

Perhaps Hazel and I need to talk about this.

The rest of the evening was far more fun. As they played dominos, which helped Abby learn her numbers, Hazel told them a wondrous tale of the *Lorax*, a creature devoted to protecting the environment. Art found it hard not to explode with laughter, yet, as she spoke, an idea came to him.

There was the issue of getting a message to his family and being certain only they understood it. What if he used pictograms, like illustrations from a book? Carved images only they knew and would spell out a message, a guide to find what he'd left behind. He made a mental note to discuss it with Hazel at some point in the near future.

Eleven

Over the next several weeks, as July turned into August, their lives fell into something of a routine. Hazel couldn't bring herself to call it a regular or normal routine, since nothing about their lives was anything approaching that. She did laundry in secret to wash out their things and hang them in their room to dry, they all worked together on the farm, the Norton boys helped too and were exceptionally well behaved, and Theo and her children came over to help as well. Arthur made sure they went to help them more than they did, and on every visit to their farm, they also went out to Aquinnah to see Ebbie and his people. It was a wonderful learning experience for Faith, and Hazel saw to it Abby went to school. Hazel also spoke to Rebecca about teaching the children sign language, and she was all for it. Given Hazel's knowledge, she volunteered to help teach it. The children enjoyed it almost as much as story time.

She tried hard to be a good and dutiful colonial wife, but she didn't have it in her. She had a tendency to speak her mind, but she didn't have a clue how to do any of the usual household chores. Baking bread was like splitting atoms for her, so forget about cooking an entire meal. She burned her fingers repeatedly when Faith showed her how to make candles, the chickens routinely escaped the coop when she fed them and gathered eggs, and she most definitely could not bring herself to kill a chicken, heath hen, or any other animal to prepare them for a meal. As far as she was concerned, the only thing keeping them alive was Faith.

There was also Abby. As bad as Hazel's household skills were, her maternal talents were ten times worse. Faith was not only self-sufficient, she was a downright expert at living in this world. Abby was another matter. While she'd lived on her own for some time, she had no clue as to proper living, and Hazel wasn't much help. She didn't know about eating right, bedtime for little kids, or anything else a mother of that era should know. Although, come to think of it, she would probably be a pretty poor mom back in the present. Once again, Faith came to the rescue. Having helped raise her younger siblings, she guided Hazel in the process. It helped that Abby was mystified and amazed at the washing machine, gristmill and butter churn. As far as she was concerned, Arthur was a magician as great as Merlin, and

Hazel was an angel merely because she showed her simple acts of kindness. It was also clear she bonded to them. She started calling her and Arthur Mamma and Papa.

The one remaining issue was theft. Someone, and Hazel was sure it was the silent boy, kept stealing food and clothes. He was a slippery one who knew the area. They never so much as caught sight of him or heard a sound, and she was sure it wasn't the Picaroons. They wouldn't come by merely to take one blanket and a couple of eggs.

Then, one afternoon, a week into August, Arthur came home from another hunt, and he wasn't alone. Joshua pulled up in his wagon, Arthur next to him, and a big black Labrador sat between them. They exchanged a few words, updated each other on their lives, and Joshua departed. He declined their offer of supper.

Watching him drive off, Hazel rubbed her chin as she chewed her lip. "Huh, does that seem odd to you?"

"What?" Arthur said. "Oh, Joshua not staying? Naw, you know Patience. What's he say about her? She has no patience?"

"Yes, but I find it a bit strange that they haven't come to visit at all in the longest time. I mean, not to be boastful, but Patience did like crowing about us to everyone. Is it me or has she seemed a little… cold of late?"

Arthur cracked a single knuckle. "Come to think of it, she has been a bit…distant. You think something could be up?"

A slight knot formed in her gut. "Well…I don't know. I'm still trying to figure out the colonial America paradigm. Tell you what, next time you go on a hunt, when you get back, see if you can chat Joshua up a bit, get some clue as to if anything's troubling her."

He nodded. "You got it."

"Oh, and Arthur, I've been meaning to tell you something," she said, squirming. "I…I'm sorry for not wanting to take Abby in. I…it's just…I've never been around little kids, so I didn't have a clue about what it would be like having one in my life. On top of that, what with us being strangers here, *true* strangers, I wasn't sure if it was a good idea to bring her into our home."

"And now?"

Lowering her head for a moment, she lifted her gaze to meet his. "Now, I can't imagine life without her. I just wanted to say that, to…to apologize."

He stepped closer and took her hands. "It's all right. To be honest, I kind of blurted it out without thinking. I was trying to find a way to get the poor thing away from that terrible life. I guess…if I had it to do over, I would have talked to you first. I *should* have talked to you first, and I apologize for not doing that."

She smiled. "Thank you for that, Arthur, but it's all right. Sometimes you simply have to dive into a situation and see where it takes you. Oh, hush now, honey, here come the yung'uns."

He turned in time to see Abby dash up to them from the side yard, Faith hot on her heels. Abby hugged and patted the dog over and over, her glee erupting from every fiber of her being

"Abigail, settle down," Faith scolded. "You'll scare the poor thing."

Abby squealed in delight and giggled as the dog licked her face. "He's funny, what's his name?"

"He doesn't have one," Arthur replied. "I was thinking…Sirius."

Hazel snorted, trying hard not to laugh. "A *black* dog named Sirius, I like it."

Faith, her hands full of dried laundry from the line, smiled and nodded. "Oh, that's a good name, Uncle. Let's see, Sirius that's in the constellation Canis Major."

Hazel turned to her. "It seems someone has been paying attention in astronomy. Very well, Sirius it is."

"Perhaps now we can catch our thief," Faith said. "Or at least scare him off."

"Now, now, child, be thoughtful and considerate," Arthur said. "After all, the poor boy is all alone."

"Fie, he has all he needs," she grumbled. "We and the other ladies leave him plenty of food. He has no need to steal. No, he does it because it's as they say, he's evil."

The air shot from Hazel's nose. Faith could be such a good girl, but she could also be far too primitive, which got Hazel's blood pressure to spike once in a while. She turned to her and was surprised to see her cower. Arthur had mentioned Hazel's need to be stricter with her, but she found it difficult.

Well, it seems I can be intimidating when I want to. "Young lady, what have I said about judging others?"

"I…um, sorry, Auntie."

"We will say no more about it. Inside and start supper, now," she snapped.

Faith zipped off, and Abby went to help her, despite not being the one in trouble. Arthur chuckled and turned to her.

"Well, well, seems your reputation is deserved."

Her eyebrows went up. "I have a reputation?"

"Word has gotten around about you punishing Phineas *and* Abby, and that you're a strict woman."

"Really? Considering how common corporal punishment is, I'd have thought I'd be seen as a softy."

"Ah, but you punished a child that wasn't yours, and, according to Phineas, you caned little Abby the moment we got home. The fact she's so well-behaved, despite being a 'hardened criminal', only serves to reinforce that belief among the citizens."

Hazel ground her teeth. "Oh, of course, Abigail is poor, she's a thief, and therefore she can't be a good girl unless she's beaten daily. I've a good mind to give them all a rather huge piece of my mind."

He chuckled and patted Sirius. "You could do it, sweetie. In fact, I'd almost be willing to pay money to see it, but—."

"Yeah, I know, I'd get in royally big trouble. Okay, I will tuck this little issue away in the back of my mind along with everything else," she said with a sigh. "You know, by the time we get home, I'm going to need about five years of therapy to get over all the...*stuff* we've dealt with."

"True, but what a story you'll have to tell," he said with a smile.

She nodded, as she agreed, and they went inside to eat. Arthur told them of his work on the hunt. Once again he'd been in the boat that killed the whale, which meant they'd get a nice share of the profits. That knot in her gut grew bigger, but she said nothing. She'd come to accept that this was part of the world they now lived in, and the knowledge the whale would have died anyway did help her to be at peace with his actions.

The next day, Arthur worked the farm, and Hazel took the girls to school. The students all smiled and greeted her as they filed inside, and she spent the morning helping Abby and the younger children with their reading. When the lessons were done, she knew what was coming, and smiled.

"It's story time, children," Rebecca said. "Let's sing the song Mrs. Mayhew taught you."

They did, most of them horribly off key, but Hazel didn't mind. She found it cute. As Rebecca had once told her, the children were good at a Dutch concert. Hazel didn't know what it meant, so Rebecca explained it was a situation where everyone sang a different tune. When they were done, she took her seat in the center of the room, and they ringed her in.

Abby raised her hand. "Mamma, what's a mango, and are there really fish of gold that nip at our toes?"

"They're called gold fish, and some will do that, but gently. It doesn't hurt. As for mango, it's a fruit from...ah, actually, I don't know, but I hear it's quite tasty."

"Will you tell us another story of Kryten and Lister, and their silly friends?" she asked.

"Oh, I'm tired of those stories," Gregory, a boy said. "Tell us about Sir Luke and the wizard Obi-wan again."

Abby shook her head. "I don't like that one. I had bad dreams about Darth Cheney, he's scary."

"All right, how about something completely different?" Hazel said. "Let me think. Ah, I'll tell you a story about the great wizard The Doctor and his struggle with the Knights of Dalek."

The children were enthralled by the tale, and after school Hazel led the girls home. Passing the fields, they saw Arthur hard at work. She took in a deep cleansing breath as they headed for the house. He looked *quite* nice stripped to the waist. His rippling muscles gleamed with sweat. She tore her gaze away, trying to put certain thoughts out of her mind, and kept walking. Her brow wrinkled, something was amiss.

Sirius was nowhere to be seen.

Has he run away? We only just got him, so I guess that could happen. I hope not. Abby already loves him dearly.

Nearing the house, a black mass next to the barn caught her attention out of the corner of her eye, and she turned. Her jaw dropped. It was Sirius. He wasn't moving. A host of terrible ideas tore through her mind as she considered several reasons for his untimely death.

"Auntie, what is it?" Faith said.

She took a step toward the poor animal but froze. *Damn, wait a minute, I should get the girls inside. They don't need to see this. Whoa, what the ...?*

Sirius lifted his head and gazed at them. Hazel gasped. A filthy little hermit-like ragamuffin was asleep *under* the dog.

Hazel bent down close to the girls and whispered, "Girls, I think we've found the Silent One. Do you see? He's right there. Now, here's what we're going to do."

She sent Abby inside to get a blanket, Faith around to the back of the barn to cut off his escape that way and to make a big noise once Hazel gave the signal, and she moved to the front of the barn, but out of sight. She looked through the barn to the small window in the back, she saw Faith come into view. Hazel signaled. Faith kicked the side of the building and shouted. Sirius yipped. Clearly the boy had pushed him off, and a moment later the dog raced out and the boy came after him. Hazel pounced.

"Got ya," she cried.

"Hey!" the little guy cried.

He wiggled and squirmed in her grip. The layers of dirt and grime made him rather slippery, and his aroma was enough to bring tears to her eyes. Faith raced to help, and Abby bounded out the door and leapt from the porch, blanket in hand.

"Settle down," Hazel said. "We wo—will not hurt you. We want to help. Girls, get that blanket on him, it's like wrestling an eel!"

It took all three of them, but they managed to pin him and wrap the blanket tight about him. Hazel sat up and held him in her arms. He struggled a bit for a few minutes but seemed to like the feel of the blanket. She rocked and sang to him in a low voice, and the girls knelt in front of him.

"What's your name?" Abby said.

The boy grunted and kept his gaze away from theirs. Sirius ambled over and licked his face. He giggled.

"Good, Sirius," Hazel said.

"Good, Sirius," the boy said.

Faith gasped, stepped back, and fell to her knees. "Dear God, it's a miracle."

"No, Faith, it's knowledge and understanding," Hazel said. She shifted him away from the girls so he couldn't see them, hugged him tighter, and whispered. "It's all right, little fellow, we will not shout or be loud, or make you look at us, and you can be with Sirius all you want. Now calm down, calm, calm."

He did. Sirius seemed to sense the boy needed him and lay down next to him. The boy became still, his breathing eased, and he smiled. He nuzzled Sirius, rubbed his cheek against the dog's back.

"Mamma, is he some kind of wild animal?" Abby said.

"No, pumpkin, he's a lost boy," Hazel said, keeping her voice low. "I think he has… troubles. Speak softly around him and don't look him in the eye. It upsets him. Child, do you have a name?"

"Auntie, he was born in the wild. He cannot—"

"Saul," he said, barely above a whisper.

Faith gasped again and almost fell over. "He has a name!"

Hazel practically growled at her. "Faith, what did I say? Quiet, speak softly. You disobey me again, and I *will* cane you, do you understand?"

"Yes, ma'am, I'm sorry," she squeaked.

Hazel smiled. "Now, lit—I mean, Saul, will you come with us, behave, and let us help you?"

"Ca-can I keep Sirius close?"

"You can keep him right at your side all you want," she said softly as she gently rubbed his head.

He nodded. Hazel began to unwrap the blanket, while Saul pulled his arms out to hug Sirius, but kept the blanket around him, which only confirmed what Hazel thought.

I bet he's autistic, but in this era, they don't know anything about the disorder. Damn, wish I knew more about it. Oh well, here's yet another thing we're just going to have to work out somehow.

"All right, first thing you're getting is a bath," she said. "Faith, get the hot water. Abby, let's see…we don't have any clothes for him."

"I'll run to the Nortons and ask them for some of the boys' clothes," she suggested.

"Why, Abby, what a wonderful idea," Hazel said. "Good girl, good idea! Yes, you go do that. Oh, Faith, after the water, get some food ready. I would imagine Saul hasn't eaten a decent meal in a while."

She nodded and headed for the back of the house. Abby glowed with delight at being praised and raced off. Hazel helped Saul to his feet, and they walked into the house. Sirius stayed right at his side the whole way. She had dozens of questions but decided not to press the boy. The fact he was cooperating with them was a huge step forward. Moving through the house, they went down to the cellar, Sirius still with them, and Saul nearly exploded with glee at the sight of everything he saw. The water flowing down the spout, it trickling around the cooler, and the water wheel turning mesmerized him. She was easily able to get him undressed and in the tub, and started the scrubbing, and did she ever have to scrub!

The amount of pure filth and soil that was literally caked and glued to his body was nothing short of amazing. Hazel was sure he lost about five pounds over the course of the bath, and his hair went from black to a sort of honey-blond. Sirius stood on his hind legs and sniffed at him. Eventually he climbed in with Saul, who squealed in delight and splashed about with the dog. Hazel pretty much got drenched.

Her first instinct was one of total revulsion. Back home, she had no nieces or nephews, she'd never babysat, and so she had no experience with small children. In fact, sitting there washing Saul's hair, she acknowledged she hadn't much cared for children at all. She sat back as he used a pitcher to rinse off, and she chewed her lip.

Huh, how about that? I'm becoming...maternal, taking in another stray. Damn, what's next? I'll want to have a baby? Ha, not here, not now. Down, girl, get your estrogen under control. Although, there is something Arthur and I can do.

Water struck her in the face.

"Hey! Why, you little dickens, you settle down," she scolded, softening her words with a smile.

"Water feels nice, I like water, feels good, want you to feel good. What's your name?"

She smiled and patted his head. "I'm Hazel, you can call me...um, let's see...Auntie. You can call me Auntie. Do you remember your mother and father? Do you know how old you are?"

"Momma and Pop gone," he said, keeping his eyes down. "They asleep, fell asleep, and not wake up. They home, still home. My ears hurt from bad noise, and I go down stairs, find them sleeping. They gave me this."

He held out a small silver pendant hanging around his neck on a long chain. Hazel squinted and checked it out. It was heart-shaped and had the golden profile of a woman in its center.

"Is this your momma?"

"Ah-huh. She said it way to find them, I able to know who my momma."

She sat back. *I've heard of primitive cultures doing things like that. Poor parents unable to care for a child give it up but put a ring or necklace or something on them as a way of identifying them later.* "What was the bad noise you heard?"

"Not know, don't know, it hurt, hurt so much, not want to hear again."

"Can you remember when they...fell asleep?"

"I...saw the summer solstice six times since then."

"You...know what the solstice is?"

He nodded, reached for another pitcher of water then poured it over his head. "Oh, feels so nice, so nice. Saw sparkly lights on longest day, heard Arthur talk to Solomon in field, said longest called solstice. Six, I've seen it six times."

"Ah...huh," Hazel said, biting her nail hard. *Damn, this kid is smart. Yeah, definitely autism. He remembers seeing it six times. So, that probably makes him nine or ten. Yeah, I'd say that's about right. Wait, sparkly lights?* "Um, Saul, what are the lights you spoke of?"

"Clear stones, they sparkle, sparkle when sun hits them, hit just right, sparkle a lot."

Hazel's toes wiggled, and her throat tightened. "Saul, dear boy, could you show Auntie these stones?"

Little footsteps on the stairs told her Abby was back. She bounded down the steps, took them two at a time, and Saul shrieked and clamped his hands around his head.

"Mamma, I got some nice things for Saul," she squealed.

"Abby, quiet and stop stomping about, it hurts his ears," Hazel snapped.

She froze at the bottom step. "I sorry."

Hazel gave her a warm smile. "It's all right, pumpkin, you forgot. Put them down there and go help Faith. We'll be up in a few minutes."

She nodded, smiled, and tip-toed up the stairs. Hazel turned to Saul. A lump formed in her throat, and her eyes grew watery. Sirius sat close to him and rested his head on his shoulder. Saul slowly lowered his hands to hug him. Hazel was amazed at the devotion Sirius showed. He sat there, let Saul dump water over both of them, and never flinched. As much as Saul loved pouring water over his head, the bath had to end. She drained the tub, got him dry, then dressed in clean clothes. His old rags weren't worth even bothering with. Then it was upstairs to sit and eat, and Saul was ravenous. He probably hadn't eaten a proper meal in months.

Hazel made a point of sitting right next to him, as he liked being close to people, but she kept her eyes straight ahead while they talked. It not only made her happy to get him to speak, but she was also overjoyed to see Abby and Faith pick up on that. They didn't meet his gaze, and they spoke softly. Based on what he told them, it seemed his parents had a farm further inland, on the other side of the cemetery, and they had probably been trying to cultivate grapes for wine. Saul's description of their fields sounded a lot like a vineyard. They'd died six years ago, and he'd wandered off to find help, but he hadn't been able to talk to anyone because they stared at him and made too much noise, so he hid among the tombs of the cemetery and had been there ever since. Arthur stomped in a moment later. Saul squirmed and shrank down next to Hazel.

"Well, well, well, and who have we here?" he said. "This our little thief?"

"Papa, shhh," Abby said. "Loudness hurts his ears."

"Oh, sorry," he whispered.

"Honey, sit, eat, and let us tell you his story," Hazel said.

He did so, taking a seat across the table from her and Saul, and she told Arthur all about him. She also noticed Saul refused to look at Arthur and wouldn't respond to him in any way. Here was yet another element to his autism. Anything Arthur wanted to ask him had to be relayed through Hazel or one of the girls.

"So, you've been alone and hungry ever since they di—went to sleep?" Hazel said.

He nodded. "Alone, but not hungry very often, not very. Find baskets, don't like baskets, feel rough, but like food, good food except when snow on the ground, not much food then. Liked it when you moved in, had people to watch, took things because I wanted to come see you. I sorry I take, you beat me?"

"That will not be necessary," she said. "If you work the farm with us, help out, and from now on do as you're told, you can stay and be part of our family."

"I do, I work, behave, do what you say, what you say. Want family, want to be part of family, miss family."

Her heart twisted like a pretzel. She'd spoken without thinking, but she didn't care. Now they were taking in yet another child, and she hadn't discussed it with Arthur first. Yet, she knew him, he was responsible and helpful, mister big hearted good guy, which was why her heart was growing closer to his. She'd agreed in an instant to take in the boy. Why was she so willing to do it? Well, it seemed those damn maternal feelings were getting in the way of her rational mind. The question facing her was where were those emotions going to take her?

"Why didn't you ever talk to us?" Faith said. "Or anyone else? We would have helped you. Everyone thought you were…afflicted or cursed. All you had to do was tell us what was wrong."

He lowered his head and squeezed Hazel. "I…I afraid."

"Afraid of what?" Faith said.

"I don't know, and so I was doubly afraid to speak because I couldn't explain why I wouldn't speak, couldn't speak."

Hazel sighed and hugged him back. "Quite the quandary. Well, maybe we can help you to learn to not be afraid, and in time you can go to school."

"Oh, I go, I follow you, go to school, stay outside and listen, and I learn. Like stories, like wizards and dragons, and land of music. Music is nice, like music, you tell story again? Tell about Pepperland and apple boppers?"

Hazel laughed. "Yes, I'll tell more stories. Huh, so, it seems I was right when I thought someone was watching us at school. It was you. When you're ready, we'll take you *inside* the school, but that's for the future. Right now, can you help us clean up from supper? After that, we'll do numbers and story time."

Saul bounced in his chair. "Yes, I help, I wash. Can I wash? Like to wash. Like water."

Faith and Abby giggled.

Arthur grinned. "It seems we have ourselves a dishwasher, girls. All right then, let's get to work cleaning up."

They did. Saul was almost as fast and hard a worker as Abby. He loved to scrub the plates and dishes, and he put his arms into the washtub as far as possible, up above his elbows, and scrubbed as hard as he could. After that, they all went upstairs for math lessons, games, and stories. Here again, it was clear Saul was quite bright. He was able to do huge sums in his head, and he listened in rapt attention as Hazel told another story. He lay on the floor with Sirius, the two practically wrapped around each other, and then it was time for bed. Abby and Faith shared the room right next to the kitchen, so they set up Saul in the room behind theirs. Saul was mystified by the bed, but liked how soft it was, and loved it when Hazel tucked him in nice and tight under the covers. That Sirius flopped on top of him was icing on the cake. Blowing out the oil lamp, she left the door ajar, said good night to the girls, and climbed the stairs to join Arthur in their room. They talked about the new addition to the family and agreed he was probably autistic.

"Do you think we'll be able to help him?" he asked.

She shrugged. "I don't know. I'm no expert, and I take it neither are you, but maybe we can at least help him to fit in better."

He smiled. "Yeah, we can do that. Wow, I wonder what affect this is going to have on the time stream? We do seem to be piling up the changes, don't we?"

"Yeah...um, Arthur, maybe we should talk about that. Aren't we in danger of creating a paradox, maybe even a pair of paradoxes?"

"Oh, I wouldn't worry about it too much. After all, consider what we've done. We've saved a girl from a loveless marriage, taken in two orphans, and got a dog."

"I...guess I'm just...concerned about them. Ah, but, I may have something that can help you and me."

Getting ready for bed, he turned to her, his eyebrows going up. "Oh? Do tell."

She told him Saul had related the story about the crystals at his house sparkling at the solstice.

"You think that could be where the light enters the cavern?" she said.

Arthur cracked his knuckles. "Could be. It's worth checking out. You think he'll be willing to take us there?"

"If I ask him and go along, I think so, but we need to be prepared he might get halfway there and change his mind."

"Why would he...? Oh, thinking of his parents might scare him, right?"

She nodded. "Yeah. So, the important thing is to *not* push him. If he does it, great. If not, we don't yell at him or complain."

"Got it," he said with a smile, rolling back on the bed and smiling. "Man, Hazel, you are something. You rescue orphans, run a house, and now help an autistic kid. Is there anything you can't do?"

"Well...I do have an issue with commitment, but I'm...working on it," she replied, joining him in bed. Cupping his face in her hands, she gently kissed him on the lips. "Arthur, I'm...I'm ready to take our relationship to the next level."

He pulled away from her slightly. "Hazel, are you sure? I don't want you doing something out of...loneliness or a hunger for human contact because I'm essentially the only man available."

"I'm sure. We've settled into quite the life here. I've watched you step up to the plate in working hard in the old fashion male role, and my love for you has grown. If you're willing, I want us to *be* together."

His response was to slip off his nightshirt and embrace her. Hazel shivered. Her body tingled with fire, and she kissed him, long and deep. She wrapped her arms about his solid frame. It seemed a month of working a farm had bulked him up, and she loved the feel of his rippling muscles. His hands played across her flesh, and he helped her to undress. Once their naked bodies were entwined, their passion built to its inevitable fiery conclusion.

~ * ~

Come the dawn, Hazel yawned and stretched, and was a bit more flexible than she had been since their temporal journey. Climbing out of bed, she ambled for the door, and was halfway down the stairs before she realized something, she was naked.

Damn, I forgot!

"Auntie, is that you?" Faith said.

Hazel let out a squeak, went up on her tip-toes, and her hands flew to cover her body. "Um, yes, I...I'll be right down."

Turning, she practically leapt up the stairs. If she touched a single step on her trip back to their room, she would have been quite surprised. Once the door was closed, she got dressed, and headed back downstairs. Arthur followed, and she was happy to see Saul hadn't run off during the night.

"Why, Auntie, you appear...different," Faith said with a smile. "You seem to have a healthy glow about you."

"I...do? Um, must be all your good cooking, sweetie."

Faith let out a soft squeal as she turned away. "Auntie, stop, you'll make me blush."

They all laughed and sat down to breakfast. After eating, they made plans for the day. Faith and Abby went off to school then Hazel and Art set off to find Saul's home. He led the way out behind the barn, beside the crops, and into the woods. Sirius stayed right at his side, Hazel followed close, and Arthur brought up the rear. He hung back so as to not scare Saul. Up the hill they went, passed pear trees, maples, and oaks, and finally the forest opened at the cemetery. Saul took off at full speed, raced among the tombs and headstones. Arthur tried to dash after him, but Hazel grabbed him as he came alongside her.

"No, wait, let him go," she whispered. "Remember, this is home to him, and he's not running away."

She was right. Zipping back and forth among the stones, Saul ran his hands over the rough and moss-covered memorials, and Sirius stayed with him. After a few minutes, Saul threw himself down in the tall grass and rolled around in it. Sirius yipped and bounced along next to him, his tail wagging, and every time Saul's face got close, he gave him a big lick, which got the boy giggling.

Getting to his feet, he walked off, heading southwest, and in a few minutes they came to a deserted vineyard. Grapes grew wild on rotting racks and the area was overgrown. Hazel could just make out the crumbled roof of a small house. He drew in on himself, became smaller, and he slowed in his pace. Sirius raced up to him and whined. Saul patted him and kept walking.

"It seems like he's going to go inside," Hazel said.

"Any idea what we're likely to see in there?"

"Well, six years, I don't expect there to be much left. What sort of wildlife you got on the island? Any large predators?"

"What, you mean like bears or cougars or something? Naw. Skunks and raccoons are about it. Why?"

"Just wondering what sort of critters might have…munched on the dearly departed. Oh, he's stopped on the porch. Come on, let's check on him."

They walked faster but didn't run. She warned it might scare him. Saul sat on the crumbled porch, Sirius at his side, and he picked up a piece of charcoal. He started to sketch something on the wall under a broken windowsill. They stepped up on the cracked and slumping boards and gazed around. The place was dilapidated and overgrown.

"Arthur, why don't you go in and check it out? I'll stay here and watch over our boy."

He nodded. "Good idea."

"Now, be careful. Don't take any unnecessary chances. I just decided I love you, and I would prefer to not lose you so soon."

"I'll keep that in mind," he said, grinning.

He entered the front door, which was so slanted he almost had to bend over to get through. She got an idea. While Arthur investigated and Saul sketched, she checked out the yard. She found the crystals she was after. There was an outcropping of them off to the left and next to the house. Hazel couldn't contain herself; she shook with glee. Brushing the dirt and grass from the highest point, she studied them. She couldn't see much—they seemed thick and cloudy. Saul was engrossed in his art, so she decided to pull one of her modern items out. She reached under her dress to her fanny pack and grabbed her little flashlight. Turning it on, she waved it over the crystals, and a thrust to her soul cut into her. She understood why the crystals sparkled.

"Hazel, you find something?" Arthur called out.

Spinning to face him, she stuffed the light in her pocket. She opened her mouth to reply, but saw Saul drop his charcoal. Arthur's loud voice upset him. She waved him over and waited until he was closer.

"Take a look. These crystals aren't any help to us."

He bent and studied them. "What the…? Wait, is that dirt under them?"

"Yeah, which explains why they sparkle when lit."

"Ahhh, I get it, the light has nowhere to go. It bounces back, and that's what Saul has been seeing."

She nodded. "Yeah. So, you find anything?"

"A few bones in and next to a rotted bed on the ground floor. I didn't dare try the stairs. It doesn't appear as if Saul has been living here, which doesn't make sense. I mean, it *is* his home. Why not stay in his room?"

Hazel chewed her lip. "Huh, maybe it was his parents not waking up. It might have spooked him. I wonder how they both died at the same time."

"I might have a clue about that," he replied. "The body next to the bed was a man's, the clothes made that clear, and his skull has a huge hole in it."

"A…hole?"

"Yeah, and there was also the proverbial and literal 'smoking gun' on the floor, a flintlock pistol."

She gasped. "What? You think it was a murder/suicide?"

He shrugged. "Could be, but he would have had to kill his wife with a knife or something else, unless she died of a disease or something. Remember, Saul said he heard a 'bad noise' and went to check on them. He didn't hear two noises, and his dad was dead by the time he got there. Those old weapons took a while to load."

"Wow. Why would they do that? Maybe guilt over his…affliction?" Hazel said.

"Who can say? Remember, we're dealing with Eighteenth Century mentality here. I think we should walk away and not tell Saul about it. Oh, and there's something else. He may not have been living here, but he's been visiting. The walls are covered in charcoal drawings like what he's doing there."

Her eyebrows went up. "Really? Um, can you watch him for a minute? I'd like to give the place a quick once over."

He agreed. She moved inside to the large parlor that encompassed the entire front of the small house. Slowly turning a full three-sixty, she saw he was right. The walls held a myriad of images, and once more a pang sliced into her heart. They were pictures of a life that might have been—Saul with his parents sharing meals, them playing happily, and his mother reading to him as he sat in bed.

Hazel never thought of herself as a weakling. She wasn't one of those people who cried at the end of *Love Story* or *Terms of Endearment*, or any other sappy 'chick flicks'. No, her kind of role model was Ripley in *Aliens*. Hazel was tough. She stood up for what she believed in, and backing down was not in her lexicon, which was why she was certain a life here would eventually give her an ulcer. However, right now, at this one moment she was a mushy, old sentimental fool like her dad. She wanted to sit down and cry. No, what she wanted to do was hug that little boy and never let go.

She was going to start right now.

Marching to the door, she paused and turned to take one last glance around. "Folks, I don't know what led you to…end things the way you did, but don't worry about Saul. We'll take it from here."

She stepped out on the porch, a new resolve burning in her heart. It didn't matter to her one damn bit if they created a paradox, two of them, or a dozen. In fact, she looked forward to it. Her attitude was, 'Bring it!' If it meant easing the pain of a single child, like Saul and Abby, she'd do it. Hazel had reached a crossroads—a transition in her life—and suddenly it was appropriate she and Arthur made love the night before. It was also most fitting for the decision to occur here. This decaying and crumbling building was the past, Saul's past, and in a sense her past.

She—*they* were leaving it behind, stepping through a doorway, a portal, and moving forward to the future. What did that future hold? She didn't have a clue, and that scared the ever-loving snot out of her. She was a woman who liked—*loved* to be in control. It wasn't that she needed to know the path before her. Arthur was that way. When he traveled, he had a map *and* GPS. For her, staring down a dirt road on a moonless night was the height of excitement, so long as she sat in the driver's seat and had a handle on things. Actually, scared didn't begin to describe the icy tendrils rippling through her. If her throat tightened down any smaller, she'd probably black out. Yet, at that moment, she didn't care. She was going to stand with Arthur, Saul and the girls, and take on whatever came at them head on.

I do believe I've come up with a family crest for us, an ant charging a bull and the words 'Bring it!' emblazoned below it. So, let's find the men folk and get on with our day.

She glanced around. Arthur was headed toward her. She scanned the porch for Saul. His latest work was sketched on the wall under a window, and again her soul surged with maternal bliss. It showed him embracing her, an expression of total delight in his face, and he'd somehow managed to draw a twinkle in his eye. If possible, she'd rip the image from the wall and hang it in their bedroom. She realized something; Saul was nowhere to be seen. Her head whipped around, her eyes desperate to find him, and she gasped.

He was next to a tree full of bees! Every muscle of her body tightened. She opened her mouth to scream out a warning but froze. If she startled him, they might attack. Arthur saw the expression on her face and turned to see what was upsetting her.

"Holy cow, what's he doing? I'm sorry, Hazel, I turned my back for a second to study the crystals, and he must have taken off."

Moving to his side, she grabbed his arm. "Don't do or say anything to upset him."

"Got ya. So, any ideas on how to get him out of there?"

"Working on it."

"Hey, I saw a nature show once where they used smoke to clear a hive. What if I start a fire?"

"Maybe, but we don't want to risk starting a forest fire. Come on, let's see if we can talk him out of there."

Slowly plodding through the tall grass, Hazel tried to figure out what to do. This was a tough situation, and Sirius added to it by staying with Saul. He was oblivious to the danger, standing next to the tree, and watched as the bees buzzed around him. Reaching into a hollow in the tree, he pulled out a gooey hunk of honeycomb and held it over his open mouth. The bees practically swarmed him, and yet he seemed without fear.

"Would you look at that?" Arthur whispered. "He's like a...bee whisperer."

"It's possible he's never been stung, which would explain him being so comfortable around them."

"Auntie, Uncle, see this is where I get sweet things from. Sweet things. You want some sweet things?"

"Maybe another time," Hazel said, keeping her voice soft and steady. "We can come back with a bowl and get some for everyone. Now, it's time to go. Come on, bring Sirius, and we'll go home."

He nodded and put the honeycomb back in the tree. Patting Sirius, he casually strolled over to them, the bees gradually dissipating from his shoulders and head like fog burned away by the morning sun. He stayed close to Hazel, and they headed back to the house, then ate lunch. Afterward, Arthur went out to work the fields with the Norton boys, and Hazel was able to work with Saul. While she was no educator, in this era she was the closest thing to an expert on autism available. So, she was going to take a shot.

First, she got Saul comfortable, which meant letting him decide where and how he sat. It was out under the biggest pear tree next to the barn. He loved hearing the wind rustle through the leaves. Next, she gave him some charcoal from the fire and some sheets of parchment and let him draw anything he wanted. She and Sirius sat next to him, and she read to him from some of Faith's books. For a while that was all she did. Then, once in a while, she asked him a question about what she'd read. At first, it was simple questions to see if he was paying attention, and then she got more creative. Her inquiries required him to put facts together or make a logical deduction or calculate something.

He never stopped drawing, and he got every question right.

Yeah, you the man, Saul. Tomorrow, we'll see about getting you in school.

That night, over supper, Hazel informed the family as to Saul's progress. Abby took it in stride as if it was nothing, but Faith was dumbstruck.

"Auntie, you were able to teach him?"

She nodded, all smiles. "That I did, and from your books. Go on, ask him something. Ask him in Latin if you like. I taught him some."

"What?" She gasped, then calmed down when Saul groaned. "I...um, *quo Vadis*, Saul?"

"*Schola discere potero*," he replied.

Faith almost fell off the bench.

"Cousin, what's wrong?" Abby said. "What did he say?"

"He said he was going to go to school to learn all he could. Auntie, I-I apologize, you are a true miracle worker, and Saul, whatever his...troubles is not cursed or afflicted. He is merely...different. I-I have sinned and sinned again."

"Now, now, Faith," Hazel said, patting her hand. "Don't be so hard on yourself, you didn't know, you only knew what your mother and the other ladies said about him."

"Where was I when my neighbor needed me, but bearing false witness against him, casting him out, ignoring his needs for charity and kindness, and most especially for love!"

Getting up from the table, Faith dashed to her room sobbing. Saul was visibly shaken and worried about her, and Abby tried to console her.

"Cousin, wait," she cried.

Hazel touched Abby's shoulder. "No, let her go. She has some things to figure out. Arthur, why don't you and the little ones clean up? I think it's time for some 'women talk' between me and Faith."

He nodded. She headed for the girls' room and lightly rapped on the door. As Patience would say, she didn't need the gift of second sight to know what Faith was doing. Hazel didn't wait for an invitation to enter and was careful to shut the door behind her. No sense embarrassing her more. Besides, her carrying on would upset Saul. Faith knelt at the foot of the bed, her face in her hands.

"Young lady, are you ready to discu...deal with your actions?"

Sniffling and wiping her face, she nodded and stood. "Yes, ma'am. Are you going to cane me or have Uncle use the strap?"

Hazel sighed and sat on the bed. *What am I going to do? The poor girl is overcome with guilt. Wait a minute, I've got it.* "Faith, I *am* going to discipline you, but not in the manner you expect. Discipline can be to punish, but it can also be to *teach*, and that's what I'm going to do with you."

"To...teach?"

"Exactly. I am giving you the task of teaching Saul all he needs to know, and *not* just book knowledge. Think about it. What's going to happen to him when he grows up? Will he be able to fend for himself? What about a wife? What woman would have him? He's going to have to live on his own, most likely, which means he's going to have to know how to cook and clean and grow his own food and take care of all of his needs. So, *you* will teach him."

"Me?"

Hazel nodded. "Yes. Consider it your act of redemption."

"I…but, I don't know if I can. Auntie, I'm no teacher. I've not mastered household chores or farming or…anything else."

"Oh, pshaw, look at this house, who truly takes care of it? Be honest, Faith, how much do I do around here, how much do I know compared to you when it comes to cooking, gardening, and everything else connected with maintaining a home?"

"But, it's your upbringing, Auntie," she said softly, as if afraid to agree with her.

"True, but my point is still valid, *you* know how to do all these things. Do you know what a master is?"

She shook her head. "No, ma'am."

"Someone who has failed more times than the beginner has even tried."

"Ohhh, that's good," Faith said. "Did someone famous say that?"

Hazel chuckled. "Well, my mother told me that. If you want some famous words, remember also something Michelangelo said, 'The greatest danger for most of us is not that our aim is too high and we miss, but that it is too low and we reach it.' So, I want you to aim high. Work with Saul, and if you find yourself lacking, remember Uncle and I will be here to help."

"Yes, ma'am!" she said, her voice strong.

Hazel smiled. Her words had the desired effect on Faith. The girl stood tall, her shoulders went back, and her head tilted up as if she was gazing off into the future. She drew in a long, slow, deep breath. Faith had a new resolve. An inner strength was building and growing within her, and she now had a purpose that gave her joy and a means of dealing with her guilt.

Hazel slowly nodded. She'd helped the poor girl. Embracing, they walked back out in time to help with the last of the cleanup then it was playtime. They played dominos, which allowed Faith to help Saul with his numbers, and Hazel told another story. When bedtime came, Faith insisted on taking care of the children on her own.

The instant Arthur closed their bedroom door, he spun to face Hazel. "What the heck did you say to her? Faith has become a…Colonial Energizer Bunny!"

Hazel grinned. "Sorry, dude, girl talk. There is a veil of silence that cloaks such conversations from the Y-chromosome."

"Geez, you're worse than the Masons," he said, smirked and gave her a kiss on the cheek. "Eh, who am I to complain? Girl, you did good. It sounds to me that Faith is going to be ok—ah fine."

"It's a good first step for her," she said, getting undressed. "Tomorrow, we see about taking the next one, and that's school for Saul."

She almost laughed when she realized how quickly she and Arthur had become comfortable with each other. They both stood naked next to the bed.

"My, my, Farmer Mayhew, it seems you've become quite buffed in your time here."

He grinned, his eyes playing up and down her curvy frame. "What, you're just now noticing that?"

Reclining on the bed, she struck a seductive pose. "Well, this is the first time I've seen you naked, with the lights on, that is."

"And how do you like...*it*, lights on or lights off?" he replied, his finger swirling around the base of the oil lamp.

"As much as I enjoy *it* with them on, I think you better douse it. I don't know if there's a...morality police in this era, but I'm willing to bet if someone caught sight of either of us in our current state, we'd be in serious trouble."

He laughed, blew out the lamp, then climbed in bed. "You're probably right. Man, talk about repressed. You know, one of these days you could stay home from school, and I could skip a few chores, and we could...you-know in daylight."

She forced a loud, fake gasp as she pulled him closer. "Why, Arthur, you wild man, what's next, whips and chains?"

He laughed so hard his vibrating stomach tickled hers as their bodies blended together.

"Hazel, that's what I truly love about you, you can make me laugh, even when my mind is focused on other...matters."

"Judging by what I'm feeling right now, I'd say your body is focused on those 'matters' as well. Now, shut up and kiss me!"

"Okay, but where?"

"Ooo, you *are* a wild man," she whispered in a husky tone. "Surprise me."

He did, and they again spent a night locked in the fires of total delight.

Twelve

Next morning, Hazel was careful to dress before leaving the room. Over breakfast they discussed school. She was concerned about taking Saul there until she had more time to work with him. Not that she said that as she didn't want to upset him. Instead she spoke of needing to talk to Rebecca about him attending. As Arthur was going on another whale hunt, there was no one to stay with Saul.

"Can't we tell him to stay home?" Faith said.

Arthur cracked his knuckles. "I don't know if it would work. He could promise to do that, be sincere, and then something as simple as buzzing bees could distract him. It's the way his mind works."

The poor girl seemed totally confused. It was clear the concept was quite beyond her. Yet, Hazel could see something else at work—Faith was trying to process a new idea. Even if she failed, Hazel couldn't help but feel proud. Faith was broadening her horizons.

"I have an idea," she said with a smile. "Saul, when you see or hear your auntie or uncle come home, you are to come home too. Do you understand?"

"Yes, I like them, they kind, I even like Uncle."

Arthur grinned and nodded but said nothing. Hazel was proud of him. He knew there were times when it was best not to speak.

"He and I like you too, and so do Abby and Faith," Hazel said. "We don't want to lose you. So, while we're away, please stay as close to the farm as possible. Can you do that?"

He nodded, still staring at his eggs. "Oh yes, yes, I can do that, I like the farm, like walking in the fields. Fields feel good. Sirius, stay with me?"

"Of course," she said. "Can you take care of him, keep him safe, and close by? We don't want to lose him."

"Oh no!" he said, gasping with concern as he turned and gazed at her. "No, not lose Sirius, we can't lose Sirius, he friend, he my friend. Yes, I watch him, I keep him close, keep him here on farm, I promise."

She nodded and shared a knowing expression with Arthur and Faith. They'd done it, they'd hit on the perfect way to keep Saul on the farm and prevent him wandering off. After that, they finished breakfast, and departed to their various destinations. As Hazel led the girls toward the schoolhouse, they waved to Arthur as he headed for the harbor, and she looked one last time to check on Saul. She smiled. He was playing happily with Sirius. Unfortunately, that represented the height of her day. When they got to school, Rebecca made her views on Saul *quite* clear.

"While I applauded your efforts, I have a curriculum to teach, and I can't change it to accommodate one addle-pated boy," she explained. "In addition, there are the parents to consider. They will object to their children being exposed to an unnatural child."

Hazel clenched her teeth, but it sure didn't feel like that. Stars danced before her eyes for a moment, and she was impressed with herself. She managed to rein in her rage with only a count of five.

"Fine, if that's the case, he will not come *inside* the schoolhouse," she said.

~ * ~

The rest of the school day was quiet and uneventful. Hazel then led the girls home. She grinned as they neared the house. Saul was happily bouncing about, flapping his arms as if trying to take flight, and Sirius was right there with him.

Saul ran to meet them. "I watch Sirius, keep him close, keep him home. I do good?"

"You did fine," she said.

"Can we walk now? Want to walk, want to go, go somewhere. We go visit home?"

She chewed on her lip. "Saul, this is your home now, remember?"

He nodded, sort of flapping his arms. "Oh yes, I know, this home *now*. Go see old home, get sweets, I like sweets."

"Ohhh, the honey," she said slowly. "Actually, that's not a bad idea. Girls, Saul has a real talent for getting honey from bees. Come on, we'll get some bowls and collect some. Now, Saul, you will be careful, do you understand?"

"Yes, careful, be careful, not scare bees. We go, go now, yes?"

Faith appeared confused. "Auntie, he can...*talk* to the bees?"

"No, no, sweetie, nothing like that. He merely knows how to act around them so they don't sting him. Come along, and you'll see."

Putting their books and things in the house, the girls got some pots and bowls, and they all hiked back to Saul's house. The girls stood in shock and awe as they watched him casually pluck honeycomb from the tree and bring it to them. They easily filled five large bowls with honey and headed home.

"Mamma, Saul is a magician!" Abby said. "He really *can* talk to animals."

Hazel laughed. "He does seem to be a bit of a Dr. Doolittle, but it's much simpler than that. He doesn't know to be afraid of the bees, and so he doesn't fear them. I think there's a lesson for all of us in that."

"You are wise," Faith said. "Where there is no fear, there is no danger?"

"No, that's not it," Hazel replied. "If you're not afraid of a bear, does that mean it's not a dangerous animal? The lesson is don't fear the unknown."

Faith nodded. "I'll try. Is Dr. Doolittle a physician you knew back home?"

"What? Oh, um, yes, he's an animal doctor, and he has a real rapport with the cows and horses and other animals, so much so that he seems to almost talk to them."

"Could he teach me?" Saul said. "I like to learn, learn more, have school lessons, I learn enough to go to school, yes?"

She nodded. "Of course, when the time is right, you'll go with us. As for the doctor, he's back in England, so you can't learn from him. Faith, would you like to teach Saul today?"

"Yes, Auntie, yes I would, very much," she chirped.

"Then you will. Abby, you and I will put the honey away, take care of the chores, and start supper. Saul, go to your learning spot and wait for Faith. She'll be along as soon as she's ready."

Saul did a little bounce-bounce and raced off, Sirius hot on his heels.

Faith headed for the door to put her bowls away but stopped and turned to Hazel. She had a troubled expression on her face.

"Um, Auntie, I'm concerned about Saul's future. What will happen when he learns he cannot go to school? Miss McCarthy was most emphatic on that point, and you agreed to abide by it."

Hazel grinned and nodded. "So I did. I said Saul would not go *inside* the school, and he will not. However, that doesn't mean he can't sit outside and listen in on the lessons."

Abby and Faith gasped.

"Mamma, that's being artful!"

"Auntie, you are truly skirting the letter of the law. Is that wise? What if she complains? What if the parents object?"

"Then we will deal with the issue when it arises. My hope is that by the time anyone notices him, the children will accept him, and everyone will understand he's just a boy who's a little different."

Faith squirmed. "That's noble, but...well, you may be expecting more of people than they can...deliver."

"Why, Faith, I'm surprised at you, having such a low opinion of your neighbors."

"I'm sorry," she said quickly. "It's merely that I know how stubborn my parents can be, and many adults on the island are like them. Remember my feelings about Saul. Were it not for your efforts, I would still think the same."

"I see your point. Well, if we fail to convince them, so be it. We'll keep him home. However, I intend to try my best."

"So, we're going to be brave?" Faith said with a grin. "We're going to go into a fight knowing we may lose but do it because it's the right thing to do."

Hazel smiled ear to ear and nodded. "Very good, Faith, you're learning. Now, you run along and teach some of what you've learned."

Faith nearly floated into the house. She practically exploded with pure glee, and then she went outside to sit with Saul. He was nestled on the branch of a pear tree, leaning against the trunk, and Faith sat on the grass under the limb. Hazel paused a moment to watch and almost laughed at Faith's expression. She clearly wasn't about to try and climb up there with him. Hazel and Abby went inside, poured the honey into some small jars with lids, so as to keep out the ants and other critters, and they set to work.

By the time supper was well under way, Arthur returned, and Saul and Faith came in to help. While they ate, Saul experienced a true breakthrough and spoke to Arthur. It was minimal, only a few words, but he did it. He was fascinated by Arthur talking about seeing a whale. When he picked up on that, he made a point of not mentioning the killing part.

"Whales big! Whales so big, yes, Uncle, very-very big?" he said, practically breathless.

Arthur smiled. "Yes, Saul, they're big, the largest creatures to live upon the earth."

"More, tell me more," he begged.

He did, and Saul got to the point where he was bouncing in his seat. Quite suddenly, he bolted from the room. Faith rose to chase him, but Hazel grabbed her arm.

"Wait, let him go. Let's see what he's up to."

Before Faith could even reply, he raced back in, paper and markers in hand. His plate and bowl were pushed aside, and he set to work. He was totally focused with no effort on their part. Even Hazel scolding him couldn't get him to reply, and so they finished eating and started to clean up. The sound of water poured into the wash tub got his attention.

"Oh, dishes," he said. "I do, I wash, I want wash, I like to wash!"

Faith giggled. "All right then, get to work, little sir, and then Auntie will tell us another story."

That got him doubly excited, and he started scrubbing. As they cleaned, Hazel stepped over to his sketches, and her jaw dropped. She silently signaled to Arthur, and he moved next to her. Saul had created a breathtaking image of a whale leaping from the water as a tall ship sailed nearby. That he was able to draw something like that from only Arthur's words was nothing short of amazing.

"We need to get him some art supplies," Hazel said in a low voice, so as to only be heard by him.

He nodded. "I agree. I'll pick up some tomorrow."

Their evening was much like the night before, until she and Arthur were alone in bed. He gave her a report on his chat with Joshua after the hunt.

"I tried to be subtle, not confront him about Patience, and sort of…hinted around us coming for a visit. He made excuses that they were busy with the farm. I let it go, and invited them to come for a visit, even stay overnight to enjoy the bounty of our feast."

"Still refused?"

"He begged off, made his apologies, and gave the excuse that he had a business deal to negotiate."

"You didn't buy it?" she said, cocking her head at him.

"Well, you remember when you were able to tell when I was upset? Joshua is the same way when it comes to lying. He doesn't do it well. Something else is up, but I can't tell what, and I decided not to press him on it."

"A wise move. Why bother rock the boat for no reason? Hey, wait a minute, you know what it could be? They might be upset that I'm not pregnant."

"Really, you think that would set them off?"

She nodded. "Could be. Remember the social dynamics of this era and community. Women are baby factories, and both Patience and Joshua are concerned with the Mayhew family's position on the island. Given how hot and bothered the Davenports have become since we arrived, they could see my failure to be with child, as the old saying goes as quite the slight to the family."

"Wow, girl, you're good."

She grinned. "I have my moments. If you want, we could tell them I am, and later say I had a miscarriage. I'm sure that's quite common in these days."

"That's not a bad idea," Art said with a nod, "and it would get them off our backs about cranking out babies. For now, let's not rush into anything, but we'll hold onto it."

"Keep it as an ace in the hole, right?"

"You got it. We'd need to make sure the miscarriage story rang true.

The last thing we'd want is island gossip that you got an abortion."

She sat up in bed, her jaw dropping. "What?" she squeaked, quite loudly, and then cleared her throat and whispered, "I didn't think those were possible now."

"Oh yes, and legal in many colonies. Under English common law, a woman could get an abortion until the quickening, which is when she could feel the baby moving."

"Wow," Hazel said slowly. "I had no idea. How do they do it, do you know?"

"If I remember correctly, the older women in the community would brew certain herbs and plants to create a broth the woman would drink, and it…caused it."

"Amazing. Why would we want to make sure no one thinks I've had one, if it's legal? Wait, I know, social stigma."

Art nodded. "Exactly. We're Mayhews, we're leading citizens in the community, we're supposed to set a good example, and there's the fact that we have no children. How would it appear for us—*you* to have an abortion?"

"Man, I had no idea life in such a simple era could be so complicated."

"I know," he replied, and heaved a sad sigh. "I wish I knew for sure what was up with them. After all, we're family, even if it's not the sort of family they think, and I'd like us to get along and get to spend time together. It…it means a lot to me to have this opportunity to connect with my ancestors."

Reaching out, she caressed his cheek. "I understand, and I wish there was something I could do to help. Maybe…I don't know, give me some time to…analyze the situation, and I'll try to figure it out what's what."

Covering her hand in his, he smiled. "Ah, there's my scientist, ready to study the social structure of a colonial family to determine what makes them tick."

"If it'll help you, my sweet, I'll do all I can," she said, swirling her index finger across his chest. "Now, how about I help you with …stress reduction therapy?"

"After the day I've had, oh yeah," he said, and kissed her, long and deep.

They enjoyed yet another night of intimate delights and fell asleep in each other's arms.

~ * ~

The next day, Art was as good as his word. He went into town and bought canvas and paints, both oils and watercolors for Saul, and his creative side exploded. He painted and sketched for hours, and some of his images were true works of art. Soon every wall of the house was adorned with his efforts, and the family debated what to do about his talent. If they showed the pictures to other people, they'd ask about Saul, and what could they tell them? In addition, there was school.

Saul would sit in a tree outside the building and listen and draw, and sing along during the music lessons, but they were careful to keep him hidden from Rebecca and the other children. Faith worried to death about him being seen, but Hazel came up with a simple answer—they made it a game of hide and seek. Saul was told to hide from the teacher and students, and if he wasn't caught, he got a sweet treat when they got home.

That was all it took to make him the world's best hider.

Faith also taught him everything she learned, and often he would communicate with Art via images. Little by little, as the wheat grew higher and the leaves changed color, Saul was able to speak to Art, Solomon, Phineas, and eventually Mr. Norton. They were fascinated to learn the Silent One was the son of their old neighbor.

"I never really knew the Turners," Ed said, as he and the boys helped Art in the field. "Let me think, they were…ah, Daniel and Chastity Turner, and their dream was to have their own vineyard."

"How long has it been since you saw anything of them?" Art said.

"Oh…must be at least ten years. Wait, as I recall, the last time Daniel came a-calling, Chastity was in the family way. After that, we had a particularly hard winter, and we lost track of them."

"Father, I remember," Solomon said. "In the spring of seventy-four, Phineas and I were playing with our friends out in the woods near the cemetery, and we found the old house."

Ed snapped his fingers. "That's right. You came back and told us about that, and I went to check for myself. The place was in such ruin we thought they'd perished some time before, and so we let it be."

Art was a bit surprised at their attitude. *Man, they made no effort to search for them? I guess they saw the place as a haunted house, and it was best to stay away. Well, at least now we know more about the little guy.*

As All Saints' Day approached, Hazel commented in private how they wouldn't celebrate Halloween, and Art got ready for the harvest. Quite the warm surge coursed through his heart. It wasn't merely the changes they'd made in Faith's life, but it was also Abby and Saul. He couldn't help but think of the life they would have had if he and Hazel hadn't come along. An icy knife thrust plunged deep to his heart. He'd almost forgotten.

Casting his gaze about the room as they sat by the evening fire, he saw happy faces bathed in the crackling light. He felt the warmth wrap about him and knew it wasn't the mere heat of the fire, it was the tender embrace of familial love. A new resolve built within him. He thought about his own family, lost to him or gone too soon because of grief. Outside was the crop of wheat in the field, *his* field, *his* crop, and as the seeds grew to maturity, a strength now germinated in his soul.

I'm going to level with Hazel and tell her everything. We're going to see about saving our family and friends. Tomorrow, when I get back from the hunt, we'll...ah, go for a walk, someplace quiet and private, and I'll tell her everything.

The next morning, after kissing his family goodbye, he headed to the harbor. Art made a point of dressing extra warm. The heavy coat came in handy as an icy blast of wind roared down from the northeast, and the ship rocked and rolled through ten foot swells. Never in his life had he been out in such terrible weather. He shook and shivered. His stomach lurched and burned, and he didn't need a mirror to know he turned several shades of green.

A monstrous shudder cracked from the bowels of the ship, and it settled lower in the water. A wave washed over the deck, Art and the crew members were tossed like seaweed on the shore, as they clung to the rigging.

A man raced up from below. "Sir, three feet in the bilge, and it's rising fast!"

Jonas turned to him. "Lay on the pumps."

"Already done, sir. They cannot keep up."

"Israel, bring us about, make for land," he said, turning to his mate.

"Sir, that means running before the wind," Israel replied.

"We have no choice. We must get to shore before we're scuttled."

Israel struggled with the helm, even as he nodded, the concern clear in his eyes. Art moved to help him. The ship turned until the wind was behind them, and the entire vessel shook and groaned. The sails snapped forward, filled with the maelstrom roaring at their backs, and every mast and spar bent like a bow preparing to fire an arrow. His jaw dropped. Never in his life had he seen such huge thick masts bend so much.

The ship tore through the waves like a bullet and shook as the deck began to warp. The planks creaked, squeaked, and buckled. They popped and snapped, and a most fearsome explosion resounded above them. He looked up in time to see the mizzenmast, the rearmost one, break at its midpoint. The top plunged toward the deck and pulled sails and rigging with it as men screamed and ran. Jonas tried to give orders, but the mainmast broke next, and Art knew there was nothing anyone could do.

"Abandon ship," Jonas shouted.

Art glanced around and saw the whale boats buried in debris. The ship was far from land, which was on the horizon, and appeared painfully small. He clung to the helm. With the deck torn apart there was no way for him to get to one of the boats. Even if he could, was there time to clear it away and get it over the side? He didn't think so. Art was a good swimmer, but not that good, and the water was freezing. His options were minimal.

Hazel, remember me fondly, and take care of the kids. I'm sorry I got you into this mess.

Taking a deep breath, he moved to the railing and jumped. A thousand icy daggers plunged into every corner of his body. The water was bone-chilling. Kicking hard, he burst from the depths, shook and shuddered in frigid pain, and splashed about. A large chunk of the ship floated by, a piece of paneling or some such thing. It didn't matter. It was big, and it was buoyant, which made it important. Swimming hard, he grabbed the flotsam, heaved with all his might, and hoisted himself atop it. As he lay there, his teeth began to chatter, and he tried desperately to rub some warmth into his body with both hands. He looked around. The ship was settling in the water, the massive waves washing over it, and crew and supplies spewed from it as if being vomited in its death throes.

Uh-oh, I'm not headed toward shore. The current is carrying me east toward the Sound.

Forcing himself up on his knees, Art seized a piece of the hull and used it like a paddle. He couldn't fight the current, but he could use it to his advantage. Maybe he could make land on East Chop or, more likely, Naushon Island.

If I end up there, how will I get home? Hold it, one disaster at a time. Let's try to stay alive and get to shore, any shore, and then I'll work of getting back to Hazel.

He kept at it, paddling hard, aiming for East Chop, even as the current had other ideas. It soon became clear he wasn't going to make it back to the island. If he was lucky, he'd land on Naushon or Pasque. After that, well, he was on his own.

~ * ~

Hazel had the oddest feeling. An empty void gnawed at her insides like a pumpkin being hollowed out. Moving about the house, she was on auto-pilot, which wasn't all that safe for her and easily burned her fingers while baking. When she heard a wagon approaching, she dashed outside. She knew Arthur was supposed to be returning, like always, but for some reason she needed to get there to welcome him. Joshua was in the wagon, no one else, and as he drew nearer a tightness squeezed Hazel's chest.

He wore a black armband.

Climbing down, he stood before her, his expression spoke of total sadness and regret, and he moved to embrace her. The tightness in her chest became a blade, and it thrust deep into her heart.

"Hazel, I need to have words with you," he said simply.

A hand reached up from her chest to close about her throat. Hazel had to clear it three times before regaining the ability to speak. "All right, what do you have to…say?"

He took her by the hand. "Not here, dearest. Inside, in private."

"What's happened?"

"Hazel, please," Joshua begged. "Let us go inside."

"Joshua, I already fear the worst. Tell me."

He did. Parts of the *Silvana* had washed ashore, along with bodies and survivors, but Arthur wasn't in either group. Long before he was done, Faith and the children joined them, and Abby wept as Faith worked to comfort her. Saul was like Hazel, frozen in shock.

"Hazel, I will stay with you tonight," Joshua said. "In the morning we will discuss…the future."

"Yes, of course," she said, turning for the front door.

"Mamma, where are you going?" Abby said.

"Hush, child," Joshua said quickly. "Stay here with us. Your…mother has…much to consider."

Hazel was dimly aware of their exchange as she plodded inside. The next thing she knew, she was in the bedroom, *their* bedroom, and she flopped onto the bed. Something was wrong with her, but she didn't know what. Her ribcage was being compressed in a vise, bones broken, flesh torn, organs crushed. Her neck inflated and cinched down, choking off her air, and her brain was shredded. Never in her life had she been so overcome with pain. No, that wasn't the right word. Calling this 'pain' was like calling Stephen King's *It*, a pleasant short story.

What's happening to me? Am I having a stroke or something?

Gulping air, she shook and shuddered, wrapped her arms around herself in a vain attempt at keeping her ribs from erupting from her flesh, and exploded into unending tears. Hazel understood. It was grief, she was feeling true deep grief for the first time in her life. She'd never lost anyone before, not even her parents or grandparents, and thus mind-shattering sadness was something she'd managed to avoid.

Until now.

She remembered the old saying about time flying when you had fun. It seemed the reverse was true. Sitting there, wail upon wail of pain erupted from her lungs, the seconds became hours. Every stab to her soul, every slash into her heart made her cry out, and her mind and spirit crumbled and cracked and bled into each other as each tear dripped from her chin. Her ears brought her an echo effect. It took several minutes, but she got her sobbing under control, and that's when she heard him.

"I sorry, Auntie, I sorry," he squeaked. "Please don't cry."

It was Saul. He was right outside the door, and he was crying too. Hazel got to her feet, took in a deep breath, and slapped herself in the face.

Time to woman up and show some guts.

Opening the door slowly, she peeked out. Saul was curled up in the corner on the left. He saw her and pulled his legs in tighter.

"I sorry, I sorry," he said.

She stepped toward him and got down on one knee. "It's all right, sweetie. You didn't do anything wrong."

"Yes I did, I must have. You sad like my mommy was before she fell asleep. It my fault then, so it my fault now. I sorry, you beat me, can beat me every day for a month."

She pulled him into her arms; her eyes filling with tears again. "No, it's *not* your fault. Uncle Arthur has...he's gone away, but it has nothing to do with you. Come on, let's go be with the family."

Getting to their feet, they joined hands and walked down the stairs to find the girls in the kitchen. Faith still comforted Abby, who softly sobbed, and Joshua was in the backyard chopping wood. Hazel could see him through the window, and she immediately went to Abby to hug her and Faith.

"It's all right to cry, girls, it's part of the grieving process. Just remember, we still have each other, and we'll get through this together."

Faith nodded. "I will do all I can to help. Father said Captain Ahab was among the survivors, although the poor man lost a leg, and he is arranging a memorial ceremony next week here in Cottage City."

"Oh, how good of him," Hazel said, her voice cracking in sadness again. She cleared her throat. "The captain survived? I thought he was supposed to go down with the ship. I...ah, I'll go ask Joshua if there's anything we can do to help and tell him to stop chopping. At this point, I think we've got enough wood to last all winter."

"I don't know about that," Faith replied. "The trees have dropped a lot of acorns, and I've seen the squirrels gathering them early. We will need a couple cords to get through the winter, and the wood will need several months to dry. I will speak to the Norton boys about cutting us some more."

Hazel nodded and headed for the back door. She didn't know about acorns and quarts of wood, or whatever, she was still mostly numb and tried to process what was going on. The cool autumn air was refreshing and helped her to snap out of her depression a little. As she neared Joshua, he stopped swinging the axe and set it aside.

"Hazel, again, my deepest regrets at your loss."

"Thank you. Please, I know the signs of winter are all around us, but you don't have to do this. Come inside. Right now, I want to be with family."

"When bad news comes, I try to stay busy. It's my way of...keeping my mind off things I do not wish to think about," he said, painting on a weak smile. He paused for a moment, scratched the back of his neck, and gazed toward the house. "Hazel, before we go inside, I would speak with you."

"Um, of course, Joshua, speak your mind. What troubles you?"

He turned, moved toward the barn as if trying to get out of earshot of the house. "It's not a trouble, it's…more a…concern about Arthur. From his letters, I gathered he was a good and loyal servant of the crown. It was why we asked him to make the appeal to Parliament. We thought his words would carry much weight with them. However, his words and deeds of late seemed…different. When I would bring him back from the hunts, we talked, and he clearly sympathized with the Colonials. Did he speak to you of his politics?"

"Me? No, of course not," she said, feeling quite an icy chill ripple up her spine. "After all, I'm a woman and a lady, and such things are beyond my…comprehension."

His eyes narrowed. "I…see. I only wondered why he *appeared* to change allegiances and thought perhaps it was all a feint, a ruse to ingratiate himself in with the likes of Isaac and the other…rebels for some reason."

It seemed as though Hazel was a suspect in one of those crime dramas she used to watch, and Joshua was the detective investigating a crime. What was he after? What did he suspect about her and Arthur? He couldn't have figured out they were from the future, yet he knew something was different about Arthur from only his letters.

"Joshua, dear cousin, I can only tell you what I know. Arthur and I deeply loved each other. I was proud to call him my husband, and I shall grieve for him every day."

"Very well, we shall speak no more of it."

They ambled inside, and Hazel tried to put concerns about Joshua out of her mind. At this moment, she had a lot more troubles to fill her time and mind. Sitting down to supper, he took stock of the new addition to the family.

"Strike me down, Hazel, have you taken in another orphan?"

"Yes, Saul's parents lived nearby and perished some time ago, and he has joined us. Please, do not press me for details, not now."

He nodded. "Of course, dear lady, we shall not speak of him until you wish."

Afterward, the evening was low-key, and while Faith assured Hazel she could tend the children, Hazel made a point of helping. She wanted to be there for them. Joshua insisted she sleep in her own bed. She didn't put up much of a fight over the issue. The bed seemed especially large and cold that night.

Lying on her side, gazing out at the star-filled sky, she took stock of her life. She was trapped in the past, in the midst of a war, and she was now a single woman. Trying to navigate this world had been hard enough when she had Arthur to help, but she was on her own now. She wondered about Patience and Joshua. Why was she so cold and distant? What had he meant when he spoke of Arthur? Did Joshua suspect something about him and by extension her? Then there were the children to care for, the farm to run, and also the biggie, the solstice next year. Without Arthur, could she get home?

Wait! Did he say a man and woman in love or two people? It's an important distinction. If it's the latter, what if I go to the cave with Abby or Saul? Could we activate it? Well...is that fair to them, to take them from their true life, and thrust them into a strange world they never could dream of? Damn, this life of mine just got a whole heck of a lot more complicated. She climbed out of bed and moved to the window. *I guess I shouldn't obsess too much about things. After all, I've got close to eight months to get through, and who knows what they're going to hold. Arthur, wherever you are, know that I love you, and will remember you always.*

Getting back into bed, she stared at the ceiling for a moment, closed her eyes, and let sleep take her. Hazel accepted that this chapter of her life was closing, as she had acknowledged that childhood had to end back when she was a teenager. Well, the first phase of her new life in this old world was over. It ended with the loss of her beloved. Now book two started, and it didn't matter what the pages held, she would face them head on. Like that old song she liked. The pen was in her hand, and the ending wasn't planned. It didn't matter. *She* would write her own ending.

About the Author

A transplanted New Englander, his first novel was *Murder on Gosnold Island*. It combined his engineering background with his love of Martha's Vineyard. Next came *Lexa and the Gordian Maze of Terra* a children's science-fiction work. It led to *Lexa and the Smugglers of Cyclo*.

Many of his short stories are on www.grubstreet.ca, and he put thirty of them into *Martha's Vineyard: My Island, My Memories*. *Dragonspeak: Drew, the Boy Who Talked to Dragons* is a children's fantasy. It was a finalist in the 2010 RPLA (Royal Palm Literary Award).

His first produced screenplay was *Wiccans' Lair*, a supernatural suspense/thriller. While not released, a representative for 20th Century Fox called it "engrossing and well-made." Andrew also acted in it and assisted in the production.

Hip Hop High is a musical set in an urban high school and was featured at the New York City Fringe Fest in 2013. The trailer is on YouTube. He's also done scripts and treatments for several television series.

He was Regional Director of Central Florida for the Florida Writers' Association, a non-profit group dedicated to helping writers, and was president of Cricket Cottage Publishing, LLC, which he recently sold.

~ * ~

We hope you enjoyed *The Long Journey Home*. If you did, please write a review, tell your friends, or check out the other offerings from Andrew and the other authors at Champagne Book Group.

A Time to Love
Lee Ann Sontheimer Murphy

Reclusive songwriter Samuel Baird lives on a remote Arkansas mountain drinking his life away. The last thing he wants is a woman to complicate things, but during a spectacular thunderstorm, a woman arrives just in time to save his life.

She says she comes from the late 1800's, and he thinks she is crazy, but Annie still manages to gain his attention and affection.

To reach a happily ever after, Samuel and Annie must overcome several obstacles, past and present to find the happiness they seek.

****

One

Whether it was the strong sunlight that streamed through the uncovered windows or the after effects of a very strange dream, Samuel Baird awoke with a jerk that brought him upright in bed. He put his hand to his chest to quiet the pounding of his heart and shuddered. Hell of a nightmare.

The images from the dream remained foremost in his mind as he put his bare feet to the floor and stumbled into the bathroom. His bladder was tight so he emptied it. The quick relief eased his body, but his mind remained uncomfortable.

Images from the nightmare lingered like an aftertaste as he fumbled to make coffee. By the time he poured his first cup, his dream had faded but he couldn't shake a strange sense of connection to the woman in his dream, a classic damsel in distress. If she was familiar, he couldn't place her. He had taken enough psych courses to wonder what the hell she represented. *Probably a combination of too much whiskey and too little sleep.* He set his empty mug into the sink with the other unwashed dishes.

He had no job or schedule to keep so he heaved his ten-foot johnboat into the bed of his pick-up. After grabbing his fishing poles from the porch, he tossed them beside the tackle box he kept in the truck.

His tires kicked up a cloud of dust as he took off without a backward glance at the cabin. He slowed as he reached the one-lane dirt track that meandered down the mountain. Too many rocks studded the surface for speed, so he inched along until he reached the blacktop where he accelerated.

At Lake Queen Wilhelmina, he parked beneath some trees near the water and hoisted the boat down to the launch. His old Evinrude motor came to life at the first tug, and he trolled out to a favorite fishing spot.

Sunshine filtered through the thick leaves overhead and danced on the lake surface. A light breeze ruffled his hair and rippled the water. He didn't want to think about his dream any more so he put it out of his head, as his mind drifted into the same easy rhythm as his casting, spinning in time with the reel on his rod when he cast or got a bite. He thought of nothing but fish until late afternoon when his stringer was full with bream and blue gill.

Time to quit. He brought the boat back to shore. Back in his truck, he kept to the speed limit on his way home and opened his window once he was on the mountain. He inhaled the cooler air, the crisp essence of the pines, and sighed with pleasure.

As he passed Tim Curtis' place, the old man, his sole neighbor, stepped off the porch with a wave. Never in a hurry since he had traded in the Nashville scene for a hermit's life in Arkansas, Samuel stopped.

"Was your fishin' any good?" Tim asked, resting an arm on the truck bed.

"Not bad. I'm havin' a fish fry tonight."

"I'll come if you got beer."

Samuel laughed. "I've one or two. Come about six if you're comin'."

"I'll be there."

Samuel drove deeper through the dense woods. Few but he and Tim dared to dwell in the wilderness below Rich Mountain. Anti-social since his divorce and the end of his advertising career came in the same week, Samuel relished the remote spot despite the black bears, rattlesnakes, and empty hours spent alone. He parked the Ford beneath the tallest of the pines that encircled the three-room cabin.

He carried his stringer to the sun-faded bench where he scaled and gutted the small bony fish. As he dumped the leavings at the edge of the woods, he almost trod on a rattlesnake stretched full-length in the sun, its pattern camouflaged among the leaves and rocks. Heart pounding, palms wet, he used the heavy hoe leaning against the shed to kill it.

Dim light inside the cabin made him blink at the change from sunshine. His hands reeked of fish and sweat soaked his clothes. A cold shower would be great, he mused, but he settled for a bath in the old claw-foot tub that took up most of the space in his small bathroom. For the ten thousandth time, he wished he had bothered to install a shower.

The water was soothing as he scrubbed away the day's odors. He dried off and tossed the towel on the floor before walking into the bedroom to dress.

I've come a long way from Nashville, in more ways than one. A mental comparison of his surroundings to the split-level ranch he'd called home in Music City put the rustic cabin on the bottom end of the scale, but he preferred it to any dwelling shared with Kimberly, his ex-wife. He didn't mind at all when she got the house, because he got the boat that had been his dad's.

When Tim arrived, Samuel was frying fish in an old iron skillet.

"Samuel, you here?" Tim stuck his head through the screen door.

"Yeah."

The old man seated himself at the small round table that marked the transition from kitchen to living room. Three mismatched chairs were grouped around it, and Tim chose the steadiest of the trio. An open bottle was in his hand.

"Hope you got plenty of beer." He took a long pull from the Bud he'd brought from home.

"Not much," Samuel said, lifting the last piece of fish from the smoking skillet. He stirred potatoes around in a second pan and brought it to the table, balancing the platter of fish in his other hand. "Bourbon's my poison, not beer. I keep it for you, not me."

As the men ate, Tim's gaze wandered to the wall above the stone fireplace. Several strings of rattlesnake rattles hung there—Samuel's trophies. "You got a new one."

"I killed another rattler after I cleaned the fish," Samuel said, eating with relish. He didn't cook often but when he did, he enjoyed the change from his usual fare of bologna sandwiches, Chef Boyardee, and frozen dinners.

"How many is that so far this spring?"

"Six or seven, I think, more than most years. I don't usually get that many all summer."

"You're lucky you nailed that one. You'll end up snake bit yet."

"I won't." Samuel snorted. The rattlesnakes gave him the heebie-jeebies but he didn't like to talk about it.

"I hope you don't. Son, you'd be dead before I could haul you down to Mena."

Samuel didn't reply to the dire prediction and filled his glass with bourbon. He drank then shuddered as the fiery liquid burned down to his gut. By the time he sat, he had lost his appetite, and Tim wasn't talking about snakes. Instead, he turned to another well-worn topic: women—and Samuel's lack of one.

"Ain't natural," Tim said, lips shiny with grease from the fried potatoes. "A man ought to have himself a woman."

"You don't," Samuel said. The liquor numbed his emotions, which felt good.

"You're thirty-five years younger than me. I had a woman, was married for more than fifty years. If I wasn't so old, I'd get one now."

Samuel sighed, and his mind wandered as Tim's words brought his bitter divorce to mind. Even after several years, the thought of Kimberly tasted sour as tainted milk.

"I haven't forgotten my fifth anniversary when the bitch told me she was having an affair with the doctor," Samuel drawled, slowing his words down to suffer one more time. "The next day, McMasters and Michael downsized, and I lost my job."

"Didn't you never hear the one about don't let one bad apple spoil the whole lot?"

"Tim, you're full of shit. We've talked about women until I'm sick of it," Samuel said, his voice lazy and without rancor. "Have another beer before you make me mad."

"Well, maybe one more. You make a good fish fry for such a mean son of a bitch."

He didn't dignify Tim's jab with a reply, but he ached inside at the sting. He couldn't see himself as either mean or a son-of-a-bitch but he was lonely and reclusive. Thinking of their first meeting, Samuel cleared his throat and spoke. "Remember my GTO?"

Tim laughed. "The one you busted the oil pan on? Sure. You ought to know better than to drive that little car down the road out yonder."

"True but if I hadn't, I'd never met you and we wouldn't be sittin' here full of fish, half wasted."

"Would have been my loss, son." The serious note in Tim's voice warmed Samuel's wounded heart. "If you hadn't bought the place, this cabin'd be a wreck by now, worse than the hotel."

An image of the first Queen Wilhelmina Lodge in ruins came as Samuel recalled the photographs he had seen at the current inn. If his memory was reliable, the old man remembered when Arkansas acquired the property and rebuilt the once magnificent Queen Wilhelmina, destroyed by fire ten years later. The State later built the present incarnation.

After Tim went home, Samuel drank bourbon until oblivion dimmed his ability to think and then his consciousness. He woke on the cold bathroom floor where he had vomited profusely in and around the commode before passing out.

Still sick to his stomach, he crawled into bed and stayed. He didn't wake until late afternoon with a raging headache and urgent need to puke. His physical symptoms didn't worry him as much as his inability to remember—something that had seldom happened before. The specter of alcoholism frightened Samuel, who grew up watching his father drink his way toward death. Realization that he seemed to be setting foot on Joe Baird's self-destructive path fueled a black pity that threatened to drown him. He was in a vicious cycle but although he marked it, Samuel didn't care enough to break it.

Tim came up the lane in the early evening. "You look like shit."

"Thanks." Samuel's voice was as sour as his churning stomach.

"I brought the mail up. Looks like you got a royalty check." Tim's voice lacked condemnation, which caused Samuel to regret his rudeness.

He was glad to receive his quarterly royalties for his single hit song, "Livin' On The Land"—his sole income. *Thank God my needs are small,* He took the envelope from his neighbor. *And thank you, Jesus, that Johnny Gale had a hit with my lyrics.* "Thanks, Tim."

"No problem. It's fixin' to storm, and I'm headin' home."

The sky to the west was heavy with black clouds, and when Samuel raised his aching eyes, he saw the first fingers of lightning over Oklahoma. May could produce some wicked storms, he mused, but he didn't care. It was just weather.

He refilled his glass. When it was empty, he drank from the bottle. The storm moved in. Lightning crackled off the mountaintops and thunder rumbled in a bass growl as the temperature dropped, and a sudden, sharp breeze raked the porch. The wind howled around the eaves of the old cabin, and a rush of wild exhilaration drove him into the yard.

Above his head, the clouds parted to unleash a downpour. He could not see or hear anything over the rush of water and roar of wind but a wild pagan joy made him limber as he cavorted in joyful dance.

"Ahhhhh!" he cried in wordless expression of his pleasure.

Jagged bolts danced like the moving finger of God Almighty. One of the flashes revealed a woman in the lane. Her knee length black hair tumbled in disarray and her ankle length dark dress clung wet to her skin. She also wore a white pinafore apron and old-fashioned button up shoes. He gaped at the woman in disbelief and shook his head. What he saw seemed surreal.

She's the woman from my dream. Damn, this is strange.

He had no more time to ponder the situation because she grasped his shirt and jerked him toward the cabin. He struggled and pushed against her hands without success because, lacking sobriety, his motor skills didn't work right. He felt her tiny hand shove the small of his back so hard he toppled.

The sodden ground smacked his face as singing electricity lifted the fine hairs on his arms. His ears roared as lightning struck the pine above them. Splinters and shards of the shattered tree flew, and Samuel tasted sap as a stray sliver touched his tongue. A large limb lay inches from his head and smoldered. The smoke made his throat ache, but he was lucky to be alive. She had saved him from injury or death.

He wiggled to his feet with clumsy motions and offered her a hand so she could rise.

"Thank you." Humility brought gratitude into his heart, swelling it with stronger emotion than he had known in many months.

"You are very welcome." Her voice was a rich alto that fell easy on his ears. "We should seek shelter."

At her suggestion, he dashed toward the porch. He retrieved his bottle and drained it to gain anesthesia from his emotion. The harsh liquor jolted his stomach and a strange sensation rocketed through him as the alcohol hit hard and fast. He pitched forward. By the time he met the floor, he was unconscious.

~ * ~

One eye opened to sunshine so bright pain shot through his head, which pounded. Rank nausea stirred, and he struggled for the concentration needed to rise. His bare feet slapped the linoleum floor and sent tremors through his midsection. Rising vomit threatened but he held it until he could hang over the commode, where he spewed, dry retching even after his stomach was empty.

Wobbling on unstable legs into the kitchen, he squinted against the brightness and fumbled to find a bottle because sometimes bourbon helped ease the hangover. Movement distracted him and he turned his head with effort to see a woman standing before the stone fireplace, disheveled and dirty but solid.

"You're real." His voice seemed loud to his ears, and he cringed at the sound.

"I am, sir."

"Who are you?" He sank into his rump-sprung favorite recliner, unwilling to stand any longer, and waited for her answer with trepidation. She looked like the woman he remembered from his fragmented dream.

"I am Annie," she said, with a curtsey. "Annie Gregory."

"I'm Samuel Baird." Polite introductions were all he could manage as pain clamped vise-like on his head. He shut his eyes to block the light and ease his discomfort but reopened them when he felt the smooth coolness of a glass against his clenched hand. "What's that?"

"Something to cure what ails you."

"I'm not sick."

"I know you are not. You have taken too much drink, and this will help."

Shrugging, he tilted the glass upward and downed the murky contents. Tasted unusual but not unpleasant. He waited for his stomach to rebel but it didn't so he put his head back, eyes shut. After fifteen minutes, the nausea was gone and so was his headache. "What was in that?"

"'Tis a family secret, sir."

"So you won't tell me?"

"No, Mr. Baird."

My God, I could use a drink. That desire made his temper short and his words blunt. "What were you doing out in that storm?"

Annie's smile crumpled, and fear darkened her blue eyes until they were almost black. "I lost my way." Her soft voice sounded hesitant to him, as if she kept something hidden.

"From where? Were you camping up at the park?"

"No, sir. I work on Rich Mountain."

"At the Queen Wilhelmina Lodge?"

"Yes, sir."

Her polite manners grated his nerves. He wanted simple answers to easy questions but she failed to give any. "You don't have to call me 'sir.' So you work up there?"

"I do."

"What's with the dress?" His gaze focused on what she wore, garments that suggested a maid's outfit in a poor stage play. He couldn't imagine any woman wanting to wear such a get-up.

"My dress?" Annie said, eyes darting around the room as if there was another. "Is there something amiss with it? I know it is wrinkled but that is from the rain."

"It's about a hundred years out of style."

"It is not. It's fashionable enough and what Mrs. Carmichael has us wear. No one has found fault with it but you, sir."

Samuel tried to envision guests that would find her costume ordinary and could not. During his one stay at the Queen Wilhelmina, the housekeeping staff had worn neat uniform slacks with matching tops.

"Are you a waitress, Annie?" Ruling out domestic service left The Queen's Restaurant as a possibility for her employment.

"Oh, no, I am not. Only waiters serve the dining room. I am but an upstairs maid. I do the odd bit of cleaning and serve ladies who come away without their own servants. You will know some do bring their girls along?"

"No." He clipped the word. Her attempts at explanation muddled things but what disconcerted him the most was his attraction toward her. Since Kimberly's defection, his approach to women had been sexual, never personal. To avoid examination of his confused emotions, he changed the subject. "Do you want me to take you back up to the Queen Wilhelmina? Or home? Where do you live?"

Annie flinched, and her face blanched but she answered. "I live in...at the Queen Wilhelmina."

He rose and groped for his keys on the mantle. "I'll go get the truck ready."

The motor failed to start. In frustration, he pounded the dash with a loud curse and tried again. At the click that confirmed the battery was dead, Samuel stomped inside to call Tim for a jump but found the phone out after the storm. Wary of snakes, he took down his single shot .410 shotgun from over the door and went out. Hiking to Tim's was the one way he could get help.

He turned to Annie. "I'll be back."

~ * ~

Annie bowed her head in acknowledgment, watching as he moved away from the cabin. When he vanished into the line of trees, she sighed and fell to her knees in silent thanks for the unexpected reprieve.

Unshed sobs had ached within her throat for hours and now, alone, Annie released them. Her harsh sobs shook her body and she buried her face in her hands. Through the hours of the night, she had waited with perfect posture, gripped with cold fear. Throughout the slow hours, she listened for sounds of a search party or even a posse. Twice, she thought she heard the muffled sound of many hoof beats but she had been wrong.

A soft wind blew through the open door and touched her face with invisible fingers. The familiar mountain breezes calmed her and her tears trickled to a halt. Annie wiped her face with both hands and rose, as her mind spun with tornadic speed. Her heart beat with such force she felt each thump in her chest and she willed herself to quiet.

The same fortitude that helped her raise her younger brothers and to survive her husband's brutality served her well now. It offered the power to push the previous night's events out of her thoughts for now so she could focus on the present. Annie stared down at the floor and saw that her feet were caked with mud from her wild flight over the mountains. Although she had washed both hands and face when preparing the remedy for her host, she hadn't considered her appearance until now.

Shame stained her cheeks as she turned on the kitchen spigot and wet a rag to wipe her feet. That Samuel Baird had running water in his home was the first odd thing she noticed. To her knowledge, the sole other place in the Ouachitas that offered indoor plumbing was the inn where she worked. With one finger, Annie touched the screens on the open kitchen window, the mesh strange to her touch. *Must have money, to have such here.*

Her stomach gnawed with emptiness and ached with want. She pressed a flat hand across her abdomen and rubbed it to ease the hunger pangs. It had been thirty hours since she'd eaten. Her full bladder sent off urgent twinges so she slipped out of the cabin to squat behind a tree. Her urine puddled then soaked into the soil. With lighter steps, Annie returned inside.

Despite her hunger, she surveyed her surroundings. The worn, sagging couch where she'd spent the night was fashioned with simpler lines than she'd seen. She plopped down in the faded recliner, wondering how Samuel made it tilt backward. Her fingers fumbled at the handle on the side. When the footrest shot up and the back tipped, she screeched with surprise. Her breath came fast as she struggled to right the chair.

Her nerves had the edge of a well-honed knife. She retreated into the kitchen, shaking. It was not the recliner that disconcerted her as much as what happened early in the storm. Images of Jake's face, twisted with rage, returned with such power her lungs froze. Her flesh crawled as she speculated on what might be happening on Rich Mountain. An urge to rip the uniform from her body was so intense Annie clutched her hands to stay it. Whatever happened, whether she returned to the Queen Wilhelmina or not, everything had shifted. She began to breathe again but with short, fast breaths that made her feel like a locomotive.

I won't think about it now. I can't and I won't. I know who he is; I saw him before. It will be fine. It must be.

The familiar task of cooking a meal steadied her. The stove was different from any she had seen but it was for cooking. She opened what she thought was the firebox but it was apparent that no fires had burned within the cavity. Perplexed, she turned a knob and saw flames lick around an oval ring. Her quick mind made the leap that it was an oven, meant for baking. Leaving it to heat, Annie opened cupboards and doors to find something to cook.

Inside a large cabinet that felt cool within, she found a pound of ground sausage. She touched milk in an unfamiliar container and found butter, formed into long sticks rather than molded. Her deft hands fashioned the meat into patties and put them in a skillet. Eyes squinting with concentration, Annie rotated another knob and smiled when flame appeared.

With ingredients found in the cupboard, she made biscuits with the recipe in her head. By the time she heard Samuel's step on the porch, Annie had fried the sausage patties, baked biscuits, and made milk gravy with the meat drippings. She cut fresh corn from several cobs she discovered, surprised to see ripe corn this early in the season.

~ * ~

His tromp through the rugged country defused Samuel's wrath, and he was in a reflective mood when he returned. The aromas of food reached him before he set foot on the porch, rousing him from his thoughts. Surprised by the smells, he felt unexpected hunger and a strange sense of homecoming, shaking his head to dispel the illusion. He lived here but it wasn't home. He didn't have one, not now and never again. He put away the shotgun and turned to Annie, who greeted him with a smile.

"I made supper for you, sir. Sausage, fried corn, and biscuits."

Speechless and moved despite his determination to remain aloof, Samuel nodded and sat. Kimberly seldom prepared meals for him and when she had, the food was unpalatable unless it came prepared from the freezer. He responded to Annie's gesture with gratitude he didn't know he felt until he spoke it.

"Thank you, Annie. Listen, Tim's phone is out, too. He'll give me a jump in the morning but you're stuck till then unless you want to walk. Sorry, but it's as good as it gets."

"I do not mind, Mr. Baird."

Samuel smeared a biscuit with butter and nibbled. As it crumbled in his mouth, he saw Annie waiting, hands folded, for a blessing. With no little embarrassment, he swallowed and said the simple grace his mother taught him. "Amen."

It was the last word spoken until the meal was over. He ate with an appetite he didn't know he possessed, feeling like a pig as he devoured two plates of biscuits and gravy. He broke a bite off his third sausage patty, savoring the taste of sage and fresh pork, and polished off the fried corn. He looked up to find that Annie had eaten almost as much as he had. Her shy smile made his heart contract, which brought him to his feet to pour a drink. He downed it as she cleared the table.

He watched as she put several pans of water to heat on the stove with curiosity. Until she poured the first pot into the sink, he had no idea what she was doing. Her actions stirred an old memory of his Granny Ballard heating wash water on the stove and he realized her purpose was the same.

"Annie, you don't have to do that." He rose from the table, which wavered with the effect of straight bourbon.

"I do if you want clean dishes."

"You've got hot water right here." He turned on the tap and filled the sink, swishing Dawn liquid around to make suds.

She grinned and glanced up at him with delight.

"That is the keenest thing I have ever seen." She rolled up the sleeves of her wrinkled dress and scrubbed his dishes until they shone. Samuel poured another drink and watched with perplexed concern. The incident over hot water disturbed him—everyone knew about such things so why was she playing dumb? As he sipped bourbon, she dried her hands and drained the sink. She went outside and he followed, parking himself on the porch to see what she intended to do.

Annie passed the bench where he'd killed the most recent snake and went behind the old well house, vanishing into the trees. His curiosity kindled and, mindful of venomous snakes, he followed with speed. By the time he reached the woods, Annie met him on her way back.

"Annie, you shouldn't go into the woods like that." Worry made his voice harsher than he intended it to be.

"But where ever else would I go?"

"To do what?" The question felt valid and receding fear fueled the scolding. "The mountains are full of rattlesnakes and there are still bears around. It's dangerous to go off like that."

She stared at him, exasperated. "I've killed many a snake, Mr. Baird, and know well about the bears. If you don't go to the woods, then where do you go?"

He tossed down the remainder of his drink in a gulp that burned his belly and gave him a rush. "Go to do what?"

Her cheeks flamed scarlet, and her voice dropped to a whisper. "Make water."

Understanding cut through the effects of alcohol. "Oh, my God!" Samuel ran a hand through his hair, dumbfounded. This woman heated water on the stove to wash dishes and went to pee in the woods. Shock and disbelief made him silent for more than a minute. Frustration choked his throat as he swallowed harsh words, choosing what he wanted to say.

"There's a bathroom with a commode in the cabin." His voice sounded short, even to himself. "You know, flush toilets like they have up at the damn hotel you work at. I don't know what game you're playing but you can't tell me you don't know about indoor plumbing."

"I do, sir." With crimson cheeks, she looked ashamed and annoyed. "It is sorry I am for not thinking you would have such here."

"Who are you? Who are you, Annie Gregory?"

"I am but a maid at the Queen Wilhelmina, Mr. Baird."

Her formal address bothered him too. "Call me Samuel, please. And tell me how long you've worked there."

He didn't miss the fear in her eyes or the tremble that shook her shoulders, but it wasn't enough to keep him from questioning her. He was not yet drunk but the booze short-circuited his courtesy.

"I have been in service at the inn since it opened last year with the grand ball in June."

"*Last* year?" he asked, making his tone sardonic. He made a conscious effort to lift one eyebrow, a habit he'd cultivated as an advertising man. "What year *was* that?"

Glee made him giddier than the bourbon. He'd sensed something off about her since the first moment, and now he had her cornered. The lodge had opened in the mid-seventies after the restored version of the original burned to the ground. *Last year, my ass! Annie should have checked her dates.* He chortled aloud as he waited to hear her answer.

"1898," Annie said, frowning at his question.

His laughter died as he shuddered, feeling cold and uneasy. Nothing in her manner indicated she was joking. Her sober eyes met his, and she wasn't smiling. *My God, she's crazy.* He rubbed his lips with the fingers of his left hand. He stared at her so hard his eyes ached and his stomach considered rejecting the meal he had enjoyed so much. He belched and tasted the sour aftertaste of his whiskey.

"That's impossible." He croaked the words and turned to the bottle for more bourbon to avoid further thought. "I don't know who you are or what you want, but you'll be gone tomorrow and I won't be sorry."

He retreated into his bedroom on unsteady legs and shut the door. He pretended he didn't hear the muffled sound of Annie crying. He went to sleep sitting upright on the bed but during the night he woke, stiff and muscle strained, to curl beneath the covers.

~ * ~

Despite the closed door, his rattling snores were audible to Annie, still awake. With palms clasped flat together as if in prayer, she gasped in uneven rhythm. Heightened senses made each perception more vivid and powerful. Her cheeks tightened with drying tears and her pulse beat hard with her heart's tattoo. The fingertips that touched her lips quivered as night breezes cooled her heated skin. Her eyes stared ahead, blind to what they saw, her mind focused on the calendar on the far wall.

I must be mistaken. To come down the mountain and skip more than a hundred years is impossible. It could not be—I could not escape my deeds so easily.

But the number in stark black beside the month of May was not 1899 and did not begin with "19" to herald the coming of the new century. The date marked the time as early in the 21st century and meant she had crossed more than a century during her dash down the mountain.

The impossibility made her skin crawl with dread but as she twisted her lips together, tasting the dry salt from her tears, Annie felt a rush of sorrow. If more than a hundred years had gone in the blink of an eye or in a flash of lightning, all she knew was lost, including her family. Grief twisted her stomach at the thought but relief tempered it to a bearable level.

The law won't find me, now I'll be safe here, no jail nor noose for me. She lay down on the rough couch, her exhausted mind closing for the night.

Comforted with unexpected salvation, she slept, solaced by Samuel's presence, the sting of his words fading away in the country of her dreams.

We hoped you enjoyed the excerpt from *A Time to Love.* This and other terrific books from Champagne Book Group are available at major booksellers and vendors.

~ * ~

Interested in getting notice of sales and special deals on books? Visit www.champagnebooks.com and sign up for our newsletter. Newsletter subscribers also get chances to win advance copies of releases before the general reader public.

www.ingramcontent.com/pod-product-compliance
Lightning Source LLC
Chambersburg PA
CBHW020955180626
46814CB00003B/1102